KEEPERS
OF THE
COVENANT

Books by Lynn Austin

All She Ever Wanted
All Things New
Eve's Daughters
Hidden Places
Pilgrimage
A Proper Pursuit
Though Waters Roar
Until We Reach Home
While We're Far Apart
Wings of Refuge
A Woman's Place
Wonderland Creek

REFINER'S FIRE

Candle in the Darkness
Fire by Night
A Light to My Path

CHRONICLES OF THE KINGS

Gods & Kings
Song of Redemption
The Strength of His Hand
Faith of My Fathers
Among the Gods

THE RESTORATION CHRONICLES

Return to Me
Keepers of the Covenant

KEEPERS

OF THE

COVENANT

LYNN
AUSTIN

BETHANYHOUSE
a division of Baker Publishing Group
Minneapolis, Minnesota

Published by Bethany House Publishers
11400 Hampshire Avenue South
Bloomington, Minnesota 55438
www.bethanyhouse.com

Bethany House Publishers is a division of
Baker Publishing Group, Grand Rapids, Michigan

Printed in the United States of America

Library of Congress Cataloging-in-Publication Data

Austin, Lynn N.
    Keepers of the covenant / Lynn Austin.
        pages cm. — (The Restoration Chronicles ; 2)
    Summary: "In a story drawn from the Old Testament books of Ezra and Nehemiah, Ezra, a Jewish scholar, is called upon to deliver his exiled people from Babylon to Jerusalem—but the fight to keep God's Law is never easy"—Provided by publisher.
    ISBN 978-0-7642-1271-0 (cloth : alk. paper)
    ISBN 978-0-7642-0899-7 (pbk.)
    1. Ezra (Biblical figure)—Fiction. 2. Bible. Old Testament—Fiction. 3. Bible fiction. 4. Christian fiction. I. Title.
PS3551.U839K44 2014
813'.54—dc23   2014017784

Cover design by Jennifer Parker

Photography by Mike Habermann Photography, LLC

14 15 16 17 18 19 20   7 6 5 4 3 2 1

To my husband, Ken,
and to my children:
Joshua, Benjamin, Vanessa, Maya, and Snir

The Babylonian army conquered the Jewish nation in 586 BC, destroying God's temple in Jerusalem and marching most of the survivors into exile. For nearly fifty years, the Jews languished in captivity, far from home. Then the Persians defeated the Babylonians, and in the first year of his reign, the new monarch, King Cyrus, issued a decree that allowed the captive Jews to return:

> "Anyone of his people among you—may his God be with him, and let him go up to Jerusalem in Judah and build the temple of the Lord, the God of Israel, the God who is in Jerusalem."
>
> Ezra 1:3

A group of about forty thousand exiles decided to make the long journey back to their homeland, led by Zerubbabel, an ancestor of King David. Most people, however, chose to remain behind in their captive lands.

After a long, twenty-year struggle, the returnees finally rebuilt God's temple, encouraged by the prophets Haggai and Zechariah who promised a future restoration for God's people. Meanwhile, the Jews who remained in captivity discovered that the window of opportunity to emigrate had slammed shut once again. For the next generation, still living among their pagan enemies sixty years after King Cyrus's decree, all hope for restoration has vanished.

Haman paced the citadel's rooftop, waiting for the court astrologers to finish their work. He despised his impotence. His destiny should be under his own control, not determined by mere pricks of light, sparkling in the midnight sky. This muttering huddle of stargazers in their night-black robes shouldn't decide his future—he should. But the request he wanted to bring before King Xerxes, supreme ruler of the Persian Empire, was much too important to leave to chance or fate.

Haman paused near the parapet to gaze down at the sentries standing watch at the king's gate. His obsession first began at that gate when an impudent Jew refused to bow down to him. The entire world bowed before Haman now that he'd earned a seat of honor above all of the king's nobles, now that he'd become the second most important man in the empire. He'd spent his entire lifetime in the king's service, yet after everything Haman had achieved, Mordecai the Jew refused to bow.

"Lord Haman . . . ?" He turned at the sound of the chief astrologer's voice. "We have an answer for you, my lord."

Haman took his time crossing to the waiting astrologers, unwilling to let them see his urgency or the power they held over him. "What do the stars say tonight?" he asked, folding his arms across his chest.

"Tomorrow will be an extremely favorable day for you, my lord. We see no opposition from the heavens to whatever you plan. In fact, the heavenly bodies all line up in your favor."

Haman struggled to conceal his relief, his triumph. He had waited weeks for this news. At last, he would be able to put his plan into place. "Good. I have one more task for you tonight. Cast the lots for me and choose a favorable month in the future and then a day of that month."

"A date for what, my lord?"

"That's not your concern. Just do it. Now."

Haman followed the astrologers down the stairs to their shadowy workroom. He watched as an apprentice readied the leather bag with twelve marked clay tiles, one for each month, then a second bag with thirty tiles to represent the days. Of course, the proper incantations had to be mumbled before they cast the lot, and Haman grew impatient as he listened to the chief sorcerer's gibberish. The tiles clicked like bones as the magi shook the bag. He plunged his hand inside and drew one out. "Twelve, my lord," he said, holding it up for Haman to see. "The month of Adar."

Haman nodded, his jaw clenched. Adar was eleven months away! He wanted to implement his plan now, not delay it for so long. But as he waited for the sorcerer to recite the second incantation and prepare to draw the lot to determine the day of the month, Haman decided that maybe the delay would be a good thing after all. It would provide plenty of time for his decree to reach every corner of the kingdom, all 127 provinces. Plenty of time for Haman to prepare for the execution of his enemies.

Day after day, each time that stubborn Jew had refused to bow, Haman's fury had multiplied until he'd decided not only to execute one man, but every Jew in the empire. Haman knew who Mordecai's people were—the enemies of his own race of Amalekites. The hatred they harbored for one another traced back to a mother's womb, where twin brothers had grappled for supremacy. The younger twin, Jacob, had stolen everything from Haman's ancestor, Esau, who was the older twin and rightful heir. It was time for Haman's people to rid the world of Jacob's descendants, the Jews, and take back what belonged to them.

The sorcerer held up a second tile. "The thirteenth day, my lord."

Haman couldn't suppress his smile. His lucky number. Born on a thirteenth day, he had come to power on a thirteenth day. Yes, the thirteenth day of Adar would do very nicely. "Thank you," he said with a nod and strode from the workroom.

Haman didn't bother going home to his bedchamber and his wife, Zeresh. He would never be able to sleep. Instead, he went to the king's council chamber and sat down to compose his edict. Even with the stars lining up in his favor, Haman needed to plan cautiously, choose his words wisely. Every Jew must die—young and old, men and women, children and infants. But Haman couldn't come right out and propose such a bold plan. He needed to use veiled suggestions and innuendoes to guide the king into reaching that conclusion, leading him there the way a hunter uses carefully placed bait to lead his prey into a snare.

When the chamberlains arrived after dawn, Haman ordered them to prepare the throne room, opening windows to let in the fresh spring air, lighting braziers to take the chill from the stone floor, arranging torches for light, plumping pillows and cushions. Everything must be perfect. Haman stood before a polished bronze mirror as he waited, composing his facial expression to show deep concern without a trace of the anticipation and elation he felt.

In due time King Xerxes arrived, ushered in by servants and pages to take his seat on his ivory throne. "Your Majesty—may you live forever!" Haman said, bowing low before him. When he rose again, Haman sat down in his seat at the king's right hand. "I trust you rested well last night, Your Majesty?"

Xerxes gave an impatient wave as if to say that his sleep habits weren't important. "What business must we accomplish this morning, Haman? How many petitioners?"

"A room full of them, Your Majesty. But before we begin, may I speak to you in private about a matter of extreme concern to me? It has to do with the stability and peace of your entire kingdom."

"This sounds very serious. Of course you may speak."

Haman waited as the pages and chamberlains scurried away, aware of the heavy thudding of his heart. "It has come to my attention, Your Majesty, that there is a certain race of people dispersed and scattered among the provinces of your kingdom whose customs are very different from all your other subjects. They worry me, Your Majesty, because they don't obey the king's laws. It's not in the best interests of your kingdom to tolerate them."

"Have they openly rebelled?"

"Not yet, but the potential is very great because they have never assimilated into the kingdom the way the other subject nations in your empire have. They don't see themselves as part of your kingdom at all, but stubbornly insist on maintaining their ethnic identity and customs. Most worrisome of all, they refuse to worship the gods of our great empire."

The king grunted. "They refuse, you say?"

"Yes. Even when threatened with punishment and death. Should we risk angering Persia's gods? Gamble on incurring their wrath?"

"Certainly not."

"There is nothing to be gained by keeping these people as subjects. There is no benefit they provide that outweighs the harm they cause." Haman paused, watching the king's reaction, trying to assess his every gesture and expression.

"What's your recommendation?" Xerxes said after a moment.

Haman wiped his palms on his thighs. "If it pleases the king, let a decree be issued to destroy this potential threat, so these people can never harm you and your empire. In fact, I feel so strongly about the danger they pose that I'm willing to put ten thousand talents of my own silver into the royal treasury to pay the men who will carry out this decree."

"That's a great deal of silver, Haman. Are these people truly that dangerous?"

"I believe so, my lord. Especially since they are dispersed throughout your kingdom like a deadly plague that could multiply and bring destruction."

The king stared at the floor, playing with the signet ring he wore on his finger. Haman held his breath, planning what he would say if Xerxes asked for proof of these accusations, or for the name of this menacing group of people. But the stars were in his favor, Haman reminded himself. He would prevail.

At last the king spoke. "I've decided to trust your judgment, Haman. If you say they are a threat to me, then I want them taken care of." He pulled off his signet ring and handed it to him. "Keep your silver . . . and do whatever you think best with these people to eliminate the threat."

Haman closed his eyes in relief and victory, clenching the king's signet ring in his fist. Once his decree went out, it could never be rescinded. Every Jew in the empire would die. "Yes, Your Majesty. I'll attend to your wishes right away."

Part I

Dispatches were sent by couriers to all the king's provinces with the order to destroy, kill and annihilate all the Jews—young and old, women and little children—on a single day, the thirteenth day of the twelfth month, the month of Adar, and to plunder their goods.

ESTHER 3:13

CHAPTER

1

BABYLON

The door to Ezra's study burst open without warning. Startled, he looked up from his scroll and saw his brother Jude on the threshold, breathless. He still wore his leather potter's apron, and streaks of dried clay smudged his arms and forehead. "You need to come right away."

Ezra held the pointer in place on the scroll to mark where he'd stopped reading. "Can it wait a few more minutes? We're nearly finished with this Torah portion, and it's a particularly difficult one."

Jude strode across the room and snatched the pointer from Ezra's hand, tossing it onto the table. "No! It can't wait. If the rumors are true, our people's lives are at stake, and your Torah studies aren't going to matter in the least!"

"I'm sorry," Ezra said to the other three scholars. "I'll be back as soon as I see what the problem is."

"All of you need to come," Jude said, gesturing to the men at the study table. "This involves all of us."

"But our work—"

"This is more important." Jude tugged Ezra's arm, pulling him to his feet. "Come on."

17

Ezra would chide his brother later for bursting in on him and his colleagues and not even allowing him time to put away the scrolls. Jude was thirty-one, four years younger than Ezra, and his temper could burn as hot as the kiln where he and their younger brother, Asher, fired their pottery. "Where are we going?" Ezra asked as Jude hurried him and the others from the room.

"To the house of assembly. The elders have called an emergency meeting."

"Can you give me the gist of the problem, Jude? We have important work to do." His brother didn't understand the seriousness of Ezra's scholarly work, studying and interpreting God's holy law, putting it into practical terms so laborers like Jude could apply it to their everyday lives. The God of Abraham had called His people to live holy lives, and Ezra's work would ensure that they didn't repeat the failures of the past, which had led to their current captivity in Babylon.

"I know all about your important work," Jude said as they strode through the narrow streets. "Why do you think Asher and I support you and give you a place to live?"

"That doesn't give you the right to interrupt me and order me around—"

Jude halted, still gripping Ezra's arm, and swung around to face him. "Did you hear what I said, Ezra? Or was your head in the clouds with the angels? This news concerns our people's lives."

"You can let go of my arm," he said, pulling free. "I'm coming with you, aren't I?"

Ezra seldom participated in community councils, preferring his life of scholarly isolation. But he sensed the urgency of the meeting as soon as he and Jude pushed their way into the packed assembly hall. Men from every strata of society had left work to gather here. *Rebbe* Nathan, the leader of Babylon's exiled Jewish community, stood on the *bimah* calling for quiet. Beside him stood an elderly Babylonian man, dressed in the robes of a royal sorcerer, looking out of place in this Jewish house of prayer. The stranger gazed around as if looking for an escape—as if the crowd might pull him limb-from-limb any minute. The mere sight of a Gentile, standing so close to where the sacred scrolls were kept, infuriated Ezra.

"What is that pagan shaman doing in our house of prayer?" he asked Jude. "It's a desecration—"

"Shh!" Jude elbowed him. "Will you forget all your holy rules for once and just listen?"

"Quiet! Please!" Rebbe Nathan said. "Everyone needs to listen!" When the men finally quieted, he turned to the elderly Babylonian. "Tell them why you've come. Tell them everything you told me."

The sorcerer stared at the floor, not at the crowd as he spoke in a halting voice. "Years ago, as one of the king's young magi in training, I was honored to know the man you called Daniel the Righteous One—may he rest in peace. Because of my great admiration for him, I wanted you to hear about this royal dispatch immediately." He held up an official-looking document. "Couriers delivered it from the citadel of Susa. King Xerxes sealed it with his own ring. It will be translated into every language and sent to satraps, governors, and nobles throughout the empire, announced to people of every nationality. The king's edict is an unalterable law in every province—" The old man paused as his voice broke. He passed the document to Nathan. "Here, you read it . . . and may the God you serve have mercy."

Rebbe Nathan cleared his throat. "This is an order to destroy, kill, and annihilate *all* Jews, young and old, women and children, in every province in the kingdom. . . ."

Horrified murmurs swept through the crowd. Ezra shook his head as to erase the words he'd just heard. *Kill all the Jews?*

"The massacre is scheduled to take place on a single day

later this year," Nathan continued. "On the thirteenth day of the twelfth month."

Ezra turned to his brother, hoping this was a mistake or a terrible joke, hoping he'd misunderstood. This couldn't be true. They would all be slaughtered in a few short months? Jude, who had a wife and two young daughters, had tears in his eyes.

"But . . . why?" Ezra asked aloud. "Why kill all of us?" What had been the point of all his years of study, all his knowledge of the Torah, all the work of the men of the Great Assembly, if their lives ended this way? Why would the Almighty One allow it?

"What's the reason for this decree?" someone shouted. "What did we do wrong?"

Rebbe Nathan wiped his eyes. "No explanation is given."

"We don't have enemies here in Babylon," another man said. "They wouldn't kill us here, in this city, would they?"

"The order allows our assassins to plunder our goods," Nathan said. "Even those men who don't hate us will join in the killing to take everything we have—homes, businesses . . ."

"And since this decree comes from King Xerxes himself," the Babylonian sorcerer added, "many in his kingdom will rush to obey it in order to win his favor. You've been declared the king's enemies."

"We have to flee!" one of the elders said. "We have to get our families out of Babylon now!"

Ezra had the same thought. He needed to race back to his study and pack all the priceless Torah scrolls, the historical accounts, wisdom literature, the scrolls of the prophets, and take them someplace safe.

"There's no place to go," Nathan said, his voice hoarse with emotion. "The executions will take place simultaneously throughout the empire. In every province."

"Oh, God of Abraham . . ." Ezra covered his mouth. He leaned against his sturdy brother, sick with horror. Panic and fear swelled like thunderclouds throughout the hall.

"What are we going to do?" someone moaned.

"Our wives . . . our children . . . we can't let them die!"

"God of Abraham, why is this happening?" Wails of grief filled the hall.

"Why not just kill us now, if that's what they want?" Jude shouted above the weeping. "Is it part of the torture to make us wait eleven months so we have to watch the angel of death slowly approach?"

Nathan held up his hands again to silence the commotion. He turned to the Babylonian sorcerer. "Please, can you help us get an audience with the government officials here in Babylon? Maybe if we begged them for mercy—"

"They'll never agree to speak with you," he replied, shaking his head. "They fear King Xerxes and his chief administrator, Haman, too much. In fact, I'm risking trouble myself by coming here and associating with you. I need to go." He tried to step down from the bimah, but Nathan stopped him.

"Wait. Who is this Haman?"

"He sits at King Xerxes' right hand, second in power only to the king."

"Do you know his full name or anything about him? Would he show us mercy?"

"I don't know. . . . Maybe his full name is there in the decree, somewhere," he said, gesturing to the scroll. "Look for yourself. I have to leave."

"Isn't there anything we can do to stop this? Do you know anyone who would give us refuge or a place to hide? We'll travel anywhere, no matter how distant."

"If I knew I would tell you. I don't want to see this happen, either. I came for Rebbe Daniel's sake, but I really must go now. I never meant to stay this long." Nathan helped him step down from the platform, and the crowd parted to let him through as he hurried away.

"How can this be?" Ezra tugged his hair and beard, the pain

a reminder that this was real and not a nightmare. How could every Jew in the empire be under a death sentence, without hope, without an escape? The God of Abraham would never do this to them. They'd suffered destruction and exile before, but God promised through His prophets that a remnant would survive, that His covenant would endure. Were the prophets wrong?

Ezra looked up and saw Nathan perusing the king's decree, murmuring the words aloud as he read it. The crowd hushed to listen. "There's no other way to interpret it," Nathan said. "The decree is final, signed and sealed with King Xerxes' authority . . . and witnessed by Haman son of Hammedatha, the Agagite."

Ezra moaned. "Oh no. There's our reason."

"Does that name mean something to you?" Jude asked. Ezra could only nod, overwhelmed by the truth of who this powerful enemy was. "Tell all of us, Ezra," Jude said, pushing him toward the front. "Listen, everyone! My brother has information. Let him speak!"

"You know this man Haman?" Nathan asked.

"No, I'm only a scholar. I've never traveled beyond this city." Ezra climbed the bimah, his steps heavy. "But I know the Torah and the history of our people, and believe me, the man behind this murderous decree—this Haman the Agagite—is our enemy."

"Tell us what you know."

Ezra needed a moment to catch his breath. "Agag was the king of the Amalekites—a tribe of people who descended from Esau's grandson, Amalek. If Haman calls himself the Agagite, then he must be from their royal family. He's their king—and now he's in a position of power over the entire Persian Empire. Of course he would want to use that authority to destroy us." Ezra had to pause again, horror-struck by what he was saying.

"The Amalekites have long been the enemies of our people. They attacked our ancestors as soon as we escaped from Egypt with Moses. They didn't care that we were unarmed or that we traveled with women and children."

"Cowards!" someone shouted from the crowd.

"That's exactly right," Ezra said. "The Almighty One commanded our first king, Saul, to completely destroy all the Amalekites. When Saul disobeyed, his kingship was taken away and given to David. We've been at war with the Amalekites throughout our history. These descendants of Esau believe that if they destroy all of the descendants of Jacob, they'll inherit the covenant blessings from God that rightfully belong to us."

"Do we have to sit by and accept this?" Jude asked. "Why not arm ourselves and fight back?"

Nathan bowed his head for a moment before looking up again. "The King will use the Persian army to enforce this decree. Even if we tried to fight, we couldn't possibly win. When the thirteenth day of Adar comes . . ." He couldn't finish. He leaned against Ezra as if about to collapse, weeping.

"Get a bench!" Ezra shouted. "He needs to sit down." The men passed one up to the platform, and Ezra helped the elderly rebbe sit on it. "Are you all right?" he asked. Nathan didn't reply. He continued to weep, his body bent double, his head in his hands.

"Isn't there anyone in the government who can help us?" one of the elders asked. Ezra realized that the man was addressing him. Everyone was looking to him to take Nathan's place.

"None that I know of," he replied. "Daniel the Righteous One was an advisor to the king when he was alive, but we no longer have an advocate in Babylon or Susa or anywhere else. Even if we did, the king sealed the decree, and the laws of the Medes and Persians can never be changed."

Sounds of mourning filled the hall again. "I refuse to accept this death sentence!" Jude shouted above the cries. "There must be something we can do besides sit around waiting to die!"

"We can fast and pray," Ezra said. "We can wrestle with God the way Jacob did at the Jabbok River as he prepared to face Esau." He spoke the correct words, giving the response that a man of faith would offer, but in that moment, Ezra's faith was so shaken, his heart and mind so engulfed by the rising river of hopelessness, that he didn't know how God could possibly save them. They were all sentenced to death.

"Do you think this is God's punishment?" someone asked. "Is it because our fathers remained here instead of returning to Jerusalem with Prince Zerubbabel?"

"It can't be," Jude said before Ezra could reply. "Isn't Jerusalem under the same death sentence we are? Every Jew in the kingdom will be annihilated!"

"We need to pray," Ezra repeated.

"What good will that do?" Jude asked.

Ezra couldn't answer Jude's question, nor did he want to argue with him in front of the entire community. "I need to go back to my study and—"

"Ezra! For once in your life, put away your scrolls and join the real world!" Jude said. "Do you think you'll be allowed to go on studying while the rest of us are slaughtered?"

"My scrolls may not help, but neither will shouting," he replied. "There's nothing any of us can do for now, except pray. Maybe God will tell us why this is happening or show us a way out. In the meantime, someone needs to take Nathan home. . . . We all need to go home." Ezra stepped down from the platform, desperate to reach the nearest door. He couldn't stay here a moment longer, listening to questions he couldn't answer, defending a God he didn't understand. The fear in the hall had become paralyzing, and he needed to escape it while he still could walk.

But when Ezra reached his study and sank onto his stool, he could only stare in stunned disbelief at the Torah scroll lying open where he'd left it. "How can this be?" he asked aloud. "God of Abraham, how can you let our enemy triumph this way? How have we angered you?" In spite of all Ezra's knowledge and learning and his ability to interpret the finest details of the law, the Almighty One seemed unknowable at that moment. Ezra lowered his head to the table, resting his forehead on his folded his arms. "'My God, my God, why have you forsaken me? Why are you so far from saving me, so far from the words of my groaning?'"

The door opened. He looked up, expecting to see his brother, but it was one of his Torah students, a young man named Shimon. "Rebbe Ezra, I don't understand—"

"Neither do I!" His words came out harsher than he intended, but he wanted to be left alone. Instead, Shimon took a step closer.

"Rebbe, you said God's punishment and exile ended when our people were allowed to return and rebuild the temple, but this decree—"

"This decree came from Gentiles, Shimon, not God."

"But the Almighty One allowed it, didn't He?"

Ezra didn't reply. He propped his elbows on the table and covered his face, hoping Shimon would leave.

"Why do the Gentiles hate us, Rebbe?"

"Because we follow God," he said, his hands muffling his reply. "Men who worship false gods want to wipe out all remembrance of the one true God and His moral laws, and so they attack us, the keepers of His Torah."

The stool scraped across the stone floor as Shimon sat down across from him. Ezra lowered his hands, resisting the urge to shout at him to go away.

"Rebbe, this decree reminds me of Pharaoh's order to throw our baby boys into the Nile. I know the Holy One spared one of those babies, Moses, but many more must have died. I asked you once why the Holy One allowed it, why He didn't save all of the babies, and you said He allowed it for a time because it served His greater purpose. You said God wanted to show the Egyptians His power, and rescue *all* of us." Ezra watched Shimon through his tears, unable to recall ever saying those words. "Could this decree be part of some greater plan, Rebbe?

Do you think the Almighty One wants to show His power to the Persians the way He did to the Egyptians?"

Ezra couldn't reply. Maybe he would arrive at a place of understanding someday, but not today. Today he was too shaken, his mind too numb to do anything but cry out in grief. He didn't want to die—not this way, not at the hands of the Amalekites, not after striving so hard all his life to study and obey God's law.

At last he found his voice. "Go home to your family, Shimon. They surely need all the comfort you can offer. I'm going to do the same." He pulled himself to his feet and wrapped the scroll in its covering. Shimon rose to help him, but Ezra waved him away. "I can finish. Go home. There won't be any classes today."

When he had put everything away, Ezra returned home to his room in Jude's house. He didn't want to talk to anyone, but Jude's wife, Devorah, stopped him in their courtyard before he could slip past her. He saw fear in her dark eyes and knew Jude must have told her about their death sentence.

"What's going to happen to us?" she asked. "If we fast and pray to the Holy One, He'll surely save us, won't He?"

Ezra glanced at his two small nieces, babbling as they shared a bowl of dates, and his brother's words from earlier that morning pierced his heart: *For once in your life, put away your scrolls and join the real world!* The king's edict wasn't another Torah passage to wrestle with and interpret but a decree that affected flesh-and-blood people. His people.

"Tell me, Ezra, please! You know the Almighty One better than the rest of us—"

"No, Devorah. I don't. You know Him as well as I do. Maybe better because you have children. You understand the need to discipline them when they do wrong, but you also understand mercy. I've watched you pull your girls into your arms and love them after you've punished them. I may know God's law and the history of our people, but I don't think I truly understand His mercy. And right now, we need to plead for His mercy."

The door from the inner rooms opened and Jude came out. He stared at Ezra as if surprised to see him. "You came home?"

"I've put away my scrolls. I'm joining what you call the real world. Tell me what you want me to do. How can I help?"

"We're going to need a new leader. Nathan is . . . well, you saw how upset he was. He fell to pieces after you left."

"You expect *me* to take his place?"

"You have more wisdom than the rest of us put together. And that's what we need right now—wisdom and . . . and guidance."

"I'm a scholar, not a leader."

"I know! I know! An expert on the God of Abraham and His Torah!" Jude's temper, always volatile under pressure, threatened to explode. "Tell us why this is happening. Why God is doing this to us, and what we can do about it. Give us answers!"

"I don't think—"

Jude stepped closer. "You asked me how you can help, and I'm telling you. We need a strong leader, a man of faith. Our faith has been shattered by this decree."

"And what makes you think mine hasn't?" Ezra raised his voice for the first time. Jude's two small daughters froze in place, clutching their bowls as if the loud voices had frightened them. Devorah bent to lift the baby, then prodded the older child to her feet, leading her inside.

"Pray about it," Jude said. "Study your scrolls. Find out what we've done to deserve this. Then, if you still refuse to lead us, pray that the Almighty One will send someone who will."

"I can do that," Ezra said quietly. "I can pray. And I can see what the law and the prophets have to say." He would start today. And he wouldn't stop searching the Scriptures until he found the reason for the decree—and the solution. But to become the leader of his people in Rebbe Nathan's place? Ezra couldn't promise such a thing.

CHAPTER
2

BABYLON

Devorah was still awake when Jude finally came to bed. As tired as she was from her day's work, the bewildering news wouldn't allow her to sleep. Her mind fluttered about like the dove that Noah had released from the ark, searching in vain for a place to land. She floundered about through stories from her ancestors' past, seeking a way to understand what the Almighty One was doing. And what He might do next.

"Do you want me to light the lamp for you?" she asked as she watched Jude strip off his tunic.

"No. It might wake the girls." He finished undressing but didn't lie down beside her. Even without the light, Devorah saw the expression of bafflement and fear on his face, the same expression she imagined on their ancestors' faces when they reached the shore of the Red Sea and heard Pharaoh's chariots thundering behind them. In the four years she and Jude had been married, Devorah had never seen her strong, dauntless husband so pale and overwhelmed. The moment he'd walked into their courtyard today in the middle of the afternoon, she'd known something terrible had happened.

"What's wrong?" she had asked, abandoning her dough in

the kneading trough. "Is it one of your brothers? Is someone hurt?" She could think of no other reason for him to be home so early or in such a state of shock.

"The Persian king has sentenced all of our people to death. Men, women, and children. We're all going to die."

"What? . . . No . . ." She had tried to embrace him, but he held her back, as if too tense to accept comfort. "But why, Jude? What's the reason for it?" He shook his head, unable to speak, then fled inside their house, refusing to say more. She had cornered her brother-in-law, Ezra, the moment he came home, hours earlier than usual. Ezra knew more about the Almighty One than anyone in Babylon, but he'd also been in shock, unable to offer assurance that God was in control.

Now she waited for Jude to lie down beside her, but he couldn't stop pacing, as if desperate to do something to change their situation. Devorah rose from their pallet and went into his arms, resting her head on his broad, solid chest. "I want to know the truth, Jude. Tell me everything about this death sentence and what we can do about it. Don't shelter me." He was a bear of a man, a giant alongside her tiny frame. Tonight he held her as if she might break, as if afraid to cling to her with the full force of his emotions. He stroked her dark hair, the color of the midnight sky, he always said.

"It's my job to shelter you," he said. "Men are supposed to protect their wives in situations like this."

She released him, looking up at him in the dark, fighting the urge to shout at him. "I don't want to be sheltered! I told you before we were married that I'm not like other women, content to live in ignorance of what's going on, letting my husband do everything and decide everything. I told you that I wanted more from our marriage than to simply cook your food and have your children—and you agreed, Jude. You agreed that I would be your partner as well as your wife. You promised you'd never hide anything from me—"

He put his fingers over her lips, stopping her, glancing at their children sleeping nearby. "You know why I agreed, Devorah? Because you captivated me. I was as helpless as Samson with his head shorn. You were right; you weren't like other women. You were an 'old' woman of twenty, for one thing."

She couldn't help punching his arm at the familiar tease. Jude was trying to distract her, and it made her furious. "That's because I was waiting for a man who would agree to my terms. And you did. You can't go back on your promise now. And don't change the subject. I'm not a child, like Abigail, who you can distract. Tell me what you know about this decree."

Jude exhaled. She could tell he was searching for words, trying to shape them in his mind the way he shaped his clay pots. He was a man who preferred action over words. But Devorah wanted to know everything, believing she had enough faith to handle the truth. She had grown up as the much-loved, only child of a scholarly father who had treated her like a son, immersing her in the stories of their ancestors, discussing the Almighty One and His Torah with her the way mothers discussed household duties with their daughters. She would have preferred not to marry at all than to live with a husband who didn't confide in her and consider her his best friend.

"If I tell you what I know, it will distress you," Jude finally said. "And I don't want you to be upset. I'm sorry I said anything in the first place."

"If you don't tell me, I may have to stop speaking to you and feeding you—and sleeping with you."

He turned away and sank down on the bed. Devorah wondered if he was going to be stubborn, but he beckoned for her to join him. "The decree came from the Persian king," he said when she had nestled beside him. "The law has been signed and sealed in his name and can never be changed or cancelled. He sent it to every province in the empire." He paused, then finished in a rush. "It allows our enemies to execute every Jew in the world—men, women, and children—on the thirteenth day of Adar. This year."

Devorah felt sick. They would kill children, too? "Our enemies?" she asked when she could speak. "We don't have any enemies here in Babylon."

He sighed again. "Have you ever heard of the Amalekites?"

"Yes, they attacked our people when we were helpless in the desert."

"Well, Ezra discovered that an Amalekite prince is behind this order of execution. And this prince—our enemy—is the Persian king's right-hand man."

She was beginning to see the hopeless trap that had been set for her people and to understand Jude's despair. She rested her head on his chest, listening to the steady thump of his heart, inhaling his familiar scent of hard work and earthy clay, wishing she could wake up and discover that this had only been a nightmare. "What do the elders say? Have they decided what we're going to do?"

"There hasn't been time. The decree came without warning. The elders are in shock. We all are. Rebbe Nathan fell apart. I'm sure you heard me trying to convince Ezra to take over for him. If anyone knows about God and His ways, it's my brother. Maybe he can figure something out, find something we did that angered God and caused this to happen. Maybe we haven't been faithful enough or haven't followed all His laws the way we should—although it's pretty hard to obey the Torah here in Babylon."

Devorah was glad she was lying down. She felt shaken by Jude's words and the fear she heard in his halting voice. When he'd first told her about the decree earlier today, it had seemed unreal to her, something that couldn't possibly be true. Was it a natural reaction to believe you'll live even when the Angel of Death unsheathes his sword in front of your face? She heard the rattle of his saber now, and it seemed as if the God she'd known since childhood had disappeared. She drew a shaky breath, trying to summon strength.

"God performed miracles for our ancestors, Jude. We both know the stories of how He parted the sea and brought water from a rock and gave us manna to eat in the desert. He made a covenant with us, promising to always be our God—and He'll keep that promise. He will!" She was trying to convince herself as well as Jude. "I know things look bad right now, but we just need a little time to find a way out. Our armies have been outnumbered before, but God always came through for us and saved us."

"Not always," Jude said. "Look where we are."

A chill went through her. Jude was right: not always. Not if her people turned away from Him and disobeyed His laws. Wasn't that why they were living here in Babylon, marched into exile under the sword of God's wrath? "We'll figure something out," she repeated.

"Maybe you should lead our people instead of Rebbe Nathan. You'll be like your namesake, General Devorah."

"Are you making fun of me?"

"No, my love," he said, pulling her closer. "If any woman in the empire could lead an army, it's you."

The baby began to stir, tossing restlessly in her bed before starting to whimper. "Did we wake her?" Jude whispered.

"No, a new tooth is bothering her. I'll rub her gums."

This planned execution of her people would never happen, Devorah told herself as she lifted one-year-old Michal into her arms. God would never allow it. If all the stories in the Scriptures were true, then the Almighty One had a plan. Her people could trust God no matter what.

Even so, as Devorah soothed her daughter back to sleep, she couldn't deny that she was terrified—not for herself but for her children. She understood Jude's compulsion to protect her, because she would die to protect Michal and three-year-old Abigail. Tears stung Devorah's eyes, but she forced them back, holding the baby closer, refusing to cry. She would be strong. And she would teach her daughters to be strong. And to trust God.

Chapter 3

THE CITY OF CASIPHIA, NORTH OF BABYLON

Reuben squeezed his eyes closed, fighting tears. He was a man now at age twelve, and men weren't supposed to cry. Even when they faced death. Especially then. Soldiers on the battlefield never wept.

"Careful!" his father warned. "Watch what you're doing. Keep the bellows going."

Reuben opened his eyes and pumped the leather bellows as Abba held the blade in the flames, slowly turning it until it glowed red-hot. "Don't stop, Reuben. . . . Keep fanning the coals." Abba knew when the metal was hot enough to remove from the fire. And Reuben knew that blowing air on the coals made the furnace burn hotter. Sweat rolled down his face and stung his eyes. His father's face and bare chest glistened with it.

At last Abba pulled the blade from the fire and carried it to his anvil to hammer into shape. Reuben rose from his crouch and wiped sweat and tears from his eyes as the clang of metal against metal rang in his ears. The racket went on and on until Abba paused to inspect the curved sickle blade he had fashioned.

"How can you just keep working?" Reuben asked him. "Why

33

bother? We're all going to die in a few months!" He coughed and cleared his throat to disguise the emotion in his voice.

"The Babylonians don't care, son. They still expect us to do our jobs."

"We should refuse. What could they do? Kill us sooner rather than later?"

Abba looked up. "You're right. We could all stop working and just wait to die. But I spend my time praying while I'm working. It helps me concentrate." He laid the blade on the anvil again and hammered it some more.

Reuben didn't want to die, but the emperor of Persia had decreed it. The date of his execution was set for the thirteenth day of Adar.

Abba paused to inspect his work again, and Reuben knew by the satisfaction on his face that the blade was finished. "See that?" Abba said, holding it up. "We'll sharpen it on the grinding stone, let the carpenters add a wooden handle, and it'll be ready to cut grain." Abba had another blacksmith who worked for him and two apprentices, but he was training Reuben himself. They would own the forge together one day—at least that had been the plan before the king's edict. Reuben vowed to burn the smithy to the ground on the night before his execution. It wasn't much, just two furnace pits and a collection of tools and worktables beneath a thatched roof, but he refused to let the Babylonians have everything after they killed him.

"What if the Holy One doesn't answer our prayers and save us?" Reuben asked. "Then what are we going to do?" He followed his father to the grinding stone in another part of the shop.

"We've been through this, son. I told you the elders have discussed it and—"

"I know, I know. But why can't we escape outside the empire? Someplace where we don't have enemies."

"The lands beyond the borders are all unknown, their people uncivilized. Besides, our enemies won't allow a mass migration of millions of Jews. They want us all dead, not relocated. We're trapped inside the city walls." Abba continued to work while he talked, sorting through his sharpening tools.

"Can't we escape and hide in the desert? Just our family?"

"I've considered that. But we would have to stay there forever and never come back."

"So? I'd rather be alive in a cave than dead here."

Abba looked up at him, his expression angry and sad at the same time. "The elders have discussed all these options, Reuben. Endlessly. They've prayed and fasted and prayed some more. None of us wants to die in a few short months, but we haven't come up with a plan that will work yet. Keep praying that we will."

"Can't we fight back?"

Abba moved closer to Reuben and lowered his voice. "I intend to fight. When the time comes, I'll fight with my last breath to protect you and our family. A lot of other men feel the same way."

"But I don't understand why—"

Abba reached for Reuben and pulled him close, his muscled arms wrapped tightly around him like metal bands, his body slick with sweat. Reuben could no longer stop his tears as he clung to him. "I don't understand it either, son. I wish I did. I can't explain what I don't understand myself."

When Abba finally released him, his eyes glistened with tears. "Go get more wood for the fire before we break for lunch. We need to make another sickle blade before evening prayers."

"Are you just going to keep working all the way to the end?"

Abba looked at the new blade for a moment, as if trying to decide. "Yes. I am," he said. "We show our faith in God when we keep moving forward even when our prayers aren't being answered. It's the highest form of praise to keep believing that God is good even when it doesn't seem that way."

Reuben didn't want to praise a God who would let them all die. He exhaled and went out to the woodpile where the air was cooler and a breeze blew inland from the nearby river. He picked up a piece of firewood and then flung it down again, as hard as he could. He knew he would die someday, but most of the time he never thought about it, living as if life would go on forever. Now all he could think about was death, wondering if he would have to suffer or if he'd die quickly. And he wondered what would happen afterward.

Reuben had cheated death once before when he and his friends had gone swimming in the flood-swollen Tigris River, misjudging the danger. Reuben had barely made it back to shore after the current swept him downstream, inhaling so much water he'd nearly drowned. But once he'd reached the riverbank and the shock and terror faded, he'd felt a thrill that had been addictive, fueling his passion for more death-defying exploits.

But this was different. His enemies planned to execute him in less than ten months, along with his family, his friends, and everyone else who was a descendant of Abraham. Maybe he deserved it. He didn't always obey his parents or follow God's laws. He often recited his prayers in the house of assembly without thinking about the words or the God he was talking to. And he had no interest in studying the Torah. So yes, he probably deserved to die—but his mother and father didn't. His two younger sisters didn't. Neither did the new baby his mother was expecting in a few months. Would his enemies kill an innocent newborn, too?

Why had life become so crazy? The God of Abraham had turned out to be as careless and unpredictable as the gods of Babylon. And the adults Reuben had trusted to have everything under control were helpless to stop this edict and completely without hope.

He finally bent to gather an armload of wood and carried it back to the fire pit. Abba stirred the coals, making a place to add the logs. "I wish we weren't God's chosen people," Reuben said as he let the wood drop to the ground. "Why can't we be like everyone else? Maybe if we blended in with the Babylonians and started going to their temples and festivals they'd let us live."

Abba shook his head. "If we deny God, our lives aren't worth living."

Reuben heard his father's words but didn't understand them. He crouched to rebuild the fire, fighting tears again. "Is it true that the king's law is final? That no one can change it?"

"Yes, it's true." Abba ran his fingers through his beard as if considering something. "Come with me, Reuben," he said when the fire was laid. "I want to show you something." He led him to the rear of the shop, separated from the work area by a partition. He pulled a crate from one of the shelves and opened the lid to show Reuben what was inside.

Swords. Four of them.

Reuben pulled one out to examine it, recognizing his father's craftsmanship. "I plan to forge as many of these as I can in my spare time," Abba said, "before the month of Adar. Would you like to help me?"

Reuben could only nod, unable to speak. Maybe they weren't without hope after all. If he had given up the day he'd fought the river's current, he would've drowned. But he hadn't given up then, and he wouldn't now. He and Abba would fight until the end. And maybe, just maybe, they would survive the slaughter after all.

CHAPTER

4

BETHLEHEM

Wait!" Amina shouted. "Wait for me!" She limped along as fast as she could, dragging her weak leg through the dirt, but her sister and the other children ignored her pleas. They ran ahead of her through the marketplace, weaving through displays of pomegranates and melons, running between stalls of reed baskets and wool rugs, laughing as they chased each other. Amina was the youngest at age eight, and she couldn't run as fast as her older sister, Sayfah. Tears blurred her vision, and Amina tripped and fell, her crippled leg collapsing beneath her. She lay in the dust, angry and bleeding, crying harder.

A gentle hand touched her shoulder. "Are you all right, dear?"

Amina sat up. Crouching beside her was the white-haired woman who owned a stall filled with beautiful woolen cloth. Her wrinkled face was kind, the skin around her dark eyes creased as if she smiled a lot. She lived in Bethlehem, not Amina's village. And she was a Jew. Amina's father hated Jews. His people, the Edomites, always had.

"You've skinned your knees," the woman said as she helped

Amina to her feet. "Come inside my booth and let me clean off the dirt for you."

"I told Sayfah to w-wait for me," Amina said, sobbing, "b-but she didn't listen!"

"Is Sayfah your sister?"

Amina nodded, drying her tears on her sleeve. The woman helped her sit on a low stool inside her booth. She was very pretty for a white-haired grandmother. "My name is Hodaya," she said as she fetched a clean cloth and a skin of water. "What's yours?"

"Amina."

"That's a lovely name." Hodaya squatted beside her, and as she lifted her hand, Amina flinched and drew back. In her experience, a raised hand was likely to strike her. "I won't hurt you, Amina. I'm just going to clean off the dirt and blood." Her hands were gentle as she worked, holding the cloth in place until the bleeding stopped. The cool water soothed Amina's stinging knees. She couldn't remember the last time anyone had treated her so kindly.

"Does that feel better?" Hodaya asked. Amina nodded. "I like to watch you and the other children play when you come to the market. I noticed you especially because we have something in common. See?" She stood and lifted her hem to show Amina her left foot, withered and twisted at an odd angle. "I can't run very fast, either," she said, smiling.

"The other girls laugh and make fun of me because I can't keep up, but I used to run even faster than Sayfah." Amina wiped another tear as it rolled down her face.

"What happened?"

"I got a fever and the sickness made my leg weak. Is that what happened to your foot, too?"

"No, I was born this way."

"Abba is ashamed of me," Amina said, lowering her voice so no one would hear her. "He won't even look at me and my ugly leg. Did your father hate you, too?"

Hodaya took a moment to reply. "I had two fathers. The one

whose blood I share was much like yours. When he saw that I was born crippled, he didn't want me. But our loving God, who created me this way for a reason, gave me a new father, the man who raised me and loved me. He was a priest in God's holy temple, and he taught me all about the God who loves you and me."

"I wish I had a nice father like that. I try to stay out of Abba's way because he'll hit me if I make him lose his temper." Amina didn't say so out loud, but she feared her father's words even more than she feared his blows. They rained on her like stones, saying she was worthless, she would always be a burden to him, she would never marry a husband and be a proper wife.

"What about your mother?" Hodaya asked.

"Mama does whatever Abba says so he won't hit her, too."

"You poor child." Hodaya reached for Amina again, and again Amina instinctively pulled back. When she realized that Hodaya was only trying to put her arm around her, she moved closer to receive the rare embrace. What would it be like to be treated this kindly all the time?

"Do you have a husband?" she asked Hodaya.

"He died a few years ago, but Aaron and I were married for many years. My sons have given me seven grandchildren."

"Abba says no one will ever marry me unless I stop limping. I've tried and tried, but I can't help it. See how weak this leg is?" Amina wasn't supposed to let anyone see her thin, shriveled leg, but Hodaya had already seen it when she'd washed the dirt off Amina's knees. Besides, the old woman's leg was shriveled and crooked, too, and her misshapen foot pointed the wrong way.

"A husband who loves you won't care what your leg looks like. A very wise friend once told me that every one of us has something about us that isn't perfect. For you and me, our differences are just a little more noticeable, that's all."

Could that be true? Were Amina's sister and older brothers and even her father imperfect in some way? It seemed unlikely. Amina held out her palms to show Hodaya how they'd been scraped, too. Hodaya poured more water onto the cloth. "Maybe you can't run as fast as the other children," she said as she wiped the dirt off Amina's hands, "but God created you to do something special that they can't do."

"He did? What?"

Hodaya laughed. "I don't know, but I'm certain you'll figure it out by the time you're my age. My husband was a shepherd. His flock grazed in the fields outside town. I learned to spin and weave the wool from his sheep and make cloth to sell."

Amina climbed off the stool after Hodaya finished and looked around at the colorful skeins of wool and piles of cloth. Hodaya had been unpacking her goods in her stall when Amina had tripped and fallen, and she continued laying out her samples now. "These colors are really pretty," Amina said, trailing her fingers over the soft fabric.

"Thank you, dear. I dye the wool myself. I love trying different ingredients and creating new colors."

Amina's father said Jews were thieves and liars, and she should stay far away from them. If her sister came back and saw her talking to one, Amina would get into trouble. But she didn't care. She liked this kind, gentle woman.

"Your hair is such a beautiful color," Hodaya said, resting her hand on Amina's head for a moment. Amina only flinched a little this time. "I would love to find a way to dye my cloth this gorgeous, coppery-brown."

"Sayfah says my hair is ugly. Hers is black like Mama's."

"Don't listen to her. It's lovely and—" Hodaya halted in surprise as a man hurried into the booth. Amina could tell by the little cap he wore and the tassels on his robe that he was Jewish. "Jacob! What are you doing here?" Hodaya asked.

"Pack everything up, Mama. We have to go home right away."

"What are you talking about? I just got here. I haven't sold anything yet." The man began stuffing cloth back into sacks as if he hadn't heard her. "Jacob, stop. What are you doing?"

"Something's happened, Mama—"

"To one of the children? To your brothers?" she asked in alarm.

"No, we're all fine." He noticed Amina for the first time and asked, "Who's the Edomite girl? Why is she here?" He glared at Amina as if she were his enemy.

"This is my new friend, Amina. She fell and skinned her knees. Amina, this is my very rude son, Jacob." He didn't respond as he continued to fold up Hodaya's cloth and take down her display, his movements hurried and jerky. Hodaya made him stop, pulling a bolt of fabric from his hands. "Jacob, I'm not packing up or going anywhere until you tell me why."

He let out his breath in a rush, the way a horse snorts when it's impatient to run. "Three elders from Jerusalem came to the house of assembly this morning with bad news. The Persian emperor has issued a decree that's . . . well, it's like something from a nightmare. We're holding a meeting right away to discuss what to do. I came to take you home."

Amina watched Hodaya's face. If her son's news upset her, the older woman didn't let it show. She rested her hand on Amina's head again, as if blessing her. "It was so nice to meet you, Amina. I hope we see each other again."

"Me too."

Just then, Amina heard her sister calling her. "Amina . . . Amina, where are you?"

"Bye," she said with a little wave. "Thanks for helping me." She ducked out of the booth and limped up the street toward Sayfah, taking her time so she wouldn't trip again.

"Where have you been?" Sayfah asked. She looked as angry and impatient as their father as she stood with her arms folded, glaring as if Amina was at fault instead of Sayfah and the others for running off. "Come on, slowpoke. Mama is finished shopping. We're going home."

Mama stood waiting at the narrow entrance to Bethlehem,

holding the produce she'd purchased. Amina tried to help, carrying a melon as she limped home, but her weak leg made it hard to keep up. She tried to show Mama her scraped knees when they arrived back in their village. "Look what happened when I fell. A nice woman in the marketplace helped me—"

But her mother wasn't interested. "Maybe you'll watch where you're going next time."

Amina helped prepare the meal, then waited out of sight while Abba and her two older brothers ate. They were the three most important people in her household and entitled to the first and best of everything. They peppered her with slaps and kicks and curses whenever she didn't move quickly enough, especially when they were tired from working in the fields all day.

She was still thinking about the Jewish weaver's kindness as she lay in bed that night. Hodaya had called Amina's hair a lovely color. She'd said there was something special that Amina could do that her sister couldn't—and she would find out what it was someday. Hodaya said she liked being different, even though her foot was even more crooked than Amina's.

Amina fell asleep thinking of her words. But sometime in the middle of the night, loud voices and cheering woke her up. She sat up, listening in the dark to sounds of laughter and celebration. It sounded like the festival her village held after the olives were harvested, but they weren't even ripe yet. When another great cheer went up, Amina climbed out of bed and peeked outside her door. Everyone in the village had gathered in the street, celebrating with torches blazing and open jars of wine. Amina's mother and some of the other women passed through the crowd with pitchers, refilling everyone's cups. Abba stood on the back of a wagon, swaying slightly as if the wagon was rolling down the road. "What a day this is!" he said, lifting his cup. "We'll be rid of those filthy Jews at last! Now they'll all die!" The crowd cheered in response.

Amina's Uncle Abdel, who had come to visit from a distant

village, jumped onto the wagon beside him, draping his arm over Abba's shoulder. "Friends, we'll take our pick of the Jews' houses and property," he said. "We can have their olive groves and vineyards, harvest fields that we didn't have to plant—"

"And sheep!" someone yelled from the crowd. "They have huge flocks of sheep!"

"That's right!" Abba said. "We'll not only reap the benefits of the Jews' labor and prosperity, but we'll be rid of them for good." His words were met with joyful laughter.

"Listen . . . listen!" The oldest man in the village shuffled toward the wagon with his arms raised, signaling that he had something to say. The laughter quieted. "I was just a boy when the Jews arrived here from Babylon with their stinking caravans. They invaded like a locust swarm, building on our land and claiming our fields and vineyards as their own. Thousands of them! That was nearly seventy years ago, and I've thought of little else all these years, except getting rid of them. At last we'll have our chance!" The people gave another roaring cheer.

Amina was wide awake now. She slipped through the door and limped barefoot across her family's small courtyard to stand by the gate. She was too frightened by the shouting and rowdiness to venture into the street, and besides, she was in her nightclothes.

"We need a plan," Abba said, "so we can take advantage of this opportunity. Everyone needs to stake his claim and determine whose plunder he wants and which Jews he intends to kill. And we'll need swords and other weapons."

"It might be better if we rounded up all the Jews first," the old man said. "We could kill them all in one place."

"Do you think they'll fight back?" Amina's uncle asked.

"They can't!" Abba replied. "That's the beauty of it! This decree comes from King Xerxes himself. Every Jew in the empire—every man, woman, and child—must be executed."

Amina didn't understand. The woman who'd helped her

today was Jewish. Why would the king kill someone as kind and gentle as Hodaya?

She watched her father drain his cup of wine, then scan the crowd as if searching for a refill. "Hey! What are you doing out here?" he shouted when he saw Amina. She backed away, careful not to trip and make him angrier. "Get back inside! Now!"

Mama hurried over and slapped Amina's face before yanking her into the house. "You heard your father. Stay inside where you belong."

"But . . . why is Abba going to kill—"

"This doesn't concern you. This is grown-up business." Mama pushed Amina down onto her pallet saying, "Go to sleep and forget what you heard."

"But the nice lady who helped me today was Jewish and—"

"What are you doing talking to Jews? You know better." Amina ducked as Mama lifted her hand to slap her again, her face still burning from the first slap. "Never trust a Jew. They do sneaky things to deceive people and disguise what they're really like. They all deserve to die." Mama left the room, closing the door behind her.

Amina was no stranger to killing and bloodshed. She'd seen Abba and the other men slaughter sheep and pigs for festivals and special occasions. She'd watched as the blood gushed onto the ground after Abba cut their throats, his hands and arms turning red and slick. The animals had squealed and squirmed one moment, then lay limp and lifeless the next. Would Abba kill the Jews the same way, slashing their throats and letting their blood soak his hands and pour into the dirt? Amina knew that people sometimes died—two children from her village had died of the same fever that had crippled her leg. But everyone was supposed to be sad when people died, wailing and mourning for them. They weren't supposed to cheer and rejoice in the streets. Amina shivered in bed as she listened to the noise outside. It took her a long time to fall asleep.

CHAPTER
5

BABYLON

Time passed with a swiftness that left Ezra breathless, the days and weeks trampling each other in a wild stampede. Ever since they'd heard the king's decree a month ago, Ezra had spent each day here in his study, searching for answers, finding none. Now, as spring began to blossom and their death sentence loomed closer, he felt a desperation that bordered on panic. Studying and teaching the Scriptures had fulfilled him in the past, but it had been an intellectual pursuit, not a matter of life and death. And he hadn't worried about time eroding, hour by hour, like a riverbank in a rainstorm.

His people had less than nine more months to live, less time than it took for a child to form in its mother's womb. He had cancelled all his classes and suspended work with his fellow scholars to study in solitude, praying and confessing, fasting and weeping and then studying some more. But Ezra was no closer to discovering the mind of God or a way to save his people. Instead, he'd discovered the vast difference between talking about God all day and talking to Him; between knowing about God and His laws, and knowing God. The more he learned, the less he understood—and the more unqualified he felt to lead his people as Jude still urged him to do.

He looked down at the scroll of Isaiah lying open in front of him. The prophet's words had blurred on the page a moment ago as he'd read them through his tears: *"O Lord, you are our Father. We are the clay, you are the potter; we are all the work of your hand. Do not be angry beyond measure, O Lord."* He had thought of his own father, a master potter, pictured his muscled hands, skilled at shaping a formless lump of clay into a useful vessel. Abba had been proud of Ezra, his firstborn son, blessed by the Almighty One to be a Torah scholar instead of a potter, and the youngest member of the Great Assembly. Abba had continually reminded his three sons of their heritage as priests, tracing their lineage back to Moses' brother Aaron, and to Zadok, the high priest in King Solomon's temple. If they hadn't been exiled here in Babylon, Ezra might be serving as the high priest of the temple in Jerusalem, the spiritual leader of his people. But his learning and his pedigree did him no good, now. He may as well make pots like his younger brothers.

He stood and rolled up the scroll to put it away. He needed to get out of his stifling study. The sackcloth beneath his tunic burned his irritated skin like fire, but he refused to remove it, a reminder to pray each time it chafed. As he walked through the quiet, meandering lanes of Babylon's Jewish community, hearing the familiar sounds of goats bleating and babies crying, only two things were clear to him—and they were contradictory. The Almighty One had made a covenant with Abraham and his descendants, an everlasting covenant that would never change; and the Persian king had decreed his people's annihilation, a decree that also could never be changed.

Ezra's steps took him to the grove near the canal where his brothers continued their father's pottery business, the towering palm trees above the clay pit motionless in the still air. He wove his way around the shimmering heat of the kiln and through the obstacle course of pottery in various stages of completion to where Jude sat at his potter's wheel, shaping a vessel on the upper wheel while spinning the lower wheel with his foot. Jude glanced up and acknowledged Ezra with a nod before returning to his work, dipping his fingers in water to keep the clay supple. The knee-high vessel he was making would be glazed and fired, then used to store grain or olive oil.

Ezra watched the clay expand and grow beneath Jude's experienced hands like a living thing, obeying the pressure of his fingers, the pull of his hands. He thought of Isaiah's words: *"We are the clay, you are the potter . . ."*

Ezra had apprenticed with his father in his younger years and knew that a pot couldn't be shaped without pressure. He also knew the importance of centering the lump of clay precisely in the middle of the wheel before beginning. If it wasn't centered, the emerging vessel would become deformed or even fly off the wheel as it spun. Ezra had never mastered the centering process, and his pots had inevitably become misshapen beneath the pressure of his fingers. Was that where his people had gone wrong? Had they failed to center their lives on God's law before being shaped by Him? Maybe if Ezra could teach the Law to his people more diligently, centering them and—

"What brings you here?" Jude asked, pulling Ezra from his thoughts. The wheel had stopped spinning, the pot finished.

"I needed to get out for a while. Get some perspective." Or was he avoiding God's echoing silence? His brother cut the pot free with a thin cord, then climbed from behind the wheel, stretching his arms and shoulders.

"Did you find a reason for the king's decree?"

"Not yet."

Jude sloshed his hands in a bucket of water to clean them off. In the pit in front of them, an apprentice treaded the oozing slime, mixing water into the clay with his feet. Two more apprentices knelt beside a wooden board, wedging the clay to force the air out before forming the clay into a pot. Ezra had never mastered the skill of wedging, either. But the Torah? He could recite large portions of all five books by memory. Jude crouched beside the boards to inspect the wedged clay, poking it to feel the texture. He shook his head. "Work it some more."

Their youngest brother, Asher, worked beside the kiln, dressed in a turban and loincloth. His lean body glistened with sweat in the intense heat. Married for less than a year, Asher had been ecstatic as he'd shared the news that his wife was expecting. Ezra remembered how he had bounced from one foot to the other as he'd announced the news. Now Asher's joy had turned to despair. He seemed to shrivel a little more each day, like a branch hanging too close to the flames, knowing he couldn't protect his wife and unborn infant. Why would God doom his child—all their children—to such a short life?

Asher left his work to talk with his brothers, unwinding his turban as he walked closer, using the end of it to wipe the sweat from his face. "I told Jude that it's a waste of time to keep making pots all day," he said. "Why not stop and enjoy the few months we have left?"

"And I told him that we still need to earn money to feed our families," Jude said.

Asher responded with a huff. "Right. Let's fatten everyone up like calves in the stall, even though we've been sentenced to death. In fact, maybe we should hold a banquet!"

"Would you rather we all starved to death before our enemies have a chance to kill us?" Jude asked. "Because starvation is an agonizing way to die, you know."

"And being slaughtered isn't agonizing?"

"Stop . . . please . . ." Ezra held up his hands.

"Is there any hope at all?" Asher asked. "That's what I want to know."

"As the psalmist wrote, our hope is in the Almighty One's

unfailing love," Ezra said. But did he really believe that, or were they mere words?

"I hope you've made up your mind to lead us," Jude said. "We need a strong leader more than ever."

Ezra spread his hands. "How can I lead if I don't have any answers?"

"Then find answers! Give us hope or understanding or something," Jude said. "You're the expert on God, the great theologian. We don't care about your doubts, just tell us what God is doing to us!"

"Have you heard about Rebbe Nathan?" Asher asked before Ezra could reply.

"No . . . what about him?"

"He resigned as head of the house of assembly. He's suffered such severe pains in his chest that he's bedridden."

"We were discussing his replacement this morning," Jude said, "and the other men requested I ask you."

Ezra groaned. "You're the natural-born leader in this family, Jude. Not me."

Jude rubbed his forehead, leaving behind a smear of clay. When he spoke, Ezra heard the emotion in his voice, the unshed tears that threatened to choke him. "I can't lead. It takes all my energy to be strong for Devorah and the girls. I can't do more than that. I can't be strong for our people, too. You need to help us, Ezra. You don't have a family like the rest of us do."

As difficult as it was to face his own death, Ezra knew this ordeal was even worse for men like Jude and Asher with wives and children. Ezra wouldn't have to spend the final months of his life struggling to console the people he loved. He could stay awake day and night as he had been doing, falling asleep at his study table with his scrolls and sputtering oil lamp in front of him. And he could mourn and weep alone instead of pretending to be strong for someone else. Yet Ezra envied his brothers now more than ever before. What would it be like to find comfort in a loving wife's arms? Who would he hold in his final moments of life?

"Ezra . . ." Jude said, breaking the silence. "You're a million miles away again."

"Sorry. My mind seems to spin in useless circles lately." He found it harder and harder to concentrate each day. And while he used to love maneuvering through legal labyrinths, exploring circuitous rabbit trails in the written and oral Torah, this dilemma had no end—or maybe the end was too final. A dead end. He massaged his eyes with his thumb and forefinger, pressing against the throbbing pain in his head.

"God is just, but He is also merciful," he finally said. "Even if we deserve this punishment, we can plead for His mercy. Either He'll spare us or He won't. I don't know what more I can do as a leader except tell everyone to fast and pray."

"There's plenty more you can do," Jude shouted. "Stop stuttering excuses like Moses and make up your mind to lead us!"

"Help us make sense of this," Asher added. "Give us hope."

"I don't want to give false hope—"

"How do you know it's false?" Asher asked.

Ezra stared at his feet, unable to meet his gaze. When he looked up again, he saw Jude's face harden as he gave Asher a nudge. "Look . . . they're back again." Jude pointed to two Babylonian men who stood across the yard from them, gesturing to the kiln and the rows of pots as if surveying the property.

"Who are they? What do they want?" Ezra asked.

"Our pottery works," Jude said. "They're planning to steal it after they kill us. Hey!" he shouted as he bolted across the grove toward them. "This is my property! I told you the other day to stay away from here!" Ezra and Asher hurried to keep up.

"Not for long," one of the strangers said. He had the gall to smile.

"That's right," the other one added. "You'll be dead in eight months and this will all be ours."

"But maybe we won't kill *all* of you," the first man said. "I think I'll keep your pretty little wife around for a while until I get tired of her."

Jude rushed the man but Asher was quicker, grabbing Jude from behind. "Let me go!" Jude shouted. "Let me kill these dogs!" It took all of Ezra's strength to help Asher hold him back.

One of the Babylonians leaned forward as Jude struggled to free himself and spit in his face. "We're the ones who will be doing the killing, *Jew*!"

Ezra trembled with helpless rage as he watched the Babylonians turn away. All his life, he had felt disdain toward Gentiles with their useless superstitions, willful ignorance, and shocking immorality. But the king's decree had transformed his disdain into hatred so violent that his body shook with it. Jude finally freed himself and wiped the spittle from his face. "I'm going home," he said, and Ezra knew it was to check on Devorah and his daughters, to reassure himself that they were safe.

Ezra retreated back to his study and closed the door, unwilling to spend another moment among his Gentile enemies, watching them go about their carefree lives, gloating as they plotted his destruction. How could the Holy One allow these *animals* to destroy His people?

He slumped down in his seat, waiting for his anger to fade. He had no desire to lead their community in Rebbe Nathan's place. He was a scholar, not a leader. But was he really stuttering excuses like Moses had at the burning bush? Ezra remembered the promise God had made to Moses, saying, *"I will be with you."*

He sat alone in his room for a long time as an idea began to take shape, fueled by his hatred toward the Gentiles. Then, before he had a chance to change his mind, Ezra rose and went out to the study hall where two scholars and a handful of yeshiva students sat talking. "Go and gather all the other rabbis and teachers for me, and any students who are available. Tell them to meet me here as quickly as possible. I have a proposal to make."

An hour later he stood before a roomful of his fellow teachers and their disciples, the memory of their enemies' taunts still fresh. "Our people are asking why the Almighty One would allow this decree," he said. "What is His purpose in this? Will He really allow all of the descendants of Abraham to die? I've been searching for answers, but the task is too huge for me to accomplish alone in the short time that remains. But working together, maybe we can find the reason why we've been abandoned. Maybe we can discover a way to obtain the Holy One's mercy." He paused to wipe the runner of sweat that trickled down his forehead, remembering the spittle on Jude's face.

"This is what I'm proposing: We will divide the holy books among as many of us who are willing, and read them day and night, scroll after scroll, searching to find out what the Almighty One has promised us, where we have gone wrong, and why God is allowing evil to win. We'll read and study the books of the law and the prophets and the history of our people, and at the end of each day we'll compare notes. Together, we'll assemble the pieces, and maybe God will reveal the bigger picture to us. When we gather for evening prayers, I'll share what we've learned with our people to encourage them. They're begging for hope and direction. In fact, it's time for evening prayers right now," he said, noticing the angle of the late afternoon sun. "If you'd like to help me with this project, meet me here first thing tomorrow."

Ezra led the way outside for the short walk to the house of assembly, his young student, Shimon, falling into step beside him. "Rebbe Ezra, I just read the Holy One's promises in the prophecies of Jeremiah. God said that only if the heavens could be measured and the foundations of the earth be searched out would He reject all the descendants of Israel."

"Good, Shimon. Very good. That's exactly the kind of promises we're looking for."

"And in another prophecy, God said that although He would

completely destroy all the nations where we've been scattered, He would never completely destroy us."

Ezra stopped to rest his hand on his student's shoulder. "You'll be a great help to us, Shimon. Thank you."

A few minutes later, Ezra climbed onto the bimah to address the assembled men, ignoring the misgivings he still had about assuming a leadership role. "I'll be leading prayers until Rebbe Nathan is well," he began, "but first I want to—"

"Why should we pray?" someone shouted from the crowd. "Isn't it obvious that God isn't listening?"

It took Ezra a moment to recover his poise. "Well . . . we can ask God to spare us for Abraham's sake, for His covenant's sake. Even if we deserve this punishment for failing to keep our part of the covenant, God is merciful and—"

"But the king's law can't be repealed!"

"True. But the Almighty One proved He was more powerful than Pharaoh, didn't He? He's more powerful than the Persian king, too, and He can rescue us—"

"Yes, He's powerful enough to save us—but will He?"

Ezra hesitated. "If it's His will," he finally replied. He knew it was an unsatisfactory answer. He and the other scholars would have to do better.

"If God loves us, how could He allow this to happen?" called out another voice. "Why did He allow the Egyptians to abuse us and throw our sons into the Nile?"

"Maybe He wants us to turn to Him," Ezra said. "Maybe we would have been content living in Egypt if Pharaoh hadn't issued his decree. And maybe we've become too content here in Babylon, too."

"Then why are the Jews in Jerusalem sentenced to die along with us?"

"I don't know," Ezra said, exhaling. He had taught his students to ask good questions and dig deep into God's Word. But these questions sprang from fear, not intellectual curiosity, and were more difficult to answer. He could understand how the congregation's terror and despair had overwhelmed Rebbe Nathan. But when Ezra remembered the two Gentiles who plotted to steal Jude's business and rape his wife, his anger hardened into resolve like clay fired in the kiln. He cleared his throat, and when he spoke, his voice came out louder than before. "The Almighty One told Abraham, 'I will establish my covenant as an everlasting covenant between me and you and your descendants after you for generations to come, to be your God and the God of your descendants.' *Everlasting*. That means a remnant of our people *will* survive. It may not be us. It may be Jews from another part of this empire. But I am certain of this: God's people *will* survive—somewhere, somehow!"

"But it *may* be us?"

"Yes. And so every day, between now and the thirteenth of Adar, we need to repent of our sins and plead for mercy. And no matter what happens, whether we live or die, we need to pray for the salvation of God's remnant."

BABYLON

Devorah knelt beside her sister-in-law's bed and wiped her forehead with a cool cloth. "You have to stay calm, Miriam. It isn't good for you or your baby to be so upset."

"But I want my life back," she wept. "The life I had before this terrible decree. The life I always dreamed of with Asher and a houseful of children. Our baby isn't even born yet, and now it will die before it has a chance to live!"

"Shh . . . Don't think about such things." Fear, Devorah discovered, was contagious. Hours could pass as she cooked meals and cared for her daughters when she would almost forget about the Angel of Death. But Miriam's panicked words made her aware of his arid whispers, the sickly vertigo of his touch. Devorah's inevitable meeting with death's angel would be bad enough, but he had no right to invade her soul now, bringing nightmares of her final moments—nightmares in which she clung to her husband and daughters, desperate to save them and herself, knowing she couldn't.

Miriam grabbed the basin and held her head over it to vomit. Ill with worry and morning sickness, she had nothing left in her stomach to bring up. "You need to lie down again," Devorah told her as she wiped her face. "Try to rest, Miriam. Think of pleasant things."

"I don't want to die! And I can't stop thinking about it, wondering how it will happen, if they'll herd us all together or come here with their swords and—"

"Stop it!" Devorah fought the urge to shake her. "Miriam, you have to stop this! You're dying a hundred times before the day finally comes—and it might not come, you know. As long as we have breath we can hope, can't we? We have to trust God."

Miriam covered her face and wept, her cries so heartrending that Devorah had to swallow her own tears. Her daughters were out in the courtyard with Miriam's mother, and Devorah determined never to let them witness such fear and grief. Asher had begged her to console Miriam, but it was proving impossible. She took Miriam's hand to try again.

"Listen, Miriam. You must know the words to some of the psalms. Why don't you recite them when you're afraid? That's what I do." Devorah tried to think of one now, but the fever of fear had scattered her thoughts. She sat by Miriam's side until she finally calmed down, then gathered up her girls and returned home in defeat.

She had only been away from home a short time, but when she came through the gate, she found Jude pacing their courtyard in his potter's apron, raking his fingers through his curly black hair. "Devorah, thank God!" he said when he saw her. He rushed to meet her, pulling her into his arms without waiting for her to put down the baby. The strength of his embrace could have crushed both of them. "Where were you?" he asked. "When I came home and you weren't here I was worried sick!"

"Visiting Miriam. Why were you worried? . . . And since when do you come home in the middle of the morning? What's wrong?"

"Nothing. I . . . I just felt like coming home."

She didn't believe him. Devorah studied her husband's face as he picked up Abigail, who was clinging to his leg. She saw worry lines on Jude's forehead that she hadn't noticed before, and she reached up to smooth them.

"Asher asked me to talk to Miriam. She hasn't been well and—"

"You didn't walk to her house all alone, did you?"

"Of course. The girls and I—"

"Devorah, no! From now on I don't want you to leave our house by yourself! Ever!"

She stared at him. He was angry over nothing. Jude had always had a quick temper, but lately it seemed nearly impossible for him to control it. She longed to argue with him and tell him that his command for her to hide at home was unreasonable, but she knew she would have to tread carefully or risk stepping on a beehive.

"The girls need a nap," she said as calmly as she could. "Stay here. I'll be right back." She took them inside and made them lie down, promising a treat if they stayed quiet and obeyed her. When she came outside he was pacing again. "You're going to wear out our pavement. It's only mud-brick, you know. . . . Now, tell me what's going on, Jude."

"This decree has me edgy, I guess. I can't bear to think of something happening to you and the girls."

She moved into his arms, at home in his embrace. He was a wonderful husband, strong yet tender, handsome yet without arrogance, generous and hardworking—and more than will-ing to love her even though she was too strong-willed to fit the mold of the ideal wife. Jude had his bad habits, of course, such as his fiery temper. But all husbands had faults and none of Jude's outweighed her love for him. Never, for even a second, did she doubt that he loved her, too. But lately he had taken on the role of overseer and guardian instead of partner, in spite of his promise.

"Listen to me, Jude," she said when she felt his muscles relax. "If you want me to stay locked up in our house all day, you have to give me a good reason why."

He was silent for such a long time that she didn't think he would reply. At last he released her. "Two Babylonians keep hanging around work, eyeing our business. They come back every day to taunt us, saying we'll be dead soon and everything will be theirs." He ran his hand over his face as if trying to wipe it clean.

"Just ignore them. They can't make you angry unless you allow them to. Don't give them that power. David didn't care about Goliath's taunts."

Jude frowned and the worry lines in his forehead deepened. "As I recall, David didn't put up with those taunts. He hurled a rock at Goliath's head and killed him—which is what I might have to do if I see those pigs hanging around again."

She ran her hands down his muscled arms to soothe him. "How will that help anything? If you kill two Babylonians, the authorities will haul you away for murder. How will you protect me then?"

"I can't stand being helpless, Devorah."

"Trust God."

He exhaled and turned away. "I don't have your faith. I need to do something! To kill them before they kill us!"

His anger seemed out of proportion to the taunts. And why make her stay locked inside the house all day? Then another thought occurred to her. "Did the men threaten the girls and me? Is that why you don't want me to leave the house?" She knew by his guilty expression that she had guessed correctly. "No wonder you're so angry." His gallantry touched her, and if it were possible, made her love him even more.

"They knew all about you, Devorah, as if . . . as if they've been watching you. Watching our house!"

Her stomach made a slow, cold turn. She felt violated without ever being touched. Living with a death sentence was bad enough, but would she have to spend her few remaining months looking over her shoulder? "I won't live in fear," she said, acting braver than she felt. "As I just told Miriam, we'll die a hundred times before the day finally comes if we give in to fear. You shouldn't worry about me, Jude. I'm stronger than you think. Trust God."

"Trust God . . . trust God," he mimicked. "You need to stop saying that, as if trusting Him is something I can just snap my fingers and do. Besides, it's pretty hard to keep trusting Him after He allowed us to be sentenced to death. Even Ezra admits that his trust has been shaken. Isn't yours? If you're honest?"

Tears filled her eyes. Yes. If she was honest. But she would never admit it to anyone, even herself. "Listen, if God isn't trustworthy . . . if everything we know about Him from Scripture is a lie . . . then we may as well sit down and die right now because life isn't worth living." She paused to wipe at her tears, frustrated that she couldn't control her emotions. "I've made up my mind to trust Him even if we all die, because God must have a reason for it. He must!"

Jude reached for her again, pulling her close. "Listen, you crazy woman. I'm glad you trust God—you have more than enough faith for both of us. But promise me that you won't leave the house all alone. Walk with one of the other women if you have to go out. Please, Devorah. Promise?"

Once again, her stomach turned with dread at the thought of being watched. "Yes," she finally said. "Yes, I promise."

BETHLEHEM

Amina lifted another shovelful of manure from the goat pen and dumped it on the pile. She paused to rest. Along with the late afternoon sounds of whirring insects and chirping birds, she thought she heard muffled hoofbeats on the dirt road and a donkey braying. She listened for a moment. Yes, the hoarse cry of Abba's donkey was unmistakable. Dread made her heart beat faster. Abba was home.

He'd been away for more than a week, and Amina had dared to relax during that time, freed from fear of him. Now she tensed, glancing around to make sure Abba couldn't find fault with anything—although he seldom needed a reason to be angry with her. She stood very still, listening for his voice and for her brothers' voices, trying to determine their mood after their long journey.

Laughter. She heard laughter, and allowed herself to exhale before stowing the shovel in its proper place and running to fetch water for the donkey. When she rounded the corner with the jug, Abba and her brothers were standing in front of the house with not one donkey but three, the animals' backs swaying beneath towering loads. Amina ran with the heavy jar and poured water

61

into the trough. In no time, the donkeys lapped up what she'd given them, and she hurried to fetch more. Sayfah brought water for the men while Mama fussed over Amina's older brothers, ruffling their damp hair and lavishing them with the affection and attention that Amina never received.

"Unload the animals," Abba told her brothers after they'd all quenched their thirst. "Carry everything inside. Carefully!"

"What is all this?" Mama asked. "What did you bring?"

Abba grinned. "Weapons. The most beautiful swords and spearheads and arrow tips I've ever seen in my life. The men of Ashdod are superb craftsmen." Amina's brothers untied the awkward bundles, stowing them in the storeroom alongside jars of wheat and olive oil and grain. She knew the sacks were heavy because it took both brothers, working together, to carry each one. At last the donkeys' backs were bare.

"I met with the leaders of several other villages along the way," Abba told Mama as Sayfah filled his cup a third time. "They have some good ideas for carrying out the king's decree and executing the Jews efficiently. I'm having a meeting here tonight so I can tell the others what I've learned and show them the weapons."

So that's what Abba's journey had been about. Amina hadn't known why he'd left or where he'd gone. Nor had he mentioned killing the Jews since the night of the celebration. But it hadn't been just a bad dream after all. Killing had been on Abba's mind all this time, which meant he still planned to kill Hodaya, the kind Jewish woman from the marketplace.

The men were hungry after their long journey, and Amina helped Mama prepare a meal and serve it right away. Abba was still in good spirits as he sat down to eat, and he called for Mama to join him in the courtyard, saying he had news to discuss. Amina and her sister stood listening in the shadows, ready to serve him if he called for them.

"I talked to the leader of my brother's village just outside

Jerusalem," Abba said. "He's very interested in taking Sayfah as a wife for one of his sons." Sayfah gave a startled cry.

"Shh . . . Sayfah, he'll hear you!" Amina whispered. Her sister gripped Amina's arm so tightly it hurt.

"But I don't want to get married!"

"Shh!"

"She will marry his third son, not his firstborn," Abba continued. "But even so, he will be a very rich man in just a few more months. There's a wealth of gold in the Jewish temple in Jerusalem, and the men from Abdel's village plan to claim it after they execute the Jews. There will be plenty of gold for everyone."

"Does this man know he will have to wait another year for Sayfah?" Mama asked. "She's only eleven and isn't a woman yet."

"He knows. But it will be a good arrangement for both of us. The deal is done."

"No!" Sayfah moaned. She leaned her head against Amina's shoulder as she burst into tears, nearly knocking her over.

"Sayfah . . . shh!" Amina begged. "Abba will be furious if he hears you." And he might take out his fury on both of them. Sayfah covered her mouth to muffle her sobs. She and Amina both knew that marriage meant becoming a slave to your new mother-in-law and obeying your husband's every whim or risking a beating. The sisters had whispered about all these things as they lay in bed at night, and they were both terrified of marriage. As difficult as their lives were as daughters, they could become much worse with a demanding husband and a mother-in-law to obey. Marriage meant leaving home and each other. And having babies.

"What about Amina?" Mama asked. "Have you made a decision about her?" Amina held her breath, waiting to hear Abba's reply.

"Not yet. I'll give her one more year to make up her mind

63

to walk without limping, and if she refuses, I'll be forced to do something about it. No one pays a dowry for a cripple."

Tears burned Amina's eyes, but she forced them back. Abba hated any sign of weakness. She silently repeated the Jewish weaver's words so she wouldn't forget them: *"God created you to do something special that they can't do."*

"Sayfah!" Abba suddenly called out. "Sayfah, come here."

She stared at Amina, her eyes wide with fear. "What should I do?"

"Dry your eyes," Amina whispered. "Hurry! You have to go to him."

"I don't want to! I'm scared."

"Sayfah, get in here!" he called again.

"He'll see that I've been crying, and he'll beat me," Sayfah whispered as she wiped her face. It was true. Her eyes were red and puffy, her cheeks streaked with tears—and a respectful daughter should respond with gratitude and joy to such an important announcement from her father.

Amina let out the breath she'd been holding. "I'll go. I'll tell him you went to the latrine. But don't take too long." She stepped out into the courtyard, trying to walk straight and tall, trying not to limp. But her knees wobbled with fear, making it nearly impossible. She stopped after only a few steps. "Sayfah went to relieve herself," she said, looking down at her feet. "She won't be long."

Sayfah entered the courtyard a minute later, a stiff smile on her face as she approached their father. She stopped several feet away, staring at the ground, not at him. "Yes, Abba?"

"Come here and let me have a look at you. . . . Turn around," he said, twirling his finger in a circle. Sayfah obeyed. "Not bad . . . not bad . . . You will be a beauty like your mother." Amina had always envied her sister's wavy black hair and wide, brown eyes. Sayfah's back was straight, her legs long and shapely, her skin a golden, tawny color. But even from where Amina stood, she could see her sister's chin quivering with fear.

"I've found a husband for you. We'll begin the negotiations as soon as this business with the Jews is finished."

Amina held her breath, silently willing Sayfah to answer quietly and respectfully, not revealing her emotions. But Sayfah's fear of marriage proved stronger than her caution. "Abba, no!" she said with a wail. "I don't want to leave home and get married. Please don't make me, Abba, please!"

His anger was swift and terrible. Amina saw him pounce, and she ran from the courtyard to hide in the goat pen, plugging her ears to drown out the sounds of Abba's blows and Sayfah's pitiful screams. They seemed to last a long, long time.

Amina held her sister in her arms later that night until she cried herself to sleep. But Amina couldn't sleep. What had Abba meant when he'd said he'd be forced to do something if she didn't stop limping? With all the drama that had taken place in her home that evening, she had forgotten all about Abba's meeting with the other village men until she heard them gathering in the courtyard. Her brothers carried the bundled weapons from the storeroom to show the other men. Amina lay awake, listening to the faint clanking of metal, the murmurs of approval.

"We bought enough weapons for everyone," Abba said. "And I talked with other village leaders about their plans. Most of them plan to surround each Jewish settlement ahead of time so no one can escape."

"Herd them like sheep into a pen," someone said.

"Jerusalem's walls and gates have never been rebuilt," Abba continued. "The Jews wouldn't be able to defend the city even if they were allowed to."

"Is it true that the temple treasuries hold a wealth of gold and silver?" someone asked.

"It's true. And we're welcome to join that fight once the killing is finished in Bethlehem."

Amina stuffed her fingers into her ears and buried her head

beneath the covers so she wouldn't hear any more. She fell asleep to muffled murmurs and laughter.

The next morning, Amina and her mother walked to Bethlehem for market day. Abba made Sayfah stay home, her punishment for showing disrespect. "Feast your eyes on all of the Jews' goods," he told them before they left. "Remember, it'll all be ours very soon."

The women from Amina's village acted friendly toward the Jews as they bartered for goods in the market square, but Amina knew it was a lie. She let the other children run ahead of her as she searched the rows of booths for Hodaya's. The piles of beautiful woolen cloth were easy to find, the weaving so much finer and more colorful than anything Amina would ever wear.

"Well, good morning, Amina," Hodaya said when she saw her. "I wondered if I would see you here today."

Amina ducked behind one of the piles where she wouldn't be seen. "I have to tell you something," she whispered. She glanced all around, her heart beating like birds' wings. "The men in our village are going to kill you. I heard my father and the others planning it. Abba bought swords and weapons and—"

"I know, little one. I know." Hodaya's gentle smile faded as tears filled her eyes. "We know all about the king's decree."

"Are . . . are you scared?"

"Not so much for myself, but I'm terrified for my grandchildren. The youngest is about your age, and I know how frightened she'll be. I hate to think that her short life will end in fear. I've lived a good, long life, but the children—" She couldn't finish. Amina reached to touch her arm as Hodaya wiped her eyes. "I'm sorry," the older woman said after a moment. "I'm trying to remain brave for their sakes, but as the weeks race by and the day draws closer and closer . . . sometimes it's very difficult." She blew her nose in her handkerchief.

"You need to run away," Amina whispered. "I don't want Abba to kill you." But when she saw Hodaya's crutch propped alongside her, she knew the elderly woman wouldn't be able to escape. Hodaya bent to give Amina a long, tight hug. Affection was so rare for Amina that she soaked it up like butter melting into warm bread.

"It's very sweet of you to be concerned for me," Hodaya said. "You have a beautiful, tender heart."

"I hate my father for wanting to kill you," she said when they finally pulled apart.

"No, don't hate him. Killing us isn't his idea. The order came from the Persian king, and there isn't anything we can do about it."

"Can't you hide?"

"I'm not sure. The men in our village have been praying about it, and some people are talking about escaping into the desert."

"You should go. And if you have trouble walking, maybe you could ride a donkey."

"Yes, sweet child. I will. I ride a donkey whenever we travel to God's temple in Jerusalem. We've been going there as often as we can to pray and beg for His mercy. I have friends there who are priests, and they believe that our God is going to save us. I don't know how He'll do it, and I know it looks hopeless right now, but they're telling us to trust God."

Amina heard laughter and running feet, and she ducked down to hide as the other children ran past. "Aren't you playing with them today?" Hodaya asked. "And where's your sister? . . . What was her name?"

"Sayfah. Abba wouldn't let her come. He's punishing her because she told him she doesn't want to get married."

"Married! How old is she?"

"Eleven. Abba chose a husband for her from another village, and she has to marry him as soon as she turns twelve. He says her husband will be rich after—" *After they kill the Jews.* Amina put her hand over her mouth, regretting what she'd been about to say.

Hodaya pulled Amina close for a moment and kissed her forehead. "You are a dear, sweet girl. Don't let the ugliness of life ever change that."

"I need to go." If she didn't, she would start crying, and Mama would ask why.

"Thank you for coming to warn me," Hodaya said. "And may God bless you for your kindness."

"I . . . I hope I see you again." Amina stood on tiptoe to kiss Hodaya's soft cheek, then hurried from the booth, her heart breaking. When she reached the end of the lane, she turned to look back at her friend one last time.

CHAPTER

8

BABYLON

Near the end of another disheartening day, Ezra stood before all the people in the house of assembly to lead evening prayers. Night would fall while they prayed and another day would end, bringing them one day closer to their execution. He cleared his throat, feeling inadequate, wondering if he would ever become accustomed to standing here as their leader. "This evening, I want to encourage you with this prophecy from Jeremiah," he began. He was desperate to feel the promise conveyed in the prophet's words, desperate to disguise his own growing hopelessness. Only eight months left to live. Thirty-two weeks. "'This is what the Lord says, he who appoints the sun to shine by day, who decrees the moon and stars to shine by night, who stirs up the sea so that its waves roar—the Lord Almighty is his name: "Only if these decrees vanish from my sight," declares the Lord, "will the descendants of Israel ever cease to be a nation before me."'"

Ezra paused to glance up for a moment, and his knees went weak. The Babylonian sorcerer who had brought the devastating news of King Xerxes' decree stood in the rear doorway. Ezra gripped the podium, trying to draw enough air to speak.

The assembled men turned to see what Ezra was staring at, and when Jude spotted the sorcerer, he quickly pushed his way toward him. "You're back! Is there more news?"

The old man showed him a square of parchment. "The king issued another decree."

Ezra longed to sit down. He didn't think he could bear more bad news. He took a shaky breath and said, "Please come forward and share it with us." The sorcerer hobbled to the front of the long, narrow hall to climb the bimah. Even after all of Ezra's hard work these past few months, studying with his colleagues day and night, praying with the Jewish community, showing them God's promises, their hope seemed tenuous, their faith as fragile as cobwebs. Were his efforts going to be undone by another decree?

The hall fell still as the Babylonian handed the parchment to Ezra. "This just arrived from Susa. I brought it right away."

Ezra was afraid to read it. He wanted to know the gist of it first, to soften the blow. "What does it say? Does it cancel the first decree?"

"No, that cannot happen. But Haman is no longer in power. The king executed him."

Excited murmurs chased through the crowd. A sliver of hope made Ezra's heart pound. "Executed! Do you know why?"

"We've heard rumors, but no one knows for certain. The first decree cannot be changed or repealed, but the king has issued a new one. Read it."

Ezra swallowed and began to read. "'By order of King Xerxes, the Jews in every city throughout his kingdom are hereby granted the right to assemble and protect themselves. . . .'" He paused to read the words again, his heart beating faster. *They had the right to protect themselves!* His voice grew louder as he continued reading. "'The Jews have the right to destroy, kill, and annihilate any armed force of any nationality or province that might attack them and their women and children, and to plunder the property of their enemies.'" He looked up, repeating the news. "We have been granted the right of self-defense! A miracle! 'The day appointed for the Jews to do this in all of the provinces of King Xerxes' reign is the thirteenth day of the twelfth month, Adar.'"

The room erupted into chaos. "What kind of craziness is this?" Jude shouted above the noise.

"What does it mean?" someone else called out.

Ezra held up his hands, attempting to quiet the crowd. "Can you explain this to us?" he asked the Babylonian.

"I know it doesn't seem to make sense," he replied. "But those of us in the governor's palace interpret it this way: Since the king's first edict can't be rescinded, he's now granting all Jews the right to strike back and defend themselves. As you know, the first decree didn't allow for self-defense."

"So we're saved from execution?" Ezra asked. He was afraid to believe it, afraid to hope.

"Not exactly. . . . No document written in the king's name and sealed with his ring may be revoked, but a new law can go into effect alongside it, and this new one—"

"Allows us defend ourselves!" Jude shouted. "We don't have to die after all!"

Another great cheer went up. The deafening noise filled the hall. Ezra leaned against the podium, weak with relief. "Praise God! Our prayers have been answered," he murmured, trying to control his emotions. "O Lord, forgive us for doubting your mercy."

Everyone began talking at once, laughing and weeping and cheering. Ezra looked down at the decree again and saw a new signature in place of Haman's: *Mordecai son of Jair, son of Shimei, the son of Kish*. He read it a second time, then a third, unable to believe his eyes. These names were Jewish. This man was a descendant of King Saul from the tribe of Benjamin— *Jewish*!

He turned to the Babylonian sorcerer, pointing to the parchment. "This name . . . Mordecai. Does he serve in Haman's place?"

"Yes."

Tears filled Ezra's eyes but he no longer cared. "Listen!" he shouted above the noise. "Listen! The Almighty One has not only heard our prayers, but He has replaced our enemy Haman, with a son of Abraham!" Once again, deafening cheers filled the hall. Ezra moved closer to the sorcerer to ask another question. "You said there were rumors concerning the reason for the king's change of heart. What are they?"

"Mind you, they are only rumors, and they may turn out to be false, but . . ." He moved closer, cupping his hand near Ezra's ear to be heard above the joyful din. "They say that the queen herself is Jewish." Ezra could only stare at the man in astonishment. He'd guessed that Mordecai might be a Jew, but the queen, as well?

"The queen?" he repeated. "The Persian king's *wife*?"

"Yes—according to the rumors she is related, somehow, to this Mordecai. If it's true, then King Xerxes issued this new decree to spare his queen's life and the lives of her people."

Ezra felt laughter bubbling up. Unable to control it, he laughed until the tears rolled down his cheeks. They truly were saved— and by a daughter of Abraham! Only the Almighty One could arrange such an astounding miracle. Below him, someone began singing a song of praise to the Almighty One. Others joined him, linking arms to dance in circles as they sang.

"I need to return before dark," the sorcerer said.

"Wait. One more question. Will this new decree go into effect everywhere?"

"Yes. The news is being sent out on swift horses to all 127 provinces in the king's empire."

"And what will happen here in Babylon? Do you know? Will the local government and the Persian army help us?"

"Not directly. But the man who has replaced Haman wields a great deal of power. The nobles and satraps and governors will likely favor you Jews because they fear Mordecai."

They feared Mordecai. And they feared the Jewish queen, the wife of King Xerxes. Unbelievable! "Thank you for bringing this news," Ezra said as he helped the man step from the platform. "We're very grateful to you."

Ezra didn't want to interrupt the celebration—the people must have a chance to rejoice—but in spite of this miracle, the reality of his community's plight still concerned him. Later, as he sat with Jude and Asher after dinner, he shared his thoughts, leaning forward across the dining mat so his brothers' wives wouldn't hear him. "I didn't want to diminish everyone's hope earlier, but we'll still need to fight for our lives. The new decree gives us the right to defend ourselves, but our enemies still have the right to kill us and ransack our homes and businesses under the first decree. And I'm sure many of them will still want to do that."

Asher smiled as he watched his wife tend to the supper dishes, as if he saw hope now for his unborn child and was reluctant to return to despair. "Maybe our enemies will be afraid to attack us now that this second order has been issued."

Jude leaned forward, as well, lowering his voice. "No, the Babylonians will still want to kill and pillage. Remember those dogs who've been eyeing our pottery works? They've been planning to steal it for months and won't accept defeat. We need to start gathering weapons right away and prepare to defend ourselves."

"But this edict is a miracle," Asher said. "Can't we trust God for more miracles?"

"Miracle or not," Jude replied, "our enemies have had more time to prepare and strategize than we've had. If we're not ready to fight back in eight months, we'll die." He turned to Ezra. "Do you think we can gather enough weapons and learn to use them in the few months remaining?"

"I have no idea."

"We aren't warriors—" Asher began.

"We'll only have to fight for one day!" Jude said, then lowered his voice again as both wives looked up from their work. "We must be ready for their attack at sunset on the eve of the thirteenth of Adar, when both decrees go into effect. And we must be prepared to fight until the sun sets again the following evening."

"Where are we going to get weapons?" Asher asked. He and Jude both looked to Ezra for the answer.

This ordeal wasn't over for him. As the leader of his people, the task of arming his fellow Jews and training them in warfare would fall to him. "I'm not a warrior," Ezra said, "but since they numbered me among the condemned, I'm willing to be numbered among those who will fight. The Almighty One helped Joshua fight the pagan Gentiles, and He'll help us. We'll need to forge weapons or purchase them and—"

"I know a Jewish blacksmith," Jude interrupted. "A very skilled one. He lives in Casiphia, where we trade our pottery. He's a Levite, in fact. I met him when I prayed in their house of assembly the last time I was there. There are dozens of Levite families in Casiphia."

"Good. You need to go there right away and talk to him, Jude. I'll talk to the other men tomorrow morning about raising funds. We'll need money to purchase weapons and other supplies—"

"No, Ezra. You need to go to Casiphia, not me." Jude glanced at Devorah before looking back at him. "I won't leave my family alone and unprotected. You can't imagine how it feels to know someone has been watching Devorah, lusting after her. You'll have to go in my place."

Ezra hesitated. Ever since hearing the good news, he had been imagining that he could return to his teaching and his studies.

"You're our leader," Jude continued. "Everyone depends on you, especially now that you've brought us this victory."

"I did nothing. It was the Almighty One—"

"He gave you this role as our leader."

"You can't abandon us now," Asher said.

Ezra leaned back with a sigh, running his hands through his hair. "But I've never traveled anywhere before. And I'll be carrying money—"

"I'll send a shipment of pottery with you. We'll hire drivers. Asher knows the way."

"It's true, I do, but . . ." Asher looked at his wife, then exhaled. "Fine. I'll go with you."

"I can get a shipment ready and hire drivers in a matter of days," Jude said. "You can be on your way before the end of the week. Will that give you enough time to raise money for weapons?"

"I suppose so." Ezra was reluctant to protest again, but the journey seemed daunting to him. What did he know about buying weapons, much less using them?

"We can bring the good news about the second decree to the Jews in Casiphia," Asher said. "Maybe they haven't heard it yet." He grinned and lifted his cup of wine in salute. Jude lifted his, as well.

Ezra lifted his but didn't drink. His head spun even without the wine. The Almighty One had answered their prayers! He would keep His promise of an everlasting covenant with the children of Abraham. They were no longer sentenced to die. The reality of their salvation astounded him, and he bowed his head and closed his eyes, feeling the same awe and gratitude that Moses must have felt when Pharaoh's chariots and horses drowned in the sea.

Today, God had granted Ezra and the others a glimpse of His power and glory.

CASIPHIA

Reuben held the sword to the grinding stone in his father's dimly lit shop as he honed it into a sharpened blade. He and Abba worked every night until they were too tired to work any longer, secretly forging weapons so Casiphia's Jewish community could go to their graves fighting. So far, they had used leftover scraps and bits of metal, but Reuben knew they were nearly out of materials.

Abba said he prayed while he worked, and tonight Reuben tried to do the same. His foremost prayer was that he and his family would survive somehow. But as the weeks passed and the thirteenth day of Adar drew closer, Reuben began praying for courage. For strength to disguise his fear and face death bravely. Most of all, he needed to control his tears and the sickening nausea that overwhelmed him every time he thought about dying. He was a man now, and he wanted to be like his father, strong in body and in heart. He wanted to make his father proud.

Reuben bent to his task, straining to see in the flickering lamplight, the grinding noise jarring his nerves. Then along with the sounds of hammering and grinding, he thought he heard the rumble of wagon wheels. He stopped and raised his head to listen. The rumbling halted in the street out front. He turned to his father. Abba held his finger to his lips in warning before scooping up the weapons they were making.

"Go see who it is," Abba whispered. "Stall for time while I hide these."

Reuben removed his leather apron and walked to the front of the open-air forge, carrying an oil lamp. The wagon parked outside was loaded with clay pots. The driver and the two men standing beside the load of pottery were Jews wearing *kippahs* and beards and fringes on their robes. Reuben felt relieved but still wary. "Can I help you?" he asked.

"Good evening. My name is Ezra ben Seraiah, and this is my brother Asher," one of the strangers said. His fair skin had never seen the sun, his smooth, elegant hands had no calluses or cuts, no dirt beneath his nails. He was neither a potter nor a caravan driver—although the younger man beside him had the lean, sun-browned look of a laborer. And they did resemble each other. "We've come from Babylon looking for a blacksmith named David, from the tribe of Levi. Do you know where we might find him?"

"My father's name is David. And he owns this smithy," Reuben said. "But he's busy. Why do you need to see him?"

"We bring very good news that your father will be happy to hear." Ezra's smile seemed kind and genuine. "Has the Jewish community here in Casiphia heard about King Xerxes' second decree?"

"No . . . there's a second decree?"

"Yes, and it's good news, son. Don't worry. Your father and the others will want to hear about it right away. And we have a business proposition to make with your father." The two men seemed trustworthy and sincere, but Reuben was afraid to hope for good news.

"Wait here, please. I'll go get him." He left the lamp with his visitors and made his way through the darkened forge, slipping behind the partition. Abba was just closing the crate, covering it with a length of burlap sacking to hide it.

"Who is it, Reuben?"

"Two Jewish men from Babylon with a driver and a wagon full of pottery. They asked for you by name. They said they have good news about a second decree from King Xerxes."

Abba hesitated for a moment. "I'll talk to them. Grab that other lamp."

Reuben followed his father outside where the stranger introduced himself again.

"I'm Ezra ben Seraiah, and this is my brother Asher. We weren't sure if you've heard the news from Susa yet, but King Xerxes has issued a second decree, giving us the right to arm ourselves and fight back on the thirteenth of Adar." It took Reuben a moment to realize what he'd just said. Abba seemed to have trouble comprehending it, too.

"Wait. Say that again, please."

"Our people will survive after all. The Almighty One heard our prayers, and now the Persian king is allowing us to defend ourselves. We're no longer sentenced to die! We have the right to kill anyone who tries to destroy us."

Abba grinned and clapped Reuben on the back. "Did you hear that, son? We're saved!" Reuben could only nod, too overwhelmed to speak.

"We've come to buy weapons," Ezra said, lowering his voice. "A fight will ensue, and we need your services as a blacksmith."

Abba didn't hesitate. "Come with me. I want to show you something." He beckoned to the men, leading them through his forge to the little alcove behind the partition. He opened the crate and showed them the weapons that he and Reuben had made. "The Jewish community here in Casiphia was already planning to fight to the death," Abba said, "even though we were outnumbered and couldn't possibly win."

The younger stranger lifted a sword from the crate. "These are beautiful."

"Thank you," Abba said. "Unfortunately, I'm nearly out of materials. I can't make many more."

"I understand," Ezra said. "We took up a collection to pay the cost of your labor and materials. We can raise more money, if needed."

Abba grinned a second time. "I'll put all my other orders on hold and start right away. But listen," he said, clapping his hands. "This news is too good to keep to ourselves. Reuben, run to your Uncle Hashabiah's house, and tell him to gather all of the men in the house of assembly, right away. Go! In the meantime, have you eaten anything?" he asked the men.

"We don't want to trouble you."

"I would be honored to have you as my guests. My wife can fix you something to eat while we wait for the men to assemble. Go, Reuben! Hurry!"

Reuben finally got his legs to move. He raced as fast as he as could through the dark, narrow streets to his uncle's house near the assembly hall, wondering why life was so chaotic. One day the king sentenced him to death, and the next day he decreed that he could fight back. Reuben was still afraid to believe it, still afraid that he and everyone he loved would die. Why did the Almighty One do such crazy things?

He delivered the message to Uncle Hashabiah—who seemed afraid to believe it, too—then ran home again. The strangers from Babylon sat in Reuben's courtyard, eating the hasty meal that Mama had prepared. "We've been praying for the Almighty One's mercy," Ezra was saying, "and He answered our prayers."

"It's not a very good answer, though," Reuben blurted out. Everyone turned to him. "We're still in danger, aren't we? We still could die."

"You're right," Ezra said. He didn't seem surprised or offended by Reuben's outburst. "Do you remember the story from the Torah when our enemies backed us into an impossible corner at the Red Sea? Pharaoh's chariots were behind us and there seemed to be no escape?"

"I know the story."

"The Almighty One came to our aid and parted the sea—but we still had to step between the walls of water. We had to take a risk and trust that God wouldn't let us all drown. It's the same now. God has parted the waters and begun our deliverance, but we have to move forward in faith."

"Rebbe Ezra is a Torah teacher," Abba explained.

"The most brilliant one in Babylon," Asher added.

"And I understand that you're Levites," Ezra said, breaking off another piece of bread. "Asher and I also descend from the tribe of Levi through the line of Aaron. Our ancestors were priests."

"Tell me," Abba said as he refilled their cups, "do you ever wish we could return to Jerusalem and serve in His temple?"

"Yes, of course. But I'm sure you know that immigration to Judah was halted sixty years ago. We're not allowed to return."

Abba grew still as he gazed into the distance, in the direction they faced every day when they prayed—toward Jerusalem. "If the king ever makes another decree like the one King Cyrus gave, I'll be the first one to leave for Jerusalem. My greatest wish is for my son to serve his true calling as a Levite."

Abba's words surprised Reuben. This was the first time he had ever mentioned such a wish. "But I like being a blacksmith," Reuben said.

"And you're becoming a very skilled one," Abba said, gripping Reuben's shoulder. "He's not quite thirteen," he told Ezra, "but he'll be a great help to me in the coming months as we forge weapons for you. But my wish for you, Reuben, is for something greater—that you could serve the Almighty One the way you were born to do."

Reuben looked away. This wasn't the time to tell Abba that

he wanted to fight, to use the weapons they'd made to kill his enemies. If Abba ever asked him what his greatest wish was, Reuben would say it was to become a man of courage and strength—to be a warrior. To make sure that no one could harm him or his family ever again.

Babylon

D evorah's stomach rumbled with hunger. How much longer would she have to wait to eat? Evening prayers were becoming longer and longer, and so were the practice drills that followed. The yard of Jude's pottery works now sported targets so the archers could hone their skills, as well as straw-filled dummies for the swordsmen. Jude channeled his worry and fear into action, and even Ezra was learning to fight. Devorah had no such release, and her helplessness frustrated her. Having no control over her life had long been her worst fear. She couldn't even take walks with the girls like she used to do, or visit the clay pits to watch Jude work. She could pray, of course, but that didn't satisfy her need to *do* something.

Jude worried for her safety, but what was she supposed to do with her fear for him? He could be killed. Asher's wife wept over the possibility of losing her husband every time Devorah saw her. "Aren't you worried for Jude?" Miriam had asked just this morning.

"Of course I am," she'd replied. "But I have to be courageous for my daughters. Instead of crying, I pray for Jude's safety."

"I have nightmares that Asher dies. I don't know what I would do without him. I know we're no longer under a death sentence, but that doesn't guarantee that we'll all live."

Devorah pushed thoughts like that from her mind. "Hasn't God already heard our prayers? He took an impossible situation and provided a way for us to fight back. We have to keep trusting Him."

"I wish I had your faith," Miriam said.

"You can start by praying instead of worrying. And pray for poor Ezra. He's going to fight, too, can you believe it? We should be worried for him. He isn't as strong as Jude and Asher. And Ezra doesn't have the temperament it takes to fight like our husbands do." But for all of Devorah's efforts, Miriam's fear remained unchanged.

The sky was growing dark. The men couldn't practice in the dark, could they? Devorah fed Abigail and Michal their supper and put them to bed. Afterward, she shifted the pots of food around on the hearth—too close to the fire and the food would stick to the pot and burn, too far from the embers and it would grow cold. Either way, it would serve the men right for taking so long.

Devorah's life had changed so drastically in only a few short months. Would it settle down again after the thirteenth of Adar, and return to the way it had been? She hoped so. But after a trial of faith like this one, she would never view life the same or take her family for granted. For now, the hardest thing to live with was the uncertainty. No one knew if their enemies would still attack them or how strong their forces would be. Or how well her own people could fight back. As Miriam had said, they might not face execution, but there was no guarantee of survival, either.

At last she heard Jude's deep voice echoing through the narrow lanes as he neared home. "There you are! At last," she said as he walked through the gate. She longed to greet him with a hug in spite of the sweat that ran down his face and soaked the front of his tunic, but Ezra was with him, and she and Jude had agreed to refrain from showing affection in front of him.

The rug was already spread for their meal. Devorah put the food in the middle of it while the men washed. They were still talking about swords and arrows as they sat down, but they paused long enough for Ezra to recite the blessing over the bread. They continued their conversation the moment they said *amen*. "Did I tell you, Jude, that the Persian governor has offered to let us confer with his experienced military officials?" Ezra asked. "They'll help us draw up plans for our defense."

"Are they going to help us fight, too?" Devorah asked.

Ezra looked at her as if surprised she was there, much less listening to their conversation. "They aren't willing to go that far," he replied before quickly looking away. She found it unnerving that he rarely addressed her directly and avoided looking at her whenever possible. She had asked Jude about it once, and he'd explained the Torah's prohibition against lusting after another man's wife.

"But I'm his sister-in-law, for goodness' sakes," she had said. "He lives here with us."

"Doesn't matter," Jude had replied. "As far as Ezra is concerned, every commandment and precept and decree and law should be taken literally."

Devorah knew she should remain quiet now and let the men talk, but she had a sudden thought. "Excuse me, but how do you know that these Persian military officials are our friends?"

Jude held out his bowl for her to fill. "What do you mean, love?"

"Just because the Persian governor favors us doesn't mean his army officers do. They could purposely give us bad advice. Or pretend to be allies and then share our battle plans with our enemies."

"She's right, you know," Jude said. He suppressed a grin as he elbowed his brother.

"Besides," Devorah continued, "the Scriptures are full of battles that our people fought under the Almighty One's direction. Can't those accounts act as a guide instead of us relying on Gentile Persian generals? Didn't the Almighty One tell Joshua how to fight the battle of Jericho?"

Ezra laid down his bread. "I haven't given the governor my answer yet. But you've given me something to think about."

"We'll have to call you 'General Devorah' from now on," Jude teased.

She frowned at him, thinking it wasn't funny. "Why not put our trust in God, not men?' she continued. "Especially when we don't know these Babylonians very well."

"Thank you. I appreciate your thoughts," Ezra said. Was he grateful or was he dismissing her? The brothers talked of other things while they ate, but the subject of fighting came up again after the meal when Ezra winced in pain as he massaged his shoulder.

"How are you getting along with that sword?" Jude asked.

"My arm aches. I'm using muscles I've never used before. At least you're used to lifting heavy pots. The heaviest thing I lift is a Torah scroll. And look at these. . . ." Ezra held out his palm to show an oozing set of blisters.

"I have some balm that will help," Devorah said. She rose to fetch it, still listening to their conversation.

"You know, our enemies may not be any better at fighting than we are," Jude said.

"Let's hope not. I never imagined I'd have to wield a sword in battle, did you, Jude?"

"Never."

Devorah gave the little pot of salve to Ezra to rub on his palm. "I'm glad we don't have a son who has to fight," she said as she cleared away the bowls. "I don't think I could bear it. It's hard enough to send my husband to war."

Jude reached for her arm and pulled her down on the carpet

beside him. "When this is finally over, maybe the Almighty One will give us a son. You know I love our daughters, but they'll grow up and move to their husbands' homes someday. But a son? A son can work alongside me and inherit my business. Sons are a blessing from the Almighty One."

"What if your son doesn't want to be a potter?" Ezra asked. His tone was lighthearted, and he wore a crooked smile. "What if he wants to study Torah with his uncle? What then?"

Devorah looked at him in surprise. Her serious brother-in-law rarely smiled. Jude laughed out loud. "Listen, if you want a son to study Torah with you, get married and have one of your own. *My* firstborn son will be a potter like his father."

Ezra scratched his beard, his expression wistful. "You know, I just might look for a wife when this is all over. One of the Holy One's first commands was to be fruitful and multiply."

Jude laughed again. "You hear that, Devorah? On the fourteenth day of Adar you can help my brother find a wife. You won't be sorry, Ezra. Don't the writings say that a good wife is a gift from God? It's about time you accepted His gift."

Devorah smiled as she listened to the men. They had given her hope. The fighting would last for a day, but after that? . . . After that, life and love and joy would return.

CHAPTER
11

BETHLEHEM

Something was wrong. Amina knew it the moment Abba stormed into their courtyard, shouting curses and throwing his staff onto the cobblestones in a rage. She and Sayfah had been sitting in the shade of the overhanging roof as they helped Mama cut up leeks and garlic, but Sayfah leaped to her feet and grabbed Amina's arm the moment they heard him coming. She pulled Amina, stumbling and limping, into the storage room to hide. They were close enough to hear him if he called for them, far away enough to be out of his sight. Sayfah's bruises were nearly healed, and neither of them wanted to risk another beating.

Amina heard one of their brothers talking to him, his voice low and cautious as if he was frightened of Abba, too. "It makes no sense!" Abba shouted in reply. "Whoever heard of such stupidity? One day they issue an order to kill every Jew in the kingdom, then they issue another one saying the Jews can fight back!"

Fight back? Amina drew a quick breath, then covered her mouth.

"What's wrong?" Sayfah asked. "What's he talking about?"

87

Sayfah hadn't been awake to hear the meetings and celebrations. She didn't know Abba's plans. And Sayfah hadn't met the kind Jewish woman in the marketplace. Maybe Hodaya wouldn't have to die after all. She'd said her God would help her—and now He had.

"I can't believe it!" Abba shouted. "We've been planning this for four months!"

"Planning what?" Sayfah whispered.

"To kill his enemies," Amina whispered back. "That's why he bought all those weapons."

"But why—?"

"Shh! I want to hear what they're saying."

"We can still kill all the Jews, can't we?" her brother asked. "And take their goods?"

"And we still have the advantage," her other brother said. "The Jews won't have much time to buy weapons. And don't we outnumber them?"

"You're right, you're right," Abba said. His temper had cooled, but he sounded hoarse from shouting. "The first edict is still the law of the land. Now we need to make sure the Jews can't buy weapons. We'll intercept all caravans and shipments so nothing reaches them. In the meantime, we can't let them suspect that we still plan to attack. Tell the women to shop in the market as usual and act friendly. We'll take the Jews by surprise."

Amina longed to run all the way to Bethlehem and warn her friend what Abba and the others still planned to do. But when she walked into Bethlehem two days later with Mama, the market square looked deserted. Amina slipped away from her sister and limped to her friend's booth, longing to glimpse Hodaya's kind, wrinkled face one last time and feel her warm arms surrounding her. But Hodaya and her beautiful cloth were gone. None of the Jews had come to buy or sell. The only merchants and customers were from Amina's village. She bent to pick up a forgotten strand of blue thread, the only thing that remained of the colorful piles of fabric, clutching it in her hand like a valuable coin. Would she ever see her friend again?

"What are you doing?" Sayfah asked, surprising her as she came up behind her.

"Nothing." Amina gripped the strand of blue wool tightly so Sayfah wouldn't see it and ask questions.

"Come on, Mama needs our help."

"I'm coming." Maybe Amina's friend had gone away to hide. Maybe she wouldn't die after all.

CHAPTER
12

CASIPHIA

Reuben crouched beside the fire, fanning the flames with his bellows in smooth, even strokes. He watched his father's every move, trying to anticipate what he might need and help him any way he could. Their work was of the utmost importance now, and may mean the difference between life and death for his people. He and Abba worked from before dawn until after dark, laboring to forge weapons in the blistering summer heat as the months continued to speed past. Reuben's anxiety grew along with the stockpile. He and everyone in his family still might die. But they also might live. He fanned that ember of hope the same way he fanned the coals, waiting for it to ignite and burn brightly.

His arms ached from the strain of the added work, and he longed to rest. But this morning he remembered something the rebbe had said a few years ago: *"We're all called to serve God."* Reuben hadn't understood what he'd meant back then, thinking he had to study all day or become a rabbi to serve God. Now, as Reuben crouched beside the furnace, feeling the fire's intense heat and watching Abba rotate the glowing metal, he finally understood. God called him and his father to serve God

90

as blacksmiths. The Almighty One chose them for this work, so their people could survive.

Reuben's apprenticeship had accelerated from all his labor, transforming his skills. Along with added knowledge and experience, his love and respect for his father also increased. Weapons now filled stacks of crates behind the partition—swords and knives, spears and arrowheads. Abba would ship most of them to Rebbe Ezra in Babylon, hidden inside wagonloads of produce. Every able-bodied man in Casiphia was now armed, too.

"Take a break, Reuben." Abba pulled the blade from the flames and turned to hammer it on the anvil. "Get a drink and cool off." Reuben could tell by the ringing sound and the thickness of the metal that the sword was nearly finished. He laid down his bellows and removed his leather apron, hanging it on the hook behind the partition before bending to ladle a drink from one of the clay jars. With his thirst quenched, he retrieved the arrow and bow he had begged from one of Abba's craftsmen and carried them to the narrow lane behind the forge where the straw target was set up. Reuben could hit it every time, so he stepped back from where he'd practiced yesterday, increasing his range. He felt the growing strength in his arms as he strung the bow and drew back the string, certain that God had created him to use these weapons as well as fashion them. *Thwack.* The wild thrill he felt each time his muscles strained to draw the bow, each time his arrow struck its mark, satisfied him more than his daring escapades with his friends.

"You've become quite a good shot, Reuben."

He turned to see Uncle Hashabiah and another elder from the house of assembly standing in the alleyway behind him. "Thank you." He grinned and hurried forward to pull the arrow from the target, hoping they would stay for a moment and watch him shoot again. They were in charge of training the men in his community.

"Is your father here? We've come to see if he has more weapons for us."

Reuben waited to reply until after he'd taken aim and the arrow had penetrated the center of the target. "Yes, we've finished a few more swords," he said. "I'm practicing so I can join you when training begins." The two men looked at each other without replying. "I heard that practice starts soon," Reuben continued. "I want to fight with you."

"You're only twelve, Reuben."

"I'll be thirteen in a few months. And I can already shoot. You just saw me. I can use a sword, too."

"Is your father inside?" Hashabiah asked again. He went into the forge without waiting for Reuben's reply. Reuben followed them, still carrying his bow and arrow, and they found Abba at the grinding stone, sharpening a new blade.

"Are the weapons ready?" Hashabiah asked.

"Yes, Reuben and I finished a few more since you were here. And the shipment to Babylon leaves tomorrow."

"Good. Will you have time to come for training tonight? I know you're busy with all of this," he said, gesturing to the forge.

Abba tested the edge of the sword with his thumb, then bent to sharpen it some more. "Yes, I plan to come."

"I want to come, too," Reuben said.

Hashabiah shook his head. "You're too young, son. The elders have decided that volunteers must be at least sixteen."

"But that's not fair! I've worked as hard as any man making these weapons. Why can't I use them, too?" He struggled to keep his voice level and not whine like a child, but the injustice angered him.

"I know, Reuben, but—"

"Don't our enemies outnumber us?" Reuben asked. "Won't we need every man we have? Tell them I'm strong enough, Abba. Tell them how I've been helping you."

Abba laid down the sword and rested his hand on Reuben's

shoulder. "You're my right-hand man, son. Strong and smart and very capable. But I was there when the elders made this decision. I'm sorry, but I agree with them."

"No! Let me fight and defend myself! The Gentiles will kill me if they get the chance. They'll even kill little children."

"I know." Abba's hand squeezed tighter. "But we need you in the second ring of defense, to guard the women and children."

"I want to fight!"

"I pray that none of us will have to fight," Abba said. "And that the Gentiles will be too afraid to attack us. But you have your whole life ahead of you, Reuben. Imagine for a moment that you're a father who loves his son very much. Try to understand why I don't want you on the front lines."

"But I can shoot—"

"I know you can. But do you understand what our enemies will do to your mother and sisters and the baby if they break through our defenses? The greatest help you can give me is to protect our women and children. Someone has to do that very important job. Promise me that you'll take care of them for me." He waited, still gripping Reuben's shoulder, refusing to look away until Reuben finally replied.

"I promise. . . . But can I at least come and watch you practice tonight?"

"Yes, you may watch."

"Wait," Hashabiah said. "I don't think that's a good idea. The other boys his age will want to come, too, and—"

"My son worked as hard as any man making these weapons," Abba interrupted. "He deserves to watch us learn how to use them."

"I understand. But I worry that we won't be able to restrain our young people's zeal for war after this is over. How can we teach our boys that self-defense is sometimes necessary but that it's wrong to hate?"

"Don't you hate?" Abba asked. His voice grew louder, angrier, as he continued. "You surely must, if you're honest. My wife just had our fourth child and the Gentiles will slaughter him without blinking an eye. So yes, I do hate them. Just as much as they hate us."

Reuben remained silent as he watched the two men. Hashabiah seemed about to argue, then shook his head as if changing his mind. "We'll take those weapons now," he said. "And we'll see you later tonight for training."

CHAPTER
13

BABYLON
THE EVE OF THE THIRTEENTH OF ADAR

E zra stood inside the shed they were using as a weapons
cache and pulled a sword from the crate. It felt heavy in
his hand. He had practiced for months against a straw-
filled dummy tethered from a rope, his arm growing strong as
he'd learned to wield the weapon. But the dummy hadn't carried
a sword or fought back. The enemies Ezra would face in a few
hours would. And they would show no mercy.

"Ready?" Jude asked.

"Yes. Let's take our positions." Ezra walked with his brothers
through emptied streets. The sun had sunk below the treetops,
below the housetops, squatting on the horizon like a fiery ball.
Today had been the longest day of Ezra's life as he'd waited for
the sun to set and the thirteenth day of Adar to begin—the day
when his enemies would attack and kill and plunder his people.
Yet it had also been the shortest day he could ever remember
with time darting as swiftly and chaotically as swallows while
he and the other men rehearsed their plans a final time. He had
left the house early this morning so he wouldn't have to watch
his brothers say good-bye to their families. So he wouldn't have

to wonder, as their wives surely did, if Jude and Asher would survive and return home. Better he died than one of them.

Ezra had stood before the people in the house of assembly this morning as their leader, encouraging them to look to the Almighty One for strength. "He holds our lives in His hands each and every day," he'd told them, "although we're seldom aware of it until we find ourselves facing danger. He knows the number of days written for each of us in His book. And so, whether we live or die in the coming hours, we can trust Him completely—because He is worthy of our trust. As Joshua prepared to fight the Gentile armies in Jericho, God told him, 'Be strong and courageous. Do not be terrified; do not be discouraged, for the Lord your God will be with you.'"

Then Ezra led the community in prayer one last time, begging for God's mercy for the coming day. "Not because we deserve it," he'd prayed, "but for your name's sake, for your glory. Let not our enemies triumph over us." And Ezra had continued to pray silently throughout the day as he'd helped construct barricades and secure their defenses and distribute weapons. He'd learned the difference, these past months, between talking about God with his students and colleagues in the yeshiva, and talking with the Almighty One, alone, on his face in prayer. If he survived the coming night and day, Ezra knew he could never go back to the way he'd approached prayer or Scripture in the past. The Torah would be a radically different book. Prayer would be intimate and sacred.

"It will be your responsibility to lead the evening prayers tonight," he had told the young yeshiva students earlier today, the boys too young to fight. "It will be the most important job you'll ever have." They would be praying right now. The sky was already darker in the east, an indigo curtain falling closed as if the disappearing sun were a weight that yanked it shut. Before long, the first stars would poke through the curtain's folds.

"Good evening, Rebbe Ezra." His young Torah student, Shimon, hurried over to greet him when he arrived at the barricade. The sword looked awkward and out of place in the young man's hand. "May the Almighty One be with you this night."

"And also with you, Shimon." He saw apprehension in Shimon's eyes and pale face, and fought the urge to send him back to his books and his studies, away from the shadow of death. But he also saw his young student's determination. Like their forefathers under Joshua's command, he and the others were no longer individuals but the people of God, fighting together.

Earlier today, the men had blocked all the lanes leading into the Jewish community. Ezra and the others would defend those entrances while the women and children took refuge in the house of assembly. The arguments over that decision had been fierce. "Our families will become easy prey if they're all grouped in one place," some had insisted. "Why not hide them throughout the community, so at least a few might survive?"

Others had disagreed, arguing that it would be easier to protect the women and children if they were all in one place. "That way, if we're forced to retreat we can form our last ring of defense around the house of assembly, guarding the women and children." And the Torah scrolls. Shimon had helped Ezra wrap them in cloth and bury them in leather-bound boxes beneath the floor of the yeshiva in case their enemies set the building on fire.

Another group of men had wanted to make a suicide pact in case the enemy broke through and all was lost. "Let's agree to kill the women and children and then ourselves," they'd said, "rather than allow our enemies to slaughter us and rape our women."

The arguing parties were unable to reach a consensus and had turned to Ezra to make the final decision. "I'm not an expert in military strategy and defensive tactics," he'd said, "but I do know how to pray." He'd become quite skilled at praying in the dwindling weeks—and so he'd turned to the Holy One before deciding. "The women and children will take shelter in the house of assembly. But let's not talk of suicide or rape or defeat. 'God is our refuge and strength, an ever-present help in trouble. Therefore we will not fear, though the earth give way and the mountains fall into the heart of the sea.'"

His assigned barricade, a crude pile of discarded furniture, broken crates, and crumbling mud bricks blocking the street, provided a shield to fight behind. He chose Shimon to climb the nearest rooftop and serve as a lookout. Ezra gazed around at the men who would fight alongside him, their faces hardened with resolve in the fading light, as if molded from bronze instead of flesh. Did he look the same? Did these men feel the same gut-twisting unease he felt as they prepared to face their enemies?

Ezra listened, tense and uneasy in the evening stillness. Even the birds had stopped twittering. No one spoke, and the unnatural silence lengthened and grew until he could no longer fight the urge to shatter it. "Remember, men, if we must die there's no greater honor than to die as the people of God." He closed his eyes and led them in the ancient creed of their faith: "'Hear, O Israel: The Lord our God, the Lord is one. Love the Lord your God with all your heart and with all your soul and with all your strength.'"

The curtain of night descended around them. The thirteenth day of Adar had begun. It was impossible to see more than a dozen yards away from where they stood. Now Ezra would wait, sword in hand.

"Do you really believe we'll survive this?" Jude asked. "That God will protect us?"

Ezra exhaled. What did he believe after months of endless soul-searching, hours of studying Scripture? He replied carefully. "I believe with all my heart that God will save a remnant of His people. Hasn't He already helped us by changing the king's heart and allowing us to defend ourselves? You were there when the governor told us how the Babylonian nobles and satraps have sided with us out of fear of Mordecai the Jew."

"Yes, but will *we* be part of that remnant? You and me and Asher?"

"God knows. . . . I pray that we will be."

Jude edged closer, lowering his voice so the others wouldn't hear. "In case you don't know it, a lot of men are upset about your decision not to plunder our enemies. I'm not sure we can restrain some of them if the battle goes in our favor."

"I explained my reasons for not taking the Gentiles' spoils. Mordecai may have followed the language of Haman's letter, but I don't think he intended for Jews to kill women and children. We only need to defend our lives. That's why I also said not to kill unless you have to."

"I think your decision was wrong."

"Yes, Jude. I know you do. We've had this argument before."

"Why should we allow our enemies to live? They'll gladly kill us. Why not be as ruthless as they are?"

Asher had inched closer to listen and join the discussion. "Remember the story of Saul and the Amalekites?" he asked. "Saul was supposed to destroy *all* of them. If he had obeyed and done what God ordered, we wouldn't be fighting them now."

"True. But in all my prayers and pleadings, I never once heard the Almighty One order us to utterly destroy them. He granted us the right to defend ourselves—that's all. Revenge is His to repay."

Jude shook his head, unconvinced.

"Don't let your hatred overrule your caution," Ezra warned him. "I hate these Gentiles as much as you do. But letting that hatred take control would be a fatal mistake."

They moved apart, and Ezra continued to wait, alert to every rustle, every shifting shadow, his sweating palm fused to the grip of his sword. Months ago, Jude had admonished him to leave his study and join the real world. Now that he had, Ezra had grown to love this group of courageous men. He had accepted God's call to lead them, and he felt responsible for them as they stood waiting to defend their wives and children. *Lord, help them. . . . Help us all.*

"I still say we should go on the offensive," Jude said, breaking into Ezra's thoughts. "Why not flush out our enemies and kill them first instead of waiting here like fish in a pond?"

"Because then we would be taking matters into our own hands. Trust God, Jude."

They settled back to wait some more.

Eventually, Ezra grew so accustomed to the soft, nighttime sounds of fidgeting men and chirping insects that he no longer noticed them—until the sounds suddenly stopped. He stood up straight, instantly alert. "Over there," Jude whispered, pointing. Ezra glimpsed movement in the distant darkness as the shadows shifted. He heard the rustle of approaching footsteps. He glanced at Jude for confirmation, and he nodded, hearing it, too. Shimon whistled the warning sign from the rooftop. The archers readied their bows.

This was it. The first attack. Ezra would signal the archers to fire as soon as the enemy came into range. He and the other swordsmen would rise up out of hiding after that first volley. Ezra's heart raced as the ominous shadows drew closer, skittering between buildings, staying under cover. He wiped his palms on his thighs. *Get control. Steady.*

"God, be with us," he whispered. Then, as the shadows materialized into a flood of enemies, Ezra shouted, "Fire!" He ducked his head as a volley of arrows slammed into the attackers. Sickening thuds and cries of pain told him the arrows had found their marks. He peered over the barricade and saw dozens of fallen men, but a tidal wave of attackers still surged forward.

Ezra shouted the battle cry, and his men rose up to defend their homes and families, fighting for their lives.

CASIPHIA
THE EVE OF THE THIRTEENTH OF ADAR

The sky was still light when Reuben and his father led Mama and his younger siblings to the house of assembly for shelter. The other men in his community were doing the same, bringing enough food and supplies for the women and children to last a full day under siege. Mama carried his new baby brother while Reuben carried extra oil for the lamps and bedding for tonight. Would anyone besides the very smallest children be able to sleep? Reuben certainly wouldn't. Every muscle in his body ached with tension and fear. The meal he'd tried to eat lay lumped in his stomach. What would happen to his family, to him, before the sun went down tomorrow night?

A short distance from the assembly hall, their progress halted. Reuben set down his bundles and followed his father forward to see why. Two large wagons loaded with household goods blocked the street and the entrance to the building like a plug in a wineskin. "What's all this?" Abba asked the well-dressed man, sitting beside one of the drivers. "You're blocking the road—and it's nearly sunset."

"I'm not leaving my valuables behind for the pagans to steal," he replied. "I'm storing them inside for safekeeping."

"There's no room inside," someone shouted at the man. "Leave them!"

"Get your wagons out of our way," another said. "Our families need to get through."

"This isn't the time to worry about your possessions," Abba said. "This is a fight to the death."

"Everything I've worked for is in these wagons!"

"And I'm trying to get my family inside! They're the only things worth safeguarding. Now move aside!" Abba stepped toward him, challenging him, but the man didn't flinch.

"You can't tell me what to do. I own men like you."

Abba was brawny and strong—and determined. "I don't care how rich you are. If we lose this fight, we'll all be dead by this time tomorrow, and our enemies will steal everything we own no matter where you store it. If we win, your goods will be perfectly safe inside your own house. Now move your wagons out of the way! The house of assembly is a shelter for women and children, not household goods."

By now, several other men had gathered around. Their tempers seemed as hot as banked coals as they waited for their enemies to become the fuel that would unleash the flames. This man, blocking their path, fanned those coals. At Abba's signal, the men grabbed the oxen and dragged them and the wagons out of way. The owner sputtered and shouted helplessly.

With the path cleared, Reuben's family hurried inside and found a place to spread their bedding. Women and children packed the hall, the mothers trying to distract their little ones with songs and games and treats. Reuben felt the tension in the air, as if a dark, storm-filled cloud was slowly rolling toward them.

"I have to leave now," Abba said. "You'll be safe here. The men will form a protective ring around the hall, and every window and door will be guarded." He held Mama in his arms for a long moment, then kissed her and each of Reuben's sisters. He pulled Reuben close for a hard embrace. "Watch over them for me, Reuben."

"I don't want to wait inside, Abba. If I can't fight, at least let me help the other men keep watch outside."

"Listen, son—"

"Please, Abba! I'll go crazy in here with the babies."

Abba exhaled. "I'll talk to the man in charge. But you'll have to obey him and do exactly as he says. And don't leave here. Promise?"

"I promise."

"Be sure to check on your mother from time to time to see if she needs anything," he added as they walked toward the entrance.

"I will, Abba."

Reuben's father talked with the chief guard, who agreed to let Reuben stand watch outside. The guards, mostly elderly men, were too old to fight but still eager to defend their families with their lives. Shortly after Abba left, the sun set. The day everyone had long dreaded had come. Reuben strained in the darkness, trying to see into the deserted streets. "It's so dark!" he said to the man beside him. "How can our men see anything?"

"They can't. But our enemies can't see anything, either."

Time passed. Nothing happened. The guards paced as they made their rounds. Reuben heard a baby crying inside the building and wondered if it was his brother. The hardest thing in the world was waiting, doing nothing.

Then in the distance, Reuben heard the unmistakable sounds of battle—swords clashing, men shouting. The guards went on high alert. "Go inside, son," the chief guard told him. Reuben had promised to obey, but he halted on the other side of the threshold to watch from the doorway. The sounds continued for more than an hour before fading away. Then a knot of figures materialized out of the darkness, hurrying toward them. Reuben unsheathed the knife he had made out of scrap metal, wishing he had a sword. Had their enemies broken through their defenses? If only he could prove his courage in battle.

"We're on your side," one of the figures called out. "We're bringing in the wounded."

Two guards went forward to help, carrying the injured men past Reuben and laying them inside the assembly hall. The women brought lamps and huddled around the groaning men to tend their wounds. Reuben craned his neck to see, praying he wouldn't see his father. Two of the bloodied men were strangers, the third a young man named Samuel who was only a few years older than him. Reuben had watched Samuel practice with the men a few days ago—now he lay gravely injured.

The thirteenth day of Adar had just begun. Hours and hours remained until it ended. Reuben went outside again, unsure how he would bear the suspense of waiting until it did.

CHAPTER

15

OUTSIDE BETHLEHEM

Amina listened from the safety of the storage room to the commotion in her family's household. Her father had been in a high state of readiness all day, barking orders, running red-faced in and out of their house, holding final, impassioned meetings with the other village leaders. He wore a sword strapped to his side, as did both of her brothers. The day they'd waited and planned for had finally come. The day when all the Jews would die.

"By this time tomorrow we'll be rich men," one of Amina's brothers said.

"Yes, but only if you keep your wits," Abba said. "Don't waste too much of your strength on the Jewish girls."

One of the other men laughed. "Let the young men enjoy the delights of conquest. They'll only be young once."

"What about the women from our village?" another man asked. "Will they be safe from the enemy's lust?"

"The Jews will never get this far," Abba replied. "By morning this will all be over, and the Jews will be dead."

"What if we lose and—?"

"We won't!" Abba's shout made Amina's skin prickle. "We

outnumber them, out-arm them. We'll move in as soon as the sun sets and finish them off."

The windowless storage room was cold. Amina wished Abba and the others would hurry up and leave so she could come out again. "Sayfah! Amina!" he suddenly shouted. They hurried to see what he wanted.

"Gather up all the blankets you can find," he said. "We'll use them to carry home the spoils." Amina did as she was told, piling them near the door. The nights were cold during the month of Adar, and she wondered how she would stay warm without her blanket. The men ate a final, hurried meal and prepared to leave.

"Remember," her father told Mama, "be ready to leave with all the other women as soon as the moon rises. You can help carry home the plunder after the battle. Wait near the market square in Bethlehem until we signal that it's safe to enter the village."

"Amina is too clumsy to walk that far in the dark," Mama said.

"Then I don't want her slowing everyone down. Stay here!" he said, pointing his finger at her.

The men left home first. A few hours later when the moon rose, the women and girls walked down the dark road to Bethlehem with sacks and blankets and pack animals, leaving Amina alone in the house. At first she waited in the animal enclosure with Abba's goats, trying to draw comfort from their warmth. But even the animals seemed to sense the tension in this long, strange night. They startled at every sound, staring wide-eyed into the darkness, bleating loudly. She finally left the enclosure and went to stand near her front gate, gazing into the shadowy street. The entire village stood empty and deserted. No lamps glimmered in the windows. Not even a baby's cry disturbed the eerie stillness, although Amina knew there must be small children and old people who'd been left behind like her. She sank down in the shadows beside the gate to wait.

Amina's life had never been a happy one, but she had endured it by living day to day, trying to forget yesterday and never thinking about tomorrow. Now for the very first time, she wondered what her life would be like after Abba and the other men got what they wanted. Would it be different from what she'd known? Would Abba be happier? Would she?

She finally went inside again and lay down on her pallet, curling into a ball to stay warm as she waited for this long, dark night to end.

BABYLON

Devorah sat on a mat in the house of assembly, singing softly to put Abigail and Michal to sleep. No one spoke above a whisper in the packed room, nor did they dare to light any oil lamps. They couldn't let their enemies know that the women and children had taken shelter here, so many of them that they'd spilled over into the yeshiva next door. Devorah paused in her tune, listening for sounds of battle in the distance. Instead she heard Miriam sniffling tears. "Crying won't help, you know."

"I'm sorry," Miriam said, "but I can't help being scared."

"I'm scared, too. We all are."

"And I can't get comfortable. My back is killing me!"

Devorah sympathized. Miriam was in her last month of pregnancy, and Devorah recalled how difficult it had been to find a comfortable sitting position when she'd been pregnant, let alone lie down on the hard floor.

"Try walking. Maybe it will help."

"How can I walk? It's so dark in here."

Devorah's daughters were asleep, and she could use a change of position. "Come on, I'll walk with you. We can circle the edge of the room. See if it helps your back." She stood and helped Miriam to her feet.

"What are you doing? Where are you going?" Miriam's mother said, clutching the hem of her daughter's robe.

"Miriam needs to stretch her legs. Will you watch the girls for me, please? We'll be right back." They threaded their way through the crowd and began a slow circuit around the inside perimeter of the hall. Only the very youngest children seemed able to sleep. The older ones fidgeted and whined as if sensing their mothers' fear and worry. Aside from the nervous rustling and whispering, the room was eerily quiet. Devorah was certain that she could hear battle cries in the distance—or was it her imagination?

"How's your back? Does walking help?" Devorah asked as they began their second circuit.

"No. It still hurts really badly, and—" She halted and gave a little gasp. "Oh no! Oh no! I'm . . . I'm all wet!"

"Your sac of waters must have broken. That means your baby is coming."

"No! Not tonight! Not here, in the middle of all this!" Miriam sank down on the floor as if her legs had given way. "I want to be in my own home, in my own bed! I want Asher close by and—"

"Miriam, shh . . . shh . . . You need to lie down. I'll find the midwife and—"

"How are you going to find the midwife in this crowd? In the dark?"

"It won't be hard." She helped Miriam to her feet, and they walked back to their places. When her sister-in-law was settled, Devorah whispered the news of Miriam's labor to all the women around her, asking them to pass the message through the room until it reached the midwife. A few minutes later, the woman made her way to Miriam's side.

"Stress can bring on labor," she told Devorah. "I wouldn't be surprised if every expectant mother in this room has her baby tonight." Devorah remembered a story from her people's history of how a priest's wife went into labor when she heard the Ark of the Covenant had been captured and her husband killed in battle. The woman had also died, as Devorah recalled. She shook her head to push aside the image, wishing she didn't know the Bible so well.

"See if you can find a private place to lie down," the midwife told Devorah. "Her labor needs to proceed in peace."

On her way to search for a spot, Devorah noticed a commotion near the door and people lighting oil lamps. She went to see what was going on and discovered that several wounded men had been brought in from the battlefront. Devorah's heart began to race. She had to see if one of them, God forbid, was Jude. She pushed toward the door and saw blood pooling on the floor, glistening darkly in the lamplight. She heard the moans of the wounded, the cries of the women, and forced herself to study the men's faces until she was sure that Jude wasn't among them.

The sight had shaken her. She had to sit down for a moment until her legs stopped trembling. When she stood again to find a place for Miriam to give birth, she knew it would have to be far away from the makeshift hospital by the door. But by the time she found a spot and hurried back to tell the midwife, word of the casualties had whispered through the crowd reaching every woman in the room.

"Asher . . . is Asher alive?" Miriam asked. "I'm so afraid for him!"

"I saw the men they brought in," Devorah told her. "I didn't recognize any of them."

"Stay with me, please!" Miriam begged. Devorah asked a neighbor to watch her sleeping daughters, then helped the midwife move Miriam to a far corner of the room. She kept calling for Asher, making herself sick with worry over him, and her contagious fear wore on Devorah, fueling her own fears for Jude.

"It's going to take several hours," the midwife said. "First babies usually do. But it would be better for you and your baby, Miriam, if you calmed down. The child can sense your tension."

Devorah tried praying with her sister-in-law, singing to her, reciting psalms. Nothing helped. The battle sounds had quieted, and Devorah didn't see any more casualties coming in, so she knelt beside Miriam's mat and took her hand. "Listen, I'm going to do my best to get a message to Asher."

"Tell him to come! I need to see him! I need to know that he isn't hurt!"

"I can't promise that he'll be able to leave the barricade, but I'll do my best."

And maybe Devorah could learn about her own husband, as well.

CHAPTER

16

BABYLON

Ezra sank behind the barricade and wiped sweat from his eyes. He still gripped his sword in his aching arm. After more than an hour of endless fighting, he and his men had repelled the first assault. He'd watched the enemy scatter, retreating into the darkness out of the archers' range. "Is everyone all right?" he asked. Fatigue and stress made it difficult to catch his breath. He saw cuts and scrapes as he looked around at his men, but nothing serious. Jude and Asher were safe. Across the barricade, however, enemy bodies littered the street. "Provide cover for us," Ezra ordered the archers. "We'll strip their weapons."

Jude held him back. "Stay here. I'll go." Jude and a handful of men finished the grim work of pulling arrows from the bodies and gathering swords from the slain, then they took cover again to await the next attack. This ordeal had only begun.

Ezra had barely known what he was doing as he'd lashed out with his sword. He remembered ordering his men to give a shout, just as his ancestors had at Jericho, and the noise had startled their enemies. In the fierce fighting that followed, he'd had no time to comprehend that he was killing people. He looked out at the battlefield now and knew that he had slain some of the dead. The thought made him shudder. But if he hadn't killed them, he would surely be dead in their place. He looked away, ordering a fresh scout to climb up to the rooftop in Shimon's place.

"I need you to be my messenger," he told Shimon after he came down. "Go around to the other barricades and bring back news. See if there have been other attacks." Ezra took a long swig of water after Shimon left, then told the others, "We need to rest in shifts. For all we know, our enemies could be sleeping through the night while we remain awake, so they can attack us in the morning when we're exhausted."

"I told you we should go on the offensive," Jude said. "Why not kill them now instead of sitting here, waiting? Otherwise, we'll have to keep this up all night and for another full day." Ezra didn't reply. He'd chosen his strategy after hours of prayer. Right or wrong, it was too late to change plans.

A while later, Shimon returned. "The enemy attacked three other barricades the same time they attacked us, but all our defenses held. The other barricades remain on alert."

"The enemy may be trying to find our weak points."

"All the more reason to go after them," Jude said. "Now the waiting will be endless. And like you said, they'll sleep but we won't dare."

"I hardly think they're relaxing out there," Ezra said. "For all they know, we might leave the barricades any minute and come after them." Jude shook his head in disgust and walked away. Ezra turned to his messenger again. "What about injuries? Were there casualties?"

"About a dozen altogether. They took them to the house of assembly for medical attention."

"I pray that none of our men dies."

"One more thing," Shimon continued. "Your brother's wife, Devorah, sent a message. She said Asher's wife is in labor."

"Oh no. Is she all right?"

"The midwife is with her. But she's terrified for her husband. They believe her labor will go better if she learns that he's okay."

Ezra nodded, aware of the deep love between his brothers and their wives, a love that made him envious at times. He walked to where Jude and Asher lay sleeping against the wall, but before he had a chance to wake them, they both opened their eyes and looked up at him in alarm. "What's wrong?" Jude asked.

"Asher, your first child is on its way. Go back to the house of assembly and wait with your wife. She needs to know that you're fine. Take a shift as a guard there, where you're out of danger."

"I want to fight. Why should other men die protecting my family?"

"Go back, for now. Reassure her that you're safe. We'll send for you when we need you."

Asher stood, his reluctance obvious. "I'll go—but I'll be back."

While the others dozed, Ezra paced the area behind the barricade, too restless to sleep. When he gauged the time to be almost midnight, he climbed to the rooftop to take the lookout position.

The sky was just turning light in the east when he saw the enemy coming—a solid block of them, more than one hundred strong. This time they carried shields as protection from Ezra's archers. They made no attempt at stealth, and their marching feet broke the stillness as they surged forward, their swords and spears extended like bayonets. They were going to storm the barricade.

"Here they come!" Ezra shouted to the men below. "Wake up! Take battle positions!" He prayed they could shake off their sleepiness.

Within minutes, the battle raged. This time the volley of arrows did little harm against the enemy's shields. Sounds of clashing swords and battle cries filled the air. Ezra longed to go down and fight, but he needed to watch for assaults from other directions. "We need reinforcements!" he shouted to his messenger. "Go to the other barricades and tell them we're outnumbered." He watched helplessly as his men fought for their lives.

Then, off to his left, a group of Babylonians ran forward with ladders. They were going to bypass the barricade and scale the rooftops. "I need help up here!" Ezra shouted.

An enemy arrow whistled past Ezra's head, barely missing. He crouched low to be a smaller target, his heart pounding at the near miss. Out of the corner of his eye, he saw his enemies prop a ladder against the house adjoining his. With no time to call for help, Ezra stood and got a running start to leap across the gap to the neighboring rooftop, landing painfully on his hands and knees. He made it just as the first invader reached the top of the ladder. Ezra slashed out at him with his sword, uttering a savage cry, then kicked the ladder backward, sending the two men who'd been scaling it to the ground. The ladder smashed into bits. Ezra ran back to his lookout position. "I need more men up here! Quickly!" he shouted. "The enemy is scaling the rooftops!" In the chaos that followed, a few enemy soldiers managed to penetrate the battle line but were eventually felled.

Hours later, Ezra's men finally defeated their attackers. Once again, he sent men across the barricade to retrieve the fallen enemy's weapons. His men had sustained casualties this time, and he sent the wounded to the house of assembly for treatment. "I'm afraid that this was only the opening salvo," he told Jude. "Now that daylight is here, the battles may be much worse as more enemies join the fight."

"I smell smoke!" Jude said, sniffing the air. "Do you think they'll start fires to flush us out?"

Ezra smelled it, too. "I doubt it. They want our plunder, remember?"

"But maybe we should prepare for it."

"You're right. Now that it's light, have the young boys fill water jars and keep them ready." A few minutes later, Asher returned.

"The attacks came on several fronts this time," he reported. "None of their forces made it past our barricades."

"What about casualties?"

Asher lowered his voice. "Dozens of our men were killed. Twice as many were wounded."

Ezra closed his eyes at the news, aching for their families. But the death toll would be devastating if they hadn't been granted the right to defend themselves. When he opened his eyes again, Asher was smiling.

"I have a son," he said.

Ezra pulled him into a quick embrace. "Congratulations. And I'm guessing it would be useless to order you to stay away from the front lines?"

"I'll defend my son's life with my dying breath."

"I pray it won't come to that."

The skirmishes continued all day, with enemy forces growing larger each time. Ezra's men continued to win, and he knew God was on their side. During each lull, he encouraged his men with prayers and words of Scripture: "'You are my King and my God. . . . Through you we push back our enemies; through your name we trample our foes. I do not trust in my bow, my sword does not bring me victory; but you give us victory over our enemies.'"

By late afternoon, Ezra's men were so weary that many of them fell asleep sitting up. He allowed them to rest in shifts but always near their posts. He ordered more guards to the rooftops. The women sent food and water to the front lines to keep up the men's strength, but each battle left a few more of Ezra's soldiers wounded. How much longer could they hold out?

The sun crawled toward the horizon. Their ordeal was nearly over. But as Ezra had feared, the enemy made one final assault before the day ended, and this time the Babylonians had recruited teenaged boys to join the attack. It seemed criminal to wield a sword against mere boys, but Ezra had no choice. He ached with exhaustion and knew his men did, too, but they fought with all their strength, well aware that they fought for their lives.

They beat back their enemies one final time, forcing a retreat. Ezra watched them disappear in the fading light and felt as if a mountainous burden had lifted from his shoulders. He turned to Jude, who had been fighting alongside him, but his brother suddenly shouted, "Hey! That's him!"

"What are you talking about?" Instead of replying, Jude started climbing over the barricade. Ezra grabbed his leg to pull him back. "Jude, stop! What are you doing? Don't go out there yet!"

"Let me go! I saw him! I saw the filthy Babylonian who threatened Devorah!" He kicked and struggled to free himself.

"No, wait. It's nearly over now. The Babylonians are retreating."

"I know! And I won't let him get away alive!" His brother was much stronger and managed to break free. Before Ezra could stop him, Jude bolted over the barricade to chase the retreating men.

Ezra scrambled over behind him, calling out to Asher and the others. "Help me! We have to stop him before he gets himself killed!"

Jude raced ahead, charging into the retreating men. "Come back and fight like a man, you coward!" The Babylonian halted and turned to face him. But so did six others. Jude hurled himself at his enemy as if blind to the danger, plunging his sword into the startled man in a deathblow.

"Jude, look out!" Ezra shouted as he ran toward his brother, his steps slowed by exhaustion. The warning came too late. Ezra watched in horror as the enraged Babylonians turned on Jude before he could withdraw his sword from his enemy's body. By the time Ezra reached him, Jude lay slumped on the ground, blood pouring from several stab wounds, including one to his gut. Ezra chased Jude's attackers, not content until he and Asher and the others had killed all six Babylonians. Then he hurried back to where Jude lay bleeding. His brother's eyes were open. He was still alive. "Bring a litter!" Ezra yelled to the men behind the barricade. "Hurry! My brother needs help!"

"Did I kill him?" Jude breathed. "Is he dead?"

"Yes, Jude. And so are all the others." Where was the litter? Why didn't they hurry? Ezra tried to lift Jude and carry him himself, but his right arm felt strangely weak. He thought it was weariness from wielding his sword for so long, but he looked down and saw blood gushing from a jagged wound on his upper arm. Only then did he notice the pain and feel faint. Asher grabbed him before he fell and eased him to the ground.

"Ezra! You're injured!" Asher tore off a strip of cloth and wrapped it tightly around Ezra's arm to slow the bleeding.

"I'm all right . . . I'm all right. Go with the others, Asher. Make sure Jude gets help." The day wasn't quite over, and they needed to retreat behind the barricade in case there was another enemy assault. Someone helped him to his feet. The pain in his arm was excruciating, and as he climbed over the barricade, Ezra knew he wouldn't be able to hold a sword again. Instead, he climbed to the roof to watch the shadowy streets for movement, praying continually for Jude.

"I need to find my brother," he told the other men the moment the sun slipped below the horizon. He found Jude lying inside the house of assembly, his ruddy face pale with approaching death. Devorah sat beside him, holding his hand, begging God to spare his life. "How is he?" Ezra whispered to Asher. But his younger brother simply shook his head, tears in his eyes.

"I'm here, Jude," Ezra said as he knelt beside him. Jude appeared too weak to speak. He gazed up at Ezra for a long moment, then looked at Devorah, then back at him. Ezra understood. "Yes. I'll take care of her, Jude."

"No, no, no, no . . ." Devorah moaned. "Jude, no! You can't die! Oh, God, please . . . please . . ."

"On my soul, I promise I'll take care of her," Ezra said. Then he rose and hurried away to give Jude and Devorah their final moments alone. But Ezra couldn't stop weeping—and he didn't care who heard him.

CHAPTER
17

CASIPHIA

Reuben hadn't slept. He'd spent all night and day on alert outside the house of assembly, watching bloodied men being carried back from the front lines. At least a dozen had died. "You must be exhausted," the man standing guard beside Reuben said. The elderly man's joints were too crippled and twisted with age to hold a sword. "Why don't you go inside and lie down, son?"

Reuben shook his head. "I can't sleep."

"Here, then. A slug of this will keep you going." The old man lifted the jar that he'd kept at his feet all this time and offered it to him. Reuben took a gulp, thinking it was water, and discovered that it was wine. Fermented wine. Stronger than anything his family drank on the Sabbath. It stole Reuben's breath and burned all the way to his stomach. He took a second gulp, then coughed. The old man laughed. "We call that 'liquid courage.' Helps your tired body wake up, doesn't it?" Reuben nodded and handed it back as the wine's warmth spread through him.

The litter bearers arrived with yet another casualty. "How's the battle going?" the old man asked them.

"We're keeping them at bay," one of them said. "They're losing more men than we are."

"Good . . . good. Only a few more hours until sunset."

A blanket shrouded the body on the stretcher. The man was dead. But when Reuben glimpsed the man's dangling arm and callused hand, he stopped breathing. He recognized that hand. He yanked back the covering and saw his father's bloodless face.

"No!" he cried out. "Abba, no!"

Reuben collapsed beside the stretcher as the men quickly set it down. He grabbed his father's lifeless body and shook him, pleading with him to live. One of the litter bearers had to pry him away. "He's gone, son. It's too late. I'm sorry."

All reason left him. Reuben struggled to his feet, the world spinning, and ran toward the battle, blinded with rage and grief. He had promised his father he wouldn't leave the house of assembly, but Abba was dead, so what good was his promise? Reuben sprinted through the deserted streets until he reached one of the barricades where a fierce battle raged. He glanced around for a sword, eager to hack his enemies to death, then spotted a bow and a quiver of arrows, instead. One of his fellow soldiers rushed over as he picked them up.

"Whoa! Whoa, son! What are you doing here? You're only a boy."

"I came to fight!"

"You're too young. Give me those." The man wrestled to take the bow away but Reuben fought back.

"Let me go! I know how to shoot."

"Let him go," another man shouted. "We need all the help we can get."

The man released him. "Fine. Do whatever you want. The archers are up on the rooftop. But don't be foolhardy."

Reuben scaled the outside stairs to the roof. Four archers stood near the parapet, firing and reloading rapidly. Reuben looked down at the battle and took his stance. He set the first arrow in place with shaking hands and drew back the bowstring, taking aim at a Babylonian, remembering his father's still, pale face. Reuben released the arrow in a burst of rage and watched it fly too far, missing its mark.

He had to calm down, take his time. He grabbed another arrow and set it in place. He drew back the string, and this time the arrow struck its target. The Babylonian toppled to the ground. Reuben reached for a third arrow and carefully took aim—then fired. He aimed and shot again and again, letting his anger and grief power each arrow. And then the quiver was empty. He looked around at the other archers. They had stopped shooting. "It's over, son," one of them said. "There's no one left to kill."

It was true. The enemy was in retreat. The mass of piled bodies below him didn't move. The sun was setting. The thirteenth day of Adar was nearly over, but Reuben didn't want to stop. He wanted to continue killing and avenge his father's death. He reached to pull an arrow from someone else's quiver, but the man laid his hand on Reuben's arm, stopping him.

"Enough. It's over."

"We need to go after them! We can't stop until we kill them all!"

"No, son. There won't be any more fighting today. Go home to your family."

His family. Abba was dead.

Reuben dropped the bow and clambered down the stairs, running back through the streets. They were crowded now with returning soldiers and women hurrying out to meet them. Families gathered their children as they prepared to leave the shelter and go home. But Abba lay dead in the house of assembly. Mama knelt beside him, weeping and mourning, the baby squirming on a blanket beside her, wailing loudly. Reuben's Uncle Hashabiah draped his arm around Mama, trying in vain to comfort her.

"He fought bravely," Hashabiah said. "Oh, how we will miss him!"

"Why did he have to die at all?" Reuben shouted.

His uncle looked up at him. "It was God's will, Reuben."

The words were an arrow to his heart. *God's will.* "Then I don't want anything to do with God!"

"Reuben, wait," his uncle called as he stormed away. Reuben didn't stop. He saw the jar of strong wine he'd shared with the old man and scooped it up. Liquid still sloshed inside. He took it with him as he kept running, returning to the barricade where his arrows had killed so many men. The sky was growing dark now, and he could barely see the enemy's lifeless bodies littering the street on the other side. He shoved a wooden crate out of the way to clear a path over the barricade.

Reuben's anger burned like fanned coals as he walked among the slain, kicking them, tugging arrows from their bodies, arrows that he and Abba had made. He searched a few bodies for valuables, and when he saw a nicely woven robe on one of the men, he yanked it off and folded it up to keep as his prize. The Babylonians owed him.

Reuben didn't need God or anyone else. He would take care of his family by himself from now on, as he'd promised Abba. At last he returned to the barricade and sat down, lifting the jar of wine and drinking until it was empty, waiting for the pain and the sorrow he felt to drain away with it.

CHAPTER
18

OUTSIDE BETHLEHEM

Amina awoke in the middle of the night to the sound of screaming. She hadn't meant to fall asleep, but she'd drifted off from exhaustion, curled into a tight, shivering ball. The terrifying cries brought her instantly awake. She leaped up, her first instinct to run into the storage room and hide. But no, thieves would look there first. She could crouch down and hide in the animal pen—but wouldn't Abba's enemies want to steal his herd of goats, too? What to do, where to go? She turned in useless circles as the screaming continued, her own panic rising along with it.

The screams grew louder, closer. Suddenly the door burst open and a figure stood in the doorway. Amina stumbled backward, desperate to hide—until she realized that the hysterical intruder was her sister. Sayfah's clothes were torn and smeared with blood. Her face was a mask of terror. Amina limped toward her, her heart pounding wildly.

"Sayfah! Sayfah, what's wrong?"

She lunged at Amina, clinging to her, squeezing the air from her. "They're coming! The Jews are coming! We have to hide!"

Amina could barely breathe through her panic and her sister's crushing embrace. If someone was chasing Sayfah, they would easily find both of them if she didn't stop screaming. "Shh, shh . . . Be quiet, Sayfah. We'll hide in here." She dragged her into the storage room, and they stuffed themselves into a corner behind baskets of pistachios and jars of olive oil and grain. Sayfah buried her face on Amina's chest to stifle her sobs as the screaming continued outside. Rumbling carts and running feet thundered past their house. "Where's Mama and Abba?" Amina whispered.

"They're dead, they're dead! Everyone's dead, and I saw . . . I saw—" Sayfah made a high-pitched, keening wail that was certain to give them away.

"Shh . . . Never mind. We're safe here."

Sayfah finally quieted, then said in a trembling voice, "We have to run, Amina! Please! Let's run!"

"I can't. You know I can't run. Not in the dark. We'll hide here until morning." She held her sister tighter, stroking her hair as they clung to each other—for hours, it seemed. Smoke drifted through the windows, making them cough. Would their enemies burn their house, their village? Why had Abba and the other men ever started this terrible war?

At last the screams and the sound of running feet tapered into silence. Any minute, Amina's parents and brothers would return home, and she could come out of hiding. But hours passed and the room grew light, and only Sayfah had returned. Amina longed to ask her what had happened, what she'd seen, but she was afraid Sayfah would start screaming again. Sayfah hadn't stopped trembling, but whether from cold or fear Amina couldn't tell.

She was getting hungry. So were the goats in the nearby pen. They needed to be milked. "Maybe it's safe to come out now," she whispered.

"Amina, no!" Sayfah tightened her grip.

"My legs are falling asleep from sitting so long. I need to

stand up." Sayfah continued to cling to her as they both stood and peeked from the storage room.

The front door to their house slowly opened. A man stood framed in the doorway, his clothes torn and bloody. It wasn't Abba or one of her brothers. Before Amina had a chance to react, the man saw them. Sayfah screamed as Amina hurried to slam the storage room door closed. She was too slow. The man crossed the short distance and wedged his shoulder inside. "Shut up, girl! Stop that noise! You want the Jews to hear you?"

Sayfah covered her mouth, whimpering as they both backed away from him. There was no place to go in the crowded room. Amina recognized the man. He was from their village.

"Are y-you looking for m-my father?" she asked him.

"He's dead. I watched him die right in front of me. Your brothers are dead, too."

Amina didn't know whether to believe him or not. "What do you want?" she asked. He didn't reply. Instead, he pushed past her, nearly knocking her down, and began filling his arms with food supplies. When he could carry no more, he hurried outside with them. Amina grabbed Sayfah's arm and pulled her from the room. "We have to hide someplace else before he comes back."

"Let's run!" Sayfah begged. "Please, we need to run!"

"I can't run." Amina dragged her sister outside to the narrow space between the rear wall of their house and the neighbor's, and they wedged themselves inside. "We can watch him from here," she whispered. "If he comes after us, then we'll run."

The man hurried in and out of their house, returning again and again to empty their family's storeroom, piling everything onto a donkey cart parked by their door. The cart was already full, but he piled more and more, taking all of her family's baskets and storage jars, their oil and grain and olives. Amina could scarcely breathe. Her father and the others had planned to steal from the Jews, but why was this man stealing from his own people?

The storage room must be nearly empty by now, but Amina watched him go through the courtyard gate once again, carrying a rope. She ducked down, holding her breath, terrified that he was searching for her and Sayfah. If only she had listened to her sister and run away last night. She heard scuffling sounds inside and the goats' frightened bleating, the man's angry curses. He finally emerged with Abba's herd all roped together, and tied them to the back of the cart. Amina ducked again as he looked all around, her heart pounding painfully. Had he seen them?

"You girls better get out of here if you know what's good for you," he shouted. "The Jews are coming." He led the rumbling, overburdened cart and her father's goats away.

The Jews were coming. But where could she and Sayfah go? Where was a safe place to hide? "He said Abba was dead," Amina whispered. "And the boys, too. Do you think he's telling the truth?"

Sayfah nodded. Tears filled her eyes, then spilled down her pale face. "We heard terrible fighting. And before we could move, the battle came right toward us. We were trapped, all of the women and Mama and me. We couldn't get out of the way fast enough, and men with swords—our own men—knocked us down and trampled right over us as they tried to get away. The Jews were chasing them, and they had swords, too. The fighting went on and on, all around us. On top of us. The men were killing each other and people were dying, and there was so much blood. . . . So I stood up and started to run and—"

"Hush, now." Amina grabbed her sister and held her tightly to make her stop, afraid she would start screaming again.

"I should have died with Mama, but I left her there and ran. I didn't want to die!"

A sob choked Amina's throat. "Is—is Mama really dead?"

"I shook her, but she didn't move. She had blood all over her! I should have helped her. I should have stayed with her but I ran away!"

"Don't talk about it anymore, Sayfah." Amina pulled her shivering sister close. The sun had finally risen, but it offered no warmth.

"Let's make a fire. I'll see if he left us anything to eat."

"But the Jews are coming! We need to run!"

"I'm too cold to run. And we need to eat something." She squeezed out of their hiding spot and kindled a very small fire on the hearth, enough to warm themselves and roast the handful of grain she'd found spilled on the floor.

"We have to run," Sayfah repeated as they ate.

"Run where? Do you know anyplace we can go?" Neither of them had traveled farther than the market in Bethlehem.

In the end, they decided it was too dangerous to venture off alone, so they hid outside again in the narrow space between the houses, hoping someone from their family would come back to rescue them. They even managed to doze for a little while, exhausted from the long, endless night and cold, dreary day. Amina awoke again at dusk. The village was eerily quiet and deserted. Were they the only survivors?

"Sayfah," she said, gently shaking her. "Sayfah, I think we should walk to Bethlehem and look for the others. Maybe they're hurt and need our help. We can't live here all alone. That man took all our food."

"But what if it isn't safe? What if the Jews kill us, too? He said they were coming."

"We'll stay by the side of the road and hide in the bushes if we see anyone. It'll be dark soon."

"But how will you walk? Once it gets dark you—"

"I'll manage. You can help me. I think we should try to find the others."

Sayfah finally agreed, and they set out like skittering mice, hovering in the shadows, watching and listening. Smoke hung like fog in the cool evening air as they left their deserted village behind. They inched their way along the familiar path to Bethlehem as if wading through a nightmare that wouldn't end, the darkening sky lit by distant flames. Dead bodies lay scattered all along the road. Jackals barked and yipped in the twilight as if calling each other to a feast, and the dark shapes of birds circled overhead. Amina longed to wake up in her bed and discover that this was only a nightmare. Instead, she limped cautiously forward, clinging to her sister.

At last they reached the narrow entrance to the market square in Bethlehem where the women had waited to collect the Jews' spoils. Sayfah began to weep as if reliving the disaster, and Amina understood why. Scores of trampled bodies filled the street, women and girls their own age, girls they had played with only a few days earlier. They were dead. All of them—dead. So were the men from their village.

"Can you show me where you and Mama waited?" Amina whispered. Sayfah shivered as she led her through the carnage. Even in the dark, Amina recognized her mother's bloody, mangled body. She was dead. Trampled to death.

"I should have died, too," Sayfah wailed. "I was such a coward!"

Amina sank down in the dirt and wept along with her sister, not caring if her enemies found her, not caring what happened to her. What difference did it make? Her family was dead, and she and Sayfah were all alone.

She might have wept until dawn, but above the sound of Sayfah's desolate sobs she heard voices. The Jews were coming. She yanked her sister to her feet as torches bobbed toward them through the streets of Bethlehem. "They're coming! We have to hide!" Amina knew she'd never make it all the way back to their village in the dark. Should they lie down and pretend they were dead? Then she remembered the kind Jewish woman she'd met in the marketplace. The weaver's booth was only a few steps away in the first row of stalls. "Come on. I know a place to hide." She tried to pull her sister into the market square, but Sayfah wouldn't move.

"No! Where are you going? We can't hide in Bethlehem. They'll murder us!"

"No one will think to look for us here. They're probably on the way to our village. Come on." She found Hodaya's deserted booth and ducked inside, beckoning to Sayfah to join her. Her sister hesitated, then followed Amina as the voices and tramping feet drew closer. They huddled in the corner, scared and shivering. They would decide what to do next when morning came.

Amina closed her eyes, her tears falling as vivid images of the horrors she'd seen played over and over in her mind. She would never be able to erase them. She tried in vain to stay awake as a second night of terror dragged on and on, but grief and hunger and exhaustion overwhelmed her. She and Sayfah both slept.

She awoke in the morning to the sound of voices. Three Jewish men stood over her. Amina couldn't breathe, couldn't draw enough air to scream. "What are you doing here?" one of them asked. Sayfah stirred at the sound of his voice but didn't wake up.

"H-Hodaya . . ." Amina stammered. "W-where's Hodaya?"

The men looked at each other. "You're that crippled girl from the Edomite village, aren't you?" one of them said. Amina recognized Hodaya's son. What was his name? "Go on . . . get out of here!" he told her. "You don't belong here."

She didn't move, couldn't run. Desperation fueled her courage. "W-we have no place to go. Hodaya is my f-friend." The men didn't reply. Amina cowered beneath their gazes, waiting to die. If everything Abba said about the Jews was true, they would surely kill her.

"I'll go fetch Mama," one of the men finally said. A long time seemed to pass before he returned with Hodaya leaning on his arm. Amina wept when she saw her friend.

"Oh, you poor child," Hodaya said, crouching to take her in her arms. As Amina moved into her safe embrace, Sayfah woke up. She crawled backward into the farthest corner, covering her mouth in fear, not making a sound. "It's all right," Hodaya told her. "You don't have to be afraid."

"Do you know these girls, Mama?" one of the men asked.

"Yes, Amina is my friend. She and her sister live in the Edomite village a few miles from here. You have to help them get home, Jacob. Amina is lame like me and can't walk very well."

Once again, Amina saw the men look at each other. "Mama, their home is gone. We burned all the local villages last night so the men couldn't regroup and attack us again. She and the other survivors will have to find someplace else to live."

"Then you have to help them find their family. Where might your parents have gone?" she asked Amina.

"They're dead," she whispered. "We're the only ones left."

"Come on, then," Hodaya said, helping her to her feet. "I'll take you home with me. You must be hungry. Tell your sister not to be afraid. She can come, too."

"You can't take them home, Mama," one of the men said. "They're our enemies."

"They're children. Look. She's shaking like a leaf."

"But they're still our enemies. The Almighty One curses those who curse us. Tell them to go back to their people. They must have relatives somewhere."

Hodaya clutched Amina tighter. "Well, until we find them, I'm taking these girls home." She motioned to Sayfah. "Little one, you'll be safe with me."

Sayfah refused to move at first, but Amina finally coaxed her to follow as Hodaya led them out of her booth and into the smoky sunlight. Amina wondered if she was making a mistake. Hodaya was kind, but her sons hated her. These were the men who'd killed Abba and her brothers. Would they kill her, too, if they got the chance? She grew more fearful as they walked, listening to them talk as if she and Sayfah weren't even there.

"You think they'll forget this bloodbath?" the one named

Jacob asked as they left the marketplace and turned down a narrow lane. "These girls will grow up to hate us, Mama. They'll look for revenge. They'll murder us in our beds."

"We need to show them mercy," Hodaya said.

"Why should we show mercy? Their people wouldn't have if the battle had gone the other way."

"But it didn't," Hodaya said. "We must do it because God is merciful. He spared us all from a horrible death yesterday."

"Our leaders will never approve. These girls are Gentiles and—"

Hodaya halted and turned to stare up at her three sturdy sons. "Yes. And you also know that I was born a Gentile. You've heard my story countless times. I was also an enemy of the Jews, but the Almighty One spared my life. And now you're going to help me spare theirs."

"We shouldn't go with them," Sayfah whispered. "I'm scared!"

"Everyone is dead, Sayfah. What else can we do?" Amina dragged her sister behind her, trusting Hodaya. When they reached the warmth and safety of her home, the aroma of bread baking made Amina's empty stomach rumble. She sat down beside the fire and accepted the food Hodaya offered. Sayfah refused to eat.

"We don't belong here," she wept, rocking in place. "I should have died with Mama."

The bloody scene from the market square sprang to Amina's mind, unbidden. She closed her eyes, trying to push it away. "Hush, Sayfah," she soothed. "Don't talk about it anymore. We're safe."

BABYLON

Jude was dead. Devorah stared at his motionless body in disbelief. It was riddled with stab wounds, emptied of blood. She had watched the life drain from him as if a door were slowly closing, shutting him off from her, shutting out the sunlight and joy, leaving her in darkness. The hands and arms that had once fashioned pottery, lifted his daughters, embraced and caressed Devorah, now lay pale and limp at his sides. She would never feel them surrounding her again.

"No . . . no . . ." she repeated. "No, this can't be. . . ." She had begged God to save him yet Jude had died. Why hadn't God answered her prayers?

She couldn't imagine life without Jude. Miriam had once said the same thing about Asher. But the unimaginable had happened. Jude was gone. Gone. Just when the battles were over and the enemy defeated, the angel of death had won after all.

Devorah felt someone take her arm, try to help her to her feet, try to separate her from her husband, but she fought him off. "No . . . no, leave me alone."

"Devorah, it's time to let go." Ezra's voice was gentle and

hoarse with emotion. "Time to go home. The girls are asking for you."

She couldn't leave him, didn't want to leave him, but Ezra gripped her tightly as he pulled her away. His eyes were red with grief, his right arm wrapped in a blood-soaked bandage. Why hadn't the Almighty One taken him instead of Jude? Ezra didn't have a wife and children.

"I can't leave my husband. I can't . . ." she sobbed as he continued to drag her away.

"I know. But we have to. We have no choice."

Somehow they reached home, where friends and neighbors waited in the lamplight to share her grief. They'd made a fire and brought food, fed Abigail and Michal, and put them to bed. Night had fallen. Devorah was surprised to see how dark it was. Yet it seemed fitting, as if the sun would never rise again. Jude had died just as the dreaded thirteenth day of Adar had ended. Why would God take him at the very end? Couldn't her prayers have protected him a few minutes longer?

Friends stayed by her side throughout the funeral and the dark days that followed. Miriam came to help, carrying her newborn son. Each time Devorah heard a footstep or a man's deep voice, she had to remind herself all over again that Jude was gone, that he wasn't coming home. A mountain of grief sat on her chest, unmoving, unmovable, day and night.

As Devorah sat in the courtyard on the third morning, rocking Michal in her arms, Ezra came to her gate. He raised his hand and lifted his chin in greeting, and the gesture was so like Jude's that for the space of a heartbeat she thought it was him. Then a fresh wave of sorrow extinguished her joy.

"I hope I'm not disturbing you," he said. He wore his right arm in a sling, and she remembered the bloodied bandage, remembered thinking he should have died instead of Jude. "I've come for my things," he said.

His things. It took Devorah a moment to understand what

he meant. Alongside the bottomless crater of Jude's absence, she'd barely noticed that Ezra hadn't come home. It wouldn't be proper for him to continue living here, even though one of Devorah's friends stayed by her side, making sure she was never alone. "Yes. Of course," she mumbled.

Ezra disappeared into his room, and she heard him rummaging around. When he came out he carried a blanket-wrapped bundle in his left hand. He paused and met her gaze for a moment before looking away. "I miss him, too," he said.

Devorah's anger broke free from its precarious tether. "Why did he have to die? Why did God take him? Can you explain that to me?"

He shook his head. "I can't. I'm sorry."

"Tell me what happened during the battle. You were with him. Did Jude look away for a moment or get careless? Did God look away? I want the truth. You owe me that." Ezra set down the bundle, and she saw how weary he looked, as if he hadn't slept, either. But she needed to know. "Tell me."

He ran his hand over his face, and again, it was a gesture she'd seen Jude make a thousand times. "There was a Babylonian man . . ." he finally said. "He'd been coming to the pottery yard, taunting Jude."

For a moment, Devorah couldn't breathe. "Yes. He told me about him. He said the man had threatened me. Is he . . . is he the one who killed Jude?"

Ezra shook his head. "No. The battle was over. The enemy was retreating when Jude saw him. He climbed over the barricade and went after him before Asher and I could stop him. He killed the man who'd threatened you . . . but the man was with six others. They killed Jude." Ezra paused for a moment, exhaling. "We avenged his death, Devorah. All the men who attacked Jude are dead."

"He thought he was *protecting* me?" she asked in disbelief. "*That's* what got him killed?" She wanted to rage, to scream at the absurdity of it, but Michal lay asleep on her lap. "I told him I didn't need to be protected! I told him to ignore the man! I told him—" She covered her mouth, unable to finish. Who would protect her now? How could she live the rest of her life without Jude? She was only twenty-five; he'd been thirty-two. They should've had a lifetime together. And she loved him. How she loved him!

She remembered talking with Jude a few months ago, trying to convince him that God was trustworthy. *"I've made up my mind to trust Him even if we all die,"* she had said, *"because God must have a reason for it. He must!"* Could she say that now? Did she still trust Him?

Devorah didn't know how much time passed before Ezra spoke again. "I'm staying with Asher and Miriam for now. If there's anything you need, please ask. I promised Jude—"

"I know. I heard you promise," she said stiffly. "The only thing I need is to know why God took him. Can you tell me that? Why didn't He hear my prayers? How can He call Himself a loving God if He let my husband die?"

She closed her eyes, fighting tears. When she opened them again, Ezra was gone.

Part II

. . . the Jews who were in the king's provinces also assembled to protect themselves and get relief from their enemies. They killed seventy-five thousand of them but did not lay their hands on the plunder. This happened on the thirteenth day of Adar, and on the fourteenth they rested and made it a day of feasting and joy.

ESTHER 9:16–17

CHAPTER
20

BABYLON

Ezra awoke in the dark, his body stiff and cold. His injured arm throbbed with pain. He sat up, not remembering where he was at first. Clay jars and storage baskets loomed in the darkness all around him. He heard the squeaking and skittering of mice. Asher's storage room. It wasn't proper to live with Jude's widow, so he had asked Asher for a place to sleep.

Jude was dead. The memory brought renewed grief. Even if Ezra had been allowed to stay in his old room, he didn't think he could bear to watch Devorah mourn or hear Jude's bewildered daughters asking, "Where's Abba? When is Abba coming home?"

He would have to go back, though. Devorah wanted to know why God had allowed such a tragedy, what the purpose had been. Ezra asked the same question and many more as he wrestled with the Almighty One. He owed it to Devorah to offer what scant insight he could provide. Everyone in their community sought answers. They came to Ezra as their leader, asking for words of advice, unloading their burdens and sorrows, seeking God's guidance. He knew the Torah better than any man in Babylon, so it was up to him to reassure them. A formidable task.

If any good at all had come from this tragic ordeal, it was

that God's people were trying harder than ever to please Him. Yet following God's laws was becoming increasingly difficult to do here in Babylon, surrounded by a pagan culture. If only Ezra could lead his people home to Jerusalem.

The growing light in the room foretold dawn's approach. He wouldn't fall back asleep now, so he stood and put on his robe, careful to shield his aching arm. The enemy's sword had slashed through skin and muscle, clear to the bone, leaving his limb so weak he could barely lift a cup. His arm would have to heal some more before he could write or do any work. He fumbled to fasten his sandals with one hand and went out for a walk in the early morning light. The streets were deserted, the wintry air cold. Asher's house bordered the edge of the Jewish community, and it didn't take Ezra long to reach the street where one of the barricades had stood. It was gone and so were the bodies of his slain enemies. What had happened to them? Had their families come to claim them? He wished he could have strewn the Gentiles' corpses across the open desert beneath the sun, food for scavengers and birds of prey. He understood the psalmist's deep hatred of Gentiles and his words: *"Happy is he who repays you for what you have done to us—he who seizes your infants and dashes them against the rocks."*

Ezra walked and walked, watching and listening as the community stirred and stretched and slowly came to life. He heard the sound of hand mills grinding grain into flour, smelled the aroma of smoke and baking bread. A woman sang as she worked the way Devorah often did—the way she used to sing, that is.

His wanderings took him to the house of assembly, and he went inside to prepare to lead morning prayers. Ezra's week of mourning ended today, a week filled with funerals and prayers for the fallen. Too many funerals. This evening a special service would honor all the men who had died: fathers, husbands, sons. Brothers. It wouldn't bring any of them back.

Eventually, the other men arrived for morning prayers, and

Ezra led them through the liturgy. Afterward he and Asher recited the traditional mourning prayers for Jude. Then he sat in the tiny room behind the assembly hall that he used for his office and reread the latest proclamation that had come from Mordecai the Jew, the Persian king's right-hand man. It told a miraculous story of how the Jewish Queen Esther had intervened to save her people. Throughout the empire's provinces, seventy-five thousand of the Jews' enemies had been killed on the Thirteenth of Adar. And now Mordecai had called for Jews in every province to celebrate the fourteenth and fifteenth days of Adar from this day forward as days of feasting and joy. They would remember it as the time when Jews got relief from their enemies, and their sorrow was turned into celebration. The holiday would be called *Purim* after the lots that Haman had cast in his attempt to destroy God's people.

Ezra could understand why Jews throughout the empire would want to celebrate, but for him, the price had been too great. He would excuse himself from the festivities. Life could never return to the way it was. His own life had changed irrevocably. Babylon was no longer home to him. He closed his eyes as he recited the words to one of the psalms of exile: "'By the rivers of Babylon we sat and wept when we remembered Zion. . . . If I forget you, O Jerusalem, may my right hand forget its skill. May my tongue cling to the roof of my mouth if I do not remember you, if I do not consider Jerusalem my highest joy.'"

When Ezra emerged from his office an hour later, one of the men from the assembly approached him. "Rebbe Ezra, please. If you have a moment, I need your advice."

"Yes, of course."

The man asked an intricate question about the Sabbath laws, explaining how he felt trapped between violating the sacred day and not angering his Babylonian employer. "We're their slaves, after all," he finished. "But what should I do?"

"Give me time to study the text," Ezra replied, "and to research what the men of the Great Assembly have written about it. I'll try to have an answer for you by tomorrow."

"Thank you, Rebbe. God bless you."

The subject of employment reminded him where he needed to go next. His brothers' pottery yard had remained closed for more than a week before the battles, then for a second week as he and Asher had mourned. Ezra walked through his community's twisting lanes, accepting greetings and condolences from people along the way, his grief as painful as the wound on his arm. When he arrived, Asher was the only person in the deserted yard. He stood beside Jude's wheel, idly spinning the upper disc with his hand. He looked up as Ezra approached and halted the wheel's motion. "I can't stop thinking about him," Asher said. "How foolish he was to go after that man!"

"I know. I had to tell Devorah the truth. She wanted to know."

"Now what?" Asher asked. "We have to live among our enemies, but what do we do with our hatred? How do I live the rest of my life with it?"

"I wish I knew. God knows I hate the Gentiles, too. If only we could get out of Babylon and live in our own land again." Ezra gazed at the long row of clay pots, waiting to be glazed and fired, and thought again of the victory celebration. He should set an example for the people as they celebrated God's faithfulness with thanksgiving and praise. But how could he rejoice?

"I told the apprentices and other potters to come back tomorrow," Asher said, interrupting his thoughts. "I need to get back to work. I came here today to look everything over."

"I was worried there might have been damage. There was no way to protect an open area like this from the enemy."

"There's no damage that I can see."

"Good. Tell me what I can do to help." He lifted Jude's leather apron from the bench beside his wheel, and slipped the neck loop over his head.

"What are you doing? Take that off," Asher said.

"I'm here to help you." Ezra couldn't tie the lower strings in back with one hand.

"How in the world can you help me, Ezra?"

"Well, to begin with, we'll need to take down those targets and the practice dummies. But starting tomorrow when the others return, I'll be taking Jude's place. He worked all these years to support my Torah studies, and now I need to support his family. I promised—"

"You can't make pots—especially with one arm."

"I apprenticed with Abba when this was his shop. I remember some things."

"Yes, but you gave it up to study Torah years ago. You're a brilliant scholar, Ezra. That's the work God wanted for you—what we all wanted for you. Now that you're our leader—"

"Someone has to take Jude's place. You can't run this place alone."

"I'll figure something out. I just need a little time to train more craftsmen. Go back to the yeshiva, Ezra."

"Listen, if I've learned anything at all these past few months, it's that I can't stay in scholarly seclusion. I need to live and work like everyone else."

"You're not a potter."

"That's true. I can't make pots as well as he did. But I can tally the accounts and talk to customers for you. And I know how to add fuel to the kiln while you make the pots and train the apprentices."

"What about teaching? What about studying Torah?"

"I promised Jude I would take care of his family, and I intend to keep my promise. I'll work here with you during the day and my students can study with me in the evening when I'm finished. I'll continue my own studies whenever there's time."

"And lead our people, too? Ezra, there aren't enough hours in the day to do all those things. How can you pile any more onto an already full wagon?"

He would make it work. His studies had taken on a new meaning these past months as he'd lived and labored with the people, sharing their trials and fears. The Torah had become a completely different book. In the past, he'd read much of it as history—the story of God's dealings with Israel. But now, after their deliverance, he knew beyond a doubt that God was with them, speaking to them every day. Ezra couldn't wait to reread the holy books with new eyes, listening for God's voice. But he would have to do it in the evening hours, after laboring in his brother's place, earning a living. He picked up a stick of wood with his good arm and carried it to the cold kiln.

"Let the apprentices do that," Asher said.

"I don't mind."

Asher gripped Ezra's left arm to stop him. He had tears in his eyes. "Why did Jude do it, Ezra? Why did he have to chase after that man? If he hadn't been so hotheaded . . . if he had just waited another minute, he would still be alive."

"I know, I know . . . I don't understand it, either." Nor did Ezra understand why, if one of the three brothers had to die, it had been Jude instead of him.

"Please go home, Ezra. Give your arm a chance to heal. Give me a chance to figure out how I can make a living here without Jude." He yanked the apron over Ezra's head. "Come back tomorrow."

Ezra did what his brother asked, walking back through the streets the way he had come. But before he returned to the house of assembly to research the man's question about the Sabbath, he went back to Jude's house to talk with Devorah. As the shepherd of God's people, he couldn't let her wander away from God in her grief.

He found her sitting in her courtyard with a group of neighbors, and was glad to see that she had other women with her, making sure she wasn't grieving alone. Devorah's expression stiffened when she saw him, a mask of anger as if he had no right to be alive when Jude was dead. "Devorah, could you please step outside the gate for a moment so we can talk?" he asked. She rose, carrying the baby in her arms, leaving the gate open.

"You asked me why God took Jude," he said, wasting no time. "Why He didn't answer your prayers. You wanted to know how a loving God could let Jude die. I asked the same questions, believe me, and I confess that I still don't know the answers. But as much as I want to blame God for allowing it to happen, I also blame my brother. He let his temper take control instead of waiting for God's vengeance, and it cost him his life. I tried to stop him—" He had to pause, the memory still fresh. "I was too late. God knows I blame myself."

Devorah stared at the ground, rubbing her daughter's back as the child rested against her shoulder. Ezra exhaled. "It's easy to have faith when we get everything we want from God, everything we pray for. But when we don't, we have to decide if we want His will or our own. We can't manipulate God by a display of faith or by our actions. Only idols can be manipulated. God is sovereign, and He will do what He wills, for His purposes. And those purposes are often hidden from us."

He glanced up again and saw a tear rolling down Devorah's face. "I admit I don't like God's will when it means that my brother has to die. God no longer seems to fit the tidy little portrait I've drawn of Him. But God doesn't change, Devorah. Only our image of Him can change—and any image we create of an infinite God is an idol."

He wanted to reach for her hand but couldn't. Instead, he rested his hand on the child's head for a moment. "The question we have to ask, the question I ask myself is, will we allow grief and disappointment to erect a barricade between us and God? Or will we allow God to be the barricade, the shelter, between us and our sorrow?"

Ezra knew his words to Devorah were true. Yet as he returned to the house of assembly, alone, he wished that his heart would begin to believe them, too.

CHAPTER
21

BETHLEHEM

Amina awoke on a soft sleeping mat in Hodaya's home, feeling rested for the first time in three days. She rolled over and saw that Sayfah was already awake, curled into a tight ball, staring at nothing. Amina wasn't surprised that the first words her sister whispered to her were, "I don't want to stay here."

Sayfah had repeated those words endlessly, ever since they'd come to live with Hodaya. Once again, Amina asked, "Why not? We have food and warm beds. Hodaya is good to us, isn't she? We're safe here."

The straw-filled mat rustled as Sayfah shook her head, shivering. "We don't belong here. The Jews are our enemies. They hate us because we're Edomites."

"But where else can we go?" Amina still struggled to comprehend that she and Sayfah were orphans, their parents and brothers all dead. Today was the first morning that she hadn't awakened in a panic, ready to scramble out of bed at the sound of her father's angry shouts.

The discovery that Hodaya lived with her son Jacob and his family—the son who had wanted to send her and Sayfah back to their own people—alarmed Amina at first. But Jacob was rarely home, working during the day with his two sons—lanky, dark-bearded young men who were about the same ages as Amina's brothers.

"I didn't say good-bye to Mama," Sayfah whispered. She always whispered now, and she spoke only to Amina. She hadn't said a word to anyone else, answering Hodaya's questions with a nod or a shake of her head.

"I don't think I did, either," Amina said, trying to remember. She had been angry at being left behind, frightened of being alone in the house at night.

"I just turned and ran," Sayfah said. "The stampede knocked Mama down, and I just left her there on the ground!"

"If you hadn't run, you'd be dead, too." All of their playmates were, the girls Amina had tried to keep up with in the marketplace, the girls who'd never waited for her.

"I should be dead. I wish I were."

"Sayfah, don't say that!"

"Why not? It's true. We should both be dead—not living here with the people who killed our family."

Amina stood and rolled up her mat, pushing aside the images of her friends' trampled bodies and matted, bloodied hair. For the first time in her life she was thankful she was a cripple. If she'd been whole, she would have died along with them. And she didn't want to die. She liked living here under Hodaya's care.

"I miss Mama," Sayfah said. "I want to tell her I'm sorry." She never mentioned missing their father. Amina couldn't deny the relief she felt at no longer needing to live in fear of him. Nor would she miss his ridicule and beatings. But would life with the Jews be any better? For all she knew, Hodaya's son might prove to be just like her own father. Or worse.

She offered Sayfah her hand to pull her to her feet. "Come on. It's time to get up." A moment later, Hodaya came to the door.

"Are you awake? You girls don't have to hide in here, you know. Come out and be part of the family."

They dressed and followed Hodaya out to the courtyard where Jacob, his wife, Rivkah, and their two sons were already eating breakfast. The family also had two married sons who lived with their wives nearby. Hodaya passed Amina a basket of fresh flatbread, still warm from baking. "Sit down, please, and help yourself." Amina obeyed, unused to sitting and eating with the men.

"Jacob just told us some distressing news," Hodaya said. "I don't want to upset you girls or cause you any added grief, but I believe you have a right to know." She gestured for him to tell it.

"We've finished digging a mass grave just outside of town. We didn't know what else to do with . . . with the people from your village who didn't survive. We're burying them today."

Sayfah laid down her bread, her face as white as linen as she blinked back tears. Amina reached for her hand.

"I'm sorry," Hodaya said. "I was afraid it would upset you, but I thought you should know. I don't think the burial is something you should see, but if you want to go and say good-bye, I'll go with you."

Amina shook her head. "I don't want to," she said, remembering the carnage outside the square. "Do you, Sayfah?" Her sister shook her head.

"I don't blame you," Hodaya said, stroking Amina's hair. "Better to remember your loved ones the way they were when they were alive. Maybe we can visit their grave in a few days, instead."

"Whenever you'd like to go back to your village and look for survivors, I'll take you." Jacob said.

Amina stared down at her lap, unsure what to say. She didn't want to go back there, especially with Jacob, a man she feared, a man who didn't want her and Sayfah. "I'll be glad to go with you," Hodaya said. "I want you to know you're welcome to live with me for as long as you'd like, but Jacob feels we should offer you the opportunity to go home to your people. I'll understand if that's what you decide to do. You must have other relatives, no? Or maybe there's something from home you'd like to bring back here to remember your family by?"

Sayfah tugged Amina's arm and leaned close to whisper. "I want to go home. We need to find our own people."

Amina was still reluctant. Should she let Sayfah go by herself? "All right," Amina finally said. "We'll go. Sayfah wants to."

A few days later, Jacob readied his donkey cart after breakfast and helped his mother onto the seat. Amina and Sayfah climbed up beside her. He led the animal as they followed the road out of Bethlehem, passing through the square by the marketplace with its terrible memories. The plaza looked the same as it had before the killing, as if Amina had only imagined the carnage. But the lingering stench of death hovered in the air. Thankfully, the road to her village was no longer strewn with bodies, and at last they rounded a curve for their first glimpse of home.

Nothing remained. The cluster of houses where Amina had lived all her life was gone, razed to a heap of blackened stones and mud bricks baked to a dull red in the fiery heat. Ghostly tendrils of smoke curled from the scattered ruins, and the wind raised clouds of dust that stuck in her throat and parched her lips. Amina couldn't guess where their house had been. She longed to turn and run, to leave this scene of desolation, but she couldn't move from her seat on the cart.

"Oh, Jacob," Hodaya breathed. "What have you done?"

"We went house to house searching for survivors before we burned it, Mama. We made sure there was no one left behind in the village. From what we could tell, the houses had already been ransacked before we got there. All the livestock was gone, too. It seems the survivors took whatever they could find and fled."

Amina remembered the man from her village who'd come

149

into her house and stolen all their food. He had even taken Abba's goats.

"But these were people's homes," Hodaya said. "Why did you have to burn them?"

"So the people wouldn't come back. They're our enemies, Mama. They planned to kill all of us, remember? How can we live peacefully alongside people who are determined to slaughter us?"

"Well, from the look of it, they haven't come back."

"No. Although they might have gone into hiding when they saw us coming."

"Where, Jacob? There's no place to hide."

Amina closed her eyes. She couldn't view the site any longer. She felt Hodaya's arm encircling her shoulder. "This must be so hard for you girls. I'm so sorry for you. But listen, before we give up, I want to do everything possible to reunite you with a family member. Are you sure you don't have relatives somewhere?"

A memory flickered through Amina's mind. "Sometimes during the harvest festival, Uncle Abdel came from another village to celebrate with us. I remember him and our aunt . . . and we had some cousins . . ."

"Do you know which village they came from?"

Amina looked at Sayfah. She shook her head. "I don't think our villages have names," Amina said.

"Was it nearby?" Jacob asked. "Because if so, it probably burned as well." Sayfah covered her face. Amina longed to do the same. It was too much to bear.

"Enough of this," Hodaya said. She gave Amina's shoulder a squeeze before letting go. "Let's go home. I don't know how many more years the Holy One will give me, but I'll take care of you girls as my very own daughters for as long as I live. Come, Jacob. Take us home." He wheeled the cart around toward Bethlehem, traveling back the way they'd come. No one spoke on the return trip as Amina clung to her sister's icy hand. Sayfah was the only family she had left, but she wasn't the same as before, as altered as their ravaged village.

"I don't want to go back with the Jews," she wept as they neared Bethlehem. But Amina did. She felt safe with Hodaya.

The moment they reached Hodaya's house and climbed from the cart, the weaver beckoned to them. "Come, girls. Follow me." She led them into the storeroom where she kept her sacks of cloth until market day. She opened several bags, pulling out bolts of beautifully dyed wool. "Pick whichever color you like, Amina. You, too, Sayfah. The first thing we need to do is make you some new clothes."

Amina didn't move. She was afraid to touch the cloth, afraid to believe she could wear clothes made from such beautiful material. Sayfah covered her mouth as if to hold back a cry.

"Do you like this one, Amina?" Hodaya asked. "Or maybe this one? This color would look beautiful with your lovely auburn hair. . . . But you choose."

Amina still couldn't move. Hodaya reached to take both of her hands. "I feel so badly for what our people did to your village. You girls have nothing. Please, let this gift show you how sorry I am. Pick one. And Sayfah, too. Please?"

Slowly, fearfully, Amina moved forward and made her choice, selecting the one that complemented her hair. She chose a lovely shade of pale gold for Sayfah, who refused to choose for herself. "We know how to sew," Amina said as she held the soft cloth in front of her. "Mama taught us how."

"Good. Because my eyes don't see as good as they used to."

"We can do other chores, too," Amina said. "We used to help Mama cook and clean and take care of the animals. Sayfah and I used to milk Abba's goats. Right, Sayfah?" Her sister didn't reply. She stared at her feet, holding the new cloth at arm's length, as if it might burn her skin.

"You girls will be a big help to Rivkah and me with three hungry men to feed. They go out to the pasturelands for long stretches of time, so we need to prepare a lot of food for their trip. And believe me, they return home very hungry!"

Amina closed her eyes, feeling dizzy as a rush of emotion flooded through her. It was all too much—losing her family and the only home she'd ever known—and yet she felt unimaginably happy, as if she'd found something she hadn't even known was missing. She wrapped her arms around Hodaya's waist, embracing the kind, gentle woman so tightly she nearly knocked her over. "Thank you," Amina said. "Thank you for everything!"

"Oh, my sweet child. I'm the one who is blessed. I always wanted daughters of my very own."

CASIPHIA

R euben chose the house he would rob with care, the same
way he'd chosen each Babylonian he'd killed when he'd
fired his arrows on the thirteenth of Adar. A wealthy
Babylonian lived here, a man who worked for the Persian government and lived alone with his servants. Children cried when
they awoke in the night and women screamed, so Reuben had
decided on an easy target the first time. The Babylonians owed
him. The Jews had been victorious a month ago, so Reuben had
a right to take whatever spoils he wanted.

He watched from the shadowy alley, waiting in the dark until
the oil lamps behind the shuttered windows finally went out.
Then he waited some more to make sure the household slept.
The cold night drizzled rain. It beaded on Reuben's hair and
shoulders, but at least the clouds hid the moon's light, making
it perfect weather for tonight's work. He shivered in his new
robe, the one he had stripped from his enemy the day Abba died.
He had washed off the blood in the river, let it dry in the sun,
then hid it from his mother. Now whenever he ventured into
the Gentile neighborhoods of Casiphia he took off his kippah
and his fringed robe—everything marking him as a Jew—so he
could walk the streets unnoticed.

Reuben had devised this plan to rob the Babylonians a week after Abba died, on the night his Uncle Hashabiah had come to his house. Reuben hadn't wanted to speak to his uncle, still furious with him for saying God had willed for Abba to die. Reuben refused to go to the house of assembly with him, refused to recite the special prayers for the dead. Was that the reason for his uncle's visit? Reuben had tried to leave, but Hashabiah insisted he stay and hear what he had to say.

"There's something you should know," his uncle began. "As your closest relative, it's my responsibility to make a decision about the forge and your family's future."

Reuben sprang from his seat. "But I'm Abba's firstborn son. It's my job to take care of our family."

Mama laid her hand on Reuben's arm, coaxing him to sit down. "Let him finish, son."

Hashabiah's face showed no emotion. He continued as if delivering a memorized speech. "Your father would be proud of you for your willingness to take responsibility, Reuben. However, I'm sure you realize you're too young to take over his blacksmith work."

"I'm not . . . I know how to do everything. Abba taught me—"

Hashabiah ignored him, addressing his words to Reuben's mother. "One of your husband's workers has offered to buy the business. The profits from selling the forge and all the tools can provide an income for your family for a long time. And he agreed to let Reuben continue working for him."

Reuben couldn't stay seated. "You can't sell my inheritance! My father made me his partner. The shop is mine and—"

"Your father is gone. You and he will never be partners." Reuben's mother covered her face and wept.

"Leave our house!" Reuben shouted, furious with Hashabiah for hurting her, for reminding her of what would never be. He lunged at his uncle, trying to push him out the door. "Go away and leave us alone!"

His uncle was stronger, able to hold Reuben back. He pinned Reuben's arms to his sides and wouldn't let go, shaking him until he stopped struggling. "Stop it! You may not want to hear this, but your mother has to. She's a widow with a young family to raise and no means of support."

Mama pulled herself to her feet and rested her hands on Reuben's shoulders to calm him. "Let him finish, Reuben. Please." He stopped fighting for his mother's sake, but he could barely catch his breath while he listened.

"The man who came to me with the offer wants to own the forge outright," Hashabiah said. "He believes you're too young at thirteen to partner with him, and I agree."

"No, I'm not! Tell him you changed your mind! Please, don't do this to us!"

Uncle Hashabiah shook his head, showing no mercy. "The deal I made is a generous one. He'll pay your mother a very fair amount every month—enough for your family to live on—until the price we agreed on is paid in full, five years from now. He'll let you continue working with him, Reuben, and once your apprenticeship ends, he'll pay you a salary. What's more, your family can continue to live in this house." He released Reuben and turned to his mother. "I'm sure you'll agree this is the best solution for everyone."

"Yes . . . it is." Her voice was so soft Reuben barely heard her above the pounding in his ears. "I don't know what else we can do. . . ."

"But the forge is supposed to be mine!" Tears filled Reuben's eyes at the injustice, in spite of all his efforts to be an adult and not cry. "Please don't sell it. I promised Abba I would take care of you, and I will, Mama. I will!"

She tried to pull him into her arms. "I know you will, Reuben, when you're older. But in the meantime, how will we live? If the baby was weaned I might be able find work as a servant but—"

"Never!" he said, shrugging off her embrace. "I'll find a way to make money so you'll never have to work. But please don't let him sell our forge. Please! I can do the smithy work by myself, I know I can."

No one listened to his pleas. Hashabiah bid them good night and left. The new owner arrived the next day.

Reuben recalled those events now as he waited outside the Babylonian's house, and they made him so angry his heart raced. He had to calm himself. He had a job to do tonight. He would show everyone what he could do.

It was time to go. He'd waited long enough. He moved out of the shadows and scaled the wall, the bricks slippery from the rain, and dropped down into the courtyard on the other side. The first thing he did was lift the bar to the gate to unlock it from the inside so he could make a quick getaway. He had watched the servants going in and out through this rear gate and he already knew exactly where the storeroom was. He crept toward it, staying close to the wall, avoiding the open courtyard, and soon reached the rear of the house. Animals stirred inside their enclosure as if sensing his approach. He halted, waiting for them to settle down again. The same soaring rush of excitement he'd felt when he'd fired arrows at his enemies pounded through his veins. His heart galloped like racing horses, his every sense alert.

Reuben gripped the latch on the storeroom door and found it locked from the inside. He climbed the ladder to the roof, careful not to make a sound, and used his dagger to dig a hole through the packed clay. The roof gave way easier than he'd hoped, but he paused as dirt and lumps of dried mud showered and thudded down inside, fearing that someone had heard him. When all remained silent and the hole was wide enough to squeeze through, he gripped the wooden roof supports and lowered himself down, dropping to the floor inside the dark interior. Reuben quickly unbolted the door, letting light into the windowless room. When his eyes adjusted, he noticed another door leading into the house. He wedged a crate in front of it to block it, then paused again, listening. No sounds from inside. He finally dared to breathe.

He turned to the rows of storage jars next, choosing one filled with grain, another with olive oil. They were heavy, but he lifted them in his arms and carried them outside to the gate, then hurried back to the storage room. He spied an empty sack on the floor and filled it with anything he could find—dried apricots, dates, pistachios, figs. He added two skins of wine, tied the sack shut, and slung it over his shoulder.

Satisfied with his loot, Reuben closed the storage room door behind him and crept back to the gate. He closed it, too, and lifted the two jars. The load was heavy, and he had to stop several times on the way home to rest, but he was proud of his night's work.

The streets remained deserted. Most of Casiphia's night watchmen patrolled near the walls, and he'd chosen a house well away from them. Even so, he'd invented a story in case anyone stopped him: Unexpected guests had arrived late at night, and he'd gone to his uncle's house for provisions. But Reuben hadn't needed to use the story. He would save it for another time.

When he reached home, Reuben hid everything inside their own storage room, then changed his clothes and went to bed. The sky was turning gray in the east; he would have only a few hours to sleep. He quickly drifted off—and the next thing he knew his mother was shaking him awake. "Reuben. Reuben, wake up." She held the jar of grain in her arms. "Reuben, I found this in the storage room. Do you know where it came from?"

"What is it?"

"It's filled with grain. It has Babylonian symbols on it."

He rolled away from her so she couldn't detect his guilt. "Maybe someone donated it to help us out."

"Who would do that?"

"I don't know. Maybe someone who knew Abba."

She was quiet. Reuben was afraid to look at her. "Well . . .

come and eat something," she finally said. "I need to talk to you before the others wake up."

Reuben couldn't imagine what she would say. She couldn't possibly know what he'd done last night, could she? He dressed and went out to where she crouched beside the hearth. She looked thinner than he remembered, and lost without Abba, as if she'd awakened in a world where she didn't belong. She gestured for him to sit down on the rug where she'd laid out his breakfast.

"Reuben . . ." She spoke his name with a sigh. "I'm very worried about you."

"Why? I'm fine."

"I found a second jar and a sack of food in the storage room. I don't believe someone would just drop them off for us in the middle of the night. Tell me the truth. Do you know where they came from?"

He couldn't lie. She may as well know. "It's from our enemies. From the men who killed Abba."

"And how did you get it?" He didn't reply. She rose to her feet, looking paler and thinner than before. "Did you steal it?"

"It isn't stolen. When people lose a war, they have to give everything they have to the victors. That's what happens after a battle. That food is for us to live on so we won't have to sell Abba's forge."

"Reuben, the forge has already been sold. It's too much work for you to manage alone."

He tossed down his bowl, unleashing his anger. "It's my job to take care of you! I promised Abba!"

"But you can't do it by stealing. Suppose you get caught? Then what? How will you take care of us from prison?"

"I won't get caught."

"You know it's wrong to steal. The Torah says—"

"The Torah also says not to kill, but they killed Abba, didn't they? They owe us!"

"Reuben, please," she said, moving closer. "Think of what

your father would say. He would be horrified to know you've become a thief."

"He'd be more horrified to know Hashabiah sold my inheritance! Abba worked so hard for that shop. It's supposed to be mine." He scrambled to his feet, preparing to storm off, but Mama blocked the way.

"You can provide for us by working, not stealing. Listen to me!" She grabbed his arm so he couldn't leave. "The man who bought the shop came to see me yesterday. He said you haven't been showing up for work."

"I don't want to work for him. He should be working for me."

"Reuben, you have to continue as his apprentice. That was part of the agreement your uncle made."

"I never agreed—"

"Listen! If you don't work as his apprentice, we can't live here."

He stared at her, stunned. He was being swept downstream against his will, drowning, just as he'd nearly done once before. Mama had tears in her eyes. "Please, Reuben."

"Fine. I'll work," he said quietly. But right now, he had to get out of the house. He squirmed away from her and crossed the narrow alley to the forge.

Everything was the same as Abba had left it, his tools all neatly in place, the floor swept, the wood piled, and it seemed as though he might appear any moment, telling Reuben to fire up the furnace and fan the coals for him. Reuben knew the man who'd bought his father's business, knew he'd be kind for Abba's sake. But how could Reuben work as an apprentice in a forge that rightfully belonged to him? He could hardly stand to be here.

He hurried out again and went to the storeroom, rummaging through his loot for one of the wineskins he'd stolen. Tomorrow. He would go to work tomorrow as promised. Today he would go down to the river and console himself with wine while he planned the next house he would rob.

CHAPTER
23

BABYLON

The air inside the house of assembly felt so stifling on this hot summer morning, Ezra might have been sitting beside the kiln at the pottery works. Yet the hall was packed with men who had come to pray in spite of the heat. The battles that had raged six months ago had brought his community closer to God, and they still came every day to worship and pray and give thanks to the Almighty One for His salvation. Ezra was grateful for this spiritual renewal. But each day as he listened to the daily Torah passage and was reminded of the Almighty One's deliverance from slavery in Egypt, he felt a growing discomfort with life here in Babylon. If only God would deliver them out of slavery once again and bring them to the Promised Land. He wiped sweat from his forehead as he listened to today's passage, praying for the Holy One to speak to him and His people:

"'If brothers are living together and one of them dies without a son, his widow must not marry outside the family. Her husband's brother shall take her and marry her and fulfill the duty of a brother-in-law to her. . . .'"

What?

"'The first son she bears shall carry on the name of the dead brother so that his name will not be blotted out from Israel. . . .'"

Marry Jude's widow?

The words stunned Ezra. He had studied this passage countless times, but it had always been an academic exercise, a history lesson. God gave this command to Ezra's ancestors when they lived in their own land, governed by their own king from the house of David. Generations had passed since those days. Surely this law was for a different time, a different set of circumstances—wasn't it? Yet he had asked God to speak to him today, and Ezra couldn't escape the conviction that He had spoken. And God's commandment was clear: Ezra had to marry his brother's widow.

Impossible. I can't do it.

"I'll put the holy book away," Ezra told the assistant when morning prayers ended. He wanted to read the passage again. He waited for the hall to empty, then carried the scroll closer to the window, rereading it in a shaft of sunlight. *"If brothers are living together . . ."* That clearly described him and Jude before the battles took place. *" . . . and one of them dies without a son . . ."* Jude had daughters, not sons. *" . . . his widow must not marry outside the family."* Devorah was very young. Surely she would want to remarry someday for security and companionship. But according to the Torah, she wasn't supposed to marry outside the family. *"Her husband's brother shall take her and marry her . . ."* God commanded Ezra to marry her! But how could he obey this law? Merely reading the words gave Ezra a shiver of guilt, as if he were betraying his brother.

He continued reading and learned that if he refused to marry his brother's widow, she could appeal to the elders, accusing him of shirking his duty. The elders could summon him, and if he persisted in saying that he didn't want to marry her, Devorah could publically spit in his face. He would be disgraced, shamed before all the people for disobeying the Torah. Ezra would be disqualified from teaching. Banned from the house of assembly. Removed as the shepherd of God's people. He couldn't expect others to obey God's law if he didn't obey it himself.

But, marry Devorah? His brother's wife?

Ezra rolled up the scroll, covered it with the special cloth, and carefully stored it in the *Aron Ha Kodesh* with the other scrolls. He walked through the streets to his job in the pottery yard, unable to stop thinking about God's command. If hot-tempered Jude had turned murderous when the Babylonian had lusted after his wife, what would he think of his own brother taking her to bed? It seemed wrong. No matter how Ezra looked at it, it seemed like a betrayal. And Devorah would likely see it that way, too.

He tried to push the Torah passage from his mind, starting his workday with the row of new pots that Asher had already shaped on the wheel. They lay drying in the sun, and he felt the clay to see if they had reached the texture of leather yet. He carried the ones that were ready to the kiln. His wounded arm had healed and his skills at all aspects of pottery making were slowly improving, but Ezra was certain he would learn faster and accomplish more if not for the steady stream of people from his congregation who came throughout the day to ask questions and bring cases involving the law for him to decide. He had just replied to the third petitioner of the day and had returned to his work on the ledger books beneath a shady roof of rushes when Asher walked over to him.

"I don't know how you can concentrate with so many inter-ruptions," Asher said, shaking his head. "The least you could do is sell a pot to every person who comes here so we'd make a profit on all these disruptions."

"I'm sorry. . . . Are my people bothering you?"

"Me?" he asked, laughing. "No, I'm getting my work done as usual, but I don't see how you cope with this all day."

"It's wonderful that the people ask questions," Ezra said.

"They want to please God and live by His Torah. The Almighty One listens to our prayers anytime, anyplace, doesn't He? And we're His priests, Asher. It's our job to listen to them."

"I know. Haven't I been trying to convince you to quit this place and go back to teaching?" He spoke kindly, without animosity.

Ezra shook his head. "You mean well, Asher, but it's impossible. I have a responsibility to you and to Jude's family." Even as he spoke the words, they reminded him all over again that the Torah commanded him to marry Devorah. Commanded him! Should he talk to Asher about it? People came to Ezra with their questions, but who could he go to with his own? He opened his mouth to speak, yet there was nothing to ask. The law was very clear.

"I'll let you get back to work," Asher said, "before the next interruption comes."

That evening as Ezra ate dinner with Asher and Miriam, a new thought occurred to him. He had a responsibility to tell Devorah about this law. She needed to know that when her time of mourning ended, she wasn't supposed to marry outside the family. She didn't have to remarry at all, of course. She could refuse to marry Ezra, and he imagined that she would. Yet she had a right to know that God had provided a way for Jude's name and his inheritance to continue after his death. Ezra had a duty to tell her about it.

He left the house after the meal and walked to the yeshiva as usual to teach his students. Tonight he was excited to share the lessons he had learned while laboring in the pottery yard for the past six months. "The Almighty One is teaching me some important lessons in my work as a potter," he told his students. "I'm reminded of the two great prophets, Jeremiah and Ezekiel, who used the picture of God as the Master Potter in their prophecies. I've learned that just as the clay must be perfectly centered on the wheel before it can be shaped, so must we center our lives on God's law as we allow Him to shape us. If we aren't centered, we'll become misshapen beneath His hands when the events of our lives spin us faster and faster like the potter's wheel. Or maybe fly off the wheel entirely." He paused, speaking to himself as well as to them. He had to center his life on the Torah—and that meant obeying the law, regardless of how he felt about it.

"But even before the clay can be shaped, it must be wedged," he continued, "a process of applying pressure in order to remove all the air bubbles from the clay. These impurities may seem insignificant, but if too many of them remain, the vessel can become distorted beneath the pressure of the potter's hands. And once in the kiln, these hidden imperfections in the pot can cause it to crack in the searing heat. I'm reminded of all our sins and imperfections, all the seemingly insignificant ways that the values and morals of Babylon creep into our thoughts and actions and cause us to become misshapen instead of the vessel God intended. We're slowly being polluted here living among the pagans, and when the heat and pressure in our lives increase, we'll crumble. If we want to be the people of God, we must eliminate the impurities from our lives and follow His law."

Follow the law. As much as Ezra wanted to forget about marrying Devorah, he knew he had to speak with her. Tomorrow.

"I'll be a little late to work today," he told Asher after morning prayers the next day. "But I promise I'll be there."

Once again, people stopped him with their questions before he could leave the house of assembly. The fall holy days were approaching, and his congregation had a renewed interest in celebrating the appointed feasts, even though they couldn't worship at the temple in Jerusalem or offer sacrifices as the Torah required. What would it be like to celebrate the holy days in Jerusalem, worshiping the Almighty One the way He had commanded? Ever since the Thirteenth of Adar, the longing for home had become a gnawing ache in Ezra's soul.

When he'd patiently answered everyone's questions, Ezra walked the familiar lanes to Jude's house. The grief he felt at the loss of his brother hadn't diminished over time. If only he had clung tighter to Jude as he'd bolted over the barricade. If only he hadn't died. . . .

Ezra was still deep in thought when he arrived and found Devorah and her two daughters just leaving their courtyard. She was beautiful, he realized, even though the light had gone out of her eyes and sorrow and grief lined her face. "Are you going somewhere?" he asked.

"We're on our way to Asher's house."

"May I walk with you? I need to discuss something with you."

"Of course. But we'll have to go slowly until Michal gets tired of walking. She wants to do it herself without any help. Jude would be so proud of her independence and—" Devorah stopped, struggling to control her emotions. "I'm sorry," she whispered.

"No, I understand. I miss him, too." He remembered how Jude used to swing his daughters high in the air, grinning as their laughter rippled around him like waves. They walked on in silence, the older girl skipping happily ahead of them as Devorah took baby steps with the younger one, holding her chubby hand.

"Don't get too far ahead, Abigail," Devorah called.

"I won't. I know the way."

Ezra cleared his throat. "I promised Jude I would take care of you, and I want you to know that I will always provide a home and food and protection for you and the girls. Always. The question is, what's the best way for me to do that?"

He glanced at her as he paused. Ezra had never allowed himself to dwell on Devorah's form or her features. "You shall not covet your neighbor's wife," the Torah said—much less your brother's. He had lived with Devorah and Jude for nearly five years, yet he couldn't have described what she looked like in any detail. Now, as he let his gaze linger a moment longer, he saw again how lovely she was, with almond-shaped eyes beneath arched brows and soft, full lips. She seemed too thin, though, and her face was still pale with grief. Jude had often praised his wife as a woman of faith. "General Devorah," he had called her the day she'd advised Ezra not to trust the Persian military officials. And she had been right.

"You've always been very kind to us, Ezra," Devorah said, "especially these past few months. I'm not sure I have any choice except to rely on you. I'm not ready to marry again, even if I knew someone who would marry me. I've heard of other widows who return to their father's house, but you know that my parents are gone, and I have no sisters or brothers."

"I know. It's perfectly fine for you and the girls to keep living where you are. That's your home." He kept his head down as they walked through the narrow, twisting lanes, not wanting to be interrupted by the people they passed. "The thing is, Devorah . . . there's a law in the Torah that covers our . . . situation." She looked up at him, waiting. "It's called the law of *levirate* marriage—*levir* meaning brother-in-law in Hebrew."

She frowned as if annoyed. "I know what *levir* means. My father taught me Hebrew."

"Forgive me. I didn't mean to be condescending." This subject was difficult enough to discuss without making Devorah angry. He lowered his voice so he wouldn't be overheard. "Are you familiar with the law of levirate marriage, then?" She shook her head. "The Torah says that if a man dies without an heir, as Jude has, then his brother has a duty to marry his widow."

She halted. "You're supposed to marry me?"

"Yes."

She quickly turned her face away, her pale cheeks tinged with scarlet. "I see. . . . Is that the law behind the story of Ruth and Naomi?" she asked a moment later.

"Yes, that's right." He tried not to reveal his surprise at her knowledge. "God provided for Ruth and Naomi by allowing

166

Ruth to marry Boaz, her husband's kinsman, since her brothers-in-law were dead—"

"I know the story. But somehow it sounds different in our time—with you and me." She shook her head, almost a shiver.

"I don't blame you for your reaction. It seems like we're betraying Jude. I was reminded of this law only yesterday, and I've barely had time to consider all the implications, but . . . I thought you should know what the Torah says."

He was relieved when Devorah bent to lift the baby in her arms. They could walk faster now. They were nearly to Asher's house, and the older girl was calling to them to hurry. Ezra wanted to get this over with.

"You don't have to make a decision right away, Devorah. Take your time. And the law doesn't force you to marry me if you don't want to. But I felt it was my duty to make you aware of the law since I'm responsible for teaching our people . . . and we . . . I mean, you . . ." *Stop talking and be quiet,* he admonished himself. He was making an awkward situation worse by going on and on about it. They finally reached Asher's gate. "I need to go to work," he said. "Thank you for talking with me."

He'd started to leave when she called to him. "Ezra?" He halted. "Why would God command such a thing?"

"I've been thinking about that, too," he said, staring at his feet, "and the simple answer is He wants to make sure widows and orphans are protected. The Torah says over and over that He cares about their welfare, and the law provides many ways for supporting them—"

"Like Ruth gleaning in the fields. The reapers are supposed to leave something for them. And farmers aren't supposed to pick their vines a third time."

"Yes. Exactly so." Again, Devorah's knowledge of the law surprised him. "If the Torah didn't require a kinsman to take care of them, widows and orphans might become vulnerable to abuse. But there's a more complicated reason, and it has to do with Jude's name and his inheritance, something that's very important to every Jewish man as part of the people of God. It's especially important to our family because we're priests, descendants of Aaron the high priest. The law of levirate marriage makes sure that Jude's memory and lineage will never die out."

"How? I don't understand."

"In a levirate marriage, our firstborn son would be Jude's, not mine." He wondered if his face had turned as red as hers at the idea of creating a son together.

"So that's why Ruth's firstborn son was placed on Naomi's knees?" Devorah asked. "And why he was declared to be hers, not Boaz's?"

"Exactly. And it's why the other kinsman in that story didn't want to marry Ruth and risk damaging his own inheritance."

Devorah sighed. "Jude was always very proud that his family had descended from priests—and even high priests. He used to tell me he traced his lineage back to Zadok, the first high priest to serve in Solomon's temple."

"I'm proud of our heritage, too. I would hate to see Jude's line disappear. Mine either, for that matter." It occurred to him that even if Devorah decided not to marry him, at age thirty-six it was time he found a wife.

Devorah seemed deep in thought, and he waited for her to speak. The sun felt merciless as Ezra stood in the shadeless street, and he felt the warmth of the cobblestones beneath his feet. "If I married someone else instead of you," she finally said, "would my firstborn son still be Jude's heir?"

"Only if he was a kinsman. I'm the closest one you have, I'm afraid. Then Asher. I'm not sure who's next in line, but I could find out for you. The Torah says you cannot marry outside the family."

"So . . . if Ruth had refused to marry Boaz, then King David never would have been born," she mused aloud. "The royal line came through a levirate marriage."

"Yes. That's true."

Devorah looked up at him, her gaze frank and disconcerting. "Is this what you want to do, Ezra? Marry me?"

Again, he felt a blush rising to his cheeks. "To be honest, Devorah, if I hadn't read this in the Torah, it never would have occurred to me to intrude on the love you and Jude shared. This law feels awkward and uncomfortable to me, and I'm certain to you, too. Jude was my brother. My friend. I know how much you loved each other, and I already know I can never take his place in your heart. I would be wrong to try."

"But God commands this?"

He nodded slowly. "Yes. And I'm convinced that obeying God's law is always the wisest and best way to live. The Almighty One knows so much more than we do. He created us. And so I have to believe that, yes, this must be the best thing to do. But only if you're willing. And only when you're ready."

"Abba taught me the importance of obeying the law," she said, almost to herself, her voice so soft he barely heard her.

"You don't need to decide right away. At the very least, wait until your year of mourning ends." She remained silent, staring at the ground as if deep in thought. He was aware of his nieces babbling in the background and realized that he would become their adoptive father if Devorah married him. He knew nothing about being a father. Jude had made it look so natural, lifting his tiny girls into his arms, showering them with kisses. "I should go," he said. "Let me know if you have any questions or . . . or if you need anything."

"I will. Thank you."

Ezra glanced up at her as he hurried away, and he was struck again by how lovely she was. He felt instantly ashamed. He was no better than the filthy Gentile who had admired her beauty. But Devorah wasn't Jude's wife anymore, he reminded himself.

He ran his fingers through his hair, scrubbed his face, tugged his beard. He was the great Torah expert, the man whose life's work was to decipher the law and put it into everyday language so people could obey it. Why study it if he wasn't going to live it? He knew God's law was good. But in this case, it was going to be very difficult to obey it.

BETHLEHEM

Amina felt the warmth of the late afternoon sun, even though she sat in the shade in Hodaya's courtyard, spinning wool into yarn with her spindle. She paused to watch Sayfah carry a jar of grain across the courtyard from the storage room, and her movements reminded Amina of a frightened animal's. After all these months, Sayfah still spoke in a whisper, still skulked around Hodaya's house as if terrified. Her unhappiness with their new life seemed to grow greater and more apparent each day while Amina's happiness sprouted and blossomed like spring flowers beneath the sunshine of Hodaya's love.

They had fallen into the household's routine easily, doing the same chores they used to do at home but without all the yelling and the beatings. Hodaya's son never treated his wife and children the way Abba had treated his family. For the first few months after she and Sayfah had taken refuge here, Amina had worried they wouldn't be accepted among the Jewish people. Would they be considered enemies because of what Abba and the other village men had tried to do? But Hodaya was so beloved by the other women in Bethlehem that her new "daughters" had quickly been adopted by the community, too. Even Hodaya's sons seemed to accept them now. Why couldn't Sayfah see that? Instead, her sister recited the same, monotonous refrain: "We don't belong here."

Amina returned to her spindle, making sure she twisted and spun the yarn into an even thickness. Hodaya had taught her how to spin the wool from Jacob's sheep after it had been to the fuller, and together they dyed it a rainbow of colors. Amina loved working with Hodaya at home, then going to the marketplace with her every week and helping in her booth. She had learned how to display the cloth in the most inviting way and to bargain with customers for the best price. Sayfah refused to go with them.

"I can still hear the screams whenever I go back there," she had whispered to Amina. She had covered her ears with her hands as she'd spoken. "Such terrible screams . . ."

"Never mind, then," Amina had quickly replied. "You don't ever have to go back."

She paused again in her spinning to watch Hodaya weave on the huge loom in its wooden frame, fascinated by how swiftly her shuttle raced back and forth, how she tightened the finished rows in one smooth, quick motion. "Do you think I could learn to weave someday?" Amina asked.

"Of course! When Jacob comes home I'll ask him to build a small loom so you can learn."

"One for Sayfah, too?"

"Yes, of course. Would you like to learn how to weave, too, Sayfah?"

Sayfah frowned and shook her head before disappearing into the storage room again. Why did she have to be so miserable? They had a wonderful life here.

"You know," Hodaya continued, "it's getting harder for me to set up my loom by myself these days. I don't see very well, and my fingers are so stiff I have trouble tying the warp threads. You girls will be a wonderful help to me."

But the best part of Amina's day was listening to the stories

Hodaya told while they worked, stories about the Jewish people and the God they worshiped. Amina had learned about the first man and woman God ever created and how they'd disobeyed Him and had to leave the beautiful garden. She'd learned about a good man named Noah, who was saved by God from a flood along with a boat full of animals. Hodaya told her about Abraham, the father of the Jewish people, who had believed in one God, not many. She learned about a shepherd boy named David who wrote beautiful songs and became a great king because he loved God. But Amina's favorite story was about a crippled man who was invited to live in King David's palace and eat at his table. Amina thought she knew how it felt to be that man and go from cursing to blessing.

"Why don't you want Jacob to make you a loom?" she asked Sayfah as they lay in bed that night. "Wouldn't it be wonderful to be able to weave beautiful cloth like Hodaya does?"

"I don't want to be like them."

Amina refused to wallow in her sister's gloom. "Living here is like paradise, isn't it? I don't ever want to leave this house."

"Well, I do!" Sayfah said. "I feel like a traitor living here. The Jews killed our family and destroyed our village. We shouldn't be friends with them. It isn't right."

"Hodaya loves us, and I love her," Amina said firmly.

"Then I don't want to be your sister anymore." Sayfah huffed and rolled away from Amina, turning her back.

"Listen, were you really happy living back home, Sayfah? Remember how scared you were when Abba started arranging your marriage?"

"I don't want to talk about that."

"You have to!" Amina sat up. "You have to remember! And you have to stop looking back and thinking everything was wonderful at home, because it wasn't. Abba used to beat us—"

"Because we deserved it. We used to make mistakes and make him angry—"

"No! We were scared all the time. Can't you see how different it is here? Why would you want to go back to the old way?"

Sayfah rolled over to face her again. "Because we don't belong here. We need to go back home and see if people are living in our village again. It's been seven months, Amina. Maybe they've rebuilt it."

"I've never seen anyone from our old village in the marketplace when I go with Hodaya."

"Do you blame them for staying away after what happened? I'm probably not the only one who's afraid to return to the market."

Amina sighed, struggling to be patient with her sister, wishing Sayfah could be as happy as she was. "We can ask Jacob to take us back when he comes home. I'm sure he would do it. But I don't understand why you want to go back when it's so nice here."

"This isn't my home and it never will be."

For Sayfah's sake, Amina did ask Jacob about it the next time he returned with his sheep. He and his sons agreed to take them to their village. Hodaya didn't come this time, so they walked, leaving early in the morning before the sun grew too hot. They followed the dusty road Amina had taken with her mother and the other women from their village every week. She'd now learned to walk with a crutch like Hodaya, and it helped her move faster and keep her balance. Her father would have hated her crutch—and if he'd seen her with one, he would have beaten her with it, then burned it in the fire.

It didn't take long to reach the site where the village had been, and Amina was immediately sorry they had come. Sayfah sucked in her breath at the shocking sight, then collapsed against Amina, nearly knocking her over. Nothing remained. Thistles and grass now grew among the ruins. And that's what they still were—ruins. In an instant, Amina began to relive that terrible night of fear and loss. She felt her sister's body trembling and knew Sayfah was reliving it also.

Jacob drew his sons away to give the sisters time alone. "Let's look around and see if we can spot any signs of people living here," he said. Amina stood in the road where the village entrance had once been, holding Sayfah's hand as she watched the men make a sweep of the surrounding area. The fields that her father and the others once tended were overgrown with tangled weeds, reaching nearly to Jacob's waist.

"The grape vines and olive trees seem to have been picked over," he told them when he returned, "but the vines and trees aren't being properly tended."

"No one lives here," his son agreed. "I doubt if this village will ever be rebuilt." Amina recalled the piles of dead bodies and knew no one was left to rebuild it.

"There. Are you glad we went?" Amina asked her sister on the way back to Bethlehem. She knew she sounded harsh, but how else could she shake her sister from her sorrow and make her start living again? "Will you please stop thinking about it now? We have a new life. A happy life."

Sayfah wiped a tear. "It isn't right. We shouldn't be happy." She quickened her pace until Amina could no longer keep up.

That evening at dinner, Jacob and Hodaya made plans to go to Jerusalem the following week for a special sacrifice and a feast. Amina asked Hodaya about it later as they washed the dishes. "It's a very sacred time called the Day of Atonement," Hodaya explained, "followed by the Festival of Booths. Every Jew who can is supposed to worship in the temple and ask the Almighty One for forgiveness. You and Sayfah are welcome to come with us."

"Is it like that other feast? The Passover?"

"In some ways."

Hodaya's family had celebrated Passover a month after Adar, one month after she and Sayfah had come to live with her. Amina still had been getting used to her new home and felt shy around all the adults, but she remembered two things: The women had worked hard, cleaning the house from top to bottom, making sure every last crumb of leaven was removed before the holiday. And Amina remembered the family's happiness as they sat down to eat and tell stories. The evening had been filled with joy and laughter and singing. In Amina's village, the festivals had been loud, raucous affairs where people drank too much and sometimes got into fights. Abba used to make her stay out of sight if they had guests, ashamed of her crippled leg.

On the night of Passover, Jacob had told how the Jews had been slaves in Egypt until God set them free, performing miracles for them and killing the Egyptians. "How long ago did this happen?" Amina had asked, remembering the battle between the Jews and her people.

Hodaya had laughed. "A very long time ago. But we tell the story every year to remember what God is like. To remember that He saves us if we trust in Him."

"I think He saved me and Sayfah," Amina had said. "I think that's why we lived when everyone else died."

Hodaya stroked her hair. "I think you're right."

They hadn't traveled to Jerusalem for Passover last year because Hodaya hadn't felt well. "But now I want to go and worship in the temple for the fall feasts," she told Amina now. "You may stay here or come with us, it's up to you."

"Is it very far?"

"The journey takes about two hours, riding in the cart."

Sayfah had been sitting right beside Amina, listening to the entire conversation, but as they prepared for bed later, Amina didn't ask her sister if she wanted to travel to Jerusalem with the others. Amina was determined to go, and she didn't care what her sister did. In the end, Sayfah reluctantly decided to come, unwilling to be left alone in Bethlehem.

When the day finally arrived, the family loaded their cart and left early in the morning, traveling with a caravan of people and family members from Bethlehem. They met up with caravans from other villages along the way, all heading for Jerusalem. Sometimes they sang songs as they journeyed, and everyone seemed to know the words, even the children. Amina rode on the seat beside Hodaya, fascinated by the gently rolling hills, the terraced vineyards and olive groves with their stone presses, the patchwork fields of wheat and barley.

"I've never traveled any farther than from my village to Bethlehem," she told Hodaya as they bumped along the dusty road.

"It's a beautiful land, isn't it?" Hodaya asked. "God told our people to worship Him at three festivals, three times a year. He wants us to rejoice and remember our history as a people and all the things He has done for us. We need to take time to thank Him for providing for us." She took Amina's hand in hers and said, "I know I've never asked you about your family's beliefs . . . but did they worship God?"

"I don't know what my family believed," Amina said quietly. "We never stopped working to rest one day a week like you do. And we never said blessings at our meals, either. Abba and the other men used to walk up the hill behind our village to offer sacrifices, but I never went with them. Mama believed in the evil eye and other superstitions. . . ."

Sayfah tugged her sleeve. "She put offerings on the altar by our gate, remember?" she asked softly.

"Yes, but who was it for?" Amina asked. Sayfah shrugged. The road began to wind up the mountain, and Sayfah climbed down from the wagon to walk alongside. When they reached the top and stopped to rest, they saw a magnificent view of the city of Jerusalem on the hill across the valley. Amina had never seen so many houses all in one place, all built of stone and perched on a steep ridge for protection. Jerusalem was ten times bigger than Bethlehem, a hundred times bigger than her village.

Hodaya pointed to a higher hill above the city and to the largest building Amina had ever seen. "That's the Almighty One's temple," she said. "That's where we're going to worship."

"It's beautiful!" Built of white stones, the temple seemed to glow in the morning sun. Amina wished she could jump down from the wagon and run all the way across the valley to see it up close. When they finally did reach the base of the temple mount, huge crowds of people stood in lines to bathe in the ritual baths and purchase sacrifices, greeting each other with hugs and laughter. She longed to be a part of it all, but she and Sayfah were Gentiles, not Jews. She halted in the busy street and pulled Sayfah to a halt beside her. "I don't think we belong here," Amina murmured.

"Haven't I been saying that?"

Hodaya kept walking at first, but didn't get far before realizing that Amina and Sayfah were no longer beside her. She turned and beckoned to them. Amina shook her head.

Hodaya limped back to her side. "What's wrong?"

"We're not Jewish."

"That doesn't matter. I wasn't born to Jewish parents, either. God provided a special courtyard in His temple where anyone can come and worship Him. He loves all people, not just the Jews."

"Then why did He let everyone in our village die?" Sayfah asked.

Lines of sorrow creased Hodaya's face. She reached to caress Sayfah's hair, but Sayfah flinched and moved away. "I don't know why, dear one. But I do know that the Almighty One loves all people, and He wants them to come to Him and be His children. Not everyone accepts His offer, of course. To be part of His people we have to live by His laws, and many people don't want to do that. Even Jews don't follow His laws all the time. But everyone who leaves their idols behind and turns to God will be accepted as His own child, whether they're a Jew or a Gentile."

Hodaya's words persuaded Amina, and late that afternoon, she climbed the stairs with the others to watch the evening sacrifice. Seeing God's magnificent temple up close, watching the priests in their gleaming white robes, listening to the Levite choir's thrilling songs as the smoke and flames ascended to heaven, brought tears to Amina's eyes and filled her with an indescribable feeling of joy and awe. She already knew the Jewish God was powerful because He had saved His people from the Egyptians on Passover, drowning all of Pharaoh's horses and chariots in the sea. He had saved His people once again on the Thirteenth of Adar. Maybe the Almighty One truly was the only God.

The music rose to a thrilling crescendo, and when the people fell to their knees before Him in worship, Amina gladly bowed down with them.

CHAPTER
25

BABYLON

Devorah awoke one morning before dawn, shivering in the cold air. A year ago she would have moved closer to Jude for warmth; now she could only curl tighter in her blanket. The ache of loneliness felt more acute in these numbing winter months. Would the rest of her life be this lonely? She was only twenty-six years old.

Her time of mourning was nearly over. The month of Adar would begin tomorrow, awakening a flood of memories yet again. They would celebrate their victory and deliverance from their enemies, then they would celebrate Passover. Devorah's home had once been filled with family, especially during the holy days—Jude's parents, Jude and his brother Ezra, his brother Asher and wife Miriam. And her home should be filled with children, like arrows in a quiver.

Devorah felt a burst of anger toward Jude for his foolish act of rage, as she had so many times this past year. Abigail, who was five, barely remembered her father. She had stopped asking about him months ago. Michal, who was nearly three, had no memories of Jude at all.

Devorah climbed out of bed to kindle the fire, careful not to

wake her daughters. Today was the eve of *Shabbat*. How long
had it been since she'd celebrated the Sabbath properly, with joy
and laughter and guests at her table? She should be teaching her
daughters the songs and rituals and showing them how to light
the Sabbath lights. Jude would be furious with her for abandoning their traditions. Every week Asher and Miriam invited
her for the Sabbath. And every week she declined. But on this
cold, late winter day, Devorah decided to accept their invitation.

When the girls were awake and dressed and everyone had
eaten, they all walked to Miriam's house to help prepare the
Sabbath meal. With each step she took, Devorah recalled her
walk with Ezra a few months ago when he'd explained the law
of levirate marriage. She'd promised to give him an answer when
her year of mourning ended, but she'd pushed the decision aside
each time she thought of it. How should she reply?

"I'm so glad you finally decided to celebrate the Sabbath with
us," Miriam said as she greeted Devorah.

"Me too. We've come to help you prepare the meal. You
look as though you could use some help." Miriam balanced
her son, nearly a year old now, on her hip as she tried to wash
lentils for the soup. She was expecting again, her belly getting
in her way each time she tried to bend or move. "Let Abigail
and Michal entertain him," Devorah said, lifting the baby from
Miriam's arms. She settled the children on the rug in a patch of
sunshine, then returned to Miriam's side. "I'll knead the bread,
if you'd like."

"That would be wonderful. But I haven't even had time to
grind the flour yet."

"Then I'll do that first. How many of us for dinner?"

"You and me and Asher and Ezra, plus the children."

Ezra. Devorah needed to decide. He deserved an answer to
his proposal. She poured a measure of grain between the stones
and began to grind. "How is Ezra?" she asked. "I haven't seen
him in months."

"He needs a wife," Miriam said, laughing as she poured water over the lentils. "He's so overworked, burdened day and night with his studies and with leading our people. They come here during dinner sometimes, asking him questions. He asked Asher the other day, 'Who can I go to with my questions?' And I told him, 'You need a wife, Ezra. She'll listen to you and help you.' And you know what he said? He surprised both of us when he said he wanted to marry. It's about time, isn't it? So what do you say, Devorah? Should we help our bachelor brother-in-law find someone?" She turned to Devorah for her reply, and her smile faded. "What's wrong? Do you feel all right?" Devorah had stopped grinding.

"Did Ezra explain to you and Asher about the law of levirate marriage?"

"No. What's that?"

Devorah resumed working, her hands moving faster, grinding harder. "The Torah says if a married man dies without an heir, his widow is supposed to marry her husband's brother."

Miriam stopped chopping. "Ezra has to marry *you*?"

"Yes. That's what the law says." Devorah felt a sudden burst of anger. "It's so unfair! First God took Jude away, and now He demands this!" She paused to control her emotions, refusing to cry. "Don't I have any say in my life? I feel like a puppet that the Holy One is manipulating with His outrageous laws."

"God doesn't really expect you to follow such an outdated law, does He? It's ridiculous! Marry your brother-in-law?"

"It's in the Torah," Devorah said with a shrug. "It seems archaic . . . but how are we supposed to know which of His rules we still have to obey and which ones don't apply to us anymore?" She remembered arguing with her father one Sabbath evening, insisting that it was stupid to sit around shivering because the fire had gone out. "*Why not kindle a fire if we're cold?*" she'd asked. "*Does God want us to freeze on the Sabbath?*"

"*You don't get to pick and choose among the laws,*" her

father had replied. *"The Torah isn't a banquet table where you only have to eat the dishes you like. If we don't obey all of the Torah's laws, then we're breaking all of them."*

"So God commands you to marry Ezra?" Miriam asked. "And you don't have a choice?"

"I have a choice. I don't have to marry him. But Ezra says this is God's way of providing a future for my children and me. And also for Jude, so he'll have an heir. If Ezra and I have a son, he's considered Jude's child." Devorah poured the finished flour into the kneading trough and scooped another measure of grain between the stones. She wondered if God would forgive her for imagining that Ezra was Jude each time she held him. For wishing they were Jude's arms around her, his lips on hers. Jude had always been stronger than Ezra, well-muscled and tanned, smelling of clay and hard work. Ezra was slender, his skin pale from sitting inside all day, his shoulders a little stooped from bending over his scrolls. But Devorah had been surprised by the change in Ezra the last time she'd seen him. After months of working outside in the pottery yard, Ezra was no longer stooped and pale.

"How do you feel about this marriage?" Miriam asked, breaking into Devorah's thoughts. "Wouldn't it seem . . . weird?"

"Yes, of course it would. I don't think I'll ever love him. I could never love any man the way I loved Jude."

"Well, I know I couldn't do it," Miriam said with a shudder. "I mean, Ezra is nice as a brother-in-law, but I couldn't sleep with him."

"But I don't know what else to do, Miriam. I want to have a son for Jude's sake, but I can't help feeling like Ezra and I would be doing something wrong, like we were being unfaithful to Jude. Ezra said the same thing when he explained all this to me a few months ago."

Miriam looked shocked. "You've been debating this for months? Why didn't you confide in me?"

"Because I kept pushing the decision aside, trying not to think about it. But if Ezra is talking about marrying another woman, I'll need to figure out how to support myself and the girls. He can't possibly support two families—although he's such a kind, generous man he would probably try."

"I had no idea he was thinking of you when he talked about getting married."

"Maybe he isn't. . . . Maybe he has someone else in mind. What do you think I should do, Miriam? What would you do if Asher had died without an heir?"

"I don't know." Miriam rested her hand on her growing stomach. "I mean, Ezra is certainly a good man, but I couldn't marry him. . . . I think you should talk to him about this, not me."

"You're right. That's what I'll do."

On the afternoon of Shabbat when lunch had ended and no other work was allowed, Devorah asked Ezra to walk with her and the girls along the canal. Other families and courting couples had come out for a stroll as well on this mild winter day. "It's hard to believe nearly a year has passed already," Ezra said as they walked.

"It seems much longer—and yet like yesterday," Devorah replied.

"So much has changed."

Devorah quickly grew impatient with small talk. She had an important decision to make. "I'm sorry for making you wait so long for an answer to your proposal," she began. "You've been very patient with me."

"You were still mourning," he said. "I understand."

Devorah exhaled. "I don't know how much Jude told you about me, Ezra, but I was older than most women when we married. I waited until I was twenty because my father spoiled me, teaching me to study the Torah as if I were his son."

"I knew your father. I studied with him for nearly a year. He was one of the finest scholars and teachers in the yeshiva. You're also descended from a priestly family, you know."

"Yes. Abba always wished his family had returned to Jerusalem when King Cyrus gave his decree years ago. Everything changed so quickly, and then it was too late to go."

"If only we could go home now," Ezra said. "I hate it here in Babylon. We're surrounded by enemies who would gladly kill us again at the slightest provocation."

Devorah bent to lift Michal, who'd grown tired of walking. "Abba discussed the Torah with me the way he did with his students, bringing scrolls home and teaching me to read them. I learned that God made Eve to be Adam's helper, which meant she was his support, his armor-bearer, his friend. And so when Jude asked to court me, I made him promise we would have a different kind of marriage. That we'd discuss everything and not keep secrets. He agreed."

Ezra smiled slightly. "Jude came to my study when he was courting you. He told me about your request and asked my advice."

"What did you say?"

"I was deep into my Torah studies at the time, trying to mine every line and word of Scripture as if digging for gold. It was a lost treasure in a sense, since our forefathers stopped following the Law and ended up here in exile. To be honest, I didn't think his question was worthy of an in-depth study compared with the weightier matters of theology and covenant living I was dealing with. But I answered him as best I could and told him I saw nothing wrong with such a marriage. I think I cited a few examples of biblical couples who hadn't worked well together, such as Rebecca, who had conspired to deceive Isaac. It seemed to me a marriage would work better if husbands and wives were partners, the way you described it. But in the end, I advised Jude to talk to one of the married rabbis since I was a bachelor and hardly qualified to advise him."

Ezra paused when Abigail suddenly stepped between them, taking Devorah's free hand in one of hers and reaching to take

Ezra's hand in the other. "I want to swing, Uncle Ezra," she said. He looked perplexed.

"She wants us to lift her up and swing her between us the way she used to do with her father," Devorah explained, setting her other daughter down. Ezra quickly got the hang of it, surprising Devorah when he laughed out loud at his niece's delight.

"Me!" Michal begged. "Me too!" She took her turn, as well.

"I've been thinking about the law of levirate marriage," Devorah said when the game ended. "If I agree to marry you, will you let me be your partner in all things? Could we have the same kind of marriage I had with Jude, based on friendship and trust? Making decisions together?"

"I—I would do my best. The greater question is, do you think you could be patient with me, a thirty-six-year-old bachelor who knows very little about being a good husband?"

"We may both have to make a few changes," Devorah said. She remembered the look that had passed between Ezra and her husband when he lay dying, as he'd clearly entrusted her to his brother's care. Jude wouldn't have done that if he didn't want Ezra in her life, would he? "I'll do it, Ezra," she said, exhaling. "I'll obey the Torah and marry you."

He stopped walking, and when she looked up at him, his cheeks had turned pink beneath his tanned skin and thick black beard. He cleared his throat. "Are . . . are you sure?"

"No . . . not entirely. But it comes down to this: Will we ignore the natural discomfort we both feel and obey God's Word, trusting that He knows best . . . or reject His law, and go our own way? I think it's going to be difficult for both of us to obey Him . . . but if we don't, I'll always wonder if we missed out on something good He'd planned for us . . . such as a son to carry Jude's name."

Ezra cleared his throat. "When?"

"After the one-year anniversary. And the victory celebration."

"Good." He started to smile, then seemed to change his mind,

turning serious. "I'll arrange the betrothal with the elders."
He started walking faster as if in a hurry to get away. Devorah
halted, making him turn back for her.

"Ezra. You just agreed we would share everything with each
other, remember? Tell me what you really think about marrying
me. Was there someone else you were hoping to marry instead?"

He frowned, shaking his head. "No, I haven't even had time to
search for a wife." He tugged his beard, looking uncomfortable,
as if his clothes itched. "How do I feel about it? First of all, you
need to understand that I find it hard to express my feelings. I've
had little practice and no one to share them with. But you were
a wonderful wife to Jude, and you're a wonderful mother to his
children. He told me you were a godly woman, very wise for
one so young, and very devout. And so I think . . . I think once
the awkwardness between us fades, along with the memories
of the past . . . well, I believe we can find contentment together.
You're right in saying we can trust God's goodness. And I'm
glad you've agreed to marry me." He finished with a shy smile,
then hurried off.

But alone at home in bed that night—the bed she'd shared
with Jude—Devorah couldn't help feeling she was being unfaithful to him. She tried to convince herself that marrying his
brother was truly an act of love for Jude, the best thing she could
do to preserve his memory. She could keep his name alive by
giving him a son and heir. Devorah didn't love Ezra and probably never would. She barely knew him. But she was so tired of
being alone. She couldn't live this way for the rest of her life.
Her daughters needed a father, a second hand to hold on to
when they walked. Right or wrong, she had made her decision.
She would obey God.

In the weeks that followed, Devorah rarely saw Ezra and didn't
have a chance to speak with him again. He was always on the
move, always busy with other people, answering their questions,
making decisions. She sat through the festivities at the house

of assembly on the Thirteenth of Adar, trying to celebrate a victory that wasn't a victory at all for her, and watched Ezra try to be a dozen places at once. His congregation continually depleted him as if plucking a tree of all its fruit.

She listened to the story of Queen Esther, the story of a simple Jewish woman who changed the course of history for her people, and a thought occurred to Devorah for the first time. Obviously God wanted to provide for her and her children through this law. And He obviously wanted Jude to have a son to carry his name. But maybe God was just as concerned for Ezra, His servant, a man who surely needed a wife and helper to carry some of his burdens. Could God have specifically chosen Devorah, who knew more about the Torah than most women, to be that support for Ezra?

A week after the victory celebration, Devorah's family and friends gathered in her home for the ceremony. Ezra presented the marriage contract that the elders had drawn up and that he'd signed. He poured wine from a flask and offered Devorah the cup that would seal their betrothal. She forced back tears, remembering her betrothal to Jude. But she would do this; she would trust God and marry Jude's brother.

Devorah's hand trembled as she accepted the cup and took a drink, committing her life and her future to Ezra.

CASIPHIA

P lease, Reuben," his mother begged. "Please come with us tonight. Celebrate with us." She stood by the door, dressed in her finest Sabbath clothes. Reuben's two sisters danced with excitement, eager to leave, their hair elaborately braided for this special occasion. Even his baby brother, perched on Mama's hip, looked scrubbed and happy. The community had spent weeks planning the festivities for the anniversary of the Thirteenth of Adar, but Reuben wanted nothing to do with it. He pushed Mama's hand away when she tried to take his.

"How can you expect me to celebrate Abba's death?" he asked. "And why are you celebrating?"

"It could have been all of us, Reuben. If the Almighty One hadn't made a way for us to defend ourselves, we might all be dead. That's what we're remembering—the fact that we're alive."

"Well, I don't feel like celebrating. I'm going out. I want to be by myself."

"You already spend too much time by yourself. Yes, this is a sad day for us with many sad memories. But that's why Uncle Hashabiah and everyone who loved your father want to be with us on this occasion."

"I just want to be alone."

Someone knocked at their door, and when Reuben opened it and saw his uncle, he turned around and walked straight out the back door and across the lane to the forge without a word of greeting. Everything in the smithy looked the same after one year. Though Reuben had loved working here with his father, he now hated his job as an apprentice, hated his new boss. He had no choice. Working here was the only way his family could remain in their home. It was a prison sentence to him.

Tonight, while his community celebrated, Reuben would do the work he really enjoyed—stealing from the Babylonians. He no longer needed to steal. His family managed to live on the income his mother earned from the sale of the forge. Instead, Reuben stole for the thrill of it, the rush of excitement he felt each time he escaped with loot the Babylonians owed him. He was good at what he did. Many nights, the only thing he stole was wine, which he drank in secret by himself. Sometimes he stole food, too, and it had become a game for him to add it to the storage room a little at a time so his mother wouldn't notice. He brought treats for his siblings—fresh dates, pistachios, apricots—telling them, "It's our secret. Don't show Mama, or I won't bring you any more." Sometimes he happened upon gold coins or something valuable, but not very often. He hid the gold, saving it to buy back his inheritance someday. At this rate, it would take years.

The noise from the celebrations faded in the distance as Reuben left his Jewish community and walked through the dark streets of Casiphia. When he finally broke into the storeroom he'd chosen—after waiting in the dark for a very long time, after watching for the lights to go out inside, after waiting some more to make sure everyone was asleep—the contents disappointed him. The storeroom contained nothing special, just the usual grain and olives and oil. Even the wine tasted weak and bitter.

As he hurried through the deserted streets afterward, heading home, he thought he heard footsteps behind him. Reuben turned to look over his shoulder, but before he could see who was following him, a dark, heavy shape rammed into him, nearly knocking him down. He recovered his balance and dropped his bag of loot so he could fight back, but three more shadows came from nowhere, surrounding him, jumping him. Reuben fought with all his strength, his heart racing in panic. He couldn't see his attackers, but if they were the Persian authorities, they would throw him into prison—or worse, cut off his right hand for stealing. Maybe even execute him.

He was no match for the four men. They easily overwhelmed him, knocking him to the ground, pushing his face into the dust, tying his hands together. One of them sat on Reuben's back, forcing the air from his lungs, pinning him so he couldn't move, couldn't breathe. He felt the cold blade of a knife pressing against his throat, then a stinging burn as it slowly slit his flesh. Reuben closed his eyes, believing he was going to die.

"You'd be wise to stop struggling," a voice hissed in his ear. "You can't win."

Reuben gave a grunt of defiance with what little air he could draw. "Let me go!"

"Not too loud now, son. You wouldn't want to attract the wrong attention with a bag of stolen loot by your side, would you?"

"Take it, if that's what you want."

"We want you, not this stuff. You're going to come with us, understand? Don't make a sound, and you won't get hurt."

"Do I have a choice?"

"Sure, you have a choice. You can stay here, all tied up beside your bag of loot, for the guards to find."

They had tied the ropes so tightly they dug into his wrists. Someone slipped a burlap bag over his head. It smelled of rotting fruit. The men hauled Reuben to his feet and gave him a shove to start moving. They huddled around him as they walked, holding him upright as if hoping any observers would mistake them for drunkards. The bag over his head was only loose enough for Reuben to see his feet and the dark street beneath them. That was all. The ten minutes they walked seemed like hours. Fear made Reuben's heart work so hard he worried it might burst. None of them spoke.

At last Reuben heard the rush of the river nearby. The air smelled of fish and stagnant water. They slowed, and one of his captors pushed Reuben's head down, forcing him to duck as they entered an airless enclosure. A heavy door thumped shut behind him. A bar slid into place. Then they pushed Reuben down onto the floor. He heard the four men talking amongst themselves, and Reuben could tell by the dullness of the sound, the closeness of the voices, that the room was very small. It smelled of sweat and unwashed bodies and mildew. If only they would untie his hands and let him fight them one at a time, he might be able to escape. But he couldn't fight all of them at once.

"What do you want?" he asked. "If you're going to turn me in or kill me, just do it."

"Neither," one of them replied, laughing. "We want you to join us. We're in the same business you are. And you're a very talented thief, you know." The man's accent was Babylonian.

"We've been watching you," a second man added. Another Babylonian. "You move as silently as a leopard. And you're quick. You get in and out without a sound."

"But we're good, too," a third Babylonian said. "Have you ever seen us watching you or following you?" He poked Reuben's arm, expecting an answer.

"No. I haven't seen you." He wanted to reach up and wipe the sticky blood off his neck, but his hands were tied. Tightly. He could barely move, let alone twist them free. The cut on his neck burned and stung, irritated by the rough sack over his head.

"You should be honored, son," the first man said. "We're inviting you to join our gang. What do you say?"

Reuben hesitated. He was at their mercy. They might kill him if he refused. He longed to tell them just how much he hated Babylonians like them for killing his father, but maybe they didn't know he was Jewish, dressed the way he was.

"Or we could simply kill you right now," a fourth voice said. "Are you ready to die, Jew?"

Reuben stopped breathing. They knew. "I can't die. I have a family to support."

"Oh, we know all about your family and your work as a blacksmith's apprentice."

Reuben was glad his face was covered so they couldn't see his fear. They knew about his mother. His siblings.

"But we're not in the business of simply pilfering food like you do," the man continued, "or maybe a couple of gold coins if you get lucky. We have bigger goals: robbing ships and warehouses, stealing from caravans and merchants. We sell our goods and make a tidy profit."

Sweat broke out on Reuben's forehead. The fibers from the bag clogged his nose and throat as he breathed. "What do you need me for?"

"You're faster than any of us at breaking in."

"And the thing is, we could use some better weapons. You know where we can get them, don't you, Jew?"

"Aren't your people and mine enemies?" Reuben asked.

"Enemies? Where did you get that idea?"

"We fought each other a year ago. Babylonians like you killed my father."

"We didn't take part in those battles. We have nothing against Jews. We'll steal from anyone!" All four of them laughed.

"With better weapons and a good break-in man, we'll be able to make a really big haul one of these days. One shipment of gold or silver is all we need, and we'll be set for life. None of us will ever have to work again. We can leave Casiphia and go wherever we want."

"Have all the women we want!" Everyone laughed again.

Reuben could buy back the forge with his share. But he took his time replying, trying not to sound too eager. "What if I don't want to join you?"

"Now, that would be very tragic. Especially since you know all about us."

"I'm blindfolded. I have no idea where I am. I'm not a threat to you."

"Come on, why keep breaking into houses, risking getting caught some night by a sleepless servant? Your luck is bound to run out one of these days. Join us, and you can have true riches."

"Tell us," one of them said. "What would you do with your share of the loot?"

Reuben didn't even have to think about it—he would buy back his inheritance. Make his boss work for him from now on. Get all of Abba's tools back. Spit in his uncle's face. But he would never tell these men his plans.

"If I were rich," Reuben said, "I wouldn't let anyone push me around or make decisions for me." He heard murmurs of agreement. "All right," he finally decided. "I'll join you, but it has to be on an equal basis. We have to split everything fairly. And I get a say in making the decisions." No one was ever going to decide his fate again the way his uncle had.

"Will you get weapons for us?"

"I'll get them, but you'll have to pay me."

"I'm the leader," the loud one said.

"Yes, but I'm your partner. Deal?"

"Deal." They pulled off Reuben's mask, and he squinted in the light. It came from a small oil lamp that barely lit the dingy, low-ceilinged room. He faced four Babylonian men, ten years older than him, squatting in a circle around him. They wore dark robes, dark turbans on their heads, their faces smudged with charcoal. All four of them stood up at the same time and pulled Reuben to his feet. One of the men untied his hands and

Reuben massaged his wrists to get the feeling back in his fingers. When they lifted the bar and opened the door to walk outside, he immediately knew where he was. Their hideout was near the first house Reuben had robbed a year ago.

"How long will it take you to get weapons for us?" one of the men asked.

"I don't know . . . maybe two weeks. I know where they're stored, but I'll have to steal one at a time so they aren't missed."

"Good. Bring them here two weeks from tonight. We'll be waiting." The man tossed Reuben a small leather pouch. Coins jingled inside as he caught it. "Here's your first payment. Call it an apology for roughing you up."

Reuben loosened the drawstring and looked inside. Gold. He suppressed a smile, needing to act tough. "I'll be back in two weeks," he said and walked off into the night, alone.

BABYLON

Devorah watched her husband swallow his last bite of supper, then rise to leave moments later, and anger boiled up inside her like water in a cooking pot. Ezra had arrived home late, long after Abigail and Michal were asleep, and the food Devorah had prepared for her new husband had grown cold. Now he was leaving again for the yeshiva, where he would study until well past midnight.

"Don't wait up," he said as he lifted the latch to the gate. As if she really intended to! Her anger spilled over as she rose to her feet.

"This isn't a marriage, Ezra. We've been husband and wife for three months now, and I never see you except when we eat and sleep. Is this what God intended when He commanded us to marry each other?"

He turned and came back, resting his hand on her shoulder as he guided her inside where they could speak in private. He obviously didn't want the neighbors to know their esteemed leader and his new bride had troubles. "No, Devorah. This isn't what God intended," he said. "I'm sorry. But there's so much work to do at the pottery yard, and then there's my work at the yeshiva and—"

"Doesn't the Torah say two people become one in marriage? We're not 'one.' We're two people living under the same roof and trying to make a baby to fulfill the law."

He winced at her blunt words. "I'm sorry," he repeated, closing his eyes. "I have obligations. Tell me . . . what do you want me to do? What do other husbands do?"

"Other newly married husbands *want* to spend time with their wives. A team of chariot horses couldn't drag them away every evening, six days a week." She bit her tongue to stop herself from comparing Ezra to Jude, who had savored every spare moment with her. Would it always be this way? Would she spend the rest of her life comparing her marriage to Ezra with what she enjoyed with his brother?

"I . . . I didn't think you would necessarily want to spend time with me," he said. "I remember how things were with you and Jude, and . . . and I know it wasn't your idea to marry me."

"It was the Holy One's idea. Which is why I intend to give our marriage a chance, putting the same time and effort into it that Jude and I . . ." Her throat swelled, and she couldn't finish.

"Devorah, I'm sorry." He pulled her close for a moment, and it still felt strange to her to be in his arms, even after three months of marriage.

"Jude is gone. We're married to each other now," she said as she pulled free again. "I don't think either of us expects to fall in love, but I do expect companionship. The Holy One said it wasn't good for man to be alone, and the same is true for women. Yet I'm home alone every night."

"I know you are. And I know this marriage was God's idea, but I wish He would show me how to squeeze more hours out of each day so I can accomplish all the work He's given me to do. And I guess . . . I guess I thought it might be too painful for you to have me here all the time."

"I want a real marriage, and I thought you did, too."

"Of course I do."

"Then why don't you ever look at me, Ezra? You always avert your eyes. I know I'm not pretty but—"

"That's not true!"

"I can see that my nose is too large, and—"

"Devorah, everything about you is beautiful." He took her hands in his. "You're as lovely as the beloved wife King Solomon describes in *Song of Songs*. 'Your neck is like an ivory tower. Your eyes are the pools of Heshbon. . . . Your nose is like the tower of Lebanon. . . . Your hair is like royal tapestry. . . .'"

If Devorah hadn't been so angry, she would have laughed out loud. Only Ezra would quote Scripture to tell his wife she was pretty. She pulled her hands free. "I know all about the *Song of Songs*. It's a love poem that's included in the holy books because God created married love for our enjoyment. As a beautiful gift. But you don't know anything about enjoying God's gift because you're never home! We're married in name only."

"Forgive me," he said, meeting her gaze. "I don't know how to be a good husband. I don't know how to relate to people except as their rebbe. Jude once told me to get my head out of the clouds and start living, but I'm still not very good at it." He raked his fingers through his hair, knocking his kippah askew. "I'm sorry. I'll try to do better," he said as he straightened it. "If I shuffle my students around, maybe I can find more time—"

"I'm not asking for my own sake, but for our child's sake."

Ezra froze. His brows lifted in surprise. "Our child? You mean . . . ?"

Devorah nodded, resting her hand on her middle. "Yes. I'm expecting a baby." This wasn't the way she'd planned to tell him, but since he was always talking to other people or running off to the yeshiva, she had no choice.

"Devorah, I . . . I don't know what to say. But I know what I would like to do more than anything else right now . . . if you'll let me. . . ."

"What?"

He drew her into his arms and held her tightly. She didn't want to cry, but she couldn't help it. Being pregnant always made her emotional. "Devorah, please don't cry," he begged. "I didn't mean to hurt you. It's the last thing I would ever want to do."

"It's okay. . . . I'm okay. . . ." She wiped her eyes.

"Listen, I have a commitment tonight I absolutely can't avoid, but I promise I'll try to make more time for us to be a family from now on."

Devorah nodded and let him go. She believed he meant well. But she also doubted he'd be able to change years of habit and priorities unless she helped him.

The next morning while Ezra led morning prayers, she walked with the girls to the pottery yard to talk to Asher. "I'm going to ask you a question," she began, "and I want you to give me an honest answer. Do you still need Ezra to work full-time here at the pottery in Jude's place, or can he return to the work he used to do?"

Asher set down the pot he carried. "I tell Ezra all the time he should go back to the yeshiva and be a full-time rebbe, but he insists on earning a living here to support you."

"Don't they pay him for leading our people and for teaching students?"

Asher shook his head. "Jude and I used to support all his Torah studies. That's why he lived with you and Jude."

"That's outrageous! The least our people can do is pay him for all his hard work! The Torah clearly says not to muzzle an ox while it's treading out the grain."

"I agree, but it's not up to me. Talk to the elders."

"Will you arrange a meeting for me with them?"

Asher laughed. "I meant it was up to the elders to decide these things, Devorah. . . . I wasn't suggesting you should really talk to them."

"I know. But that's exactly what I'm going to do. Can you arrange it for me? Without letting Ezra know?"

Asher had the look of a man who had let the reins slip from his hands and was racing downhill in a runaway cart. "I—I suppose I can, but do you really think it's wise to go behind Ezra's back?"

"In this case, I have no choice. You know your brother. He would never dream of speaking up and asking for such a thing himself. And if I tell him I'm going to talk to the elders, he'll never let me do it. But someone needs to speak up on his behalf. He works night and day, Asher. He's never home. The people are wearing him out."

"I know. You're right. I'll see if I can arrange a meeting for you."

"Thank you. And please make it soon." Before she lost her nerve.

Three days later, Devorah found herself in the house of assembly after morning prayers, facing the community's twelve elders. If she allowed herself to dwell on it, she could feel very intimidated by this somber group of men with stern faces, but the justice of her plea gave her courage. Asher had arranged for them to meet without Ezra's knowledge, as promised, and he stood by her side, looking as though he'd rather be anyplace else but here.

"This is highly unusual," one of the men began.

"I know," Devorah replied. She lifted her chin and spoke the words she'd carefully rehearsed. "When my first husband, Jude, was killed on the Thirteenth of Adar, I couldn't understand it. Jude was strong and brave and knew how to fight. Ezra was the inexperienced brother. Yet Jude died and Ezra was spared. And so I've decided the Almighty One must have spared him for a reason."

She saw several of the elders leaning forward, drawn into her story, and it gave her courage. "I know you'll agree that Ezra is a dedicated leader. He's also an outstanding scholar and teacher. My husband has a unique gift for inspiring his students and making the Torah come alive. And when he leads the people of our community, he's leading them closer to God. His work has eternal value, wouldn't you agree?" Several men nodded as if inviting her to continue.

"But in order to support his family he makes pots all day. He has no choice. I believe he's wasting a very precious, God-given talent by doing that work. And so I've come to ask if there's some way our community could allow him do what he was created to do without allowing his family to starve. I'm willing to live on less so Ezra can do God's work, but he's a responsible, hardworking man, and he would never agree." Devorah paused, avoiding telling them bluntly they ought to pay him. Men rarely liked being told what to do, especially by a woman. Let them think of it themselves.

"People are always coming to speak with my husband, at all hours of the day, and he never turns anyone away. But he is so very tired. And he has no time to pursue his own Torah studies—the work he loves most of all. I just wondered how often it is in our people's history that a gifted scholar like Ezra comes along. Once in a lifetime, maybe? Isn't there anything you can do to help him?" She let the silence stretch for a moment, then said, "Thank you for listening and for and considering my question."

She left the room, her steps unhurried, and returned home to wait. She had no idea what would happen—or what Ezra's reaction would be when he found out. Jude's hot temper had sometimes been troublesome, but at least she'd always known what he thought and if he was angry and why. Ezra's quiet, self-contained nature was maddening. But one way or another, she would soon know exactly how Ezra felt about what she'd done.

Ezra stared down at the ledger books without seeing them. A dozen times a day he was distracted from his work at the pottery yard by the realization he was going to be a father. What did he feel? Joy? Wonder? Disbelief? All of those and yet something more: a sense of awe that this might be how God felt when He'd created mankind.

Devorah said she wanted a real marriage, wanted to spend more time with him. Was it possible she could love him one day? Never as much as she'd loved Jude, certainly, but was it possible? And how did he feel about her after three months—after creating a child together? Sure, he had very little time to spend with her, but he also knew he was afraid to let himself fall in love, afraid he could never measure up to Jude, afraid his presence reminded her of what she'd once had and lost. He'd been fulfilling his duty as a husband and little more. Amazingly, Devorah wanted more.

He tried to return to his computations, then noticed a knot of men making their way across the yard, coming toward him. He silently groaned. Not another interruption. But as the men drew nearer, he realized they were his community's elders. He shot to his feet, afraid something had happened, and hurried toward them. Asher saw the men, too, and left his wheel and the pot he'd been shaping to join him, wiping his hands on a rag. Asher wore a faint smile on his face, as if he was going to make a joke and ask the elders if they'd come to purchase pottery.

"I hope it isn't bad news that brings you gentlemen here," Ezra said.

"Not at all," the chief elder replied. "We've come with a proposition for you."

"A proposition?"

"Yes. Would you consider resigning from your work here? On behalf of our community, we would like to pay you to be our full-time rebbe and leader."

Ezra stared. He couldn't have been more surprised if they *had* come to purchase pots.

"I don't understand."

Asher's smile spread into a grin. "It's simple. No more pottery-making, Ezra."

"From now on your job will be to lead us and teach us," the elder continued, "and make sure we follow the Torah. That job should occupy all your time, along with your own studies."

"We've worked it out so you can spend your days teaching the next generation of leaders and scholars," a second man added. "It's what you've been doing for more than a year, but by not paying you for your work, we were doing God and you a great disservice. We must not allow you to waste the great mind He has given you on ledger books and pottery sales. Your gift comes only once in a lifetime. Maybe two lifetimes."

Ezra turned to his brother, struggling for words. "I don't want to abandon you, Asher. There's too much work here for you to do alone."

"We've done very well this past year," Asher said. "I think I can find someone to take your place. I have to learn to trust God, too."

Ezra turned back to the elders, surprised to see them smiling. "I-I don't know what to say. You've taken me by surprise. . . . Thank you, Asher. And thank you—"

"Don't thank us," the chief elder said. "Thank God. And your wife."

"My wife? What do you mean?"

"Devorah came to me and asked if I needed you at the pottery yard," Asher said. "Then she took the initiative and went to see the elders."

"She reminded us of all the work you do for our people," one of the elders continued. "Teaching us, leading us. And she pointed out that God called you and spared you for a reason—and it wasn't to make pottery."

"She even said she'd be willing to live with less so you could do God's work, but you felt responsible to support your family."

The chief elder turned to face him. "So what do you say, Ezra? Will you accept our offer?"

"This . . . this is such a surprise. But of course! Of course I will." He reached out to grasp the chief elder's hand, too stunned to think what to do next.

His wife—*General* Devorah—had gone to battle for him. She had dared to approach the elders on her own to speak for him. The knowledge left him speechless.

Devorah was washing sticky date juice from Michal's hands when she heard Ezra return home. Ever since she'd gone before the elders, she'd worried about what their reaction would be—and what her husband's would be when he found out. She finished wiping Michal's fingers and turned to greet him. The moment she saw his face, she knew something had changed. He must have spoken with the elders. He must have learned what she'd done. He seemed to be searching for words, and as she waited for him to speak, his stillness unnerved her. She prepared to defend herself if he was angry. She would point out all the reasons why she'd done it.

"You went to the elders," he said quietly.

"I did."

"You told them they should pay me for the work I do?"

"Not in those exact words. I simply reminded them of all the things you already do for this community and of all the study time you're missing because you have a family to support and—"

"You told them God spared me for a reason, and they were making me waste the mind God gave me creating pots."

"That's . . . yes, that's the gist of it." She still couldn't tell if he was angry or not. His Adam's apple bobbed as he swallowed, and she could see he was becoming emotional. But was it anger or something else?

"You would do that for me? Speak up like that? A woman, going alone in front of all the elders?"

"Well, the elders hardly scare me since I'm married to the

204

leader of our entire community, the most brilliant man in Babylon—"

He pulled her into his arms, cutting off her words. "I . . . I don't know what to say."

"You're not angry, then?"

He laughed, a rare and wonderful sound considering all the pressures he faced. He hugged her tighter. "No, I'm not angry. I was shocked at first. But I'm proud of you. I feel blessed to have such a wife." He pulled back, still holding her, and looked into her eyes. "You did a brave, beautiful thing for me, Devorah. A very loving thing. You're a wonderful, strong woman—my partner and helpmeet. . . ." His eyes glistened. "My . . . my wife."

CHAPTER

28

Casiphia

Reuben finished work at the end of a long week, storing his tools in their proper places, straightening his work area. His mind wasn't on his labor, though, but on the plans he and his partners had for later tonight. The ship docked at one of Casiphia's wharves was rumored to carry gold amongst its cargo. "This could be our big chance," one of his partners had said. "We can all retire after tonight."

He removed his leather apron and hung it on the hook behind the partition, smiling in anticipation. But he halted, his smile fading when he saw his uncle standing inside the forge talking with his boss. Reuben clenched his jaw and started walking again, his shoulders braced, intending to walk past them without speaking.

His boss stopped him. "Whoa, son. Stay another minute. I have something for you, and I asked your uncle to come here for the occasion. Hold out your hand."

When Reuben obeyed, his boss dropped four silver coins into his palm. "What's this for?"

"As of this week, you're no longer an apprentice, but one of my workers." He grinned and slapped Reuben's back. "Those are your first week's wages."

"Congratulations, son," his uncle said. "I'm told you do fine work."

Reuben knew he should be happy, but he wasn't. It would still take years to earn enough to buy back his forge, even with a weekly wage.

"Say something, Reuben," his uncle urged.

He shook his head, refusing to show gratitude to the men who had stolen his inheritance. If he opened his mouth now, it would be to shout and curse at them.

"Come to evening prayers with me," Hashabiah said. "It's only right to thank the Holy One on such an important occasion. And I'd like to honor you with a celebration dinner afterward in my home. Your mother and sisters are invited, too."

Reuben forced himself to stay calm, just as he did when breaking into one of the many homes he'd robbed. "I don't want anything from you."

Hashabiah tilted his head as if talking to a child. "Listen, I can understand why you're angry with me—even though I acted in your best interests. But don't cut yourself off from the entire Jewish community. Fellowship is the lifeblood of our people. Besides, now that you're no longer an apprentice, you'll want to get married in a few more years. You can't expect a future father-in-law to agree to a betrothal if you never pray with us, or if you're not part of us."

"I don't care about any of that." Reuben's jaw felt so tight he thought the bone might snap. He longed to bolt.

"Come back to prayers, at least."

"What for? I don't believe in your God."

Hashabiah's friendly façade changed to a concerned frown. "Do you know what the Torah says about a wayward son, Reuben? A son who continually rebels and refuses to repent? He can be expelled from the community at best—stoned to death at worst. I'm not asking for myself, but for your mother's sake. The Torah says—"

"Don't you dare preach to me! What does the Torah say about giving away another man's inheritance?" Reuben tried to push past them, but Hashabiah stopped him.

"For you father's sake—"

"Don't talk about my father! He was a better man than you'll ever be. You have no right to even speak his name!"

"You're bringing shame on your household. Your mother has suffered enough. It's time you settled down and—"

"Why should I settle down? What for? Nothing we do in life matters anyway. It's all a game of chance. One minute we're living happily, and the next minute the king issues an edict and our enemies can kill us. Then we die. The end. Don't tell me what to do. I'm fourteen now—old enough to live my own life."

He twisted free and ran across the lane to his room, hurrying in case his uncle decided to follow. Reuben grabbed the bag with his Babylonian clothes and left again, walking through back alleys and deserted lanes to the hideout where his gang met. He was early, the first one there, and he sat down to wait for the others. They had become his friends, the men he called Ram, Nib, Bear, and Digger. Reuben didn't know their real names and didn't care. The secret life he had with them was worth far more than what his Jewish community could offer. As for a bride, Bear promised to find girls for Reuben when he was ready. And after tonight, he would have much more than four silver coins jingling in his pouch.

His temper had a chance to cool while he waited, and by the time three of the others showed up, Reuben was ready to work. "The ship docked late this afternoon, just as expected," Ram told them. "The crew didn't have time to unload the cargo before night fell. Nib is watching it for us right now, and once the sailors go ashore for a night of drinking, we can get to work."

They left after dark, and Reuben felt a thrill of excitement as he walked toward the river with the others. They stayed in the shadows, their faces blackened with charcoal. This was the biggest job they had ever attempted—with the biggest payoff.

The boat lay at anchor in the river a hundred yards away, but they didn't dare approach it directly. And they would have to wait some more. The hardest part of any job they did was waiting, being patient. But it was the most important part. They kept watch until a group of sailors left the vessel, laughing as they went ashore for the evening.

"Are you sure you can swim that far?" Bear asked, cocking his head toward the bobbing ship.

"I'm sure." Unlike his friends who were built like brick walls, Reuben was slender and wiry. He would swim out and climb up the anchor rope to board the ship and check for guards.

"You remember the signal?" Digger asked. Reuben nodded. His friends were nervous. He was, too. The dock was still deserted, but in the taverns nearby, the sound of carousing grew louder.

"Good luck," Bear said.

The spring air felt cold as Reuben slipped off his tunic, stripping down to his undergarment and belt, which held his knife in its sheath. He waded into the water. It felt warmer than the air and stank of rotting fish and bilge. He ignored the garbage floating near the riverbank and dove in all at once, quickly swimming toward the ship. A few minutes later he reached the anchor rope and paused to catch his breath, giving his friends time to creep down the pier in the dark and get ready to board at his signal. When he got his breath back, he climbed up the anchor rope, hand over hand, his arms strong from his work in the blacksmith shop. He could smell the pitch used for caulking as he slipped over the rail onto the deck, wet and shivering. He unsheathed his knife, gripping it in his fist.

Except for the sound of boards creaking as the boat swayed on the waves, everything was quiet. No voices. No footsteps.

Reuben quickly searched the deck for guards, then whistled the all-clear signal. His friends came on board like slithering shadows. They crept to the hatch, and Bear led the way below, sword in hand. Reuben followed them down the rope ladder, grateful to be out of the wind even though the stuffy air below deck stank of sweat and tar. Before his eyes had a chance to adjust, he heard a shout, then sounds of a scuffle. More cries and shouts followed, then the clash of swords. He tightened his grip on his knife, wishing he could see. Should he go forward or wait? Reuben wasn't a coward. He would gladly fight with his friends if he could see what was happening and be sure they wouldn't attack him by mistake in the dark. He heard a terrible scream, and the next thing he knew, one of his partners appeared out of the gloom and shoved him backward toward the ladder. "Go, boy! Move! Move!"

In his haste, Reuben's knife accidently slipped from his shivering fingers. He bent to search for it, but Ram kept pushing him. "There's no time! Get out of here! Now!"

He scrambled up the rope ladder and onto the deck as shouts and footsteps thundered behind him. Reuben ran to the rail and dove from the boat to swim to safety. When he came up for air, he saw his partners in a shaft of moonlight, leaping in behind him. Bear was the last to jump, and it looked as though his tunic and hands were covered with blood. A flood of sailors poured out of the hold, yelling at them to stop, waving their weapons. A whistling sound split the night as an arrow whizzed past Reuben's head. He dove beneath the surface and swam underwater, paddling as hard as he could, staying down for as long as he could. He surfaced only long enough to draw a breath, then swam some more, until he was far away from the pier and the ship. When he came up again, the sailors still milled around on deck, barking orders, but there was no sign of his partners.

Reuben waded ashore downstream, dripping and cold. The frigid night air made his teeth chatter. He hurried to the hideout as quickly as he dared, staying out of sight, knowing he would draw suspicion wandering the city streets in his wet underclothes. By the time he reached their hovel, he was shivering so hard he could barely walk. He quickly changed into his Jewish clothes and looked around for fuel, hoping to build a fire. The door opened and Digger stumbled inside, wet and bedraggled.

"What happened on the ship?" Reuben asked.

"A dozen sailors were waiting below deck, guarding the cargo. Too many for the four of us. They jumped out of hiding as if they knew we were coming."

"Bear had blood all over him when he dove into the water. Is he okay?"

"I don't know. He stabbed one of the guards. Killed him, I think. He told us to run. I think Nib might be hurt, too. Good thing there wasn't enough room below decks for the guards to swing their weapons, or it would've been much worse for us."

"I saw Bear jump into the water empty-handed. Did he leave his sword behind?"

"He had to. We were lucky to get out of there with our lives."

Reuben's father had made Bear's sword. It bore his distinctive mark and could be traced to his blacksmith shop. Reuben felt his empty sheath and remembered dropping his knife. It bore Abba's mark, as well.

Digger had changed out of his wet clothes, preparing to leave again. "Listen, kid, you'd better get out of here."

"I was going to make a fire to warm up and dry off."

"No time. We need to disappear for a while."

Reuben left without a word and went home, stunned by their failure, worried about the aftermath of this disastrous night.

Each day that followed brought more worries as Reuben waited for the Persian authorities to arrive at the shop with the marked sword and dagger. Did the sailors get a good look at Reuben in the dark? Could they identify him as one of the robbers?

Three days later, he was sharpening a plow blade when Uncle Hashabiah entered the forge, carrying a cloth-wrapped bundle. Reuben forced himself to stay calm, fighting the urge to run at the look of grim determination on Hashabiah's face. He spoke with Reuben's boss for a moment, then beckoned for Reuben to step outside. Reuben took his time, trying not to look like a guilty man.

"The Persian authorities came to talk with our elders yesterday," Hashabiah said. "They were asking questions."

"What about?"

"Among other things, this." He unwrapped the cloth to reveal Reuben's dagger. "I know it's yours, Reuben. I've seen you with it. It has your father's mark on it."

"Yeah, that's mine. I lost it a few months ago. Where'd you find it?" He reached for it, but Hashabiah pulled it away.

"I can't let you have it. The authorities found it at a robbery scene onboard a ship, along with one of your father's swords— one of four that were stolen from our storeroom. Naturally, the Persians think we were involved in this attempted robbery, men from our Jewish community."

"Were they involved?" Reuben asked, feigning innocence.

Hashabiah stared at him intently. "This looks very bad for you, Reuben. This is your dagger. The thieves had one of your father's swords. If you were involved in this robbery I can try to help you, but I need to know the truth."

Reuben fought to control his emotions so his voice wouldn't tremble when he spoke. "I don't know how you ended up with my dagger. And I don't need any help from you. I didn't do anything wrong."

"A sailor was murdered that night."

"Was he Babylonian? Because if so, I don't care and neither should you."

"Reuben—"

"I'm done talking now."

Hashabiah caught his arm to prevent him from leaving. "Can you look me in the eye and swear you weren't involved?"

Reuben glared at him, face-to-face. "I didn't rob any ship, and I didn't kill anyone. Now leave me alone!"

He broke free and returned to the grinding stone to finish sharpening the plow blade, working slowly until his hands stopped trembling. He told himself anger made his hands unsteady, not fear. Nothing would happen to him. They'd never prove he was involved. But he couldn't risk joining his friends until this blew over—and he would miss them. He hoped Bear and Nib had survived their wounds.

The sailor's death unnerved him. Reuben had agreed to a robbery but not a murder. How had his life come to this place? If only Bear hadn't killed a man.

BETHLEHEM

The wagon Amina rode in stopped at the top of the Mount of Olives to wait for the rest of the caravan of travelers from Bethlehem to catch up. The climb up from the village of Bethany on the other side of the mountain had been long and steep, but Amina never tired of this view of Jerusalem, spread out on the opposite ridge with the temple perched on Mount Zion. "Isn't it beautiful, Sayfah?" she asked. She wasn't surprised when her sister merely shrugged. Amina thought of it as The Golden City. She loved the creamy color of its stones and the way the sunlight made them glow. A curl of smoke rose from the temple's altar, and Amina anticipated the fragrant aroma of roasting meat and incense. They had come for the Feast of Weeks, celebrating the day the Almighty One gave Moses the Law on Mount Sinai, fifty days after saving them from Pharaoh's army. Amina had been saved from certain death, too, just like the Israelites.

One of the men in their caravan from Bethlehem began to sing, *"I rejoiced with those who said to me. 'Let us go to the house of the Lord.'"* Others quickly joined him in the familiar tune: *"Our feet are standing in your gates, O Jerusalem."* Amina knew almost all of the songs and loved singing them on the Sabbath and at festivals. Sayfah never sang.

At last the rest of their caravan reached the top of the Mount of Olives, and they all started downhill to cross the valley together. Just outside Jerusalem, they paused again to shop in the local market square at the foot of the ramp leading to the City of David. The bazaar was much bigger than the one in Bethlehem, with Jews and local people and even foreign merchants shouting and haggling as they bartered their goods. The beautiful, exotic wares fascinated Amina and she slowed her steps, linking arms with Sayfah as she slowly limped along. Her sister pulled her to a stop in front of a booth selling painted pottery. "Look, Amina! Those pots are exactly like the ones we had at home, remember?"

Amina saw the longing on Sayfah's face as she traced her fingers over the glazed design, a longing Amina didn't share or understand. She was about to reply when a voice suddenly said, "Do you girls like what you see? Are you buying?"

Amina looked up at the owner, then froze in horror. *Her father!*

He was older than she remembered, with more gray hair than brown, but he wore the tunic and turban of her people, the Edomites. *It couldn't be!* Abba was dead, wasn't he? Amina whirled away, yanking Sayfah's arm as she prepared to run from him and disappear into the crowd, dragging Sayfah with her.

"Hey, wait!" he called after them. "You girls . . . Sayfah!"

Sayfah halted when she heard her name.

"We have to run! We can't let him catch us!" Amina tried to break free, but Sayfah wouldn't let go. The man was out of his booth now, hurrying after them, and when he finally caught up, Amina was relieved to see it wasn't their father after all. This man was shorter than Abba had been, but the resemblance was very strong. He was Abba's brother, Abdel. Their uncle. Amina still longed to run.

"Hey! Aren't you my nieces—Sayfah and . . . ?" He snapped his fingers as he tried to recall Amina's name. "You look just like your mother, Sayfah—a real beauty. And I would know you anywhere because of your . . ." He gestured to Amina's crippled leg. "Everyone thought you girls died in the fighting last year."

"We're the only ones left," Sayfah said. Amina glanced around, still searching for a way to escape, and saw Hodaya hurrying back to look for them, leaning on Jacob's arm. Amina ran to her, clinging like a vine on a trellis.

"What's going on?" Jacob asked. "Do you girls know this man?" Their uncle had his hand on Sayfah's shoulder.

"Of course they do. I'm their uncle, Abdel."

"Is that right?" Jacob asked, looking to Amina for confirmation. She nodded.

"What do you Jews think you're doing with my nieces?" he asked before Jacob could speak again. "If you've made them your concubines, I expect full payment as their next-of-kin!"

Amina spoke up, knowing Sayfah never would. "Hodaya and Jacob were kind enough to take us in and give us a home when we were all alone."

"Then it's lucky for you that I saw you today and recognized you. You aren't orphans, you know. You don't have to stay with these Jews anymore. You belong with your aunt and me. It's time to come home to your own people." He gestured to his booth, then beckoned to them to follow.

Amina's body trembled so hard she could barely stand. Did he expect them to simply walk away with him after all this time? The thought made her sick. Jacob would surely turn them over to Abdel to be rid of them. And even if Hodaya came to their defense, Uncle Abdel would never listen to her. The men in Amina's village took no notice of what a woman had to say.

"Just a minute," Jacob said. "If the girls want to go with you, they're certainly free to do so. But I think the decision should be theirs."

"They're girls!" Her uncle scoffed. "They don't get to decide where—" He stopped as he seemed to catch himself. "Of course you'll want to come back to your family, right, Sayfah? Come on." He still gripped Sayfah's shoulder and tried to steer her away. Again, Jacob came to their defense, separating Sayfah from their uncle.

"Let's not discuss this here and now," he said. "I'm sure the girls must be shocked to learn they have relatives after believing they were orphans for more than a year."

"What are you talking about? They knew they had relatives. What kind of trick are you trying to play?" Abdel was shouting now, reminding Amina of the fear and abuse she'd endured for the first eight years of her life. She clung to Hodaya, trying not to cry. Again, Jacob surprised Amina by answering quietly and calmly, standing up for them.

"The girls didn't remember which village you were from and had no idea how to contact you. But listen, we're on our way to the temple right now, and it's a holiday tomorrow. We'll meet you back here in two days. That will give your nieces a chance to decide what they'd like to do. What do you say?"

"What guarantee do I have that you're not going to steal them away and disappear? How do I know you're not abusing them? If you've taken them as wives—"

"They're much too young to be anyone's wives," Hodaya said, speaking for the first time.

"My mother adopted Amina and Sayfah as her own daughters," Jacob said.

"How do I know you're telling the truth?"

Jacob stepped toward him, confronting him face-to-face. "Because I'm giving you my word, that's how. Or you can ask the girls yourself—do you want to go with your uncle now?" he asked, turning to Amina. She shook her head. Sayfah seemed too stunned to reply.

"We'll return to your booth in two days," Jacob said firmly.

"We'll let you know their decision then. Good day." He gently turned Sayfah around and prodded her up the street saying, "Let's go, girls." Amina followed in a daze. Neither Jacob nor Hodaya said another word about the incident as they climbed the steps to the temple.

Amina had been looking forward to seeing the priests in their pure white robes, watching the beautiful rituals, and hearing the Levite choir sing, but now she was too upset to enjoy any of it. Her heart flapped wildly like a bird caught in a net at the thought of living with her uncle. As fear slowly overwhelmed her, she could barely breathe. She didn't want to leave Hodaya and return to her own people. Ever! But what could she do? She and Sayfah were Edomites, not Jews. Didn't her uncle have a right to them?

Gradually, the deep, rich sound of the music began to calm Amina. When her panic faded and she no longer wanted to run and hide where her uncle could never find her, she listened to the words of the psalm the Levite choir sang: *"You are my hiding place; you will protect me from trouble and surround me with songs of deliverance."* Amina knew what she needed to do. She would pray to the God who lived in this magnificent temple and beg Him to help her and protect her. Maybe He would save her the way He had saved His people from the Egyptians. The way He had saved her and Sayfah and Hodaya on the Thirteenth of Adar.

Amina closed her eyes, praying silently as the column of smoke from the sacrifice rose to heaven. *Please, Almighty One. Please hear my prayer and let me stay with Hodaya. I promise to worship you all my life. To follow all your laws. . . . Please . . . please . . .*

Later they returned to Johanan's home, where Hodaya and her family always stayed when they came to Jerusalem. Hodaya had grown up in this house, and Johanan, the man who lived here, was her nephew. He and his brother, Joshua, were temple priests. Hodaya got swept away as she greeted her old friends and prepared for the special meal that began at sunset. But she took a moment to pull Amina and Sayfah aside and say, with tears in her eyes, "I will miss you dearly if you go away and live with your uncle. I will be overjoyed if you stay with me. But you girls must decide for yourselves what you want to do."

The Feast of Weeks lasted late into the night, but Amina couldn't enjoy it. She silently pleaded with the Almighty One to rescue her from her uncle the way He had rescued the Jewish people from Pharaoh. Hodaya made Amina feel loved and valued for the first time in her life, but she'd be nothing but a miserable cripple again if she returned to her people. She didn't have a chance to talk to her sister until later that night, when she and Sayfah were alone in bed. "What are we going to do about our uncle?" she asked, wishing with all her heart that Sayfah felt the same fear and revulsion toward him she did.

"We'll go with him, of course," Sayfah replied. Amina's stomach rolled over at her words. "It's a miracle we finally found him."

"But I don't want to live with him!"

"We have to. We're betraying Mama and Papa by living with their enemies. The Jews are the ones who murdered them."

"Uncle Abdel hates me because of my leg. Did you see the way he looked at me today? Just like Papa used to. He didn't even know my name. And remember how Papa used to tell me I was worthless? The Jews never treat me that way."

"The Jews aren't family, Amina. Of course we have to go home. How can you even think about staying here?"

"Please! I don't want to go back there!" How could Amina make her sister understand the terror that strangled her at the thought of living with their uncle? "Don't you remember how Abba used to beat us? How we lived in fear of making a mistake and angering him every day of our lives?"

"You're exaggerating. If he beat us it was because we deserved it."

"Nobody beats us in Hodaya's house. Don't you see the difference?"

"The difference is that we don't belong here, Amina. I should have died with Mama and the others, but I didn't. Now my place is with Uncle Abdel. And so is yours."

"No, please! I don't want to leave Hodaya! Please!" She began to sob. "Please don't make me go with him, Sayfah. You can go if you want to, but please let me stay with her."

"We're sisters and we belong together, with our own family."

"Sayfah, please—"

"Stop begging! I'm the oldest, and you have to do what I say."

"I'll die if you make me go back with him!"

"And I feel like I'm dying here with the Jews. I still can't forgive myself for leaving Mama and the others and running away. This is my chance to make it up to them, don't you see?"

"Sayfah, our parents left me behind, all alone, in our house that night. They never wanted me because I'm crippled. But Hodaya loves me, and I love her. You can go with Uncle Abdel if you want, but please let me stay with Hodaya. Please!"

"We can't separate now after everything we've been through. Our family has been shattered into pieces already. This is the right thing to do, Amina. We're going home with our uncle."

Amina lay awake all night, tossing on her mat and praying to Hodaya's God, promising to serve Him for the rest of her life if only He would save her. *I finally found someone who loves me, Lord. Please don't make me leave Hodaya! I don't care if Abdel is our uncle, he doesn't worship you. And I want to worship you!*

Amina couldn't eat anything the next day and didn't sleep on the second night, either. Sayfah packed her bag early in the morning as if eager to leave, and she made Amina pack hers, too. When Jacob said it was time to return to meet their uncle,

Amina began to cry. "You poor, sweet girl," Hodaya said, holding her tightly. "Here, take my hand, and I'll walk there with you." They set out together in a drizzling rain. The dreary streets glistened, and the wet building stones turned the color of ripe wheat as if the city wept along with her.

"I don't want to leave you," Amina sobbed as they walked. "But Sayfah says I can't stay." Would she ever be allowed to come to the golden city of Jerusalem again or worship at the temple?

"Be brave," Hodaya whispered. "Ask the Holy One to make you strong."

Much too soon, they reached the market square, which wasn't very busy on this gray, dreary day. Amina's uncle stood in front of his booth with his arms folded, as if he'd been watching for them. He stepped in front of them as they approached. "I've been thinking about it," he said before Jacob could speak. "Since you say you've grown attached to my nieces, I'll take Sayfah and let you keep the crippled one."

Amina felt a jolt of shock at the cruel rejection—and yet salvation! She felt Hodaya's arm around her shoulder, drawing her close.

"Give me the money that's due me when she's old enough to marry, and you can keep her."

Amina began to weep, knowing she didn't have money to buy her freedom, knowing Jacob had never wanted her. Time seemed to stand still as the two men stared at each other. Then Amina watched in amazement as Jacob unfastened the pouch from his belt and handed Uncle Abdel some coins. "Will this compensate you for your loss?" he asked, his tone scornful. Abdel closed his fist around the coins and nodded. "I'll pay your bride price, too, Sayfah," Jacob said, turning to her. "Are you sure you want to go with him?"

"Yes. I'm sure," she said, and for once she didn't whisper.

Amina broke free from Hodaya and ran to Sayfah, hugging her tightly, wondering if she would ever see her sister again.

221

She couldn't stop her tears, which were a mixture of sorrow at their separation and joy at her salvation.

"Where is your village?" Jacob asked Amina's uncle. "Where are you taking Sayfah?"

"It's just across the valley there," Abdel said. "At the foot of the mountain."

"And you know where we live in Bethlehem," Jacob told Sayfah. "You'll always be welcome if you ever want to come back and visit us."

It was time to part. Amina released her sister and limped back to Hodaya's side, taking her hand again. In spite of all the pain she felt in this moment, a tiny flame of joy warmed her heart. The Almighty One, Hodaya's God, had answered her prayer. He had rescued her.

Her God.

CHAPTER
30

BABYLON

Devorah was in labor. Ezra heard her crying out in pain as he paced his courtyard with Asher, and he suffered along with her. "Why is it taking so long?" he asked. "I wish I could do something to help."

"Hey, this is nothing!" Asher said. "My wife had our first child on the Thirteenth of Adar, remember? We were fighting for our lives when she went through this. I not only was concerned for Miriam, I was worried sick that the enemy would break through any minute and slaughter all of us."

"I'm sorry. I'm sure it was much worse for you. It's just that . . . what if I lose her? Women die in childbirth, you know. I don't know what I would do without Devorah." He had married her only a year ago, and already he could barely remember what his life had been like before or how it had felt to be alone, unable to come home to Devorah's smile, her loving arms. How had he lived without the softness and sweetness of Devorah lying beside him at night, without her gentle words as she smoothed his hair and beard or rested her hand on his shoulder? He had never imagined such contentment—but did she still think of Jude? Was she closing her eyes and pretending Ezra was him?

223

He heard another scream and wanted to break down the door and help her. He was glad he'd sent Abigail and Michal to stay with Miriam so they wouldn't have to hear their mother suffering. "I went so many years without a wife," he said, "and I used to be envious of you and Jude. I never imagined it would be so . . . so . . ." He tugged his beard as he searched in vain for the words to describe the fear and worry and distress he was experiencing. Would he have taken Jude's advice to join the real world if he'd known how costly it would be? He had experienced much less drama and emotion, much less risk in the world of his studies and scrolls—yet Ezra knew the happiness he shared with Devorah was worth it. Devorah—his wife. "Do you think she's okay?" he asked Asher.

"Listen to yourself. You sound like a man in love."

"Is this what love feels like?"

"Yes. And I'd be very surprised if you didn't love her after all the things she's done for you."

But did Devorah love him?

Finally—finally—the terrible screams stopped and Ezra heard the fragile cry of a baby. "Oh, thank God," he murmured. "I need to sit down." Asher laughed as Ezra sank down on his niece's stool. The newborn was still wailing loudly when one of the women came out to find him. "You have a son, Rebbe Ezra. *Mazel tov.*"

He sprang to his feet. "Is Devorah all right?"

"She seems to be."

"May I see her?"

"It's not a good time right now." The woman went back inside.

"What did she mean, Asher? She *seems* to be all right? Don't they know?"

"Just be patient. They'll call for you when they're finished."

"But you've been through this twice now. What do you think she meant? Why is it taking so long?"

"Ezra. Did you hear what she said? You have a son! Mazel tov!" Asher grabbed him in a bear hug.

Yes, he had heard. And he'd thought of Jude. "He isn't my son, you know," Ezra said, smiling for the first time. "He's Jude's son. God rewarded Devorah for obeying the law and marrying me." He was beginning to relax when Devorah cried out again. "She's still in pain, Asher! Something must be wrong!"

Asher sighed as if exasperated. He pushed Ezra toward the gate, away from the house. "Come on, you need to go for a walk or something. Maybe you'll feel better if we go to the house of assembly and pray."

"No. I'm staying right here. She might need me." He ran his hands through his hair, knocking his kippah to the ground, then bent to pick it up again. "I couldn't bear to lose her, Asher. You're right. I do love her. She listens to me talk when I know I must be boring her. And she really seems to enjoy discussing the Torah with me. She knows so much about it. In fact, she's brighter than some of my students. And sometimes when I'm so tired from answering questions and solving problems and deciding cases all day, she knows just how to lift me out of my slump and encourage me. She's a real woman of faith. I never imagined we would grow so close—after all, she married me out of duty. But it's such a joy to come home to her every evening and receive her affection." He looked up at Asher, who grinned and shook his head as if amused. "What? What did I say?"

"I'm going to give you a word of advice, Ezra. When this is over, tell her. Tell Devorah what you just told me."

The baby, who had been quiet for several minutes, suddenly began to wail again. "Something's wrong with the baby!" Ezra said in a panic. "We need to pray!" He sank down on the stool again, burying his head in his lap as he pleaded with the Almighty One for his wife and newborn son. If only God would give him a chance, he would take Asher's advice. He would tell

Devorah that he loved her. He would be a husband to her the way God was a husband to Israel. "Please," he begged. "Please . . ."

After what seemed like hours, the door to the house opened again. Ezra leaped to his feet as one of the women came out. "Devorah is asking to see you."

Dread engulfed him. The words sounded so ominous, as if his wife was about to die and needed to speak with him one last time. He hurried into their room, fearing the worst. Devorah lay on their mat looking exhausted but beautiful, her long, dark hair damp and tangled around her face. She held their new son in the crook of her arm . . . but . . . Ezra thought he must be seeing things. She had an infant in each of her arms. Where had the second child come from? He opened his mouth to ask, but nothing came out.

"Twins," she said, smiling. "Identical sons." She looked radiant. Ezra knelt down beside her, longing to hold her, kiss her. Thank her. But her arms were full with two tiny, fragile babies. Were all newborns so small? "He is the firstborn," she said, nodding toward the boy closest to Ezra. The baby had a piece of yarn tied around his wrist.

"That means he's Jude's son," Ezra said, stroking the child's dark hair.

"And this is your firstborn son," she said, indicating the other one.

"I can't believe it," he murmured, wiping his eyes. "My son! Did the Almighty One feel this much joy when He created mankind?"

Devorah smiled. "Yes, I think He must have."

Ezra knew as he gazed at his wife and infant sons that he would do anything for them—even lay down his life for them. But the knowledge that his family was trapped here in Babylon, surrounded by pagan enemies, made it difficult to catch his breath for a moment. He had to find a way out, a way to take them home to Jerusalem.

"What's wrong?" Devorah asked. "Your face just went pale."

"Nothing . . . I'm—I'm overwhelmed with joy." He wouldn't share his fear with her and overshadow their happiness. "God gave you a double blessing, Devorah. You obeyed God's law and married me, and look how He has blessed you! And Jude, too!"

"And He has blessed you, Ezra."

The thought astounded him. "Yes! Yes, He has! We must redeem both boys as firstborn sons, as the Torah commands."

"I would like to name our older son Judah—if you agree."

"Of course. I would like that." He bent to kiss Devorah's forehead. "You know I'm not good with words, but I realized something this afternoon while I was waiting. . . . I don't know when it happened, but I've stopped thinking of you as Jude's wife. You're my wife now. *My* wife, and a truly remarkable woman in every respect. I'm a better man because of you. I've grown to care for you, Devorah. I know I'll never take Jude's place—"

"Stop," she said softly. "I'll always think about Jude and love him. And I'll remember him every time I look at his daughters. But Jude would want me to be happy with you. And I am."

"You are? . . . With—with me . . . ?"

She nodded, smiling. "When I decided to talk to the elders about your work, I was surprised to realize that more than anything else, I wanted to make you happy."

"You have, Devorah! Tell me your heart's desire, and it's yours."

She sighed, looking exhausted. "The strength to raise our two sons, for now. . . . And then . . . a long life by your side."

Part III

12 YEARS LATER
THE 7TH YEAR OF ARTAXERXES

*Ezra had devoted himself to the study and
observance of the Law of the Lord, and to
teaching its decrees and laws in Israel.*

EZRA 7:10

CHAPTER
31

BABYLON

Ezra watched the setting sun at the close of the Sabbath day from the rooftop of his home and felt more than his usual sadness at the end of this day of rest. The darkness that slowly approached from the eastern horizon bringing heavy clouds would soon extinguish whatever light the moon and stars offered tonight. The clouds seemed prophetic, mirroring the heaviness that hovered over his soul when he prayed for the people he loved.

His family gathered around him—his wife, Devorah; his adopted daughters, Abigail and Michal, now lovely young women in their teens; his twin sons, Judah and Shallum; and the three younger daughters born to him and Devorah. Ezra kindled the *havdalah* light and recited the prayers that ended the Sabbath and ushered in a new week. The tradition helped draw a clear line between Sabbath time, consecrated to God, and ordinary days—a dividing line between the holy and the common. God chose His people to be a holy nation, a light to the Gentiles, but the ever-darkening sky that crept toward Babylon seemed an ominous picture of the increasing darkness that threatened to extinguish God's light.

"Amen," he said at the end of his prayer, and Ezra heard one of his children sigh as if relieved the long Sabbath day of rest had finally ended. All seven children scrambled to their feet, eager to return to activities forbidden on the Sabbath. "Judah and Shallum, please wait here with me," Ezra said. "You girls may go downstairs and help your mother."

He motioned for the boys to sit down again and noticed Shallum glancing up at the clouds.

The cool wind rustling across the rooftop threatened rain, blowing the clouds toward them. Ezra usually enjoyed studying Torah with his sons on Sabbath afternoons, but he hadn't studied with them today, too grieved by the report he'd received about them just before Shabbat began. The twins stared down at the clay roof tiles, not at him, knowing what was coming. "Look at me, please," Ezra said. They looked up, their black hair, brown eyes, and twin faces so identical that only family members could tell them apart. Eleven years of experience had taught Ezra the twins' individual mannerisms and quirks. They would be Sons of the Commandments at the end of this year, responsible for their own souls before God. The thought made Ezra shudder.

"Did you think you could skip your lessons at the yeshiva and I wouldn't hear about it?" he asked now. "Why weren't you in school on the eve of Shabbat?"

"We weren't prepared for our lesson, so we went for a walk," Judah said. He was older by a few minutes and usually took the lead.

"We didn't plan it," Shallum added, as if to soften the news. "We saw a ship down by the canal and went to watch it being unloaded."

Ezra saw Judah nudge his brother, and they exchanged a quick look—Judah signaling Shallum to be quiet, as if they were hiding something else. "Tell me the truth," Ezra said quietly. "Did you also walk into the city? Into Babylon?"

"Yes, Abba." They answered together, as they so often did.

Ezra used to find it amusing that they thought alike and said things simultaneously, but not today. One of them, acting alone, never would have summoned the courage to skip class, let alone wander among the pagan Babylonians. But together they were fearless. He thought of how the Holy One had confused the world's languages at the Tower of Babel, saying, *"If as one people speaking the same language they have begun to do this, then nothing they plan to do will be impossible for them."*

"We knew you would be angry, Abba," Shallum said.

"And yet you chose to go anyway?" They wouldn't meet his gaze. "You're right, I am angry." And along with his anger he felt fear—fear for his sons' spiritual well-being as well as their physical safety. "The Babylonians are our enemies. Did you stop to think it could be dangerous to wander among the Gentiles? They hate us. They tried to annihilate us barely two years before you were born. They will do it again if they get the chance. Not only that, but I'm the leader of our Jewish community. I stand before the governor as the Minister of Jewish Affairs in Babylon. Did it occur to you that you could be a target for our enemies because you're my sons?"

Judah heaved a sigh of frustration. "Sometimes it's very hard to be your sons, Abba."

"Yes? How so?" He waited to hear more.

"Everyone expects us to be perfect all the time because you are," Shallum said.

"And you expect more of us than other fathers do," Judah added.

"Don't you ever get tired of trying to be perfect, Abba? We do."

"And we're not perfect! We just wanted to get away on our own for once and explore the city."

"We knew you'd find out and you'd have to punish us but—"

"But we decided it was worth it, just to have a day off. There. That's the truth, Abba."

Ezra closed his eyes for a moment at their painful words. How many times had God's people willfully defied God's law for the immediate pleasure it promised? Was this a taste of the fear and pain God felt when His children disobeyed Him? "So tell me," he said with calm control, "did you learn anything on your walk? On your day off from trying to be perfect?" They didn't reply. "What did you think of the city?"

"Parts of Babylon are very beautiful," Judah said. Enthusiasm sparkled in his eyes and voice. "And it seemed very . . . exciting, especially compared to our community."

"And you, Shallum?" Ezra asked. "What did you think?"

"You won't like hearing this, Abba, but . . . the Gentiles seemed very nice. We got lost and one of them told us how to get home. A stranger."

"Did these 'nice' Gentiles know you were Jewish? Were you wearing your head coverings and tassels?" Again, they didn't reply. Their faces wore identical expressions of guilt. "I didn't think so," Ezra said. "These 'nice' Gentiles killed your father, Judah. They would have killed your mother and sisters and everyone else in our community if the Almighty One hadn't saved us."

"So, do we have to stay locked away in our community for the rest our lives?" Judah asked.

"The Almighty One can protect us from danger if we live in obedience to Him," Ezra replied. "The greater threat the Gentiles pose is that their beliefs and practices will slowly creep into our way of thinking and acting. The Torah continually warns us to separate the clean from the unclean, the holy from the common. That's why we lock ourselves away, as you put it. We stay away from Gentiles and live according to the Torah to help restore the fellowship with God that was lost when Adam and Eve were banned from *Gan* Eden."

Judah gestured to the huddle of dull, mud brick houses below them. "This doesn't seem like Gan Eden to us, Abba,"

"Did the city of Babylon seem more like Eden to you?"

"No," they said in tandem. But their slumped shoulders and somber expressions were unconvincing.

"It's not Eden, but their buildings are much more magnificent than ours," Shallum said after a moment. "And they have parks with lots of trees."

A gust of wind blew across the rooftop, nearly snatching Ezra's kippah from his head and bringing the first few drops of rain. He secured his head covering and continued on, determined to get soaked rather than curtail this conversation. "You're right, boys; I do demand a lot from you. As a family of priests, we have an even greater calling to demonstrate God's holiness in our lives and to help others live it. Your direct ancestor, Seraiah, who was exiled here when Jerusalem was destroyed, was the High Priest under King Zedekiah—"

"And before him, Hilkiah was High Priest under King Josiah," Judah cut in. "And Zadok served in the first temple under King Solomon. We know, Abba. You've told us many times before."

"And you're tired of hearing it?"

"It's just that . . . we aren't priests," he said with a shrug. "And I don't see how we ever will be unless we decide to build a temple for the Almighty One here in Babylon."

"Never!" Ezra wanted to shout at the absurdity of that thought. "A temple to the Holy One can never exist side by side with temples to idols. The Holy One's temple must be in Jerusalem, the place God commanded."

"It's just that . . . we know we'll probably end up being teachers, like you," Shallum said, "or maybe potters, like Uncle Asher. So I don't see why we have to learn all the temple rules and regulations like the ones we skipped the other day."

It took a great effort for Ezra to control his temper. "No matter what work you do as adults, you still have a responsibility to live by the Torah. So please explain to me about these passages you decided to skip."

"They described things we're supposed to do if we lived in

the Promised Land," Judah said, "like setting aside the Year of Jubilee and bringing sacrifices to the temple and celebrating the feasts by killing lambs and bulls and waving branches."

"Since we don't live in Jerusalem," Shallum added, "I don't see why we have to learn all those things. We'll never get to do any of them here in Babylon."

Ezra had no idea how to reply. He longed to shout at them and lecture them, reminding them that he was responsible for their souls for only a few more months, and then they would be accountable for their own souls before God. If only he could pack up his family and leave Babylon for good and return home to the land God promised them. But that was impossible.

"I don't hear any regret or sorrow for what you've done," he finally said. "And that grieves and disappoints me."

"We're sorry for disappointing you," Judah said. Shallum nodded in agreement.

"But you're not sorry you went? What I hear you saying is that escaping from your boring lessons for a day and seeing Babylon was worth being disciplined, as far as you're concerned. You'll take whatever punishment I dole out, but at least you had a day of freedom. Am I right?"

"It's hard having such a wise father," Judah said after a pause. Now they were trying to manipulate him, taking advantage of his love for them, a fierce love Ezra never imagined he would feel. "Unfortunately, my wisdom is failing me at the moment, and I can't think of a suitable punishment to make an impression on you. Five strikes with the rod? Ten? Do you know what the Torah says to do with wayward sons?"

"Stone them," they said in unison. But Ezra saw no fear on their faces. They were well aware of how much he loved them. Even so, fear of losing his sons to the evils of Babylon felt like a crushing weight on his chest. What if he spent his lifetime helping the people in his community follow God, yet ended up losing his own sons?

At last he exhaled. "To make up for missing your lessons, you will have to go to the house of assembly in your spare time and read the portion you skipped. When you're prepared, you will present the lesson to me instead of your teacher, and we'll see if we can find relevance in those passages for your lives here in Babylon. Of course, you'll also keep up with your regular yeshiva lessons."

"That's a lot of extra study, Abba," Shallum said.

"We're preparing for our *bar mitzvah*, too," his brother added. But Ezra could tell by their expressions they were relieved, thinking this was the only punishment they would receive.

"I know it's a lot of work. And I'm expecting even more. I'm very troubled to learn that Babylon has such a powerful attraction for you, and your studies and your life in our dull community do not. When you finish the portion you skipped, I want you to search God's Word and find three passages for me that speak to your discontent. Three examples of people who were dissatisfied with God's commands and provision. And then tell me what God said—and did—about their discontent. This is the 'learning' part. I will let you know what the punishment part will be after I've had a chance to pray about it."

"Yes, Abba. May we go inside now?" The rain was falling harder, the drops thick and chilling.

"Yes, go inside."

With a house as small as theirs, Devorah easily overheard every word her husband and sons had said. "Won't the boys resent the Torah even more if you use it as a punishment?" she asked when they were alone in their room that night, the room that used to be Ezra's when he was single. He sank onto a stool near the door to remove his sandals, and she could sense the heaviness of his heart.

"I'm not using it to punish them. The Torah is God's Word.

237

They need to hear God teaching them these lessons, not me. Hopefully, they'll find it more difficult to disappoint the Almighty One than to disappoint me."

"They're young boys," she said as she spread out their sleeping mat. "Didn't you ever crave a little excitement now and then when you were their age?" He didn't answer her question, and when she looked up and saw his puzzled expression, she smiled. "Let me guess—your idea of excitement was studying a new passage of Scripture. Am I right?"

"I loved to study and could never get enough of it. I wouldn't dream of cutting class. Jude and Asher wandered into mischief occasionally, but . . . Forgive me. I sounded pompous and prideful. Did you hear our sons' accusation that I was too 'perfect,' and they were tired of being perfect? I'm very far from perfect!"

"You don't need to convince me," she said, laughing. "I'm your wife. And to be honest, I was the same as you, growing up. I wouldn't have done anything to displease my father."

"I'll have to discipline the boys, of course, but how? Will the rod accomplish anything? And then what? I can hardly watch over them day and night or make them my prisoners."

"I know you have to punish them. But can't you show mercy, too? You're an expert at applying the Law, but doesn't the Almighty One temper His law with mercy?"

"If I thought mercy would make as great of an impression on them as their adventure in Babylon did, I would gladly offer it. If fear of breaking the law didn't deter them, I'm not sure what will. That's the trouble with living here in Babylon—all the lines between right and wrong, good and evil, holy and common are starting to blur. I wish our sons saw those lines as clearly as the line between Shabbat and ordinary days. . . . If only we still lived in our own land."

"But we don't. We live in Babylon, and our children will become adults here."

"Yes. And who knows what they'll grow up to be. Their true

calling and heritage is to be priests, but that can't happen. I feel so desperate, Devorah, so afraid we'll lose them if we don't do something. They see their excursion into Babylon as simply a day of skipping classes, but it's so much more than that."

Devorah stopped preparing their bed and came to him, holding him in her arms to soothe him. "But, Ezra, the lessons they skipped—I heard the boys say those portions of the Torah don't apply here in Babylon. And in a way, they're right."

"Yes, and it worries me that they've figured it out already at their young age. How far will they take it in the future? Will they continue to exclude portions of God's Word if they don't think they need to follow them?"

He let his arms drop from around her, and she knew he needed to pace while he talked and thought. After more than a dozen years of marriage, Devorah had grown accustomed to Ezra's need for solitude. He was not as demonstrative with his affection as Jude had been, yet she knew he cared for her—and valued her opinion. He considered her one of his most trusted advisors, an honor more precious and meaningful to her than his embraces.

"Do you see it, Devorah? The gradual assimilation, the daily compromises we make when we think the little things don't really matter? If we aren't careful, we'll wake up one morning and discover we aren't a separate people anymore. We'll look and act and talk just like the Gentiles. This incident with our sons—how do we know it isn't the first tiny step away from God?"

She walked to where he stood again and caressed his face, smoothing his beard, which was flecked with gray now like his hair. Rain drummed hard on the flat rooftop above them. "Come to bed, Ezra. I know God will show you what to do about the twins." She removed her outer robe and climbed into bed. Ezra sank down beside her a moment later and tried to get comfortable, but she doubted he would sleep.

"It isn't just our sons' truancy," he said after a moment. "I've been praying about the apathy of our people for a long time now, and asking God what He wants me to do about it."

"Apathy? That's a very strong word."

"Yes, but do you remember what it was like in our community after we defeated our enemies on the Thirteenth of Adar? We were all working together then, and everyone had a renewed passion for God and a desire to serve Him."

"I think part of it was fear that if we disobeyed Him again He might not save us the next time," she said.

"True, but I also believe there was genuine spiritual renewal going on. It was easy to rise up in faith and heroism when we faced a clear-cut enemy. It's much harder to resist the enemy of gradualism and assimilation, much harder to maintain a passion for God when we're bogged down in the daily routine of life."

"Yes, I can see that."

He rolled over to face her. "Our ancestors must have experienced spiritual revival after they were delivered from slavery in Egypt, because in that first flush of excitement they told Moses, 'We will do everything the Lord has said.' I don't see that zeal anymore. I see apathy. If people follow God's laws at all, it's out of habit or legalism, not love. Some of us are no better than the Gentiles, ignoring God and His laws and then creating our own image of what God is like and what He wants from us."

"Ezra, the women I know just want to raise their families in peace. And you can't blame the young people for craving a little excitement now and then, can you? They long for something different."

"I don't want any of our children to adopt the apathy and carelessness of the people here in Babylon. Our sons think of this place as their home, but it isn't. The land of Israel is their home. I don't want them to grow up among these filthy Gentiles, do you?"

"No, but there's nothing we can do about it. We live side by side with them."

"Did you hear Shallum say the Gentiles he met were nice? *Nice*, Devorah! Their generation has already forgotten how much the Babylonians hate us. I hate Gentiles and their pagan ways, and I don't want our family anywhere near them!"

"We can't hold our sons captive. They'll be adults soon."

"I know," Ezra said with a groan. "But listen, Devorah: If I long for a better life for my children, a holy life, wouldn't God want the same thing for us, His children?"

He left their bed a few minutes later, but Devorah didn't go to him. She knew her husband well enough by now to know he needed to wrestle with God alone to find answers to his questions. Besides, Devorah had work to do tomorrow, a home and a family to care for. She sighed and went to sleep.

CHAPTER
32

Ezra's words haunted Devorah as she went about her work the next day. Was it true her people were growing apathetic toward the Holy One? That they were slowly becoming like their Gentile neighbors? She thought Ezra's opinion was a little harsh, but as she stood in line at the well with her water jug, waiting for her turn, the conversation she overheard between two Jewish women changed her mind.

"Did you have a nice Shabbat?" one woman asked the other.

"It's a day like all the others to me," the second woman replied, waving her hand. "My husband's employer is a Gentile, and he'd never dream of giving us a day of rest."

"But you could still keep the Sabbath, couldn't you? And not work?"

"Why bother? We live in Babylon, not Jerusalem."

The dismissive words shocked Devorah. She made her way home again, balancing the jar on her head, and thought of the burdens Ezra carried for their entire community.

Later, she made her way to the open-air market to shop for produce, the noisy bustle of bartering and vendors shouting out the virtues of their wares assaulting her from a distance. The air smelled of spices and ripe leeks and fresh fish. As she squeezed between the tightly packed booths, through crowds of

Jews and Gentiles, she met a friend she hadn't seen in months. "Have you been away?" Devorah asked her. "We've missed you in the house of assembly."

"No . . . It's hard to get there regularly with the children and my husband's work. You know how it is. . . ." Devorah didn't reply, but she wondered if Ezra had been right when he'd accused their people of apathy. Devorah and her friend talked about their families for a while, catching up as they haggled with vendors and sniffed melons for freshness. "Your twins will come of age later this year, won't they?" her friend asked as they sorted through a mound of fragrant garlic. "Aren't they the same age as my son?"

"Yes, their bar mitzvah is at the end of this year."

"Have you decided on an apprenticeship for them yet? Or are they going to work in the family pottery yard?"

"Ezra wants them to continue studying in the yeshiva."

"What for?" she asked, with a look of surprise. "Won't they need a trade in order to make a living someday?"

Devorah bristled. "Ezra studies and teaches and he makes a living—"

"That's different. He's our leader. But why would he want your boys to study something as outdated and impractical as the Torah? What good is it for everyday life here in Babylon?"

Devorah was too stunned to reply. Her friend said good-bye and they parted, but afterward Devorah was more attuned to the swirl of activity around her. Jews mingled with pagan Gentiles as if there were no differences between them, as if the Thirteenth of Adar had never happened.

Walking home again, the conversation she overheard between two Jewish women stunned her. "I'll be planning a wedding for my daughter soon," one of them said. "My husband is arranging a betrothal for her with his boss's son."

"I thought his boss was a Gentile," the other replied.

"He is. But he's a good man. And he has always treated us kindly."

Devorah halted and turned around. "Excuse me for interrupting, but how can you allow your daughter to marry a pagan?"

"I want her to have a happy life. She'll have servants and a lovely home and will never lack for a thing as long as she lives."

"You think servants and wealth will bring happiness?" Devorah asked.

The woman gave her a scathing look. "I think you should mind your own business."

That night after supper, as her daughters cleared the table and washed the dishes, Devorah remained seated beside her husband. "I've been thinking about what we discussed last night—about our people's apathy and the danger of assimilation with the Gentiles. I guess my eyes were closed to it, but I see what you mean now, Ezra. I paid attention today while I was in the market and at the well, and I can see the danger our children face. But what can we do about it?"

"I prayed about Judah and Shallum all night," he said, lowering his voice. "And when I finally did fall asleep, I had a nightmare. I dreamt the Gentiles were coming to kill us again, but our children didn't have any weapons, no way to defend themselves."

Devorah felt cold at the thought. "When our ancestors were on the way from Egypt to the Promised Land, our enemies attacked us and tried to kill us. When that didn't work they hired Balaam and tried to put a curse on us. That plan also failed, so they decided to be friendly to us and invite our young people to their festivals. They enticed us with the offer of 'freedom' and with sexual immorality, and thousands fell for it. We ended up destroying ourselves. That could so easily happen again, Ezra. We can't escape the Gentiles' influence. They're all around us."

"I know. We don't belong here. We belong in the land God gave us."

"But He exiled us here. What can we do if He won't let us go home?"

"God did let some of us go home, remember? Under Prince

Zerubbabel? Maybe He'd make a way for the rest of us to return, too, if we asked."

"Wouldn't that take a miracle?"

"We serve a God of miracles." She could see his growing excitement. "That's the answer, Devorah, don't you see? We need to pray—all of us, every day—and ask God to open the door for us to return the way He did eighty years ago with King Cyrus's decree. That's the only way we can ever truly protect our children."

"Do you think God will answer such a prayer?"

"Why wouldn't He? Nothing is impossible for Him. But if He did, Devorah, would you go with me? Would you help me move our family back to our homeland where we belong?"

She took a moment to reply, knowing it would mean an enormous sacrifice and incalculable changes to leave the only home she'd ever known and travel across a vast, dangerous land. But the risk of having her daughters marry Gentiles or seeing her sons enticed by Babylon seemed deadlier. "If God worked a miracle and moved the Persian king's heart a second time," she finally said, "we would be fools not to obey. Our parents and grandparents never should have remained behind the last time."

Ezra gripped Devorah's hands. "God sent Moses and Aaron to Pharaoh to demand our freedom. We need to ask the Persian king to let our people go."

"Who would dare ask such a thing? He's even more powerful than Pharaoh was."

He met her gaze. "I would go if the Holy One sent me."

She gave a nervous laugh, frightened at the thought of her gentle, humble husband confronting the empire's ruthless leader. "The boys skipped one day of school and you're Moses now?" she asked. But she could see Ezra's determination.

"Do you agree that we need to get our family out of Babylon?"

"Yes, of course, but—"

"The Holy One declared that our exile had ended when King

Cyrus issued his decree. So why are we still here? God promised Abraham that the land would be ours forever. Of course it's His will for us to go home. We need to be courageous enough to ask for our freedom." Ezra rose from the table to pace in the courtyard. "The twins were right; there are so many commandments in the Torah we can't obey here. And they were born to be priests, not potters in Babylon." He paused and turned back to her. "Will you pray with me, Devorah, and convince others to pray? We need to ask God for a miracle."

"Do you think this dream is even possible?" She felt overwhelmed and excited and afraid all at the same time. "And are you really the one who should talk to the Persian king?"

"I don't know. But I'm not going to stop praying about it until the Holy One shows me if this is what He wants me to do."

Ezra sat in the yeshiva with his head bowed, his eyes closed, praying for the Almighty One's guidance while his sons studied the lessons he had assigned them, putting in another long evening of work by lamplight. He heard them talking with each other as they prepared, discussing their ideas, bickering over sources. Then their chatter halted. Ezra looked up. "We finally have the three examples you asked us to find, Abba," Judah told him. "We found people who were discontented with their lives."

"And a verse for each one," Shallum added, "showing what God thought of their disobedience."

"Very good. I'm listening." Ezra sat back in his seat, arms folded.

"In the first book of the Torah, Adam and Eve wanted to taste the forbidden fruit," Judah said. "They weren't content with what God gave them and wanted more."

"And the Torah says, 'The Lord God banished him from the Garden of Eden to work the ground from which he had been taken,'" Shallum read.

"Good. The Holy One takes our rebellion very seriously, wouldn't you say?" The boys nodded in tandem.

"The second example comes from the fourth book of Moses," Judah said. "When Israel was in the desert, some of the people became discontented with following God's rules and eating manna all the time, and so they decided to feast with the Moabites and take part in all their forbidden rituals."

"So the Lord told Moses, 'Take all the leaders of these people and kill them and expose them in broad daylight,'" Shallum read.

Ezra nodded. It was the same example Devorah had mentioned when they'd talked earlier in the evening. "Again, it's pretty clear how God felt about their discontent, don't you think?"

"Yes, Abba."

"Our last example is from the fifth book of the Torah. It tells what will happen whenever any of us become discontented. The Holy One lists all the blessings we can expect if we obey Him, then all the ways we'll be cursed if we don't. And most of the curses have already come true, Abba. That's why we live here in Babylon and not in the Promised Land."

"But we decided to choose a verse for this one that also shows God's mercy," Shallum said, "because God is a compassionate and gracious God. The verse says, 'Even if you have been banished to the most distant land under the heavens, from there the Lord God will gather you and bring you back. He will bring you to the land that belonged to your fathers.'" Shallum finished and looked up from the scroll, waiting.

Ezra couldn't speak. From the mouths of his own sons, God had shown him His will. *The Lord God will gather you and bring you back.* The Almighty One would open the door for His people and bring them home.

"Isn't the last example good enough, Abba?" Judah asked when Ezra hadn't replied.

"It's perfect, son. Let's go home."

Ezra wasted no time convening a meeting of the community's elders the following day. Rain was falling, misting through the open windows and making the meeting room damp and clammy. According to the Torah, rain was a blessing from God—and Ezra prayed for God's blessing on what he was about to propose.

"We've finished our work of studying how the law applies to our lives," he began. "Now we need to live it. But my own sons have pointed out to me how impossible it is to do that here in Babylon. God commands us to bring sacrifices to His temple. Impossible. He commands us to make a pilgrimage to Jerusalem three times a year to celebrate the appointed feasts. Impossible. Why would the Almighty One give us laws that are impossible to fulfill?" He paused and studied the faces of the assembled men before continuing. "The answer is, He wouldn't. He doesn't expect us to do the impossible, so there must be a way to obey Him. My sons also reminded me of God's promise, 'Even if you have been banished to the most distant land under the heavens, from there the Lord God will gather you and bring you back. He will bring you to the land that belonged to your fathers.' I believe God keeps His promises. And I believe He wants us to return home to Jerusalem. Now. All of us. With our families."

"Now?" one of the elders asked. "Who will lead us? We don't have Moses or a royal descendant like Prince Zerubbabel this time."

"All you have is me," Ezra replied. "And we have each other. I believe God is calling us to return to our land, and I'm asking for your support and prayers. When the Holy One first asked me to lead you fourteen years ago, we were in a fight for our lives. I studied the Torah day and night with the other scholars, trying to learn about God in order to save our people. We figured out that we weren't keeping the terms of His covenant—and we still aren't. Maybe that's why our enemies nearly prevailed over us. We need to return home and live by the laws of the Torah. We need to keep the Sabbath and the appointed feasts.

We need to appoint judges who will govern the Promised Land by God's law. And we need to bring our offerings to the temple, for our children's sakes as well as our own. It's the only way to safeguard our families' futures. We have to put into practice what we know from the Torah. We have to keep our side of the covenant we made with God."

"How can we possibly convince King Artaxerxes to set us free?"

"I don't know, but we have to do it. We can't let the Hamans of this world threaten us again. We may have survived the sword the last time, but now we stand in danger of perishing by assimilation. We must return to our land where we'll be free to live by the Torah. It's the only way to avoid the divine curse. It doesn't matter if we read the Torah every day if it isn't evident in our lives. But if God grants us success, gentlemen—and I believe He will—then we can return home and live in our land."

"Do you have a plan?" one of the elders asked. "We're still under Persian authority, you know."

"Prayer is our greatest weapon, just as it was when we fought Haman's decree. That's why I've come to all of you. When we've prayed and sought guidance, a group of us will travel to Susa together and convince the king's officials to take our side. Fourteen years ago, God appointed a Jewish woman as queen of Persia. He appointed a Jew named Mordecai as the king's right-hand man. We don't know if they're still in power with a new king on the throne, but if God was able to put His people in important positions back then, we can trust Him to have someone in Susa who'll hear our petition and help us."

"And you're going there yourself, Ezra? As our spokesman?"

"Yes. And I'd like all of you to come with me. My plan is to ask for an audience with King Artaxerxes and petition him for permission to return to our land."

"What if the king refuses?"

"Or even worse, what if he interprets our request as an act of rebellion? We'll be back to making bricks without straw."

"It's a very long journey to Susa," someone else added. "We'd be away from our families and our work for months."

"That's true, but do you believe it's worthwhile to take those risks? Isn't any sacrifice we made worth it to finally return to our land? I'm sure you realize what's at stake if we don't succeed—we'll lose the next generation of young people. Within a few more years, we'll die out as a people just as surely as if Haman's decree had killed us."

Ezra looked around at the gathered men. He had said what he'd come to say. He tugged his beard for a moment, then asked, "Who's with me? And more important, who's with God?"

One by one the elders rose from their seats to stand in solidarity with him. Every man supported him. "Praise God," Ezra whispered. "Praise God."

CASIPHIA

Reuben awoke with a pounding headache. He had celebrated with too much wine last night, and the noise his younger brother and sister were making outside in the courtyard, laughing and teasing each other, sent a jolt of pain through his temples like a hot poker. How would he cope with the clanging and pounding in the forge all day? Then he remembered why he had celebrated last night, and he smiled to himself. He didn't have to work another day for that thief who had stolen Abba's forge. Reuben would be his own boss from now on. At last.

He sat up and felt beneath his straw mattress for his money pouch, gripping it in his fist when he found it. He'd slept with it nearby, knowing how easily thieves could creep inside a house during the night, stealing while people slept.

Outside, his sister gave another shriek of laughter. Reuben lay down again and covered his eyes, wondering if his gang of friends felt as lousy as he did this morning. Probably worse. Reuben thought he remembered Bear and Digger bringing Babylonian prostitutes back to their hideout, but his memories from last night were hazy. He had stayed out until nearly dawn and wouldn't have come home at all if he hadn't waited for more than fourteen years for the day he could buy back his inheritance. He had enough money now. Owning the forge had been Reuben's goal for so long he couldn't imagine what he would do tomorrow or the next day. He wouldn't steal anymore, that was certain. It would be too risky once he became a respected blacksmith with his own business to run. He listened to his fourteen-year-old brother's laughter and imagined them working together as he and Abba once had.

There had been lean years for Reuben and his gang of friends, especially after the disastrous ship robbery when Bear and Nib were injured. For a long time, the gang had stolen barely enough to live on. But the warehouse they'd robbed last night had yielded a cache of gold, plenty for each of them, even after dividing it five ways. If his Uncle Hashabiah knew all the things Reuben had done, he would say, "Stone the wayward son!" But Reuben didn't care. His goal was finally within his grasp, as close as the money pouch he gripped in his hand.

The door to his room creaked open. "Reuben, you'll be late for work," his sister called.

"Stop shouting. I'll get up when I feel like it."

"But you're supposed to be in the blacksmith shop. Your boss—"

"Go away! I'm not going to work today." *Or ever again,* he added to himself. He rolled over and fell asleep.

The sun was high above his house when he finally rose. Reuben washed and changed out of his sour-smelling tunic. He refused his mother's offer of food, his stomach still roiling, and crossed the lane to the blacksmith shop. His boss sat in the alcove behind the partition, reviewing his accounts. He glanced up at Reuben and frowned. "You're late. Your sister said you were sick."

Reuben tossed his bulging money pouch onto the table with a satisfying clunk. "I've come to buy back my father's shop. You'll find more than enough gold in there to pay for it."

"My shop isn't for sale," he replied. "I finished paying your family the agreed-on price years ago. The smithy is mine now."

"And I'm telling you to name your price. You know this place is rightfully mine. I want to buy it back."

"You can't possibly pay me what it's worth. I know the salary you earn, and I know you help support your family on that pay. You couldn't have saved enough during that time to—"

Reuben grabbed the bag and yanked open the drawstring, dumping the contents onto the table. The stolen coins clinked against each other as they poured out. "Look! I have more than enough!"

His boss's eyes widened. He looked uneasy as he shoved the pile of coins back toward Reuben. "I don't know where this came from . . . it doesn't matter. I'm not interested in selling my shop for any amount. It will be my son's someday."

His son's. Rage squeezed Reuben's chest, making it hard for him to breathe. The man's son worked alongside his father as an apprentice the way Reuben once worked beside Abba. The injustice infuriated him. Reuben had to leave—he would lose control and punch the man if he didn't. He scooped up the coins and poured them back into the bag.

"Reuben, wait!" He heard his boss calling after him. "You have work to do." Reuben kept walking, brushing past the man's scrawny son as he stalked through the forge. The boy held one of Abba's best hammers, and Reuben had to fight the urge to snatch it from his hand and pound him with it.

Uncle Hashabiah was to blame for this injustice. It was his responsibility to straighten out the mess he'd created. Reuben walked to Casiphia's market square where his uncle sold imported cloth, trading with merchants from throughout the Persian Empire. Hashabiah was bargaining with a merchant over a cartload of brightly dyed linen when Reuben interrupted him.

"I need to speak with you."

"Is everything okay, Reuben?"

"No, it isn't," he said with icy calm. "You stole my father's smithy from me, and now you need to help me buy it back."

Hashabiah's brow creased in a frown. "Give me a moment to finish my business. Then we'll talk." He motioned for Reuben to wait in the rear of the booth where he kept a pile of cushions and a small table to serve refreshments to his customers. Hashabiah had sons of his own who worked with him, but they were nowhere to be seen. Reuben listened to the two men bartering, each trying to squeeze out the best deal, and he knew his uncle was capable of driving a hard bargain. Hashabiah could force the man to sell the forge to Reuben if he made up his mind to help him.

Reuben's temper had a chance to cool while he waited, and he vowed to control it. He was no longer a boy who wept with rage at his impotence; he was an adult who knew what he wanted and was determined to get it. He had worked hard and waited patiently for this day, and no one was going to stop him.

At last his uncle finished his business deal and sank down on a cushion across from Reuben. "What brings you here? Why aren't you at work?"

"I'm ready to buy back Abba's blacksmith shop. You have to help me."

"How can you possibly buy it back?"

"I have money. More than enough." He dropped the money pouch onto the table. "You brokered the deal the first time—ask him to sell it back to me."

Hashabiah picked up the heavy pouch and loosened the drawstring to look inside. "Where did this come from?" he asked, lowering his voice.

"That's not your concern." Reuben snatched it from him, tying the pouch onto his belt again. "Did you ask him where the money came from when he bought my father's shop fourteen years ago? What difference does it make?"

"It makes a huge difference." Hashabiah's frown deepened.

"I've been worried about you for a long time, Reuben. I fear you've acquired this gold through illegal means and—"

"Listen, I'm no longer a child you can shake your finger at. I'm twenty-six years old. You committed a sin against me when you arranged this deal fourteen years ago, and now you owe it to me to make it right."

"I don't think he's willing to sell, Reuben. There's nothing I can do."

"You can't? Or you won't? Maybe you and I should go talk to Casiphia's elders. I'd like to explain to them how you cheated me out of my inheritance after my father died a hero's death."

"The elders know all about the arrangement I made for your family. I consulted them after your father died and asked their advice. I wanted you and your mother to be taken care of properly. The elders agreed this was the best solution."

"If they agreed, then you're all a bunch of thieves and crooks. Is it any wonder I have no respect for any of you?" Reuben's anger grew hotter in spite of his best efforts to control it. "My father built that shop with his own hands. Those are his tools, his anvil, his grinding stones. The smithy is all I have left of him, and I want it back. I can pay for it. You owe it to me to help me."

"My conscience is clear in this matter, Reuben," Hashabiah said, spreading his hands. "But in the years since your father died, you've earned a reputation in this community as a black sheep. Even if you did buy back the shop, I'm not sure anyone would do business with you. You never attend prayers at the house of assembly. In fact, you didn't even come to hear your own brother read the Torah for the first time when he became a Son of the Commandments. He looks up to you, but you're hardly a good example for him to follow."

"Can you blame me for not attending after the way you and the elders treated me?"

"And when one of your sisters was betrothed," Hashabiah

continued, "you weren't among us to help make the arrangements or provide the dowry. I took care of everything for her out of my own resources—and I have daughters of my own to provide for."

"Why didn't you ask me? I could have paid for her."

"Because we don't know where your money comes from, Reuben. How could the Holy One bless a bride who starts her marriage with a stolen dowry? You're not part of our community. You live here and work here, but that's all. You don't worship with us or pray with us or celebrate or grieve with us. You don't follow the Torah. Your mother says she has no idea where you go or what you do when you go out at night."

"You've been spying on me? Asking questions about me?"

"No. It's the other way around. Your mother has come to me countless times, asking for help. She believes you've been stealing. She's worried you're becoming a drunkard. She told me about your Babylonian friends, and she fears she's losing you to their bad influence. I never told her how the authorities found your dagger at a murder scene because it would break her heart. But I did tell her that if I knew how to draw you back to us, I would gladly do it. And it's true, I would."

"Make him sell me my inheritance, and maybe I'll start coming to prayers again."

"Reuben, if he doesn't want to sell—"

Reuben shot to his feet. "I know there's a law in the Torah somewhere that says you have to give back a man's inheritance. It can never be sold permanently—right?"

Hashabiah thought for a moment as he stood, as well. "In the Year of Jubilee, yes, property must be returned to its original owner. But that only pertains to the ancestral property we inherit in the land of Israel. We can't own land in Babylon."

"Abba owned that blacksmith shop!"

"No, not really. We pay fees and taxes to the Persians for

our land and businesses." He gestured to his own booth. "The Persians can reclaim this anytime they want to."

"I don't believe you."

He let his breath out in a rush, as if Reuben had punched him. "Listen, may I give you some advice, Reuben? You've become a very fine craftsman, so I'm told. If owning your own forge is so important to you, why not use your money to buy another one? Rejoin our community and earn back our people's trust, and I'm sure you'll make a fine living. An honest living."

Reuben shook his head. "It wouldn't be the same. My father built that forge himself. He worked hard for every tool he owned, and he wanted me to inherit everything."

"We're getting nowhere," Hashabiah said. "Look, I'm going to explain something to you, and I hope you'll listen—really listen. Our inheritance isn't composed of physical things like tools and blacksmith shops. Our inheritance is the covenant our ancestors made with God—"

"I'm leaving." Reuben started to go, but Hashabiah grabbed his arm, stopping him.

"When you forsake your true inheritance as a son of Abraham, you're killing our people just as surely as our enemies did when they killed your father. One lost descendant of Abraham means that all the generations that would have come from you will be lost, as well. Do you understand what I'm saying? You're accomplishing what the enemy failed to do fourteen years ago. You're finishing their work and letting our people die out, one by one. Is that what you want?"

"Let me go," Reuben said in a low voice.

Instead, Hashabiah's grip tightened. "The inheritance you need to reclaim, Reuben, is your covenant with God. And I will gladly help you do that." He finally released Reuben, waiting for his reply. But Reuben was too furious to say another word. He strode from the shop, nearly knocking over a customer on the way out, the pouch full of gold bouncing heavily against his side as he walked. He may as well give it away to the beggars in the streets for all the good it would do him, or to the ragged Babylonian children asking for alms to buy bread.

He kept going, heading for the hangout he shared with his friends—his only true friends—hoping to find leftover wine from last night. What good was all the gold in the world if he couldn't have the one thing he wanted most?

CHAPTER
34

BETHLEHEM

Amina knew Hodaya was dying, but she wasn't prepared to let her go. "What will I do without you?" she asked as she knelt beside her, listening to her gasping breaths. Hodaya's hand felt cold as it lay between Amina's.

"Lean on God." Amina had to bend close to hear Hodaya's whispery voice. "Lean with every step you take . . . just like you lean on your crutch. . . . You're God's child."

Hodaya passed in and out of consciousness during her last days, but she seemed at peace, not struggling against the angel of death. Hodaya's family gathered around her, hungry for their last moments with her. When Amina took her turn sitting beside her, she could tell something was bothering Hodaya. "Please tell me what's wrong," Amina said when they were alone. "You know I would do anything for you."

Hodaya struggled for words, as if trying to put her thoughts together. "Sayfah," she finally whispered. The name came out like a sigh.

"My sister? What about her?"

"Make things right."

Amina looked away, knowing what Hodaya meant. Her

259

parting from Sayfah fourteen years ago had been too abrupt. Neither of them had been willing to give in to the other, and so they'd separated. Amina hadn't heard from her sister since. For a long time, she'd resented Sayfah for choosing their uncle instead of the new life they had with Hodaya. Why couldn't Sayfah understand Amina's unwillingness to go where she was treated cruelly, unloved and unwanted? In the first years after Sayfah left her, Amina had been afraid to visit or make contact with her, fearing Uncle Abdel would change his mind and force Amina to live with him. She avoided the market outside Jerusalem whenever they visited the city so she wouldn't run into him. But Amina was a grown woman now, twenty-two years old. It was time to mend the rift with her sister. Her adopted family had taught her that celebrating the Day of Atonement and asking the Holy One for forgiveness meant asking others for forgiveness and making amends.

"I'll do it," she promised Hodaya. "I'll find my sister and make things right."

A few days later, Hodaya died in her sleep. The grief Amina felt was even greater than when her parents had died. She wept for days along with Hodaya's family, finding comfort in the arms of Jacob's wife, Rivkah, whom Amina had grown to love.

A month later, when Amina's new family traveled to Jerusalem for the Feast of Weeks, she asked Jacob to take her to Sayfah's village. "I promised Hodaya I would visit my sister and make amends," she told him. "Would you take me? I've been wondering what happened to Sayfah."

"Of course," Jacob said. "You should have asked me sooner, Amina. Why did you wait so long?"

"I was afraid to go, afraid my uncle would change his mind and force me to stay."

"I understand. And I want you to know I will never allow that to happen."

She and Jacob and his oldest son left Jerusalem at dawn the

morning after the feast. As she limped along beneath clear, early-summer skies, she fluctuated between anticipation at seeing her sister and dread at seeing her uncle. They reached the village entrance a few hours after dawn, and Jacob spoke with the elders who were seated there. "We're looking for Amina's uncle Abdel and sister, Sayfah. Do you know where we can find them?"

"Sayfah lives in her husband's home, not with Abdel. You will need to ask her husband's permission. I will take the girl there because she is an Edomite, but you Jews must wait outside our village."

"I'm sorry," Amina told Jacob. "I promise not to be long."

"Take your time, Amina. We'll wait."

As soon as she entered the village, Amina longed to turn around and run back. It was so much like the village where she was born with the same low, mud brick houses, the same style of pottery and clothing. The villagers were Edomites like her, and the people who stared at her as she limped past resembled the ghosts of her lost family. They had the same facial features Amina's family had—that she had. She even saw a child with her own reddish-brown hair color.

Sayfah gave a little cry when she recognized Amina and set down the toddler she held as they fell into each other's arms. "I thought I would never see you again," Sayfah wept, clutching her tightly. She looked the same, only taller and older, and even more beautiful than she had as a girl. She was a woman now, twenty-five years old, and resembled their mother.

"You're so beautiful!" Amina said when they finally released each other. "The elders told me you're married now. Is this your son?" She gestured to the wailing child clinging to Sayfah's leg.

"Yes," she said, lifting him again. "I have two sons older than him, too. I live here with my husband and his parents."

Sayfah's house was simple but larger than the one where they had grown up. Judging by the array of cooking pots and the beautiful hearth and outdoor oven in the courtyard, Sayfah's husband was more prosperous than Abba had been.

"What about you, Amina? I suppose you've married a Jew by now?"

"No, I'm not married."

"Good. You've come back to find a husband among your own people."

"No," she said quickly. "No, I came to see you and find out if you're all right. It's been much too long. And . . . and I also wanted to ask you to forgive me for not moving here with you. The way we parted seemed much too abrupt."

Sayfah looked away for a moment before turning back. "I was very angry with you, at first. But it was cruel of Uncle Abdel to say he didn't want you, and I knew you were probably better off with Hodaya. She understands how things are for you, being a cripple."

"I also came to tell you Hodaya died a month ago. I thought you'd want to know. She was so good to us, adopting us when we were orphans."

"Yes. She was good to us. I'm sorry to hear she died." Sayfah paused, playing with a strand of her son's dark hair. "But if Hodaya is gone, you have no one but me. Hodaya's sons never wanted us."

"Jacob and the others have changed. I'm part of their family now. And I worship the Jews' God, in His temple in Jerusalem. I'm here for one of His feast days, in fact."

"How can you worship with them? You aren't Jewish."

"After you left, Hodaya told me that Uncle Abdel may not want me for his child, but the Holy One did. The more she taught me about Him, the more I wanted to learn all the Jewish customs and beliefs, so I could worship Him." Amina didn't tell Sayfah how the Almighty One had answered her prayer to rescue her from their uncle. That salvation had been the seed of her growing faith.

"So that's it? Now you're Jewish?"

"I'll never really be Jewish by blood, but Hodaya took me to the *mikveh* to wash. Then I made the required offering and—" She paused at the sound of men's voices, shouting inside the house. Sayfah flinched as she glanced over her shoulder, and Amina saw a momentary look of fear in her eyes.

"Is he calling for you? Do you want me to leave?" Amina asked.

"No. It's okay. Please stay a little longer." But the loud voices brought back memories for Amina of the fear and abuse she'd suffered. Thankfully, the years of peace in Hodaya's home now outnumbered those years.

"Tell me about your life, Sayfah. Are you happy?"

"Uncle Abdel made a good match for me, considering I'm an orphan with nothing to bring to a marriage. My husband is a good man. I hope to bear him many more sons." Amina noticed that Sayfah hadn't answered her question. "How about you? Are you happy?" Sayfah asked instead.

"Yes. I work as a weaver like Hodaya, and I love it. In fact, before Hodaya died, our woolen cloth was in such demand with so many orders to fill, we didn't need our booth in the market-place."

The men began shouting again, sending a current of fear through Amina. "I need to leave," she said. "Jacob is waiting for me. The festival ended yesterday, and we're traveling home to Bethlehem this morning. But I'm so glad I came." She hugged Sayfah once more.

"Will you come and visit me again? My husband won't let me visit you since you live in Bethlehem with Jews."

"Yes. I would love to come again."

On the way home, Amina thanked Jacob for taking her and for waiting for her. They caught up with the rest of his family, and she chattered on and on about Sayfah from her seat on the cart. "I didn't get to meet her husband or her other two children, but I saw her youngest son, and . . . Oh, dear! I never asked my nephews' names."

"I'll take you again," Jacob assured her. "I'm glad your sister is happily married and doing well." He turned serious for a moment, then said, "You know, I asked Mama several times if I should find a husband for you. Mama always said you weren't ready yet."

"It's true, I wasn't. I didn't want to leave Hodaya. She needed my help, especially these past few years. And there was so much I still wanted to learn from her."

Jacob reached up to rest his hand on Amina's arm. "Please don't think I'm trying to get rid of you, because that's the last thing I want to do. But would you like to marry and have a home and children of your own someday?"

"Yes . . . I think so. . . . But I don't see any suitors knocking on your door, asking for my hand. I know I have two things against me—I'm crippled, and I'm a Gentile. I'll always be an oddity."

"Mama was both of those things, too."

"I know. But she arrived as a baby, not as an enemy refugee after a terrible war."

"Would you like me to make inquiries about a husband? I've seen your devotion to our God. You're accepted as one of us now."

The cart rocked as it hit a rut in the road, and Amina gripped the seat. She took her time as she formed an answer to his question. She knew nearly all the eligible men in Bethlehem. She'd grown up with them, traveling in caravans to the feasts and gathering for local celebrations. She'd seen them in the marketplace when she'd worked there with Hodaya and had never felt a spark of love or attraction for any of them—at least not the way Hodaya had described falling in love with her husband, Aaron.

"Hodaya told me your father fell in love with her just the way she was," Amina finally replied. "She told me to wait for a man who loved me, too."

"I understand. But just say the word, and I'll talk to the other fathers about finding that kind of a husband for you."

The offer filled Amina with fear rather than anticipation, especially when she recalled the shouting in Sayfah's house and the look of fear on her sister's face. "No, thank you. . . . Maybe when I've finished grieving."

"Whatever you decide, Amina. But please know you don't have to leave my home. You're welcome to live with Rivkah and me just as when Mama was alive. You're part of our family."

"Thank you." His warm words brought tears to her eyes.

"Mama loved you very much, you know," Jacob said. "You were the daughter she and Abba never had."

"I know." And as they traveled on, Amina grieved all over again for the kind woman who had saved her and made her part of her family, the woman who had brought her into the family of God.

CHAPTER
35

BABYLON

Devorah clung to her husband as they lay in bed, unwilling to let him go. Alone in their room with the children asleep, she finally had a chance to say good-bye to him in private. The hottest days of summer had passed, and Ezra would leave in the morning for the long, hazardous journey east to the Persian capital of Susa. He and a delegation of Jewish elders would make inquiries with the proper officials and ask for an audience with King Artaxerxes. They would request permission to return home to the Promised Land. Devorah couldn't imagine it; Babylon was the only home she'd ever known, while Jerusalem was a far-off place she'd only read about in the Torah and sung about in psalms.

As she held Ezra for what might be the last time for many months, Devorah recalled her last night in Jude's arms, and the loving words he had whispered to her. She'd had no idea it would be their last night together.

The brothers were very different, and her marriage to each man was also different. She'd loved Jude from the very beginning and never doubted he loved her in return. She'd married Ezra in obedience to the law, not for love, wanting a son to carry Jude's name. She never dreamed she would grow to love Ezra or find so much joy with this quiet, introspective man, the father of her children. Devorah often thought of her first husband, but she had now been married to Ezra nearly three times as long as to Jude.

She listened to Ezra's steady heartbeat as she lay in his arms and knew he was still awake. "You're not sleeping?" she whispered.

"I can't. I'm nervous and excited and hopeful and cautious all at the same time."

"Do you suppose that's how Moses felt the night before he went to speak to Pharaoh?" she asked, trying to lighten his mood.

"Perhaps." She heard the smile in his voice. "I'm wishing I had his miraculous powers. A staff that transformed into a snake might help. Or the ability to turn the Euphrates River into blood."

"You have the same God as Moses on your side."

"That's true."

"I wish I knew how long you'll be gone."

"You'd better plan on at least six months. But long or short, we're determined to wait in Susa and not give up until our petition has been heard and granted."

"I don't know how to say good-bye for that long." She nestled closer, savoring his warmth, realizing how very much she would miss him. "Tell me the truth, Ezra. Is this trip dangerous? Could you die?" She hadn't dared to ask before now, but with his caravan loaded and ready to leave at dawn, she needed to know.

"It's a two-hundred-fifty-mile trip, so I suppose there are certain dangers along the way. I don't know much about traveling since I've only been out of this city once before, years ago, to visit Casiphia. But I think the biggest danger is the risk the Persian king will interpret our petition as a bid for independence from the empire and as rebellion against his authority—in which case I suppose he'll execute us."

Devorah shuddered. "I promise I'll pray every day and ask the Holy One to keep you safe."

"Thank you, but it's much more important to ask God to give us success in convincing the king."

"Fine. I'll tell the Almighty One Ezra's safety doesn't matter—only his petition."

He tightened his arm around her shoulder, laughing softly. "All right, Devorah. You may ask for both. . . . If I'm successful, and the king grants another decree like the one under King Cyrus, you'll face the daunting challenge of leaving Babylon and traveling to Jerusalem to start a new life. This is the only home you and our children have ever known. Jude and your parents are all buried here. Does it bother you to leave here?"

"My grandfather wished he could return to the Promised Land. He would often say, 'I wish I could go home.' The way he talked about Jerusalem made me long to see it, too. But I sometimes wonder if we're too old to start a brand-new life. I'm thirty-eight and you're nearly fifty. There are so many unknowns in such a journey."

"But do you want to go with me, Devorah? I can't leave tomorrow without asking you that question. I want you by my side when I return to Jerusalem more than anything else—but you don't have to come. You can stay here with Jude's son and raise him here, if that's what you want."

She started to speak, but he stopped her. "No, listen. I know you didn't love me when we married. And I know we've been too busy in the years since then to talk about our feelings for each other very often. One of my greatest failings as a husband is that I'm not very good at expressing how I feel. But I want you to know I've grown to love you, Devorah—more than I ever could have imagined. God knew what He was doing when He made you my wife. I've never dared to hope you could love me as much as Jude. But I'm thankful every single day that you agreed to marry me."

Devorah's eyes filled with tears. She hugged Ezra tightly, struggling to control her overflowing emotions so she could speak. "You've shown me your love, Ezra. Jude grabbed a sword and fought to protect me from a physical enemy. You're willing to fight an invisible enemy, not only for my sake but for our children's sakes. You're taking your life in your hands and daring to approach the king—for us. That's love." She released him and pulled back to take his face in her hands and look into his eyes. "I never thought I would love any man as much as I loved Jude. But I do love you, Ezra—just as much as him. Maybe more because we've had more years together." Tears filled his eyes at her words. "I'll miss you when you're away and grieve your absence just as I grieved for Jude. And of course I'll go with you to Jerusalem. There's no doubt in my mind that my place is by your side."

"I'll miss you," he whispered.

"And I'll miss you, too. More than words can say."

Neither of them slept well, and morning came much too soon. Devorah held her husband one last time while they were still alone for one final, tearful good-bye. "I hate that my work takes me away from you for so long," Ezra said. "I hate leaving you and the children all alone. I'm so sorry."

"Asher will look after us. Your work is more important. When God grants you success, it will change our people's lives. It will change history."

"Amen . . . I think I understand why God said, 'It's not good for man to be alone.' You show me a side of the Holy One I don't see in myself: His compassion. I'm too hard on people, too impatient with them. I'm always afraid if I show mercy, people will use it as an excuse to sin. You've helped me temper the law with His grace. And you've made countless sacrifices so I could do the work God gave me. And now I'm asking for one more. Can you forgive me for leaving you?"

"Of course I forgive you. Just be safe. And come back to us soon."

He started toward the door, and Devorah bent to fold up their bedding. But Ezra halted and turned back to her. "I've been trying to think of what to say to our children, and it's almost harder than planning my words to the King of Persia. I know they're too young to understand the importance of what I'm doing. The twins, especially, seem resentful that they have to share their father with the entire community. And now my work will take me away for many months."

"They aren't resentful. It's just hard for them to be the sons of such a great man."

"I'm not a great man. I'm a servant of God, as we all are. It's just that He has called me to serve Him as a leader."

"The boys don't understand that now, but someday they will. They're good children at heart and not rebellious in a bad way. I know they love and admire you."

"I may have to miss their bar mitzvah. Will they forgive me for that?"

"Ask them."

She set aside the bedding and held him close one last time, then went out to the courtyard to fix breakfast. Ezra had decided to leave right after eating, the way he always did, as if merely going off to another day of work. Ezra and the twins would walk to the house of assembly together to pray, then the boys would go to the yeshiva, and Ezra would leave for Susa. Devorah whispered a prayer for him as he prepared to give them his parting instructions.

"As I get ready to leave for Susa to ask the king of Persia to let our people go," Ezra began, "I've been thinking about Moses. He had two sons, just as I do. Do you remember their names?"

The twins thought for a moment. "One was Gershom . . ."

" . . . and the other was Eliezer."

"Yes. Very good. And what are they remembered for?"

The boys looked at each other, dumbfounded. Devorah didn't know the answer, either. "We've never heard anything about them," Shallum finally replied.

"And maybe that's a good thing," Ezra said. "Too often, we hear about a person only when he does something wrong or something great. And that's my wish for all of my children. I hope I hear stories about your greatness when I get home—or else nothing at all."

"We promise, Abba." The boys grinned, and Devorah knew they understood their father's attempt at humor. But where would she find the wisdom to deal with the twins all alone while he was gone?

"I know I can count on you boys to take care of your mother and sisters for me," he continued. "But don't be in a hurry to grow up. I'll miss so much as it is. Most painful for me is not hearing you read Torah for the first time in the house of assembly. I hope you can forgive me for not being there on such an important day. Sharing your father for the Holy One's work can be your offering to Him, your sacrifice. All of us would like to do great things for God, brave and memorable things, but He's asking you to live without your father for several months. Can you do that willingly?"

"Yes," Judah said. "But we'll miss you, Abba." Shallum nodded.

"Pretend I'm in the next room. Live as if I were." He stood, and Devorah knew he wanted to leave before they all began to weep. First, he said a tender good-bye to Jude's daughters. Abigail was seventeen and betrothed to a fine young man from the community. Ezra had made the arrangements, but he didn't know if he would return in time for her wedding. "I'm sorry, Abigail. It's such an important day for you, and I should—"

"It's okay, Uncle Ezra. I understand." She gave him an embrace.

"And you, Michal. You will be a grown woman by the time I return. Maybe you'll be in love by then, as well."

Devorah watched Jude's daughters hug Ezra good-bye, knowing how much they'd grown to love him, the only father they remembered. And he loved them, too. Then he knelt down and opened his arms to their three youngest daughters. "Come here," he said. "Look, I have tears in my eyes. See? Remember these tears when you're angry with me for being so far away. Remember how very sad I was to leave you. Only the Holy One could take me away from your mother and you. For no other reason would I leave you. But I believe God commands me to go and speak to the king. Sometimes He asks us to do very hard things, and we must obey Him."

Devorah wiped her eyes, thinking what a tender, softhearted man Ezra was beneath the tough, unyielding exterior he presented to their community. And also how much he had changed in the years since they'd married. They gave each other one last, lingering hug. "Be safe," she whispered. Then she stood with her daughters at the gate, waving to him as he walked to the house of assembly with their sons.

"We won't let Abba out of our sight again when he comes home, will we Mama?" her youngest daughter said.

"No, we certainly won't." She had lost Jude, and now she was losing Ezra. But he had never been hers to keep. He belonged to the Almighty One and to the people He'd been called to lead. He turned and gave a final wave, wiping tears from his eyes, before disappearing around the corner.

THE PERSIAN CAPITAL OF SUSA

Ezra stood in the courtyard outside the king's throne room, waiting for his audience with King Artaxerxes. After weeks of traveling and months of waiting, the day he'd hoped for had come at last. Ezra had fasted and prayed in preparation for this meeting, and now he felt weak with hunger. Even so, he had vowed not to eat today until he'd spoken to the king.

The enormous royal palace covered an area as large as Ezra's entire Jewish community of tightly packed homes in Babylon. Built on three hilltops, the compound had been designed to fill the king's subjects with awe—and it accomplished that purpose. Ezra had only glimpsed it from a distance before today, and as he had crossed the bridge to enter the gate to the immense palace, his knees began to tremble. Security was tight, and he was surprised to learn that ever since the days when Mordecai was in power, the king entrusted his safety only to Ezra's fellow Jews. It seemed a good sign.

Ezra and the other elders had passed through an outer courtyard, then followed the chamberlain through a maze of hallways. They'd glimpsed the enormous *apadna* used for formal ceremonies, its towering pillars taller than any trees Ezra had ever seen, each topped with a pair of carved bulls. He and his delegation had ended up here in a smaller, inner courtyard where they'd been told to wait.

The elders who'd accompanied Ezra this morning remained silent, aware he had a lot on his mind and heart. He knew he should rehearse his speech and review everything the king's seven advisors had told him about approaching the great ruler of the Persian Empire. They had explained about body language and government protocol and cultural taboos and expectations. But all Ezra could think about was Devorah, and how very much he missed her. He longed for her words of encouragement to keep him from getting disheartened, her kisses, her embrace to strengthen him. He thought of his sons and daughters, as well, wondering if raising their seven children alone these past four and a half months was becoming too much for Devorah. Would she remember to ask Asher for help with the twins if she needed it? Ezra had just closed his eyes, trying to picture Devorah's face, when he heard his name being called.

"Ezra ben Seraiah."

He whirled around to face the chamberlain. "Yes?"

"His Majesty will see you now."

Ezra's knees went weak. He took a moment to whisper a final, desperate prayer as he smoothed his hair and beard and straightened his rumpled tunic. *God of Abraham, give me the right words to say. Move the king's heart to let our people go home.* It was all he had time for. The chamberlain opened the door, and Ezra walked down a hall and through two more sets of doors, alone.

The king's advisors had counseled him to go alone, saying it would be better for Ezra to approach King Artaxerxes un-accompanied. He would appear less threatening as a solitary petitioner making the request on behalf of his people. Ezra's first surprise was that the room was more modest than he expected.

When he'd first arrived in Susa and saw the city's magnificent palaces and buildings, he'd felt insignificant in comparison, the rustic leader of an unsophisticated, enslaved people. He saw idols everywhere, and it was impossible to avert his eyes because there was no place else to look. Susa was a city of splendor—it was the only word to describe it. But this modest throne room where King Artaxerxes sat waiting for him wasn't designed to impress the visitor with the king's might and power.

Ezra remembered to halt a respectful distance from the throne, remembered to bow low the way the advisors had instructed him. *The hand of the Lord our God is with me,* he told himself. He swallowed, found his voice, and said, "Your Majesty, King Artaxerxes, I am Ezra ben Seraiah, your humble servant."

"You've come with a petition?" the king asked.

"Yes, Your Majesty."

"You may rise." Ezra stood and handed the document he and the elders had drawn up to the chamberlain. The servant carried it to the king.

"Summarize this petition for me," Artaxerxes said as he scrolled through it.

"Your Majesty, I'm requesting that you allow my people, the Jews, to return to our homeland of Judah in the Trans-Euphrates Province. We were exiled when the Babylonian king, Nebuchadnezzar, invaded our nation nearly 130 years ago and carried us to Babylon. One of your predecessors, His Majesty King Cyrus, allowed some of our forefathers to return and rebuild the temple of our God. We're now requesting permission for more of us to return so we may worship the God of our ancestors in the city where our forefathers are buried."

The king glanced at the petition, then asked, "What does my empire stand to gain from granting your request?"

Ezra wasn't prepared for this question. But he recalled that the Persians had recently suffered a defeat by the Egyptians, and he scrambled to think of a way to use that information in his favor. "If you study a map of the Trans-Euphrates Province, Your Majesty, you'll see that my nation of Judah sits at the crossroads of that region. If you allow us to return, my people will establish a secure foothold in the province for you, a buffer state, on the border of Egypt. Not only can we be your eyes and ears in that region, but you could benefit from having our powerful God as your ally. The current population of Judah is very small, but a restored population would provide you with military and economic advantages. Our God has promised to prosper our people if we live according His laws, and if we prosper, then you and your empire also prospers."

"Is that your motivation? You're asking this for the good of my empire?"

Ezra's heart skipped a beat. The advisors had warned him to swear his allegiance to the Persian king as often and as heartily as he could. But Ezra couldn't lie. "No, Your Majesty," he said, shaking his head. "I confess my sole motivation is to serve my God. Loyalty to Him comes first and foremost. My people want to please Him and live in obedience to Him under the terms of His covenant with us. We can't do that as long as we're exiled from our homeland and our temple. The God we worship has given us very specific directions for how to live and serve Him, and many of those laws are impossible to keep in Babylon. Our God promises to bless us and prosper us when we live by His rules, and that's what we're asking to do. Of course, we will be greatly indebted to you if you allow us to emigrate freely, and we will be loyal, faithful servants to you in return."

"Did you say some of your people have emigrated before?"

"Yes, about eighty years ago under King Cyrus. His decree gave our fathers permission to go up to Jerusalem and rebuild God's temple. My petition asks you to allow more of us to return and to establish the province of Judah under the laws of our God."

"Are you asking to govern this region yourself?"

"No, Your Majesty. No. I am one of the Almighty One's priests, the descendant of a family of priests. I wish only to fulfill that calling. I also serve as a teacher, specializing in matters concerning the laws and commands of our God. My people were carried into exile because we failed to obey those commands, and so my goals are to investigate the state of things in Judah, to make sure the province is governed by the Torah, and to teach people to fear and obey our God."

"Suppose I grant only you permission to go?"

Ezra caught his breath. "That would be unacceptable. I speak on behalf of many others who also wish to serve our God and live according to His laws."

The king silently studied Ezra's written petition, then looked up at him again, his eyes cold. "Are you requesting anything else from me for your journey? Travel expenses? Soldiers for protection?"

Ezra hadn't thought to ask for a military escort, trying to keep his petition short and simple. Now he was afraid to ask for an escort or expenses, fearing they would make his petition too costly for the king to consider, especially after his military losses. "No, Your Majesty. I'm not asking for anything else. The gracious hand of our God will be with us."

The king handed the petition to the chamberlain. "Put this with the others. . . . I will consider your request, Ezra son of Seraiah, and give you my decision when I'm ready. You may go."

Ezra bowed again. "Thank you, Your Majesty. And may the God I serve prosper your reign."

As soon as he returned to the courtyard, Ezra sank down on a bench, his legs too unsteady to carry him further. The others quickly gathered around him. "What happened? What did the king say?"

"He asked me a few questions, then said he would consider our petition and let us know. Our meeting flew by so fast and . . . and I can't even remember everything I said. I tried to keep it simple, but I wasn't prepared for some of the questions he asked."

One of the elders turned to the king's advisor. "What happens now?"

"Now you wait."

Ezra returned to the house in the Jewish section of Susa where he and the elders had been staying. As they waited for one week, then two, Ezra's mood went up and down, from hope to despair and back again, as if riding a cart through mountainous terrain. He spent some days thinking about the temple, imagining himself serving as a priest alongside his sons, picturing his family in Jerusalem, God's holy city. Other days, he resigned himself to living the remainder of his life in Babylon if the king rejected his request.

He missed his family. Whenever Ezra found himself worrying about Devorah and his children, he would try to pray and turn them over to the safety of God's hand. But sometimes the burden of fear and worry would descend as he imagined his sons standing at the foot of the great ziggurat in the center of Babylon, gazing up at it with admiration. He would recall the Persian king's cold stare and be certain he would refuse their petition. Again and again, Ezra would close his eyes and pray, trying to focus his thoughts on the Holy One's promise: *"Even if you have been banished to the most distant land . . . God will gather you and bring you back,"* and trust that He would show mercy and return His people to Jerusalem.

Midway through the third week of waiting, one of the king's messengers arrived where Ezra and the others were staying. Ezra's heart began to race the moment he saw the Persian. "Do you bring good news?" he asked.

"The king's seven advisors will meet with you and your delegation tomorrow in the council chamber," he replied.

Ezra felt a stab of disappointment. The meeting would be with the advisors, not the king. In the council chamber, not the palace. "I hope this isn't a bad sign," he told the others. *Tomorrow.* How would he ever sleep tonight?

"Whether it's good news or bad," one of the elders said, "at least we can finally return to our families."

Ezra rose at dawn the next morning to pray, then walked with the others to the council chamber. He tried to read the advisors' faces for a clue to the king's decision, but it proved impossible. At last the chief counselor entered and handed Ezra a document. "The king addressed this letter to you," he said. "Personally."

"To me?" Ezra slipped his thumb beneath the Persian king's official seal to read the letter out loud, his heart racing with a mixture of excitement and dread:

> "'Artaxerxes, king of kings,
>   To Ezra the priest, a teacher of the Law of the God of heaven:
>   Greetings.
>   Now I decree that any of the Israelites in my kingdom, including priests and Levites, who wish to go to Jerusalem with you may go . . .'"

Ezra had to pause as a flood of emotion choked him. The king was allowing them to go! He closed his eyes and silently praised God. When he could continue, he cleared his throat, reading the blurred words through his tears.

> "'You are sent by the king and his seven advisors to inquire about Judah and Jerusalem with regard to the Law of your God, which will be in your hand.'"

He had to stop again. Not only would they be allowed to return, but they had permission to accomplish what Ezra had hoped for most—permission to govern their nation according to the standards of the Torah. He wiped his eyes so he could continue to read.

"'Moreover, you are to take with you the silver and gold that the king and his advisers have freely given to the God of Israel, whose dwelling is in Jerusalem . . .'"

Ezra looked up. "He's giving us gold and silver?" he asked in astonishment.

"Yes," the chief advisor said. "Keep reading. The letter explains why."

"' . . . together with all the silver and gold you may obtain from the province of Babylon, as well as the freewill offerings of the people and priests for the temple of their God in Jerusalem.'"

"We never asked for all this," he said to his companions. "Money from the province of Babylon, too? We wouldn't have dared to imagine such generosity." He cleared his throat and looked down at the letter again.

"'With this money be sure to buy bulls, rams, and male lambs, together with their grain offerings and drink offerings, and sacrifice them on the altar of the temple of your God in Jerusalem.'"

He had to pause again. "I don't know what I said to move the king's heart this way. He wants to sacrifice to the Almighty One." Ezra shook his head in speechless wonder before returning to the letter.

"'You and your brother Jews may then do whatever seems best with the rest of the silver and gold, in accordance with the will of your God. Deliver to the God of Jerusalem all the articles entrusted to you for worship in the temple of your God. And anything else needed for the temple of your God that you may have occasion to supply, you may provide from the royal treasury.'"

Ezra wondered if he was dreaming. As he continued to read the letter, it explained how the king had ordered the treasurer of Trans-Euphrates Province to supply whatever Ezra asked for—enormous amounts of silver and wheat, wine, olive oil, and salt without limit. Artaxerxes claimed he wanted to gain the Holy One's protection and favor, asking, *"Why should there be wrath against the realm of the king and of his sons?"* Furthermore, the priests, Levites, and temple servants would be exempt from all taxes, tribute, and duty.

"'And you, Ezra, in accordance with the wisdom of your God, which you possess, appoint magistrates and judges to administer justice to all the people of Trans-Euphrates. . . .'"

He looked up at the chief counselor again. "Wait. Why am I singled out, here? Surely the king doesn't mean that I'm in charge—"

"It's exactly what he means. King Artaxerxes has appointed you governor of the province of Judah. He was impressed that you didn't try to flatter him or lie to him in order to gain what you wanted. He said such integrity was rare in his empire."

"But I'm not qualified to be governor. I never asked to be in charge. Not of the entire province."

"That's precisely why he appointed you—because you didn't ask to rule. The king doesn't want leaders who grasp for power and pose a threat to his sovereignty."

"But Judah should be governed by a descendant of our king, from the House of David."

The counselor shook his head. "King Artaxerxes doesn't want your king or your princes or any of their descendants to sit on the throne. He wants you."

"You must accept the position, Ezra," one of the counselors urged. "If you refuse, the king might change his mind."

Ezra lowered his head, tugging his beard. "All I asked for was permission to return to Jerusalem and be a priest. I want to study Torah, not run a province." But he would obey the king's order because it meant his people also could return home. They would live securely in their land and serve their God.

"Is that the end of the letter?" another elder asked. Ezra shook his head and finished reading.

> "'And you, Ezra, administer justice to all the people of Trans-Euphrates—all who know the laws of your God. And you are to teach any who do not know them. Whoever does not obey the law of your God and the law of the king must surely be punished by death, banishment, confiscation of property, or imprisonment.'"

"Does he mean . . . I'm to teach God's law to all the people of the province? Not just the Jews?" Ezra asked.

"Yes. By order of King Artaxerxes."

Ezra dropped to his knees in the council room, his heart so full it overflowed. "Praise the Almighty One," he said, lifting his hands. "The hand of the Lord our God is surely on us!"

Ezra thought of Devorah and his children again as he and the elders hurried back to the Jewish section of town to relay the good news. He longed to see his wife, never imagining he could miss someone as much as he missed her. He wondered how quickly he and the elders could pack up and go home.

"Good news!" he told his fellow Jews. "The king has granted our petition! Today we have seen God's promise fulfilled."

Ezra made a copy of the king's letter that night, adding it to the journal he'd kept since leaving home:

Praise be to the Lord, the God of our fathers, who has put it into the king's heart to bring honor to the house of the Lord in Jerusalem in this way and who has extended His good favor to me before the king and his advisers and all the king's powerful officials.

On the return trip, Ezra pushed his caravan to travel as far and as fast as they possibly could each day, resting only on the Sabbath. He had watched the moon's phases and realized it still might be possible to arrive home in time to see Judah and Shallum become Sons of the Commandments. On the final week of the journey, he prodded everyone to start moving before dawn each day and didn't stop traveling until well after sunset. He would have gladly run all the way home if he'd had the strength. They reached the blue-tiled gates of Babylon on the very evening of his sons' bar mitzvah, and Ezra left the caravan behind to race to the Jewish section of the city alone, praying he wasn't too late.

The house of assembly was packed for evening prayers when he arrived. Ezra stood in the rear to watch, too dusty and sweaty from his final, frantic sprint to venture further inside. Tears of joy and pride filled his eyes when he saw his sons standing side by side on the bimah with the Torah scroll open in front of them. Shallum was about to read the passage Ezra had practiced with him, but he halted, distracted, when he looked up and saw his father. Judah saw Ezra, too, and as the boys grinned at him and gave a little wave, other members of the congregation turned around to see why. Ezra smiled as he wiped his tears and motioned to Shallum to keep reading. He listened with pride as both his sons read flawlessly.

Afterward, everyone gathered around Ezra in the plaza outside. He saw his beautiful wife and couldn't wait to hold her in his arms. But first he quieted the crowd, saying he had an announcement to make. "The hand of the Lord our God was upon us, and the king of Persia has granted our petition. Sons and daughters of Abraham, we're going home to the Promised Land!" The huge cheer that followed this news was deafening.

At last the crowd dispersed and Devorah came to him, taking his arm as they walked home with their children. She looked up at him and smiled. "I think I'd better start packing."

CHAPTER

37

BABYLON

E zra tried not to awaken his household as he crept through the gate into his courtyard on weary legs. The sun had set hours ago, and he assumed everyone was asleep by now, but he saw a lamp burning, the coals on the hearth glowing faintly, and Devorah sitting beneath the stars as she waited up for him. "I'm sorry I'm so late," he said. "I had no idea what an enormous undertaking it is to move thousands of people from Babylon to Jerusalem. There's still so much to think about and plan and organize, and we're leaving in a matter of days and—"

"You missed supper," Devorah said, rising to greet him with a kiss. "Again! I saved you some soup. It's on the hearth, so I think it's still warm. And there's bread, too. Are you hungry?"

"Yes. I completely forgot to eat."

She shook her head at him, a mild rebuke. "If you keep skipping meals, you're going to starve to death right here in Babylon and never make it to Jerusalem." She gestured for him to sit and ladled out a bowl of soup, setting it and the bread in front of him. "Did you forget how to sit down and eat a decent meal?" she asked when he remained standing. "Shall I feed it to you, too?"

Ezra managed a smile as he sank down. It felt good to relax.

The fragrant smell of lentils and onions made his stomach rumble as he lifted the first spoonful to his mouth. "People keep changing their minds, Devorah—we're staying, we're going, we're staying—what can I do with such people?"

"I wouldn't want your job," she said. "It's hard enough getting our household packed and ready. I wouldn't want to be responsible for thousands of people and all their baggage. No wonder you're exhausted. No wonder you haven't been sleeping."

He ate several more spoonfuls and tore off a piece of the bread. The warmth of the hearth beside him dispelled the night air. "Please don't share this with anyone, Devorah, but my biggest concern is safeguarding the gold and silver we're transporting. King Artaxerxes donated enormous amounts, plus more gold from the province of Babylon and all the freewill contributions we've collected. I have no idea how we'll get it there safely."

"What did Prince Zerubbabel do when his group traveled to Jerusalem with the temple treasures? They had huge quantities of gold and silver, too, didn't they?"

"Yes, but King Cyrus sent Persian soldiers to guard the prince's caravan."

"Won't we have soldiers this time?"

"I was ashamed to ask the king for them after assuring him our God keeps His hand on everyone who looks to Him. How could I ask for human protection after such a testimony?"

She looked at him for a long moment. "Do you believe what you told the king? That God protects His people?"

"Of course, but—" He saw her smiling. "Oh. I see your point."

"Everyone is praying, aren't they?" she asked. "The Almighty One already performed a miracle to bring this about. I think you can stop worrying, Ezra."

"You're right, you're right." But after finishing his soup and bread, he found himself worrying all over again. "I've been so overwhelmed that I haven't had time to ask if you need my help here at home."

"The children helped me pack."

"And what about Abigail and her new husband? They're still coming, right?"

"They wouldn't miss this trip for anything."

"And Asher and his family?"

"Your brother is ready—but he's still fussing over all the things he'll need to learn once he gets there to serve as a priest. You should hear him." She mimicked Asher's nasal whine as she said, "'Studying Torah and killing lambs at my age? Maybe I should just make pots in Jerusalem, instead.'" Ezra smiled at Devorah's imitation, easily imagining his brother's frenzied fussing. "Asher's sons are looking forward to being priests, too," Devorah continued. "And so are our sons, by the way."

"Just like our ancestors," Ezra said in wonder. "It's so amazing. A few months ago I worried about our boys turning into Babylonians. Now they'll be priests! Only God could have performed such a miracle. But what I don't understand is why every Jew in the empire isn't packing to come with us. Why remain in exile and live among these filthy Gentiles when we can return to our homeland? I just tallied the final numbers a little while ago and I was astounded by how very few of us have chosen to return."

"We were exiled well over one hundred years ago, Ezra. I guess a lot of people think of Babylon as their home now." She picked up his empty bowl. "Are you still hungry? There's more soup."

He shook his head. "Everyone is free! We can leave this idolatrous place. Everyone should leap at the chance to go home! I told the Jews I met in Susa they were free to come, too, but none of them are joining us."

"You can't condemn those who remain behind, Ezra. God is the judge of their hearts and motives. You provided the opportunity and helped open the door. Now they're accountable to God for the choices they make. A lot of Jews have prospered here. They probably don't want to give it all up for the unknown."

"But they've seen how quickly our lives can change, how unexpectedly a new king can come to power and give our enemies a chance to destroy us. Are our people's memories that short? We commemorate Haman's terrible decree every year on the Fourteenth of Adar. What am I doing wrong? Weren't my speeches inspiring enough? How can I convince more people of the need to leave this place?"

"Remember what God told Samuel when they demanded a king?" Devorah asked. "He said, they aren't rejecting you, they're rejecting God."

Ezra rubbed his tired eyes. "Rejecting God is even worse."

"Are you sure you don't want more to eat?" Devorah asked, gesturing to his bowl.

"I'm sure," he said with a sigh. "I've lost my appetite."

"Come to bed, then. And stop worrying. Trust God."

Four days later, Ezra led his family and a long line of wagons and camels and donkeys through the towering blue and gold gates of Babylon. He didn't look back. They traveled for only a few days before setting up camp near the Ahava Canal to wait for Jews from other cities to join them for the nine-hundred-mile journey.

Devorah looked exhausted as they ate dinner after the first leg of their journey. She went into their tent to put the children to sleep and didn't come back. Ezra knew she had probably fallen asleep alongside them. He couldn't relax enough to sleep, so he sat across the campfire from his brother Asher, who was keeping the coals alive on this cool spring night. Ezra opened his journal and began to write in the dim light:

Because the hand of the Lord my God was on me, I took courage and gathered leading men from Israel to go up

*with me. I assembled them at the canal that flows toward
Ahava, and we camped there three days. . . .*

He paused to read over the lists of family heads as he recorded
them in his journal, and he made a startling discovery. "Asher!
There aren't any Levites traveling with us! Not a single one on
any of these lists!"

"What difference does that make?" Asher asked, poking the
coals with a stick.

"I've been commissioned by the king of the Persian Empire
to offer his sacrifices and to draw our nation back to God—and
there aren't any Levites to help do that. Levites are integral to
our worship as assistants and musicians. We need them to be
teachers and judges. What am I going to do?"

"You can't really blame them, can you?" Asher asked. "Aren't
most of their tasks menial ones? Who would want to leave the
comforts of Babylon to be a temple servant?"

"No task is menial in God's sight. We all have a part to
play. As the psalmist wrote, 'I would rather be a doorkeeper
in the house of my God than dwell in the tents of the wicked.'
And that's one of the Levites' most important jobs—to serve
as temple guards and doorkeepers." He lowered his voice and
added, "In fact, we could use them right now to help guard all
this treasure we're hauling. I wish I knew where to find some
Levites so I could convince them to come."

Asher continued poking the coals, then suddenly looked up.
"Hey! What about that city where we bought the swords? Remember? Weren't there several families of Levites who'd been
exiled there?"

"You mean Casiphia?"

"Yes. That blacksmith . . . what was his name? He told us he
was a Levite, remember? And he had a son."

"We're not far from Casiphia. I'll send a delegation of elders
there first thing tomorrow to try to convince them to come."

"Why not go yourself, Ezra? You can be very convincing. I gave up Abba's pottery business to come with you, didn't I?"

"I can't leave the caravan," Ezra said, lowering his voice again. "I feel responsible for all this treasure we're carrying. In fact, Devorah suggested I call for a day of fasting and prayer to ask for God's protection. But you could go with the delegation in my place. You could recruit the blacksmith we met and his son."

"Sure. I'll go," Asher said.

Ezra stayed up long after Asher went to bed, compiling a list of twelve trusted men to send to Casiphia, including nine elders and two of his fellow scholars. He hoped the scholars could convince the Levites of the importance of their calling.

As the smoldering fire gave away the last of its heat, Ezra recorded the names of the men he'd chosen in his journal and went to bed.

CASIPHIA

Reuben's life had fallen into a numbing routine of stay-ing out late, drinking too much, sleeping until noon, and then waking up to do it all over again. He knew his mother was frustrated and worried about him, but as long as he supported them—using the stolen gold—he figured she had no right to criticize him. After all, he was an adult, twenty-seven years old. Tonight as Reuben ate dinner with his family, Mama skirted around the subjects they usually argued over and raised the subject of marriage.

"Don't you ever think about settling down and finding a nice wife, Reuben? There are so many lovely girls to choose from in our community. And I could use a daughter-in-law's help around here," she added, "now that your sisters have married and moved to their own households."

"I know you miss them, Mama. But no, I'm not interested in marriage. I like things the way they are."

"But you don't seem very happy to me."

"I'm fine. Don't worry about me." He sopped up the last bite of stew with his bread, eager to leave and end this conversation.

"Your boss keeps asking me when you're coming back to work."

"Never," he said calmly, setting down his bowl. "I already told you I'll never work for him again. And I also told you not to worry—I have enough money for us to live on for a long, long time."

She rested her hand on his knee. "It isn't only the money. I hate to see you just . . . drifting . . . all day. You go out every night who knows where, and—"

"And I'm going out tonight, too." He rose to his feet, stretching his back and arms as he stood. His friends were making plans for another big robbery, and he'd offered to help them. Reuben still had his cache of gold from the last robbery and didn't need to steal, but his friends had spent nearly all of theirs in lavish living. They were good companions and the only friends Reuben had, but stealing no longer thrilled him. Now that his father's shop was lost to him, he had no other goals. If Mama were to ask him what he wanted in life, he wouldn't know what to say.

He was preparing to leave a few minutes later when a stranger arrived at his family's gate. "Are you Reuben ben David?" the man asked.

"Who's asking?" He tensed, ready to run, always fearing the day when the authorities would come to arrest him. Should he answer the man or turn around and bolt through the rear door? His younger brother stood a few feet away, watching and listening. The stranger smiled.

"I don't know if you remember me or not, but my name is Asher ben Seraiah. My brother Ezra and I visited your blacksmith shop about fifteen years ago to purchase weapons for the Jewish community in Babylon."

Reuben shrugged, vaguely remembering the night the two men had come. "I guess so. Why?"

"You were just a boy, I suppose. But your father said your family descended from the tribe of Levi. I don't know if you've heard the news, but King Artaxerxes is allowing us to return to our homeland in Judah." The man wore a stupid grin on his face as if Reuben should be thrilled to hear the news.

His younger brother pushed forward. "Yes! They told us about the decree in the house of assembly." And Reuben's brother, who prayed with the other men every day, had told Reuben about it. But the news had nothing to do with him.

"I've come to Casiphia looking for Levites who want to join us and return to the Promised Land," the man continued. "I'd like to invite you and your father to come with us and serve in the Holy One's temple in Jerusalem."

"My father is dead," Reuben said. "He died in battle on the Thirteenth of Adar."

The stranger stopped grinning. "I'm so sorry to hear that."

"Who is it, Reuben?" his mother asked, coming up behind him.

"Someone from Babylon. They're looking for Levites to go to Jerusalem with them."

"Oh! Please, come in," Mama said. "Let me fix you something to eat." She opened the gate and led the man inside, gesturing to where they had just finished eating. "Please, have a seat. We heard that some of our people were returning to the Promised Land. Are you traveling with them? Are you part of that caravan that's camped by the Ahava Canal?"

"Yes, ma'am, I am. My name is Asher ben Seraiah. Please, don't fuss," he added, but Mama was already laying out bowls of stew and olives and dates, and a basket of bread.

"Run and fetch Uncle Hashabiah," she told Reuben's brother. "Tell him about our guest. Reuben, sit down and be hospitable for a few minutes while I get our guest something to drink." She hurried off to the storage room before Reuben could protest.

"So, you must be a Levite, too, Reuben. Are you interested in joining us?" Asher asked.

"What do you need Levites for?" He edged toward the gate,

unwilling to sit, needing to leave before his uncle arrived. Reuben would find it hard not to spit in Hashabiah's face.

"Well, Levites serve in the Almighty One's temple in many capacities—as guards, as singers and musicians, as assistants to the priests when they offer the holy sacrifices. It's a very important and sacred calling. And for now, any Levites who join us will be entrusted with guarding the wealth of gold and silver our caravan is transporting."

At the mention of gold, Reuben suddenly became interested. "You're carrying gold? What's it for?"

"The donations are to help us get settled in Judah and to purchase sacrifices for the Holy One's temple. It's the Levites' job to guard the temple's treasures. And you certainly look like a strong, capable young man, just right for the job."

"Who's guarding the gold now? Don't you have Persian soldiers traveling with you?"

"No, we decided to take care of it ourselves. Your tribe has a long, important history of security work like this. Solomon's temple had a wealth of gold, too, and the Levites were always the custodians of it. They also served as singers and musicians. Can you sing, by any chance?"

"No. I'm a blacksmith. At least I was."

"We certainly could use a fine young man like you. Do you know how to use a sword?"

"Yes, of course I do."

"Great! Would you consider coming with us? Believe me, you'll be a valuable member of the Holy's One's temple staff."

"I don't think so."

"Why not, Reuben?" Mama asked. She had returned with a skin of wine and stood off to the side, listening. "Why not consider it since you don't want to work in the shop anymore? You seem so unhappy here, and this would give you a fresh start."

"There's nothing in Jerusalem that's any different from here," he replied. The last thing he wanted to do was travel nine hundred miles with a group of people he despised, to worship a God he no longer believed in. But he didn't speak those thoughts out loud, unwilling to hurt his mother. "I'm not interested. I'm going out."

"Nice seeing you again, Reuben. Let me know if you change your mind. We need you!"

He hurried away without bothering to reply, determined to meet up with his gang in their usual hideout. But as he walked through Casiphia's streets he couldn't stop thinking about the caravan to Jerusalem. What would it be like to travel far away and visit new places? There was nothing keeping him here in Casiphia anymore. Unlike his uncle, who considered him a wayward son, Asher ben Seraiah had called him a fine young man and said he could make an important contribution. The only people who had ever told him he was valuable were his father and the Babylonian friends who'd recruited him for their gang. The idea of serving as a Levite guard would have been tantalizing except for the fact that it involved his fellow Jews and their religion.

"You're late tonight, Reuben," Bear said in greeting. "What kept you?"

Reuben ducked his head as he entered the cavelike room. In spite of all the money his gang had stolen over the years, they'd never fixed up their hideout near the river. It was still the same cold, dreary room they'd brought Reuben to on the night they'd asked him to join them. His friends slouched around on the same damp, tattered cushions, passing a skin of wine.

"I had a visitor—all the way from Babylon," Reuben replied. "He's with a caravan of Jews on their way to Jerusalem."

"Why was he visiting you?" Digger asked as he passed Reuben the wineskin.

Reuben gave a short laugh. "He was trying to recruit me to come with them and guard a shipment of gold they're transporting."

"Hey, I heard about the caravan," Nib said. "They're camping near the Ahava Canal, aren't they? I heard they had thousands of people with them."

"Yeah, I guess so. The man told me they're transporting a load of gold and silver to Jerusalem. A 'wealth' of it, he said. They don't have enough men to guard it, so he asked me to come along and help."

"If he only knew," Bear said, laughing. Reuben thought it was amusing, as well.

But Digger didn't seem to think it was funny at all as he leaned toward Reuben, his expression serious. "Hey, no joking, Reuben. If they're really carrying a poorly guarded shipment of gold, we could strike it rich!"

Bear's smile faded, too. "He's right. And if they're asking you to help guard it, why not do it, Reuben? You could be our inside man. Find out exactly where the gold is kept and come up with a plan for how to steal it. Then tip us off."

"I don't know . . . I still have a bag of gold from our last robbery. I don't have anything to spend it on."

"Well, maybe you're not interested in a wealth of unguarded treasure," Ram said, "but we are!"

Bear punched Reuben's arm playfully, making him spill his wine. "Come on, Reuben, think about it. Help us pull this off."

"Or at least play along for a while and check it out," Nib said. "See if this is a job the five of us could do."

"I already told the man I wasn't interested," Reuben said.

"Well, tell him you changed your mind. Come on. Please? When are we ever going to get another chance at a wealth of gold?"

"Do it for our sakes, Reuben."

"A least go back and find out some more details."

With all his friends pleading with him, Reuben's resolve weakened. "I'll think about it," he said. And he did, for the rest of the evening as his friends discussed the other robbery they were planning. After a long night of drinking and nursing his hatred for his uncle, Reuben made up his mind to seek revenge. "Okay. I'll do it," he told his friends. "I'll tell the man that I'll join his caravan, and I'll figure out a way to rob it."

"Excellent!"

"You're our man!" they all cheered him, slapping him on the back.

Reuben didn't care much about the gold, but he longed for the satisfaction of robbing the people who had robbed him, especially if his uncle decided to go along. Besides, the treasure was going to God's temple—the God who had let Abba die.

Reuben rose early the next morning and asked where he could find the man named Asher ben Seraiah who had come to Casiphia. When he learned he'd spent the night with Uncle Hashabiah, Reuben nearly changed his mind. He would have to face his uncle and convince him as well as the stranger that his desire to go to Jerusalem was sincere. His steps dragged as he walked to Hashabiah's house, wondering if his enthusiasm last night had been influenced by too much wine. But he decided to see it through. His friends were counting on him.

"Let me talk to Asher ben Seraiah," he told Hashabiah when he met Reuben at the door.

"Why?"

"That's none of your business." Reuben stared angrily at his uncle until he finally led Reuben inside. Asher sat in a patch of sunshine in the courtyard, talking with a group of men Reuben didn't recognize. "I've changed my mind about joining the caravan," Reuben said when Asher rose to greet him. "I've decided to come with you."

"That's wonderful! I'm glad to hear it. We—"

"Just a minute," Hashabiah interrupted. "Why would you want to move to Jerusalem and work in the temple after you've rejected God all these years? Why have you suddenly decided to join us again?"

"I'm a Levite. Asher said they needed Levites."

"Will you take your whole family, then? Your mother and younger brother?" Hashabiah asked.

Reuben felt a jolt of alarm. He couldn't take them. He planned to steal the gold and run. After that, he could live anywhere he pleased—anywhere but home, that is. He could never go home. It would be obvious that he'd been involved in the robbery. "My family won't want to come," Reuben said quickly.

"I'll ask them," Hashabiah said.

Reuben didn't want to arouse his uncle's suspicion any further. "She can do whatever she wants," he said with a shrug. "But I'm going. How do I sign up?"

"It's simple," Asher said, moving past Hashabiah. "Pack your things as quickly as you can and come with us. Just make sure all your debts are paid and you have no unfinished obligations. We can't have people running off and neglecting their responsibilities."

"There's nothing keeping me here." He would give his mother the bag of gold he had saved. It would provide plenty for her and his brother to live on. He and his friends would soon have much more.

"Wonderful!" Asher said. "I can't tell you how happy I am that you're joining us." Reuben felt a momentary twinge of guilt for planning to rob such a jovial, naïve man. But when he glanced at his uncle and recalled how no one in his community felt guilty for robbing him of his inheritance, his misgivings vanished.

"I'll go pack," Reuben said, turning to leave.

His uncle stopped him. "Forgive me for being suspicious, Reuben, but you haven't been part of us for a long time, and now you're—"

"Listen, I'm not asking for your permission," Reuben said. "I'm telling you to put my name on the list."

"What about—?"

"I'm a Levite. I've been invited to come, and I'm coming. That's all I have to say."

CHAPTER
39

NEAR THE AHAVA CANAL

Insects buzzed and hummed in the twilight as Ezra sat with his family outside their tent after the evening meal. Asher and the other emissaries had returned from Casiphia with good news, and Ezra wanted to record all the details in his journal:

Because the gracious hand of God was on us, they brought us Sherebiah, a capable man, from the descendants of Mahli son of Levi, the son of Israel, and Sherebiah's sons and brothers, eighteen men; and Hashabiah, together with Jeshaiah from the descendants of Merari and his brothers and nephews, twenty men. They also brought 220 of the temple servants—a body that David and the officials had established to assist the Levites. All were registered by name—

"Excuse me." Ezra looked up to find a man standing over him. He hadn't heard him approach. "Are you Ezra ben Seraiah?" he asked.

"Yes."

"My name is Hashabiah. I'm one of the Levites from Casiphia. I need to speak with you about my nephew, Reuben ben David."

"Please, have a seat," Ezra said, gesturing to a place beside the campfire.

The man shook his head. "Thank you, but I'm afraid this won't be a pleasant conversation."

Ezra stood, his unease growing at the man's somber expression. "Is your nephew having second thoughts about coming with us?" he asked.

"No, he still wants to join the caravan, but I'm sorry to say none of us from Casiphia is willing to vouch for my nephew, myself included. He's a troublemaker and has long been suspected of being a thief—if not worse. He has hung around with a rough gang of Babylonians for years, avoiding his fellow Jews."

Ezra's concern deepened at the mention of the hated Gentiles. "Yes, go on."

"Reuben makes no attempt to follow the Torah. He hasn't prayed with us or attended our celebrations or other events for fifteen years. He's more Babylonian than Jew, I'm sorry to say, and I believe he'll have a bad influence on other young men."

"How old is he?"

"Twenty-seven."

It took Ezra only a moment to decide. "We can't allow him to come."

"I tried to stop him. But Reuben insists that your brother Asher invited him to join us. He also says he met you once before, a long time ago."

"Send him here," Ezra decided. "Tell him I'd like to speak with him."

"I should warn you, Rebbe, my nephew can be quite unpleasant. And he has a very bad temper."

"Then the sooner we get this over with the better." Ezra asked his family to go inside the tent and give him a moment of privacy while Hashabiah went to fetch his nephew. Ezra paced in front of the fire while he waited, his journal forgotten. He

LYNN AUSTIN

would have to be firm with Hashabiah's nephew, letting him
know that anyone who didn't keep the law was not welcome.

The young man who arrived was tall and well-built, towering
over Ezra by a full head. If his temper was as bad as Hashabiah
said, then Ezra would be no match for him. Reuben wore no
kippah on his unruly dark hair, no fringes on his robe—both
very bad signs. His face wore the bristly stubble of an unkempt
beard and an angry expression. "I understand we've met before,
Reuben," Ezra said in greeting. "Forgive me, but I can't place
where."

"My father, Daniel, was the blacksmith who made weapons
for you."

"Ah yes." Ezra could almost recognize the boy he'd met in the
man who stood before him. "How is your father? Is he coming
with us, too?"

"My father is dead. He died in battle on the Thirteenth of
Adar."

Ezra stroked his beard, shocked by his words. That certainly
explained a lot of Reuben's anger. He would've been a boy at
the time. But it also raised a perplexing question—why was Reuben hanging out with Babylonians after they killed his father?
"I'm very sorry to hear about your father, Reuben. From what
I remember, he was a good man and an excellent blacksmith.
But tell me, what made you decide to come with us?"

"Your brother said you need Levites. And on the night you
visited our shop, I remember my father wishing we could serve
in the temple like our Levite ancestors did. He would've wanted
me to come."

Surprisingly, Ezra did remember the incident. The brawny
blacksmith's eyes had glistened as he'd voiced his wish. And
hadn't that been Ezra's wish for his sons, as well, the reason
that he'd petitioned the king of Persia? The blacksmith's longing had seemed impossible at the time, but not any longer.
Reuben's father had worked hard to furnish the weapons his

301

people needed and had died a hero. Ezra hated to turn away the son of such a fine man, but if Reuben didn't follow the Torah, he wasn't welcome. His own uncle had accused him of being a troublemaker.

"There's nothing to tie me down here," Reuben continued. "I'm not married—and my uncle forced my mother and me to sell Abba's blacksmith shop against my wishes. I would like a new start."

"So it isn't because you want to follow God's Torah?"

"I just told you my reasons."

Ezra sighed. At least Reuben was honest and didn't try to embellish his motives. But Ezra needed to be firm. "Listen, Reuben. The Persian king's decree authorized our return in order to govern Judah by God's law. That includes all the rules and regulations given in His Torah. The decree specifically says whoever fails to obey God's law must be punished by death, banishment, confiscation of property, or imprisonment." Reuben looked away. "Your uncle tells me you don't like rules, and you never worship with the other men. If we allow you to come, you'll have to live by every letter of the law. Can you honestly swear to me you'll do that?" Ezra waited, but Reuben didn't reply. "I didn't think so. You need to return to Casiphia, Reuben. Good evening."

Ezra saw Reuben's surprise, as if he hadn't expected to be turned away. Then his surprise turned to anger as he whirled around and left.

Devorah came out of their tent as soon as Reuben was gone. "Why did you send that young man away? I thought you needed more Levites."

"We do. But we only want men who are going to follow God's law, otherwise they'll pollute the land." He sat down again to resume writing in his journal, but Devorah stood over him, her hands on her hips. He looked up. "What's wrong?"

"You showed mercy to our sons when they broke the law. Why can't you show mercy to him?"

"It was different in our sons' case."

"How? Tell me how it was any different? Except that Reuben doesn't have a father to stand up for him."

Ezra swallowed an angry reply. Her interference and persistence annoyed him. He'd promised before they married to listen to her and consider her opinion, but tonight her outspokenness chafed. "There's a reason why we're told to stone the wayward son, Devorah. And Reuben's own uncle said he's a thief and a troublemaker."

"I didn't see a troublemaker, I saw a son of Abraham. And even if he was a troublemaker in the past, why not give him a chance to repent? He could change in the right environment, you know. Isn't God showing mercy to our people and giving us another chance?"

Ezra stood and rested his hands on her slender shoulders. "Devorah, don't you remember how this all began? The reason God first prompted us to return to Jerusalem was because our own sons were enticed by Babylon. We wanted to draw them away from bad influences and back to God."

"Exactly. You didn't turn our sons away after they disobeyed God's rules and skipped classes. Instead, you tried to change their environment. Doesn't Reuben deserve a chance to leave pagan Babylon, too? Why not show the same concern for this fatherless boy that you showed our sons?"

"Reuben's uncle refused to vouch for him."

"Where's the proof of his uncle's accusations? Where's the second witness? I've never known you to judge a person so quickly and so harshly, Ezra. I was very surprised by your decision."

"I was asked to give a judgment tonight, and I did."

"Just like that? Without asking the Almighty One's advice?"

"Reuben admitted his motivation wasn't to obey the Torah."

"How do you know the same thing isn't true of other people in this caravan? Reuben may have wandered away from the faith, but at least he's trying to take a step in God's direction. Why won't you help him, Ezra? Give him a chance to learn God's laws. Suppose God remembered our past mistakes and rejected us?"

Ezra couldn't reply. Very few of his community's elders ever dared to question his decisions this way, and it pricked his pride to have the rebuke come from his wife. He took a breath, then said, "Sometimes it's difficult to find the right balance between following the law and offering mercy—"

"You were all law, Ezra. You showed no mercy at all."

"Even if you're right, and I was too harsh, it's too late to change my mind. I already sent him away."

"Then maybe you need to find him and tell him you're sorry. Tell him he's needed and wanted. Isn't the Almighty One overlooking our past and giving us a second chance?"

"What if his uncle's suspicions are correct and he turns out to be a bad influence?"

"What if God is wrong about us and we abandon His law all over again? Give Reuben a chance to change, Ezra, and for God to change him. Grace can do that, you know. When God showed mercy and spared our lives fifteen years ago, look how we responded. Show Reuben God's grace and let it transform him. This young man lost his father. Suppose our sons lost you? Wouldn't you want someone to show them mercy instead of threatening them with 'death, banishment, and imprisonment'?"

"I asked him if he was willing to obey the rules and—"

"And you didn't even give him a chance to reply before sending him away."

It was true. There was nothing more Ezra could say. As much as it irritated him to admit it, Devorah was right. He would have to surrender his pride, find Reuben, and give him a second chance. He whispered a prayer for wisdom and went to find him.

Casiphia's Levites had camped at the northern edge of the caravan, and Hashabiah rushed forward to greet Ezra as he approached. "I've come to talk to your nephew Reuben again," Ezra told him.

"He's over there." Reuben sat all alone, apart from the others, staring at nothing. Ezra prayed for strength and the right words to say as he walked over to him.

"I came to apologize for being so short with you a few minutes ago," Ezra said. "I was wrong to speak to you that way, and I'm very sorry. If you would still like to join our caravan to Jerusalem, you will be welcome."

Reuben unfolded his long legs and rose to his feet. "What about all the rules you talked about?"

"You'll have to obey them, of course. But I'm hoping you'll be drawn to God and that as you get to know Him, you'll obey His rules for the same reason most of us do—because we love Him and want to please Him."

Reuben gave Ezra a quizzical look. "What do you mean?"

"Aren't those the same reasons you obeyed your father's rules when you lived in his household, Reuben? Because you loved him and wanted to please him?"

"I suppose."

"You told me you wanted a new start. Ideally, repentance should be motivated by our desire to return to God, not because we want to try something new. But I hope you'll at least try to get to know the God who loves you. I would be honored to teach you about Him myself." For the briefest of moments, Ezra thought he saw Reuben's eyes glisten. "If you're willing to forgive my earlier gruffness, please come back to my tent tomorrow morning, and we'll talk about finding a job that suits you." He rested his hand on Reuben's muscular arm for a moment, then walked back to his tent.

Reuben arrived the next morning as Ezra was finishing breakfast, and he couldn't blame the young man for looking wary and suspicious. "Have a seat, Reuben," he said, gesturing to the rug. "This isn't an exam. I just want to talk to you and get to know you." He waited for Reuben to sit, folding his long legs beneath him. "So. You're coming with us to Jerusalem. It's settled. Now we need to find the best task for you as a Levite. Everyone has a place and a job in God's kingdom. What are you good at doing? Tell me about yourself."

"I'm sure my uncle already told you all about me."

"Yes, and unfortunately it wasn't complimentary. He said you were a troublemaker and a thief. Is that true?"

"I had to steal. Abba died a hero, saving us, and my family had no way to live. I'm his oldest son. I did what I could." Reuben was quiet a moment, then added, "I'm sure my uncle didn't tell you the whole truth, though. He stole Abba's blacksmith shop from me and sold it to someone else. It was my inheritance, and he refused to help me buy it back!"

"He stole it? Your family didn't get paid for it?"

"We got money to live on, but he had no right to sell it!"

"How old were you then, Reuben?"

"Thirteen."

Ezra tugged his beard as he searched for words. "I can imagine how much you missed your father. My brother Jude died in the war, too. I've missed him every day since. I took over his responsibilities, caring for his family and working in his place, but I was fortunate to be an adult. I had a way to earn an honest living. Who knows what any of us might do if we were in your situation."

Reuben's chin trembled with emotion, but he didn't speak.

"But there's no longer any reason to steal, is there?" Ezra waited until Reuben shook his head. "Good. Because that's one of God's Ten Commandments. I'll be happy to teach you the other nine, along with all the laws and rules we talked about yesterday. You don't need to learn them all at once, of course. We can start with the basic ones. It's going to be a long journey, after all, so we'll have plenty of time to talk along the way. Would that work for you?" He waited until Reuben nodded. "Now, tell me what you like to do, Reuben. What are you good at doing?"

"Fighting. Doing whatever it takes to survive. I'm not afraid of anyone."

"You should be a guard, then. One of the Levites' duties is to stand guard in the temple. Will that suit you?"

"I would like that." He managed a smile, and he was a good-looking young man when he did. But anger seemed to seethe inside him like a carefully tended furnace.

"I noticed you were camping by yourself, Reuben. Why is that?"

"I don't want anything to do with my uncle."

"Go get your things, then. You're welcome to camp alongside my family and me. You'll find my wife an excellent cook." Ezra knew she was listening.

Reuben's angry frown softened. "Thank you."

Ezra removed the kippah from his head and handed it to Reuben. "How about if you start with this? You're one of us now."

"Why do men have to wear these?"

"It's a symbol of humility and our submission to the Almighty One, a reminder that He's always watching over us."

Reuben nodded his thanks but walked away without putting the head covering on.

Devorah came out of their tent as soon as Reuben left. "You were right," Ezra told her. "Thank you for convincing me to give him a second chance. I took your advice and showed him mercy, and I think I really reached him. I'm going to teach him to follow God."

Devorah didn't return his smile. "*You're* going to teach him, Ezra?"

"Yes." She shook her head again, hands on her hips. "What now? I thought you were on this young man's side?"

"I am. But *you* can't change his heart. Only God can do that."

Ezra watched in stunned silence as she went back inside the tent. He had expected her approval and praise. Now he felt totally perplexed. Would he ever understand this wife God had given him?

CHAPTER
40

JERUSALEM

Amina stood in the temple courtyard, watching the joyful thanksgiving procession as people presented their offerings from the wheat harvest. She was visiting Jerusalem with Jacob and his family for the Feast of Unleavened Bread, and she never tired of watching the beautiful ritual. She closed her eyes, listening to the Levite choir as they sang, *"Taste and see that the Lord is good; blessed is the man who takes refuge in him."* Amina had taken refuge in the Almighty One and she was truly blessed.

When the rituals at the temple ended late that afternoon, Amina walked with Jacob's family to the home of Hodaya's nephews, Joshua and Johanan, where they always stayed when they visited Jerusalem. The men were priests, sons of a famous prophet and man of God named Zechariah. Their home, built of uncut stones with a sprawling central courtyard, perched on the ridge high above the Kidron Valley. Amina loved rising early to help prepare breakfast whenever she visited and watching the sunrise over the Mount of Olives. She was helping prepare dinner for the last evening of the celebration when Johanan returned home with exciting news.

"We've just received word," he said, "that the king of Persia has allowed our fellow Jews still in exile to immigrate home to Judah. Their leader is Ezra ben Seraiah, a descendant of several important high priests in Solomon's temple. He's bringing dozens more priests and Levites with him to serve along with us."

"More settlers?" Jacob said. "That's wonderful news. We've been outnumbered by the Gentiles for much too long. Maybe with more manpower we can finally stop the spread of Edomite people into southern Judah."

Amina felt her face grow warm at the mention of her people. But Jacob didn't even glance at her, as if he'd long forgotten her origins.

"When do you think the new settlers will arrive?" his wife, Rivkah, asked.

"According to the letter we received, they already left Babylon," Johanan replied. "A letter travels much faster than a caravan with thousands of people. We can probably expect them in three or four months, certainly before the fall feasts."

"The fall feasts . . ." Joshua repeated. "I don't think we have enough robes for dozens of new priests and Levites to serve alongside us on Yom Kippur. And of course they'll want to participate. That's why they're coming."

"You're right," Johanan said. "We'll need to hire more weavers to make cloth for their robes and sashes and other garments. If we start right away, the garments might be done in time. Aunt Hodaya could have helped us but—"

"Amina is a skilled weaver, too, you know," Jacob said.

Amina felt her cheeks grow warm again as everyone turned to her.

"Would you consider staying here and working with our weavers?" Joshua asked her.

"You mean, move here? To Jerusalem?"

"Yes. You're welcome to live here with us."

"But . . . you know I'm not Jewish, don't you?"

"Neither was Aunt Hodaya, by birth. My father prophesied that one day the Lord would be king over the whole earth, over all people. And he said people from all nations would one day come to Jerusalem to celebrate and worship the Almighty One. You're the beginning of that fulfillment, Amina. . . . So will you help us?"

Amina thought her heart would burst from joy. "Of course! If you really think I can do it."

"The others can teach you. The cloth is a special crosshatch weave described by God in the Torah. The robes are woven in one piece without any seams except for where the sleeves are attached. And the colors are made with special dyes. "

"I've always admired the priests' beautiful garments," Amina said, "especially the high priest's robe with red, blue, and purple colors. It's so striking." She tried to hold back the tears brimming in her eyes.

"God commanded us to create garments that were dignified and beautiful—as precious as the garments of royalty," Joshua said.

"Did we say something wrong, Amina?" Johanan asked. "You're crying."

She shook her head as she wiped her eyes. "I-I'm just so happy!" she managed to say. She never imagined she would be able to give something back to the God who loved her and had saved her. While growing up she'd been pushed out of sight and told she was worthless. Now she couldn't contain her joy and wonder at being accepted and valued. Needed. Loved.

When the holiday ended, Amina returned to Bethlehem to collect her things, including Hodaya's big loom and clay weights. Jacob helped her move everything back to Jerusalem, and it didn't take Amina long to settle into the priests' beautiful home on the ridge. The next few weeks were busy ones as she adjusted to her new life and learned how to make the special crosshatch weave for the white linen garments. She set up her loom in the House of the Weavers near the fuller's field. There the flax would be spun into six-ply threads, bleached or colored using special dyes, then woven into garments. She had so much to learn. Ordinary priests wore three separate garments—a turban, breeches, and an ankle-length outer robe all made from linen. The high priest's sash was woven from a mixture of threads: twisted linen, gold wire hammered extra thin, and wool dyed sky-blue, purple, and crimson.

"How do they make these beautiful colors?" Amina asked as she examined the wool.

"The blue and purple dyes come from a special sea snail found in the Great Sea," the chief dyer told her. "They're very costly, which is why these colors are used only for royalty or priests in the Almighty One's temple. The crimson dye comes from a certain kind of worm, and it's very costly, as well."

Amina began weaving a priest's robe, constructed in one piece without seams. Another weaver would add a binding of woven work around the neck, but the lower hem would be woven-in, not sewn. "How will I know how long to make each robe if I'm weaving in the hem?" she asked.

"You won't know until the new priests arrive and we find out how tall each man is. Then the garments can be completed and sent to the chamber of the wardrobe in the temple."

Amina loved her work. But as her days moved into a happy routine, she often gazed across the valley toward Sayfah's village, wishing she could see her sister again. She had promised she would return, but so far it hadn't been possible.

"Would you please help me arrange a visit with my sister?" she asked Joshua one evening. "I'm worried she might forget everything she learned from Hodaya about the Almighty One. More than anything else, I want her to worship our God, too."

"Of course, Amina. I can have one of our servants escort you. You can take my donkey."

"Your servant will have to wait for me outside Sayfah's village. But I promise not to visit for too long."

"That won't be a problem."

Sayfah seemed overjoyed to see Amina again. They spent time catching up with each other, but the visit passed much too quickly. Sayfah never stopped working the entire time, so Amina worked alongside her, helping Sayfah and her mother-in-law with the chores. "I wish you could stay longer," Sayfah said when it was time for Amina to leave. "Why don't you come back for the festival at the end of summer and stay with me for a few days?"

"What kind of festival is it?" Amina pictured the wonderful Jewish rituals and feasts so rich with meaning.

"It celebrates the final harvest—like the festival our village used to hold every year for the olive harvest, remember?"

"That was years ago. I really don't remember much about it. What do people do at your festival?"

"What difference does it make? I'm inviting you to be my guest. Since when are you so picky, questioning every little thing?"

"Well . . . it's just that . . ." Amina didn't know how to begin explaining about foods that were acceptable and foods that were forbidden, how they had to be prepared properly and served on certain plates, and how the meat couldn't be sacrificed to idols. For all of these reasons, Jews were forbidden to eat with Gentiles like the Edomites.

"Please say yes, Amina. It will give us more time to spend together. The women prepare everything ahead of time so we can relax and visit without worrying about cooking on the day of the feast."

"Like Hodaya used to do before the Sabbath?"

"I guess so." Sayfah smiled slightly and added, "Maybe you'll have a chance to meet some young men from our village. You need a husband, Amina. You're already 'old' at twenty-three. You don't want to live all alone or marry a Jew, do you?"

"I haven't met anyone I want to marry, Jewish or not. And

I probably will live alone. Not very many men want a crippled wife."

Sayfah didn't seem to hear her. "I can introduce you to my husband's cousins. In fact, I know several men from our village you should meet."

Amina didn't know how to reply. An Edomite husband would never allow her to worship the Jews' God or go up to His temple.

"Please come, Amina. It'll be fun. There'll be food and music and dancing. . . ."

"I don't think I'll be doing any dancing," Amina said, gesturing to her leg. Sayfah gave her an exasperated look. "I came here to visit you, Sayfah, and talk with you and catch up on your life," Amina said, taking her sister's hands. "I wouldn't be comfortable at a big social event like that festival. Please don't be mad, but I know I'd have a terrible time."

But Sayfah was mad, Amina could tell. She yanked her hands free. "Sometimes you don't even seem like my sister anymore."

"That's because we've taken different paths. Edomites and Jews are very, very different, and we live in two completely different worlds. I'm not . . ." She paused, searching for the right words. "Please don't take this the wrong way, but sometimes I don't feel like an Edomite anymore."

"Don't say that! You can't join our enemies, Amina. It's bad enough you live with them. What if there was another war between us? Then what would you do?"

"I don't know . . . I mean . . . I don't think of you and the people in your village as enemies. But it isn't as simple as you make it sound. Mama and Abba were ashamed of me, and then Uncle Abdel rejected me, too. Why would I live with people who didn't want me? The Jews accept me the way I am. They make me feel . . . worthwhile." She had planned to tell Sayfah about her work weaving robes for the priests, but she changed her mind. Sayfah would never understand.

"If you don't want to be part of our people," Sayfah said,

314

"then don't bother coming to see me anymore." She turned away, angry. Amina couldn't leave this way. She had to patch things up. She limped after her sister, catching her arm.

"Wait. I don't want hard feelings between us. We're sisters. If this festival is important to you, then I'll gladly come." The prospect of mingling with Edomite men still terrified her, but Amina would be safe from their advances since none of them would want a crippled wife.

Sayfah turned to her again, smiling at her words. "Good. And plan to stay overnight with us. The festival will end very late. Tell whoever brings you here that someone will walk with you back to Jerusalem in the morning."

Amina forced a smile. She didn't want to attend Sayfah's festival, but she didn't want to offend her sister, either. Hodaya had asked Amina on her deathbed to make things right. "All right, Sayfah," she said. "Tell me the day and month, and I'll come."

NEAR THE AHAVA CANAL

Reuben finally saw the caravan's stash of gold and silver. Not just pounds of it, but tons of it—more than he ever could have imagined. Rebbe Ezra showed him the special tent where it was kept under guard. The treasure would fill the saddlebags of more than thirty camels once the caravan began to move. Reuben's friends would be overjoyed. He and his gang would never have to steal again.

They had arranged a signal—the call of a mourning dove—so they could meet at the outskirts of the camp after the fires went out each night and the people had settled down in their tents to sleep. Reuben would walk to the northeastern edge of the encampment and wait in the dark for the signal. Accustomed to moving silently at night, he was able to slip through the slumbering camp without being seen or heard. He waited for the signal, then followed it through the dark, rough terrain to where Digger waited. His friend grinned when he saw Reuben, motioning for him to follow him a short distance to where the others sat near the canal beneath a clump of palm trees. They slept beneath the stars, not daring to light a fire or pitch a tent and draw attention to themselves. Bear stood and greeted Reuben heartily. "You made it! Hey, look at you! You look just like a Jew now, with your little hat and fancy robe."

Reuben snatched the kippah from his head, embarrassed. Bear gave the tassels a playful tug. Rebbe Ezra's wife had sewn them for him. Reuben's father had worn blue fringes just like these on his robes as reminders of God's law. "I had to dress this way," he told Bear. "They nearly sent me home unless I agreed to obey all their picky little rules." He still couldn't get over how Rebbe Ezra had changed his mind about letting him come. The leader of the entire caravan—the head over all of the men, including Uncle Hashabiah—had returned to Reuben and apologized. Reuben had never met anyone like the rebbe, so intense, so religious, yet willing to admit he was wrong, willing to trust Reuben and give him another chance. It took a big man to do that. It was something Reuben's father would have done.

"I've come up with a plan," Reuben said. "Right now, everything in camp is closely guarded, and I haven't been assigned my shift as a guard yet. I suggest you follow the caravan for a day and wait until we camp the first night. Everyone will be exhausted, and the camp will be set up more haphazardly."

"That's crazy," Nib said. "A day's journey will put us in the middle of nowhere. How—"

"No, Reuben's right," Bear interrupted. "The middle of nowhere is perfect. They won't be able to track us in the dark or even know which way we went until dawn."

"I'll make sure I'm on guard duty," Reuben continued. "I'll watch to see where they stash the gold after they unload the camels. I'll wait for your signal at dusk and meet up with you just like tonight to draw you a map of the camp. Wait until after midnight for the robbery. Don't make a scene or attack any guards. I'll help you sneak into the tent so you can grab as much gold as you can carry and get out again—fast!—before anyone notices. Got it? We'll need to put some distance between us and the caravan before morning."

"It's a good plan, Reuben," Nib said, "but why take just one armload of gold? Why not make several trips and load up a string of camels and packhorses?"

The idea made Reuben's stomach turn with dread. "Don't get greedy, Nib. The longer the robbery takes, the greater the risk of getting caught. Two or three sacks of gold apiece should be plenty." Digger and Nib seemed about to argue further, but Bear held up his hand to cut them off.

"Reuben's plan is a good one. We'll follow the caravan and meet you at the edge of the camp at dusk so you can tell us where the gold is. Just make sure you're assigned to guard duty, Reuben."

"I will. The caravan will probably break camp early tomorrow morning," he told his friends before parting. But it didn't. The following day, the people and pack animals and tents all remained at the campsite near the Ahava Canal.

"Why aren't we traveling?" Reuben asked Rebbe Ezra shortly after dawn. "What are we waiting for?" The rebbe had invited him to travel and camp with his family, and Reuben hadn't wanted to raise suspicion by refusing. He brought his bedroll and meager collection of belongings to the leader's site and slept there.

"I proclaimed a fast today," Rebbe Ezra replied, "so we could all humble ourselves before God and ask Him for a safe journey for us and our children and our possessions." The campfire that Ezra's extended family shared hadn't been lit. His wife and the other women weren't preparing breakfast. Even the smallest children weren't eating.

"Some of our scouts have found evidence that we're being watched and followed," the rebbe's brother Asher added. "They've shadowed us ever since you and the other Levites from Casiphia joined us. We need to ask the Almighty One for help."

One of Ezra's twin sons turned to his father. "Why would our enemies follow us, Abba? What do they want?" The boys, who were about the same age that Reuben had been when his father died, looked identical.

"They're after the Almighty One's gold, I imagine," Ezra replied. "But it's more than that. We're on a divine mission, and the enemy wants to prevent us from teaching the Torah and worshiping God." The men brought out their phylacteries, preparing to pray, and Reuben watched Ezra wind the leather strap around his arm as he spoke. "I was ashamed to ask the Persian king for soldiers to protect us because I had assured him the gracious hand of our God is on everyone who looks to Him. And His great anger is against all who forsake Him."

"I guess our enemies forgot what God did fifteen years ago to those who tried to harm us," Asher said. "We fasted and prayed for protection back then, too, and God heard us."

Reuben didn't want to think about the fact that he was on their enemies' side this time. "What good does fasting do?" he asked to hide his unease.

"It reminds us how dependent we are on the Holy One," Ezra replied. "Each time we feel hungry, we remember to trust Him for all our provisions, including our safety. Would you like to join us in prayer, Reuben? Have you ever put on phylacteries?"

"Yeah, when I turned twelve."

"Do you remember how to do it?"

Reuben nodded. He also remembered watching his father do it every morning and longing to be like him. He'd been thrilled on his twelfth birthday when he was finally old enough to wear them. And Reuben also remembered the proud look on Abba's face as he'd helped him wind the leather strap around his arm for the first time. Poignant memories of Abba seemed to sprout everywhere in this camp. Reuben couldn't wait to steal the gold and leave—and drown those memories in a bottle of wine.

"Then you must know we begin with our statement of faith,"

Ezra continued. "'Hear, O Israel, the Lord our God, the Lord is One—'"

"Yes, Abba taught me. But I'd like to pray by myself today, if that's all right with you."

"Whatever you'd like, Reuben."

He hurried away so he wouldn't have to hear these men asking God for protection—from him and his friends. His gang didn't intend to hurt anyone, Reuben assured himself. And a few bags of gold apiece would scarcely be missed. From his vantage point on top of a small rise, he watched Ezra praying with his sons—and remembered praying with his own father. Could Abba see him from wherever he was? Did he know what Reuben was planning to do? Reuben's heart felt as empty as his stomach, and he didn't know why.

Throughout the camp, everything halted as thousands of people gathered in small groups to pray. To Reuben, who only pretended to pray, the day seemed endlessly long. He wanted to get this robbery over with, but he would have to endure another long day of traveling and waiting and worrying tomorrow before finally making his escape. He had nothing to do to occupy his time, so he wandered restlessly around the encampment, his empty stomach rumbling. What would he do with his share of the gold? And with the rest of his life?

When he returned to Ezra's campsite late that afternoon, the rebbe was beaming. "The Almighty One has answered our prayers," he told Reuben.

"How do you know that? We haven't traveled anywhere yet."

"True. But I'm convinced—in here," he said, thumping his fist on his chest, "that God already answered our prayer. All the people and goods in this caravan will arrive safely in Jerusalem. Now come with me, Reuben. I've asked the Levites to gather and weigh the silver and gold before we entrust it to their keeping."

The task took several hours. Reuben and the others crowded inside the tent or around the open doorway to watch as each bag of gold and silver was weighed on a set of scales. The totals amazed him: 650 talents of silver; 100 talents of gold; silver articles weighing 100 talents; 20 golden bowls worth at least 1,000 darics. Reuben had thought if he and his gang stole a few bags apiece they would never be missed. But the gold was being carefully accounted for—which meant that once he disappeared, they would know exactly how much was missing and that he had stolen it. Even if he and his friends managed to escape without being caught, he would be a wanted man for the rest of his life.

"Now that the weighing is finished," Ezra said afterward, "it's time to consecrate all you Levites for the task God has given you." Rebbe Ezra made Reuben sink to his knees along with the others and remove his kippah as the rebbe anointed each of their heads with oil. Ezra finished the ceremony with a prayer, asking God to guard and protect each man as they offered themselves to do His work. Reuben rose to his feet again when the prayer ended.

"Stand proud, gentlemen," Ezra said. "You, as well as these articles, are now consecrated to the Lord. The silver and gold are a freewill offering to the Lord, the God of your fathers. It belongs to Him. Guard these treasures carefully until you weigh them out in the chambers of the House of the Lord in Jerusalem and turn them over to the priests and Levites there. The Lord has entrusted you with His work."

Reuben didn't feel proud as he returned to the campsite with Rebbe Ezra. The fast had ended, but he had no appetite. "Is something wrong, Reuben?" Ezra asked as he watched him push food around on his plate.

"I'm just not very hungry." He excused himself and went to sit alone on the same little rise overlooking the canal. Ezra came looking for him as soon as the meal ended.

He sat beside Reuben in the sandy grass for several minutes without speaking, gazing down at the dark ribbon of the canal.

"I know you're an intelligent young man, Reuben," he finally said. "You must have a lot of questions you would like to ask. So I want you to know our faith in the Almighty One allows for questions—and even doubts. That's how students learn in the yeshiva, remember? The best students are the ones who aren't afraid to ask questions."

Reuben picked up a small stone, tossing it from one hand to the other as he tried to gather his thoughts. "You said today you knew God had answered your prayers. You keep talking about God as if you know Him personally, as if you've seen Him and you know He's real."

"In a way, I do know Him. God gave us His Torah so we can learn all about Him. Anyone who reads it will get to know Him."

"How do you know the Torah isn't made up?"

"Ah! A very good question." Ezra grew animated as he shifted to face Reuben, gesturing broadly as he talked. "Let me explain it this way. If you or I or any other man was going to sit down and make up a book that supposedly came from God, a book filled with wisdom and stories and laws from this made-up god, what kinds of things would we put in this book? First of all, we would fill it with heroes to emulate, right? Men and women who never doubted or did things God didn't like, and who showed us how to truly live. But what do we find in the Torah? Imperfect people. Adam and Eve, who had everything we could ever dream of in Paradise, disobeyed God and were driven out. Our revered patriarch, Abraham, told lies and sometimes doubted God. He fathered Ishmael because he didn't trust God to keep His promises. Moses, our great liberator, tried to play God and killed a man. He argued with God and even told Him, 'No!' He doubted and feared and disobeyed. You must have learned all these stories, didn't you?"

"Yes. I studied to become a Son of the Commandments."

"Be honest then: Would you include such people and all their faults in a book that was supposedly from God if you had the opportunity to edit out these unflattering details?"

"I guess not." Another memory of his father sprouted to life, unbidden. Abba had loved these tales of their ancestors. He had joyfully recounted the story of the exodus from slavery every year at Passover. *"This is our past, Reuben. We learn about God from these stories of our past."*

"So, Reuben," Ezra continued. "Let's look at what the Torah promises about our people's future. All wonderful things, right? Hardly! In the third book of Moses, God says, 'I will scatter you among the nations and will draw out my sword and pursue you. Your land will be laid waste, and your cities will lie in ruins.'"

"You have the Torah *memorized*?" Reuben asked in astonishment.

"Much of it, yes," he replied, as if it was nothing at all. "Now, think about it, Reuben. This is exactly what happened to our people. You and I know firsthand this came true because we are among those who've been scattered to faraway places. In the fifth book of Moses it says the same thing: 'You will be uprooted from the land . . . then the Lord will scatter you among all nations, from one end of the earth to the other.' No man in his right mind would put such predictions in a holy book. Who would follow it if they knew these things were going to happen to them? And it gets worse. You and I also lived through our enemies' attempt to wipe us from the face of the earth fifteen years ago, right?"

"They killed my father."

Ezra nodded. "God also predicted we would be hated wherever we were scattered. In the fifth book of Moses it says there will be no rest for our feet, no matter where we go. 'You will live in constant suspense, filled with dread both night and day, never sure of your life.' And He says, 'You who were as numerous as the stars in the sky will be left but few in number, because—'"

"Wait. Why should we follow a God who lets all these terrible things happen to us?"

"Good question. And the rest of that verse gives us the answer. God allowed it 'because you did not obey the Lord your God.' But here's the really good part, Reuben. The Holy One also promises that our people will endure, generation after generation, and that He will always be our God. He told Abraham, 'I will establish my covenant as an everlasting covenant'—that means *forever*—'between me and you and your descendants after you for the generations to come, to be your God and the God of your descendants after you.' Only the Almighty One would dare to make such a prediction because it's so unlikely to come true. Where are all the other peoples and nations of the past? Where are their gods? The Assyrians are gone. So are the Canaanites and Hittites and Jebusites. Yet against all odds, in spite of being scattered and hated, we, the sons of Abraham, have endured."

Ezra paused to give Reuben time to absorb everything he was saying. The sun's glow had faded in the west. The first stars had begun to appear. *"God's tiny beacons,"* Abba had called them, *"to light our way through the darkness."*

"Yes, God predicted we would be scattered and hated," Ezra continued. "But He also promised we would return to our land. The Torah says, 'When you and your children return to the Lord your God and obey Him with all your heart and with all your soul . . . then the Lord your God will restore your fortunes and have compassion on you and gather you again from all the nations where He scattered you.' And you and I are part of this caravan right now, Reuben, returning to our land, because the Holy One promised we would be an eternal nation in His sight. What do you think are the odds of this coming true after we've been scattered and hated for so many generations?"

And outnumbered. Reuben recalled how outnumbered they'd been on the Thirteenth of Adar, and yet they'd been victorious. "It does seem unlikely," he conceded.

"So who wrote the Torah, Reuben—God or man? If we conclude that any man setting out to make up a religion would never write such a book, and that the odds are slim we would endure as a nation in spite of such terrible predictions of our future, then we have to conclude God is the One who wrote it." Ezra leaned closer, meeting Reuben's gaze. "And if the Almighty One Himself, Creator of heaven and earth, wrote it, wouldn't we be wise to study it and live by it? That's what we're going to Jerusalem to do. To rebuild our nation according to His law. To be keepers of His covenant."

Reuben was nearly convinced—and yet he didn't want to be. He'd chosen his own path, and his mind was made up. "Does the Torah explain why my father had to die?" he asked. "And why his shop was stolen from me?"

Ezra tugged on his beard for a moment. "The Torah insists God has a plan—for us and for His world. Sometimes we can't see what that plan is until all the events have played out in their entirety. It's like trying to predict the end of a story before the tale is finished. And for us, 'the end' might not come for many more years. I asked the same question about why my brother Jude had to die. I still don't know all the reasons, but I'm beginning to see how his death might fit into God's plan."

"How? What do you mean?"

"Well, for instance, after Jude died, the law commanded me to marry his widow. I had been so wrapped up in my studies I hadn't thought about marrying. Maybe I never would have. But I obeyed the law and married Devorah, and we had twin sons and three daughters. That unexpected gift and the enormous love I feel for my children gives me a glimpse of the love God has for us, and it propelled me to want a different life for them than living in Babylon. My children belonged home, in the Promised Land. So I traveled to the capitol of Persia and spoke to the king. He issued his decree, and now we're on our way home. Would all this have happened if Jude had lived? Would we be on our way out of exile and back to Jerusalem this very minute? I don't know. Because he did die—and here we are."

A memory came to Reuben of the day he'd stood beside his father in the blacksmith shop, scared and angry about the death sentence decreed for their people. Abba had tears in his eyes as he'd told Reuben they needed to trust in God's goodness even when they couldn't see it. *"We show our faith in God when we keep moving forward even when our prayers aren't being answered. It's the highest form of praise to keep believing God is good even when it doesn't seem that way."* And then Abba had bent over his anvil and continued to work as if to confirm his trust.

"Maybe it's too soon to see all the reasons why your father died," Ezra said, "and how they're all going to work together into something good. We're not to the end of your story yet. But I believe God wanted you to come with us. You were chosen by Him to make this journey. Your father said he would be the first one in line to come if God ever made a way. So ask yourself why you did decide to come—and then ask yourself if your reasons had anything to do with the loss of your father."

Reuben looked away. They had everything to do with losing Abba. His true reason for coming was to help his friends steal the caravan's gold. And he never would've joined the gang or become a thief in the first place if his father had lived.

"How long have you been living apart from the Torah?" Ezra asked.

"Since Abba died. Fifteen years ago."

"And how has your life been since then? Are you content with it? Has it been blessed?"

Reuben thought of the pouch filled with gold he'd left behind for his mother. It had been worthless to him. He thought of his dreams, all unfulfilled, and how his only friends were a gang of Babylonian thieves. He could never go home again after this robbery. Instead, he would return to the dark, damp hideout with them to drink wine for the rest of his life. The empty place in his heart would probably never be filled.

When he didn't reply, Ezra stood and said, "Why not give the God of your forefathers a chance? Serve Him. Live by His Torah. Apart from Him we're doomed to live our lives in darkness that's even blacker than this night."

CHAPTER
42

NEAR THE AHAVA CANAL

Stars filled the sky when Reuben heard the first rustlings of movement inside the tents. Rebbe Ezra announced last night that the caravan would break camp at dawn and begin the journey to Jerusalem. Reuben hadn't slept well on the hard, rocky ground. His bed was out in the open behind Rebbe Ezra's tent, and his blanket offered scant protection from the chilly spring night. He'd awakened every hour, it seemed, Rebbe Ezra's words rolling around in his mind like pebbles in a bucket. Had God really written the Torah? Was Reuben doomed to live in darkness if he didn't obey it? And if God had a reason for allowing Abba to die, was it so Reuben could move to the Promised Land?

Abba. Reuben's thoughts always returned to Abba. He would've been so proud yesterday to see Reuben consecrated as a Levite. But Abba wasn't here. And Reuben didn't want to be here, either. Today would be his last day with the caravan. Tonight he would escape with enough gold to live on for the rest of his life. He still had no idea what he would do with it.

Rebbe Ezra's wife and daughters were kindling a fire and fixing breakfast when Reuben rose. The rebbe and his sons had removed some of their possessions from the tent to load onto the cart. "Need help with that?" Reuben asked.

"Oh, good. You're awake," Ezra said. "If you wouldn't mind, Reuben, could you help the other Levites load the gold onto the camels this morning? It might take a while, so I'll tell Devorah to save you some breakfast."

Reuben agreed, grateful for any excuse to get away from the rebbe and his disturbing lectures. The bags of gold were heavy, but Reuben was one of the strongest workers. His gang of friends would be lucky if they could carry two bags apiece, especially Bear with his bad arm. The camel drivers prodded each ornery animal to kneel while a load was placed on its back, then drove it to its feet again, the camels bellowing and protesting. Strung together by ropes into a long line, the camels waited to begin the journey. By the time the Levites finished their work, the entire caravan was preparing to leave. Reuben hurried back to Ezra's camp for the promised food.

"I enjoyed our discussion last night," Ezra said as Reuben gulped his breakfast. "You're welcome to travel with my sons and me today if you have any more questions you'd like to ask."

The last thing Reuben wanted was to raise more disturbing questions to interrupt his sleep—and his concentration. He needed to be alert for what he and the others planned after midnight. "Thank you, Rebbe, but I think I should stay close to the camel train and the gold today."

"Yes, of course."

The caravan followed the Euphrates River all day, and the steadily falling rain turned the road—trampled by thousands of feet, loaded wagons, and pack animals—into a quagmire. The mud splattered Reuben's legs and the hem of his tunic and clung heavily to his sandals. All day while they traveled, Reuben tried to make sense of Rebbe Ezra's words. Was the Almighty One real or wasn't He? Reuben knew He was. Abba had believed in Him, and besides, the world revealed too much evidence of a Creator to believe otherwise. The kippah he now wore on his head reminded him he lived beneath the gaze of an all-knowing God. But was His Torah true with all of its laws and rules—like not stealing? *"Apart from Him we'll live in darkness,"* Ezra had insisted. Reuben remembered sneaking around Casiphia's dark streets, feeling empty, even with a bag of gold tied to his belt. Would more gold really fill that emptiness? *"Why not give the God of your forefathers a chance?"* Reuben pushed all these thoughts aside and kept walking. He was committed to his task tonight. And he certainly didn't belong here with the other men and women in this caravan. There was nothing for him in Jerusalem.

Unused to so much walking, Reuben's legs were weary by the end of the long, first day, his feet aching. When the caravan finally camped for the night, he helped pitch the tent to house the treasures, making careful note of the landmarks surrounding it so his friends could find it in the dark. He felt jumpy and on edge as he ate the evening meal with Rebbe Ezra and his family, twitching at every little sound, barely tasting his food as he gulped it down. He finished quickly, then made an excuse to leave again, walking to the northeastern edge of the camp where he'd agreed to contact his friends. He waited in a drizzling rain for Digger's signal. Just like before, he followed the sound and met up with his gang a short distance away. They greeted him jovially, but he cut them off, impatient to give them instructions and leave again.

"Listen, they know the caravan is being followed," he began. "You're not being very careful."

Bear waved away his concerns. "It won't matter after tonight. Did you find out where the treasure is? And how much there is?"

"They have tons of silver and gold. I watched them weigh it yesterday. And I can tell you exactly where it is because I helped them unload it tonight. But they also have more guards now. Armed guards."

"You're one of them, right? You can get us in and help us load up?"

"That's the plan. But you'll need to be quiet and quick. Grab a couple of bags each and get out of there. I can't distract the other guards forever."

"Listen, Reuben, that plan isn't going to work now. We're going to need a longer distraction. You have to buy us more time."

"Why?"

They looked at each other—guiltily, Reuben thought. "We recruited a few others to help us out—"

"What? No!"

"This is the biggest haul we'll ever have a chance to make— *tons* of gold, you said. We need to take advantage of it."

"No! You weren't supposed to recruit anyone else. It's supposed to be just the five of us."

"Look, not only can we carry more gold this way, but the Jews have thousands of men traveling in that caravan, don't they? What if we have to fight our way out? We need more help."

Reuben took a step back, holding up his hands. "I never agreed to this."

"Well, we decided to make a slight change in your plans. And you weren't around to consult with us."

"How many others? And where are they now?"

"Out there," Bear said, gesturing vaguely to the darkness beyond their camp. "Don't worry about how many. They're all well-armed."

Reuben felt sick. "It wasn't supposed to happen this way. Send them back home. Tell them you changed your mind. It's risky enough to sneak the four of you in and out with sacks of gold. Stealing any more than that is going to be impossible. I don't want anyone on either side to get hurt."

Nib wore a sly grin on his face as he tugged on the tassels

dangling from Reuben's robe. "You aren't joining them now, are you, Reuben?"

He brushed Nib's hand away. "They have women and children with them. I don't want to put them in danger. Look, send the other men away. Tell them the robbery is off. All we need is the five of us, got it?"

Digger and Ram started to protest, but Bear stopped them. "Fine. Whatever you say, Reuben. Just don't turn traitor on us now. Remember, we're friends."

"Right. We're friends. But you're going to have to do this my way or not at all." He hadn't told them yet how to find the tent with the gold, hidden among thousands of other tents. He could walk away right now and call the whole thing off. But if he did, they would probably overpower him just like they had on the night he'd met them, forcing him to tell. They'd keep Reuben here, pressing him for details until he helped them rob the caravan. They would never let him go.

"Give me your word you'll send the others away," he insisted. He waited for each of his friends to raise his hand and swear. Only then did he tell them how to find the gold.

Reuben walked back to camp with a sick feeling in his stomach. Why did they have to recruit more men? What were they thinking? They'd been carried away by greed, obviously, and they hadn't been thinking. Could he trust Bear and the others to send these extra men away as they'd sworn to do? Reuben scrubbed his face with his hands, wishing he'd never gotten involved with this robbery to begin with. He didn't even want his share of the gold. But it was too late to back out now. He made his way to the treasury, his feet dragging, and approached the chief Levite.

"I'd like to volunteer to stand guard tonight," Reuben said. "I'm not tired at all."

"Are you sure? After all the walking we did today?"

"I'm sure. I don't need much sleep."

"Go get a weapon, then." The man gestured to the smaller tent beside the treasury where the weapons were stored. Reuben ducked inside and nearly collided with his uncle.

"What are you doing here, Reuben? You aren't one of the assigned guards."

"I volunteered. I need a sword."

His uncle studied him for a long moment, and Reuben's temper flared beneath his scrutiny. He was about to unleash it when Hashabiah said, "I have a special sword for you, son." He carried the oil lamp to an open crate and searched through it for a moment before pulling out a sword and handing it to him. "Here, use this one. It belonged to your father."

Reuben stared in disbelief. This was the sword Abba had made for himself, the one he had fought with on the Thirteenth of Adar. Reuben helped him make it. Abba had engraved his own symbol on the handle along with the words, "Dedicated to God." The sword disappeared after the battle, and Reuben thought he'd never see it again.

"I've wanted to return it to you for a long time, Reuben, but I've been too worried about you. Now . . . now Rebbe Ezra believes in you . . . and so do I."

Reuben mumbled his thanks and quickly left before his emotions overwhelmed him. He strapped the sword onto his belt and took his assigned position among the other Levites guarding the perimeter of the tent. Time crawled as he watched the shadows for any sign of movement. Reuben's anxiety soared. Midnight seemed like hours from now. After this robbery, he would be shackled to his gang forever, an outlaw for the rest of his life. Where could he go? Where would he live? And had Bear really sent the other men he'd recruited back to Casiphia?

The more Reuben thought about it, the more he realized that even if Bear tried to dismiss these unknown mercenaries, they probably would never agree to turn back without the promised gold, especially after a long day's journey. Greed caused men to do terrible things. The Jewish people's enemies had attacked them on the Thirteenth of Adar because they'd wanted the Jews' plunder. They would have murdered every man, woman, and child to get it. Men like these Babylonians would think nothing of killing innocent people in this caravan for their gold.

Reuben drew the sword from its scabbard. His hand fit perfectly on the hilt that Abba had made. He closed his eyes for a moment, feeling linked to Abba, who had died defending his fellow Jews from their enemies. Why was Reuben helping them? Rebbe Ezra and the other men had fasted and prayed for an entire day, asking the Almighty One to protect the caravan. According to Ezra, God had already answered that prayer. Had the Almighty One foreseen the defeat of Reuben's gang?

What should he do? Reuben reached up to run his fingers through his hair and knocked the kippah off his head. He bent to pick it up, and as he replaced it, he knew the Almighty One was watching. This gold belonged to Him.

Still gripping his sword, Reuben left his post and jogged over to the nearest guard. "Listen to me. There's going to be a robbery attempt tonight. Stay alert while I go get more help." He hurried to the next guard and the next, telling them the same thing. They looked baffled, but there was no time to explain. Instead, Reuben ran through the camp to Ezra's tent. "Rebbe Ezra!" he called from outside the door. "Get up! Please! I have to speak with you." The rebbe emerged a moment later wearing only his tunic, his hair tousled.

"Reuben . . . ? What's going on?"

"We need more guards at the treasury. Now. A gang of Babylonians is going to rob us tonight."

"What? How do you know?" As Ezra was speaking, Asher crawled out of his tent next door.

"What's going on?"

"The gang of Babylonian thieves from Casiphia that I used to work with are planning to rob your gold. That's why I convinced you to let me come. I know you can't possibly forgive me for playing a part in this, but I've changed my mind. I want to help you, not them. Please, gather more men and weapons as fast as you can. We have to guard the Holy One's gold."

"I'll wake the other men," Asher said. He ran to each of the surrounding tents, calling for the men to wake up.

"How many robbers are coming?" Ezra asked as they hurried back to the treasury. The rebbe hadn't taken time to dress or grab his sandals and walked barefooted.

"I don't know. They didn't say how many. There were only supposed to be four of them, plus me. But they changed plans on me and recruited more men to help. And they're armed."

"Should we light torches? Scare them off?" Ezra asked.

"No." Reuben knew how determined his friends were. "They'll only wait and come back another night and we'll be forced to live in fear. The best thing we can do is lie in wait tonight and surprise them."

"Good. That's what we'll do."

"Rebbe . . . I'm so sorry—"

"Never mind about that right now. We have work to do."

More men poured from their tents to join them. Ezra urged them to be quiet, to get weapons, find places to hide, and wait for the attack to begin. All the swords in the armory were quickly taken up. The rest of the men gathered clubs and knives. They hid in the shadows, silently waiting to spring out when the robbers appeared. "Let us do the fighting when the enemy comes," Ezra told Reuben and the other guards. "You Levites need to stand your ground and guard the tent so nothing is taken during the distraction of the battle."

"But I want to fight!" Reuben said. "This is my fault and—"

"Guarding the treasure is your only task. You've been consecrated to do it," Ezra said, then disappeared into the shadows with the other men, still barefooted. Reuben didn't know how many men Bear had recruited, but more than one hundred Jews now crouched in the shadows where they couldn't be seen, including Rebbe Ezra and his brother. If any of these men were injured or killed tonight, it would be Reuben's fault.

He took his position in the open where his friends expected to see him, clutching the hilt of Abba's sword tightly in his hand. His heart thudded painfully inside his chest. Could he attack and kill his friends? He hoped he wouldn't have to. He hoped they would scatter and run.

At last he saw movement between the tents. A mass of dark shapes crept forward toward the treasury, crouching low. Reuben couldn't see their faces, but he thought he recognized Bear's barrel-shaped body and massive shoulders. Then he spotted Digger, tall and gangly. They were his friends—Bear and Digger and Nib and Ram—and with them, were at least twenty other men. Swords glinted in the scant light. They intended to kill all of the guards. And maybe Reuben, too.

"Now!" Reuben shouted when he could see Bear's face.

Bear looked at him in surprise. "You betrayed us?"

"You swore it would only be the four of you!" It was all he had time to say. Chaos broke out as the Jews sprang from their hiding places and the battle began. From where Reuben stood guarding the tent, he could see men fighting in the dark and hear the clash of swords along with battle cries and moans. It had to be nearly impossible to skirmish on a dark, moonless night with little space between the crowded tents. He longed to join them but remained at his post, tense and alert.

Suddenly Reuben saw movement on his left and heard a ripping sound as one of the Babylonian mercenaries slit through the goat-hair tent with his sword. The man was taking advantage of the chaos to go after the gold. Reuben rushed him, sword drawn, and within seconds he was fighting for his life against a much larger and more skilled Babylonian. His enemy was relentless, and just as Reuben began to tire and lose ground, one of the other Levite guards came to his aid. Together they killed the man. "Thanks," Reuben breathed. He wondered if the other Levite knew this attack was his fault. Would he have helped him if he had?

Reuben returned to his post and saw Babylonians falling all around him, one after the other. The battle seemed to go on and on, just as on the Thirteenth of Adar, but at last the fighting stopped. Bodies lay strewn all over the ground. Were Bear and Ram and Digger and Nib among them? Reuben didn't look to see. He didn't want to know. He listened as Ezra took a quick tally, and although a few Jews had been wounded, none had been killed.

Reuben sank to the ground, still gripping his father's sword. He wanted to weep, but whether from grief or relief he didn't know. As the men cleared away the bodies, and the excitement died down, Rebbe Ezra came to crouch beside him. "Thank you, Reuben."

"For what? Planning to rob you? For telling my gang about the gold you're carrying and how to find it?" He exhaled, disgusted with himself.

"Why did you change your mind?" Ezra asked quietly.

"I don't even know." He stared at the ground, ashamed. He still wore the kippah on his head, a symbol of his submission to God. "I'll be returning to Casiphia in the morning," he said, "but I would like to keep my father's sword, if that's all right."

"You're going back to the Gentiles? Why?"

"I don't belong here with men like you."

"Reuben, you did the right thing tonight. You fought well. We could use a strong Levite guard like you."

"I don't think the others will agree with you, especially my uncle. Once they find out I was involved—"

"Let me worry about that. For now, not too many men really know what went on last night. And I'm willing to give you a second chance."

Reuben couldn't meet his gaze. "Why?" he asked softly. "I lied to you and tried to rob you."

"Because the Almighty One is a God of second chances. None of us deserves to be forgiven and set free from exile. But He did forgive us and made a way for us to return and serve Him in Jerusalem. He'll forgive you, too."

Reuben could only shake his head, unable to comprehend such an offer after what he'd done.

"Would you like a new beginning, Reuben? A chance to start all over and make different choices this time? . . . I think you do, or you wouldn't have warned us last night or fought alongside us." Ezra stood and gripped Reuben's shoulder for a moment. "For my sake, please reconsider. I don't want you to turn back. Look at this night as the death of your past. Let tomorrow bring a new beginning."

Reuben nodded, glad no one could see his tears in the dark.

CHAPTER

43

Four months after leaving Babylon, on the fourth day of the fifth month, Devorah stood on a rise overlooking Jerusalem for the first time. Ezra had pulled their donkey cart to a halt to gaze in awe at the view neither of them ever dreamed they would see. Tears blurred her vision as she silently praised the Holy One.

To anyone else, the sight would have been unremarkable—a cluster of stone houses and buildings, all built from creamy Jerusalem limestone. But to Devorah, who had sung about Jerusalem and read about it all her life, this was the city of her God. The holy temple stood on a hill in the distance, a column of smoke rising from the altar. The setting sun bathed the sanctuary in golden light as if it shone with God's glory. Below the temple on another hill was Jerusalem, a mere remnant of the magnificent city of King Solomon's day or of Judah's last kings, but she and Ezra were here to help rebuild it.

Devorah reached to take her husband's hand in hers. "It's so beautiful here! The mountains are so lush and green."

"'As the mountains surround Jerusalem, so the Lord surrounds His people,'" Ezra recited. She saw him wipe his eyes as their children gathered around them and knew this was an emotional moment for him, as well. "That's the temple over there—do you see it?" he asked. "The Holy One's temple. From now on, we can worship Him the way He commanded us to in His Torah. We'll celebrate the sacrifices and new moons and festivals."

"It's too wonderful to even believe," Devorah said. "I feel like I'm dreaming."

"When can we see the temple up close, Abba?" his son Shallum asked.

"We're probably too late for the evening sacrifice today. We have to set up camp first. And then wash and change our clothes, of course, before we can go up to worship."

"When do Shallum and I get to be priests?" Judah asked. "And sacrifice animals?"

"Not for a few more years, I'm afraid. You have a lot of studying to do first. But I'm glad to know you're so eager to begin."

On that long-ago day when the twins skipped classes, Devorah couldn't have imagined it would lead them here. "Being a priest isn't a job to take lightly," she said, ruffling Judah's dark hair. "Priests stand between the Almighty One and His people as intercessors. Your lives must be exemplary, you know—and that includes obeying your parents as the fifth commandment says."

Judah gave a weary sigh. "We know, Mama."

She returned her gaze to the temple. "I can't believe we're really here."

"I've seen dozens of temples to false gods in Babylon and Susa," Ezra said, "but this one, humble as it is, puts all of them to shame. I never thought I would be privileged to see it and to worship the Holy One here in Jerusalem."

"Let's go, then," Shallum said, tugging his father's sleeve. "Everyone else is passing us by!"

Ezra smiled at his son's enthusiasm and yanked on the donkey's bridle to start him moving again. As the children ran on ahead, he leaned closer to Devorah as if unwilling to be over-heard. "I admit I'm overwhelmed by the task ahead of me. I hesitated when asked to lead our fellow Jews in Babylon—now God has given me the responsibility of leading the entire prov-ince of Judah."

"But you don't have to do it alone. You've always depended on the Almighty One, and He has never allowed you to stumble."

"I'm under no illusions the people here will respond eagerly to my leadership. Enforcing the laws given in the Torah isn't going to be an easy task. But I know from the writings of the prophets and from the history of our people that our future depends on our willingness to keep God's covenant—and that means much more than merely attending the ritual sacrifices at the temple."

Devorah could barely concentrate on her husband's words as she gazed around, marveling at the view. Green hills rolled into the distance all around her with terraced vineyards hugging their rocky slopes. Groves of olive trees rustled their silvery leaves as if in greeting. But Ezra had chosen this moment to confide his thoughts and fears, and she leaned closer to listen. "Have you decided where to begin?" she asked.

"Not exactly. The job of teaching the people is going to be an enormous one. If Reuben is typical of other young men his age, then their knowledge of the Almighty One and His Torah is sketchy, at best."

"I'm glad you convinced Reuben to come with us."

"My decision to give him another chance is still meeting with opposition from some of his fellow Levites. He'll have to prove himself, and that may take time."

As they neared the city, a delegation of elders came out to greet Ezra, wanting to welcome their new governor and other leaders. He surrendered the reins of their cart to the twins, and Devorah continued on without him to their campsite in the Kidron Valley. The sun had set by the time they chose a spot to set up their tent, and Devorah was hot and weary, the children whining and quarrelsome. She assigned chores and set about preparing dinner with her sister-in-law, Miriam, but tears filled her eyes again as the day's accumulated emotions caught up with her. "What's wrong?" Miriam asked when she saw Devorah wiping her cheeks.

"I don't even know," she said, laughing. "I'm overwhelmed and amazed to be here—and frightened at the thought of all the changes ahead. Where do we start?"

"I know what you mean." Miriam sighed as she bent over the kneading trough to mix the dough for flatbread. "It would have been so much easier to simply stay in Babylon where we had nice homes and a good life and everything we needed. Now we're camping in tents, cooking over piles of sticks, and starting life all over again. Our children are cranky and uneasy about all the changes, too, and I don't blame them."

"I'm sure things will get better in the days ahead."

"Do you really believe that, Devorah? I mean, just look at all the work ahead of us. We're unaccustomed to this rustic life."

She sighed, wiping her eyes again. "To be honest, I'm too tired at the moment to face what's ahead. But where would our people be if Abraham and Sarah hadn't left their comfortable homes at God's command? Or if we had remained in Egypt instead of leaving with Moses?"

"The Almighty One certainly likes shaking things up and forcing people to move."

"Yes. And I admit, I've argued with Him about it in the past. I was furious when Jude died . . . and I nearly turned away from God in my grief."

Miriam paused to lay her floury hand on Devorah's arm. "Oh, Devorah! I'm so sorry. I never imagined—"

"Of course not. I went to great pains to hide how I felt. Then I struggled all over again when Ezra told me I was supposed to marry him, according to the law."

"I admire you for being willing to do it. I don't think I could have obeyed."

"It was very difficult. But we went from being reluctant strangers to finding peace and contentment with each other—and love. I love Ezra, and I never thought it could happen."

"And it's obvious to everyone in the family he loves you, too."

Devorah laughed again. "Our marriage isn't perfect—he still bristles when I offer my advice on things before he asks. And he especially chafes when I tell him I think he's wrong. But I wonder where I would be right now if I hadn't trusted the Almighty One to know what was best for me? If I had continued to fight against His will?"

"Probably not here in Jerusalem, living in a tent by a stream and trying to cook a meal without a decent hearth."

Devorah laughed. "No, probably not. But I'm glad I'm here, in spite of the hardships. And I know we can trust the Almighty One to bless us and our children and grandchildren because we obeyed Him."

Ezra made sure the tent housing the treasury was secured with a team of guards in place before retiring to his own tent. The heavy weight of responsibility for transporting the Holy One's gold and silver was nearly over.

At dawn, after bathing and changing into clean clothes, he and his family walked up to the temple for the morning sacrifice, joined by thousands of other pilgrims from the caravan. He watched in awe, moved beyond words, as the priests sacrificed a lamb for his sins, and for his peoples' sins. Then one of the priests lifted a coal from the altar of sacrifice and carried it into the sanctuary where he would use it to light the incense. The altar of incense stood before the Almighty One's throne room, the Holy of Holies, and the prayers of God's people would ascend to heaven along with the incense. Ezra closed his eyes and lifted his hands in prayer, asking for the strength and courage to lead and teach his people. Devorah was right; he could only undertake this enormous task with God's help.

Afterward, he returned to his campsite with his family. It was the eve of the Sabbath, and everyone worked to prepare for the day of rest that would begin at sunset. That evening and throughout the next day, the entire caravan feasted and rejoiced, thanking the Almighty One for a safe trip and a new beginning. For Ezra, it was a Sabbath unlike any other he had ever celebrated. He was in the land promised to Abraham, settled by his ancestors, praising the Holy One in His temple. Ezra spent the day resting for God, knowing that in the days ahead, he would need to rest on God for all his needs.

When the Sabbath ended, Ezra assembled all the Levites, including Reuben, and they delivered the huge offering of silver and gold to the priests to be stored in the temple treasury. He felt the weight of responsibility lift from his shoulders at last, as if he had carried each bag of gold himself, every mile of the way. He felt content as he sat outside his tent after dinner that evening, writing in his journal and watching his sons play a game in the dirt with pebble-sized stones. Devorah sat across the small campfire from him, combing their youngest daughter's hair.

The hand of our God was on us, he wrote, *and He protected us from enemies and bandits along the way. So we arrived in Jerusalem, where we rested three days. On the fourth day, in the house of our God, we weighed out the silver and gold and the sacred articles into the hands of Meremoth son of Uriah, the priest. . . . Everything was accounted for by number and weight. . . .*

He halted, looking up at Devorah so abruptly she asked, "What's wrong? You look as though you've seen a ghost."

"What if I hadn't listened to you, Devorah?"

"What do you mean? I hope you're always listening to me," she said, smiling. "I really hate being ignored, you know."

"We weighed the gold and silver into the temple treasury today and every ounce of it made it here safely, thank God. But what if I hadn't listened to you and shown mercy to Reuben? What if you hadn't convinced me to apologize and give him another chance? That band of Babylonians could have easily overpowered our guards. Every one of those Levites standing guard that night would probably be dead. And who knows how much gold would have been stolen." He watched her work for a moment, her beautiful hands braiding their daughter's dark hair into a long plait. "Did I ever thank you, Devorah? If not—thank you."

"I simply did my job as your wife—your helper." She finished her task and pulled their daughter close, kissing the top of her head before releasing her. The tender gesture moved Ezra.

"And you do your job wonderfully well," he told her. "The law is of utmost importance to me—I'm commissioned to vigorously defend it and teach it and enforce it. But I need you to continually remind me that although God is always just, He administers His justice with mercy and compassion. So, thank you."

Devorah laughed. "You're welcome." She rose and kissed the top of Ezra's head, too, before ducking into their tent. He closed his eyes, thanking God for the gift of his wife, even though she came to him through a time of great pain. Without her, he would've been a weaker leader.

As Judah's new governor, Ezra knew his first priority was to ask the Almighty One to forgive His people. To wash everyone clean, so to speak, the way they had washed away the dust and sweat of their long, four-month journey. Only then could he set up his new government and rule according to the Torah. Using some of the donated gold and silver, Ezra organized a convocation at the temple for the returned exiles, sacrificing burnt offerings to the Holy One: twelve bulls for all Israel, ninety-six rams, and seventy-seven male lambs; then twelve male goats for a sin offering. "We have so much to be thankful for," he told his family. He would offer his own thank offering in addition to the others.

On the day of the convocation, Ezra invited Reuben to walk up to the temple mount with him and his family. Ezra had grown very fond of this young man over the past four months, and as he vigorously defended him against the other Levites' mistrust, he'd begun to think of him as a son. But when they reached the top of the mount, Reuben would go no farther than the outer court. "Why not?' Ezra asked. "You belong in the court of men with me and the others."

Reuben shook his head. "I don't deserve to worship with the other men. I've done so many things wrong in my life."

"Go into the courts without me," Ezra told his family while he remained behind with Reuben. "When are you going to stop punishing yourself?" he asked. "Don't you believe God will forgive you if you ask?"

"I don't even know how to ask."

"That's what these sacrifices are for—so we can all plead for forgiveness. Every one of us has sinned and broken God's law."

"But none of you has done the terrible things I have."

Ezra exhaled. "I see your heart, Reuben. I see how very sorry you are—and God sees it, too. Maybe if you made a sin offering of your own and confessed your sins, you would feel forgiven. You can offer a lamb or a female goat—"

"I would love to, Rebbe, but I don't have money to buy an offering. I gave everything I had to my mother before I left Casiphia."

"Well, once you begin your duties at the temple, you'll be getting paid from the peoples' tithes."

"My duties? You can't possibly want me to serve in the temple after what I did."

"Of course we do! Reuben, listen to me." He gripped Reuben's shoulders, praying he would hear him. "There are four steps that show true repentance, and after you've completed them, you are forgiven by God and by all of us. First, you need to acknowledge you've done wrong. You've done that already. Repeatedly. Second, you must be willing to confess it. You will do that when you bring your sacrifice to the priest, confessing the particular sins the sacrifice will atone for. Third, you must be willing to abandon your sin—leave it behind, walk in a brand-new direction. I think it's safe to say you're going to abandon stealing?" Reuben nodded. Ezra released him and patted his back. "Good. Then the fourth step is to make restitution whenever possible."

"How do I pay back all the people I stole from in Babylon?" he asked, spreading his hands.

"You can't. But you can live a life of generosity toward people in need from now on. Only you and God ever need to know you are repaying that debt."

"Should I wait until I've earned a wage as a Levite and then make an offering?"

"Yes. And one more thing, Reuben. Once the sacrifice has burned into ashes on the altar, your sin is nothing but ashes, as well. The Holy One forgives us—and we have to believe it in faith. That means leaving our past in the past, not agonizing over it, not bringing it to life in your memory again and again. We must forget it the same way God does—'As far as the east is from the west.' That's how far in the past our sins will be."

Reuben lowered his head, staring at his feet. "Thank you, Rebbe."

Ezra rested his hand on Reuben's back, gently pushing him forward. "Now, come on. My family is waiting for us. And the Almighty One is waiting to forgive our people."

CHAPTER

44

JERUSALEM

Reuben was back in school again and eager to learn. He stood in the temple's outer court after the morning sacrifice with the other thirty-seven Levites from Casiphia and listened as one of the chief Levites explained their duties and responsibilities. "God separated the tribe of Levi from the other eleven tribes at Mount Sinai," he began, "and charged them with the service of God's holy tabernacle—and now His temple. You serve in place of the firstborn sons of Israel. As you may know, our firstborn sons belong to God because He spared Israel's firstborn during the last plague in Egypt when the firstborn sons of Pharaoh and all the other Egyptians died. Now each firstborn son must be redeemed at birth, and you Levites belong to God in their place. In the fourth book of Moses God says, 'The Levites . . . are the Israelites who are to be wholly given to me. I have taken them as my own in place of the firstborn. . . . I have given the Levites as gifts to Aaron and his sons to do the work at the Tent of Meeting on behalf of the Israelites and to make atonement for them.'"

Reuben followed the chief Levite as he led the group on a tour around the perimeter of the temple mount, pointing out

348

the twenty-four locations where they were commissioned to keep watch: Levites guarded twenty-one of the posts; priests guarded the other three. One of their tasks would be to open the sanctuary doors in the morning and close them again at night. "The fourth book of Moses says we bear the responsibility for offenses against the holy sanctuary," the chief Levite said. "This is holy ground, God's dwelling place. Anyone other than priests and Levites who comes near the sanctuary must be put to death."

They continued walking, then stopped again near the special platform built for the Levite singers and musicians. "Those of you who are musicians will serve here, leading the people in praise to Almighty God. Praise is an important component of worship, and we're privileged to lead it."

They moved on until the chief Levite halted again in front of the temple treasury. "You may know that when Moses divided the Promised Land among the sons of Israel, the tribe of Levi wasn't given any land or inheritance. You'll be paid from the tithes and offerings the people give to God. Their prosperity is your prosperity, their suffering is yours also."

It occurred to Reuben the gold he would have stolen from the caravan was for the operation of the temple. He would now be paid with the treasure he had rescued and guarded for the past four months.

"The cities given to the Levites are spread throughout the land," the man continued, "including the cities of refuge, where some of you will serve as judges. Your tribe is scattered in the midst of all the other tribes so you can set an example as God's servants, elevating yourselves spiritually in order to lead the people to God. Our territory is much smaller than the original Promised Land divided among the sons of Israel. But the principle of living and serving among the people remains the same. Rebbe Ezra and his fellow scholars will teach you the finer points of the law in the coming months so you can help teach others."

As Reuben listened, the role of a Levite seemed truly daunting, requiring much more of him than standing guard. Even so, he was grateful to be here, grateful for the chance to begin his life again. He only wished his father could have served alongside him.

"You will also be called upon to assist the priests with the sacrifices, especially during the annual feast days when thousands of people make pilgrimages to Jerusalem. You'll be divided into smaller groups for this part of your training and learn your duties from the priests themselves."

Later that day, the chief Levite sent Reuben and his new Levite friend, Eli, to the House of the Weavers just below the temple mount to be fitted for their new white robes. Every step of the process took place in this enclosure, from spinning, bleaching, and dying the wool and flax, to weaving the cloth and tailoring the garments. A dozen looms of various sizes were set up in the courtyard, and the weavers worked beneath the shade of a rush roof. Most of them wove white linen cloth for the robes and other garments, but a few were making the brightly dyed sashes of purple, crimson, and blue wool the priests and Levites wore.

Reuben paused to watch, amazed by how quickly their shuttles flew. And sitting among the women like a flower among weeds was a beautiful young woman with russet-colored hair. She was much younger than the other weavers, yet obviously just as skilled. Her graceful fingers moved in perfect rhythm as she worked, and the pure white cloth grew inch by inch on the loom.

His friend Eli nudged him in the ribs, interrupting his thoughts. "Are you interested in learning to weave, Reuben? Or does that pretty girl over there interest you?"

"I was noticing how skillful she is. I wonder if I'll ever learn to do my work that effortlessly."

"Are you sure you didn't also notice how pretty she is?"

Reuben gave an embarrassed grin. "Yes. I did notice that, too."

"Why don't you talk to her?" Eli said, nudging him again. "She isn't married, you know."

"How do you know that? Do you know her? What's her name?"

Eli laughed. "I never saw her before. But I know she's single because she isn't wearing a head covering like married women do."

"Oh. Of course." That's why Reuben had noticed her auburn hair—the other women's heads were all covered.

"Who's next?" the tailor called from the doorway.

Reuben went inside the building and removed his sandals to be measured. The chief Levite had explained how each robe was woven in one piece, including the hem, and would be tailored to each man's height. He had also explained how they would perform their duties without shoes, showing reverence for the temple's holy ground.

"You're a tall fellow!" the tailor said. "And muscular, too. How did you get to be so strong?"

"I worked as a blacksmith in Babylon." As he spoke the words, Reuben was surprised to discover he could recall his years with his father and be reminded of what he'd lost without anger or bitterness. His father would've rather Reuben inherit this calling as a Levite than to inherit his blacksmith shop. And if his uncle hadn't sold the shop, Reuben never would've left Casiphia and come to Jerusalem.

"Are you planning to work as a blacksmith here, too?" the man asked as he stretched his measuring cord from Reuben's head to his feet.

"No, I'm needed at the temple. They say there's a shortage of Levites."

"Your name?"

"Reuben ben David."

"All done. You may go. Send in whoever is next."

Reuben was nearly to the door when he turned and asked, "When should I come back for my robe?" He was thinking of the girl again and hoping he could gather his courage by then and talk to her the next time he returned.

"You don't have to come back," the tailor said. "We'll deliver your new robe and other garments to the chamber of the wardrobe when they're finished."

"Oh . . . well, thank you."

Back in the courtyard, Reuben was again drawn to the girl, watching her while he waited for his friend to be measured. She was slender and petite, her skin fairer in color than the other Jewish women around her. She looked up and noticed him, and he saw her cheeks flush before she quickly looked away.

The woman working alongside the girl frowned as she called to him. "Do you need something, young man?"

"No. I'm just waiting for my friend. I've never seen cloth being woven before." He wished the girl would've spoken instead of the woman. He would've liked to hear what her voice sounded like. More Levites arrived to be measured, and the courtyard became crowded. Reuben's friend emerged from the building and beckoned to him.

"You ready to go?"

No. He would've liked to stay longer. He could have watched the beautiful young weaver all day. He chided himself for his lack of courage as he walked back to the temple mount. He should have spoken to her, learned her name. How would he ever find her again?

Later that day, Reuben received his first wages as a Levite. He made his way to Rebbe Ezra's tent that evening after the meal and found him sitting outside with his wife and children, writing in his journal. The summer night was warm, and the rebbe invited him to sit with them.

"I finished my first week of training as a Levite, Rebbe. They paid me today."

"Wonderful! How are you enjoying your work?"

"I won't officially start working until my robe is finished. I went to be measured for it today. But I think I'm going to enjoy it. Being a guard suits me." His years of moving in the shadows, staying alert to every little sound and movement, had prepared him well for the vigilance required as a guard, especially when he was on night duty.

"I must say you look very happy, Reuben. There's no greater joy in life than to find and fulfill God's purpose for you."

"Yes, Rebbe . . . I came to talk to you because I'm going to buy a lamb for a sin offering tomorrow with my pay. I hope it will help me feel like my past is truly gone."

"I hope so, too. Remember, we talked about how your offering isn't accepted unless accompanied by true repentance. That means living in a way that shows gratitude. But you also need to understand you aren't buying God's forgiveness. You can't buy or earn forgiveness with any amount of money or with thousands of sacrifices. It's a gift, Reuben."

He nodded. But he had a lot more to learn about the Almighty One and His ways. "What should I expect tomorrow, Rebbe?"

"The sacrifice will be very bloody, as you already know. Think of it as a taste of your own death as you watch. The animal dies, taking our place and showing us what we would deserve if God were to judge us. The sacrifice represents the death of our physical side and allows our spiritual nature to draw closer to God. The Hebrew word for sacrifice is *korban*, and it comes from the root word meaning 'to come near' or 'to approach.' Our ability to draw close to God is what sets us apart from the animal kingdom. We raise ourselves above their level and dedicate ourselves to Him."

Reuben would be drawing near to the Holy One tomorrow. He couldn't imagine it.

"You've seen dozens of sacrifices by now," the rebbe continued. "You probably know that for each of the daily offerings we give portions of flour, oil, salt, and frankincense. All four parts of creation come together in worship: the priest represents humanity; the bull or the lamb represents the animal kingdom; the flour and oil come from the plant kingdom; the salt is from the inanimate world. In God's temple, all creation unites in harmony and worship."

At dawn the next morning, Reuben's hand trembled as he placed it on the lamb's head and confessed his sins. He watched the animal die in his place. Reuben couldn't pay back all the people he'd stolen from, but he promised God he would live generously, as the rebbe had advised him to do. As the aroma of his offering rose to heaven, Reuben was ready to start a new life, as pure and spotless as the new robe he would soon wear as he served God.

JERUSALEM

Ezra knew he shouldn't feel intimidated as he prepared to face Jerusalem's elders and chief priests—after all, he'd stood before the king of the entire Persian Empire. Yet as he entered the long, narrow throne room and walked between the rows of pillars supporting the high roof, he was under no illusion the elders gathered here would embrace him with open arms. They had welcomed him readily enough on the first day, but this would be his first official meeting with them since arriving in Jerusalem as their new governor.

He had made it his business to learn something about the elders and chief priests he would be working with, and he'd learned that Eliezer, the elderly chief priest who brought the meeting to order, was the son of Jeshua, the high priest who had returned to Jerusalem eighty years ago to rebuild the temple. The leaders sat in a semicircle while Ezra stood before them. The vacant throne of judgment where King David's heir once held court was behind him, but Ezra would never attempt to occupy such an honored seat.

"I don't mean to seem impertinent," Eliezer began, "but who are you to come to Jerusalem and tell us what to do?"

Ezra remained calm. "Are you asking for my credentials, my ancestry, or my authorization?" When no one replied he said, "I served with the men of the Great Assembly in Babylon as their youngest member. As you may know, that esteemed body of men spent years studying the Torah and issuing rulings on how to apply it to our everyday lives. I am a descendant of Aaron from the tribe of Levi. My ancestors served as high priests in Solomon's temple from the time it was built until it was destroyed. Would you like their names?"

"That won't be necessary."

Ezra usually avoided confrontations like this, preferring the solitude of his studies. But being forced to explain himself angered him and fueled his courage. This time, no matter how intimidated he felt, he wouldn't try to back away from the task of leadership God had given him like he had before the Thirteenth of Adar. "You've all seen a copy of King Artaxerxes' decree," he continued, "authorizing me to govern. I didn't seek this position. When I petitioned the Persian king to allow our people to return home, I hoped to serve as a priest like my forefathers. Nevertheless, the king commissioned me to lead, and he appointed me governor. I intend to lead to the very best of my ability—God helping me."

Eliezer's smile looked cold and insincere. "The regional governor of Trans-Euphrates won't be happy to hear of your appointment. We've dealt with him and his royal satraps in the past, and they'll view this as a loss of their authority and power over the territory of Judah."

"That's exactly what it is. And I didn't expect them to be happy about giving up their sovereignty. Nor will they be pleased when they learn the king's decree requires the treasurers of Trans-Euphrates to supply whatever finances I ask for. I'll be delivering the king's orders to the royal satraps and governors in the coming weeks and making my requests. If any of you wish to join my delegation, you're welcome to do so." Ezra wasn't surprised when no one accepted his offer. They seemed prepared to throw him to the Gentile rulers all by himself.

"It seems to us," one of the elders said, "that if authority is granted to govern the province of Judah, it should be Prince Eliakim, Prince Zerubbabel's grandson and heir. Shouldn't he represent us and govern us instead of you?"

Ezra knew exactly which man in the gathering was Prince Eliakim, heir to the throne of King David. But the fact that he hadn't chosen to sit on the throne or to question Ezra himself indicated the elders and chief priests were the real power behind the puppet prince, a power they seemed reluctant to relinquish. Ezra gave a slight bow in deference to Prince Eliakim before replying. "I've looked into this matter, and it's my understanding that the governor of Trans-Euphrates has ruled over Judah ever since Prince Zerubbabel died. The Persians no longer recognize the right of his heir or our royal family to rule in his place—am I correct?" The prince nodded, conceding it was true. "I specifically asked King Artaxerxes to allow Judah's kings to govern instead of me, but he refused. So here we are. This is the way it will be for now."

"Are you moving into the governor's residence?" the prince asked. "And living here?"

The question surprised Ezra. "No, I intend to build a house for my family just like all the other men who've returned with me."

"That would be a mistake, Rebbe Ezra," the chief elder said. "If you want to legitimize your claim as ruler—"

"This decree I'm carrying legitimizes my authority to rule," Ezra said, waving his copy of the decree.

"Yes. You've made that clear," the elder said. "But in the eyes of Judah's neighbors and the people of this land, you will need to make a conscious display of that authority by living here. This hall will serve as a place to conduct court business and meetings with other officials. The banquet hall and your staff of servants will provide a place to offer hospitality on behalf of our nation. Of course, if your wife is willing to cook for a delegation of royal satraps all by herself, we won't stand in her way."

Ezra tugged on his beard. He had always resisted the trappings of power and privilege when he'd served as the leader of the Jewish community in Babylon. But in this instance, he knew he would have to concede. "Very well. I'll move my family into this residence if that's what you advise. But I want to make it clear I will not be asking the Persians for political nationhood. For now, Judah continues to be a province in the Persian Empire. I'm here to forge a *spiritual* nation. To govern this province by the laws given in the Torah."

Ezra hoped the questioning would end soon so he could get on with his business. He hated the political maneuvering of secular leadership and had little patience for it. But these men would serve in his administration in the coming days, and he needed them as allies, not enemies. What's more, the Holy One was "compassionate and gracious, slow to anger," and Ezra's public life, as well as his personal life, needed to measure up to that ideal. But Eliezer wasn't finished with his questions.

"I see the Persian king's decree commands you to 'instruct those who don't know the law.' How do you intend to do that?"

"By doing what I know how to do best—teaching. I'm hoping there are priests and Levites among us who are well-versed in the law and who'll be able to assist me in this. If not, I will have to instruct the teachers first. I also intend to appoint judges—men who are masters of the law and can sit alone in judgment—and laymen magistrates who can preside over civil cases in tribunals."

"How far do you intend to exercise your authority outside of Jerusalem?" someone asked. Ezra recognized the man as a self-proclaimed tribal chieftain from Keilah, who currently governed a group of villages in that region. He likely saw Ezra as a threat.

"I intend to travel to every town and village within the borders of the province of Judah. I understand they extend from Jericho and the Jordan River in the east, to Azekah in the west, to Bethel in the north, and to Keilah and Kiriath-arba in the south. The teachers and magistrates I appoint will cover the same territory. Anyone wishing to continue as an elder or a leader—and of course as a priest—will need to know the Torah thoroughly and follow it to the letter."

The more Ezra spoke, the more disturbed Eliezer seemed to become. The elderly priest had all he could do to remain seated, and when he finally spoke, his voice rose to nearly a shout. "Come now, Rebbe Ezra! Let's be practical. Do you honestly expect all the people in Judah to obey you?"

"No, I expect them to obey the Almighty One. I'm hoping they'll do so willingly, especially when they see the blessings He promised for those who keep His covenant."

"But there are Gentiles living among us—Samaritans and mixed-race peoples and Edomite clans who've migrated north to settle in Judean territory over the years. How are you going to make them obey? Are you prepared to enforce the part of the king's decree that says whoever doesn't obey will be punished by death, banishment, confiscation of property, or imprisonment?"

"The people of Judah and the other provinces have been forced to comply with Persian law for some time now. That hasn't changed—and neither has the punishment they inflict on lawbreakers. As God's covenant people, we Jews have always been responsible for living according to His law—that hasn't changed since the day Moses received it on Mount Sinai. Nor have the punishments spelled out in the Torah changed.

"As for the Gentiles . . ." He paused, remembering the pagans who had slaughtered his brother. "The Holy One promised the Gentiles would be blessed through us. Perhaps this decree is a fulfillment of that promise, because if the Gentiles obey God, He promises to bless even them." Although Ezra admitted only to himself his doubt that the pagan Gentiles would ever turn to God. In fact, his continuing hatred and distrust made him hope every last Gentile would retreat from his province when they learned about the high standards they would have to live up to under the law.

Ezra looked around, trying to gauge the men's reactions. The chief priest was clearly disturbed about something, but he seemed to have run out of questions for now. Some of the men actually looked pleased with what Ezra had told them so far. "If you have no further questions, gentlemen, I have one of my own. Where are we in the schedule of tithing and the Sabbath years?"

"What do you mean?" Eliezer asked. "The people have been bringing a tithe of their grain, new wine, and oil, as well as the firstborn of their herds and flocks to the temple every year since we rebuilt it."

"Good. But every third year, the tithes are to be stored in the towns and villages so they can be distributed to the Levites and to the poor, the fatherless, and widows. And every seventh year the land is to be given a rest. We are forbidden to sow or prune or reap our land during the Sabbath year. And after seven Sabbaths, the Lord declares a Year of Jubilee."

"Nothing like that was established when our ancestors returned and rebuilt the temple," Eliezer said.

"Then it needs to be. One of the indictments against our ancestors leading to our exile was their failure to give the land a rest. God allowed us to be carried into captivity so the land would finally have its Sabbaths. We need to calculate the years back to the last known Year of Jubilee and figure out where we are in the cycle. And proper tithing must begin at once."

"The people are poor, Rebbe Ezra. The additional burden of not planting and harvesting every seven years will be crippling. You can't expect to enforce this—"

"Perhaps they're poor because they haven't been giving the Almighty One His tithe. You know the covenant curses for disobedience: 'Your basket and your kneading trough will be cursed. The fruit of your womb will be cursed and the crops of your land, and the calves of your herds and the lambs of your flocks.' But prosperity and blessing are promised to those who obey God. If we carefully follow all His commands, 'the Lord your God will set you high above all the nations on earth. All these blessings will come upon you and accompany you if you obey the Lord your God.'"

Some of the men shook their heads. Most looked skeptical. Why couldn't they understand this? "Do you believe God sovereignly controls nature?" Ezra asked. "And it is God who makes our crops flourish and brings famine?"

"Yes, of course, but—"

"Then why can't you trust God and follow His command to give the land a Sabbath rest?" No one replied. But if these men, Judah's elders and chief priests, didn't understand this basic principle, Ezra knew he was going to have a lot of work ahead of him to teach everyone else.

"Our service and our worship of the Holy One doesn't just take place in the temple, gentlemen. God wants us to give Him sovereignty over *every* area of our lives. We need to obey every word of God—not just because we want His blessings or we fear His judgment, but because His instructions are the very best way to live in this precarious, turbulent world. We are to be His example to the nations. Do we all understand that?" He waited, but no one spoke. "Good. Then let's get to work on this calendar issue right away in obedience to the Almighty One."

46

Ever since Reuben saw the pretty girl who worked in the House of the Weavers, he had watched for her among the worshippers who came to the temple every day. His assignment was to guard one of the Huldah gates near the southern entrance to the temple mount, and although he knew it might be nearly impossible to spot one woman among a crowd of hundreds, he refused to give up. The morning sacrifice was about to begin and most of the worshippers had already made their way into the inner courts, leaving the outer courtyard nearly empty, but Reuben scanned it just the same—and caught a glimpse of a woman with auburn hair standing near the barrier separating the outer courtyard from the Court of Women.

Was it really her? Reuben couldn't quite tell. He left his post for a moment, circling around to try to see her face. Yes! It really was her, standing all alone. Why didn't she join the other women inside the Court of Women? Was she waiting for someone?

Reuben knew he was supposed to be working, staying alert and on guard watching over the temple precincts, but he couldn't stop staring at her. The sacrifice had begun, and he could smell roasting meat from where he stood and hear the songs of the

temple musicians carried to him on the breeze. The deep voices
of the Levite choir sent chills through him as they sang: *"Be at
rest once more, O my soul, for the Lord has been good to you."*
Yes, the Lord had been good to him, giving him this new life in
a new land. But he was lonely. If only he could find someone
to love, someone as pretty as that girl.

Reuben was still keeping one eye on her when the sacrifice
ended. As the auburn-haired girl started to leave, she turned
around so quickly she tripped and fell to her hands and knees
on the pavement. Without thinking, Reuben left his post and
rushed to help her.

"Miss! Are you all right?"

"I think so . . ." He caught a glimpse of one of her legs before
she pulled down the hem of her robe to cover it and noticed it
looked thin and withered. Reuben quickly bent and helped her
to her feet. She was so small and slender, she seemed to weigh
nothing at all. The top of her head barely reached to his chin.
For the first time, he noticed the crutch she had dropped, and
he picked it up and handed it to her.

"Are you all right?" he asked again.

"Just a few scratches," she said, brushing dirt off her hands.
"I'll be fine. Thank you." Her voice was as light and delicate as
she was. "I'm usually not this clumsy," she said, looking embarrassed. "I must have tripped over these uneven stones. Thank you
for helping me." She started to limp away, but Reuben couldn't
let that happen. He was supposed to be working, especially now
that the sacrifice was over and large crowds of people spilled
out from all of the courtyards, but Reuben didn't care if he got
into trouble. He had to find out more about her. He couldn't
let her disappear again.

"Please, let me help you with the stairs, miss. There are so
many to go down."

"You don't need to do that. I come here every day, so I'm quite
used to the steps." He kept pace with her as she limped away,

the crowd jostling both of them. "Believe it or not, today was the first time I've ever tripped. I don't know what happened."

He glanced back at his post, but the exiting crowds blocked it from sight. The gate he guarded was purely ceremonial, he told himself. It wasn't as if he was safeguarding the treasury. "I'm Reuben ben David. What's your name?"

She hesitated. Maybe she wasn't supposed to talk to him, a stranger. Maybe they needed to have a chaperone or something. Or maybe she was simply shy. "Amina," she finally said. Her name was as beautiful as she was.

"Amina," he repeated. "I'm one of the new immigrants from a town in Babylon called Casiphia." They were nearing the stairs, and he wished she would slow down.

"Yes, I saw you the other day when you came to be fitted for your robe." She looked up at him before quickly looking away again, long enough for Reuben to see that her eyes were a beautiful shade of amber, and her cheeks flushed a pretty shade of pink. "Your robe came out well," she added.

Reuben felt a hopeful thrill—she had noticed him! "I was watching you weave that day," he said. "You're very good at what you do. In fact, maybe you're the one who made my robe."

"Maybe," she said with a little smile. Much too soon, they reached the top of the stairs leading from the temple mount down to the city. "You really don't need to help me," she said. "I know you must have work to do. But thanks again." She turned to go.

"Amina, wait!" She stopped and looked up at him, then moved aside so other people could descend the stairs. "I'm new at following all the rules and laws in the Torah," he said. "I didn't learn them back in Babylon, so I don't know the proper thing to say or do, but . . . but I would really like to see you again. I don't have very many friends here, and I'd like to get to know you better. Is . . . is that possible?" Her smile faded and she looked immeasurably sad. "Did I say something wrong?" he asked.

"No. And you're very kind to ask. But if you knew more about me, you wouldn't want me for your friend. You're a very important man with a wonderful ancestry as a Levite, and I'm . . . what I mean is . . . I worship your God, but I'm not Jewish by birth. I'm an Edomite."

"Is that why you didn't go inside the Court of Women?"

"I'm not allowed to go in because I'm crippled." She spoke without self-pity, merely stating the facts. Her face wore such an expression of sweetness and innocence that Reuben wouldn't have cared what her reasons were. He couldn't stop staring at her.

"I don't care about any of those things. I would just like to talk to you some more and get to know you. I'm all by myself here in Jerusalem. My family stayed behind in Casiphia, and I'm making new friends little by little, but I still get lonely and . . . Could we meet someplace and talk—when I'm not on duty?"

She smiled, and Reuben's heart sped up when he realized she was going to say yes. "Do you know how to get back to the House of the Weavers?" she asked.

"I think I could find it again."

"Why don't you come there and talk with me when you have some time off?"

"Thank you, Amina. I will! I'll . . . I'll see you soon." He raced back to his post, breathless. He felt as though he floated on air the way an eagle does, high in the sky, its wings outstretched, carried by the wind. Reuben couldn't remember ever feeling this way before. Amina had invited him to visit her! He had no idea what he would say to her, but she was so delicate and graceful and pretty he would be content to just sit and gaze at her while she worked.

"Where have you been?" another guard asked as Reuben hurried past. "And why are you grinning like that?"

"Am I?" Reuben realized he was—and he couldn't stop. The attraction he felt toward Amina was a new feeling for him. What would it be like to hold her in his arms? To gather her thick russet hair in his hands or kiss her sweet mouth?

He was happy. And hopeful—two emotions he hadn't felt since his father died. Reuben recalled one of his last conversations with his mother, and how she'd asked if he ever thought about settling down and getting married. He was settling down here in Jerusalem, but getting married? It hadn't occurred to him until now. Yet that's what people his age did, didn't they? Rebbe Ezra had just told him the other day that marriage was His plan and His gift. God had commanded Adam and Eve to be fruitful and multiply.

The temple courtyards were nearly empty now as Reuben returned to his post. He had a clear view of the top of the massive altar and the billowing smoke rising from it. As he watched it ascend into the clear morning sky, a prayer formed in his heart: *I know I don't deserve a beautiful woman like Amina, but please . . . if it's possible . . . could I have her for my wife?*

CHAPTER

47

JERUSALEM

Stop it, Amina chided herself. *Just stop it.* She needed to concentrate on her work and stop daydreaming about the handsome Levite. Reuben—his name was Reuben ben David. He said he was lonely and wanted to talk with her, and so she had invited him to come here to the House of the Weavers. That had been three days ago. Now she couldn't stop glancing up at the doorway as she sat at her loom, waiting, hoping he really would come.

She returned to her work with a sigh and passed the shuttle through the vertical warp strands—back and forth, back and forth. The crosshatch weave was very familiar to her now, and she could do it effortlessly. She thought back to the other morning when she had tripped like a clumsy oaf—and how Reuben had scooped her up effortlessly and set her on her feet. It had been very kind of him. Her heart had fluttered like bird's wings at the nearness of him. And when he'd asked if he could talk with her and get to know her, Amina had scrambled to think of a reply. She wanted to say yes, but she didn't have a home to invite him to, or a father to arrange such a meeting, or family members to serve as chaperones. The House of the Weavers was the only place she could think of for them to meet. Besides, Amina had no experience with young men her age, and she hoped that talking here in her familiar work surroundings would make it easier for her.

Reuben said he was lonely, but she couldn't imagine why he had chosen her. She had nothing to offer a man like him with such an impeccable family pedigree. She glanced at the gate again, then felt like kicking herself for foolishly hoping. If the loom hadn't been so heavy and unwieldy, she would have turned it around so her back would be to the gate. But even then she knew she would continue to turn every time she heard footsteps.

Stop thinking about him. He isn't coming.

The late summer weather was warm, and she loved working outside in the languid sunshine. The older women all around her talked of their families and husbands as they wove and spun, but Amina didn't join their conversations very often, too ashamed to tell them about herself or admit she was an Edomite. The woman seated at the loom facing hers was telling everyone about her newest grandchild when she suddenly looked up at the gate and stopped mid-sentence. "May I help you with something?"

Amina looked up, too—and there he was! Reuben had come to see her, just as he'd said. "Reuben . . . welcome . . . I-I mean, come in." Why was she was stammering? He looked nervous as he stepped into the courtyard. "These are my friends," Amina said, introducing each woman by name. "And this is Reuben ben David. He's a Levite." Amina saw the other women exchange knowing smiles. They returned to their work without speaking. Amina hadn't realized how awkward it would be to talk to him with all the other women listening.

"Please, come sit over here in the shade," she said, pointing to a place beside her loom. She had imagined she could continue weaving while they talked and it would help her feel at ease, but now that he was so near, her palms had become slick with sweat. She laid the shuttle aside and folded her hands in her lap, hoping he wouldn't notice they were trembling.

"I'm sorry I couldn't come sooner," he said, "but they assigned me to the night shift for the past three days."

"It must be hard staying awake all night."

"Not for me. I prefer the late night hours." He hadn't stopped staring at her since he appeared at the gate. She wanted to study him in return, but he had come here to talk, hadn't he? Amina searched for something to say.

"I-I hope you don't mind meeting me here."

"Not at all." He smiled, and the courtyard seemed to whirl in circles.

"I couldn't invite you to my home, which would be the proper place to meet, because I don't live in Jerusalem. I live in Bethlehem."

"How far away is Bethlehem?"

"Not far. It takes about two hours to walk there. I've been living in Jerusalem for the past few months while I help make robes for all the new priests and Levites, and the cloth for all your other garments. We're nearly finished, and then I'll be going back home to Bethlehem." He frowned, his handsome smile fading. "What's wrong?" she asked.

"Is it possible you could stay longer? I would really like to get to know you."

Why did he keep saying that? Amina needed to tell him the truth about herself, but not here, not in front of all the women she had worked alongside for the past several months. She hadn't wanted to stand up or walk in front of Reuben again, knowing her withered leg and limping steps repulsed most men, but the sooner he heard the truth and left, the sooner she could stop thinking about him. And stop hoping.

"Let's go out there and talk," she said. She planted her crutch on the cobblestones as she always did when she needed to help herself up, but Reuben quickly took her arm and helped her to her feet. He opened the gate for her, and they walked up the lane a little way, out of earshot of the others but where they could still be seen. The street wasn't busy this time of day, with only a few pedestrians coming and going between the shops.

"You seem like a very nice man, Reuben. Someone I would like to talk with and get to know. But I need to tell you about my past. You may decide to change your mind. . . . I'm . . . I'm not Jewish—"

"Yes, you told me the other day."

"I was born to an Edomite family. My people are the enemies of your people. On the Thirteenth of Adar we went to war against each other. My father planned to kill every Jew in Bethlehem and take their plunder. Instead, he and everyone else in my family died except for my sister, Sayfah, and me."

"My father also died that day. The Babylonians killed him. But his death and the war had nothing to do with you, Amina. You would have been a child."

"I was eight years old. A very kind Jewish woman adopted me and raised me as her own daughter. She died not long ago, but I still live with her family. My sister decided to go back to our people and live with our uncle, but I fell in love with the God of the Jewish people. He's the One who saved me as a child, and I worship Him now. I could never go back to the Edomites even if they wanted me—which they don't, because I'm a cripple."

There. She had told him everything. Reuben seemed to search her face, and she held her breath, waiting for the familiar words of rejection. "Why would any of those things matter to me?" he finally said. "I want to be your friend."

Tears stung her eyes. "B-but a man of your standing, a Levite who serves the Almighty One, shouldn't be associating with someone like me."

He looked away for the first time, and her heart sank. She heard him draw a breath, and when he finally spoke, he stared down at his feet, not at her. "Amina, I'm not who you think I am.

I'm a fraud who has no business serving in the temple. I need to tell you about the terrible things I've done in the past, and once you hear them, you won't want to be with me, not the other way around." She watched him in silence as he chose his words, and something about him made her heart beat wildly, the way it did when she was frightened or out of breath from climbing a hill. She didn't understand it because Reuben didn't frighten her, in spite of his confession that he'd done terrible things.

"After my father died, I turned away from the Almighty One. I became a thief. I broke into people's homes and stole from them. I didn't need to do it. My family had enough money to live on if we were careful. And I earned a little money working as a blacksmith. I stole because I enjoyed it, for the thrill of it, and because I found out I was good at it. Later, I joined a gang of four other thieves. Four Babylonians. We robbed ships and warehouses and places like that, then spent our money getting drunk. In one of our robberies, an innocent man was killed. But even that didn't stop me. The only reason I signed up to come to Jerusalem was to help my friends steal gold from the caravan. The Holy One's gold."

"But you didn't steal it," she said, guessing the ending.

"No. I changed my mind. I betrayed my friends and told Rebbe Ezra about the plot. He should have arrested me then and there—or at least sent me back to Casiphia. Instead, he said God would forgive me if I asked. And he said God still wanted me to serve as a Levite."

"That's the most amazing thing about the Holy One, isn't it?" Amina asked. "His forgiveness! The Jewish family who adopted me has been telling me how much He loves even Gentiles like me—and how the sacrifices at His temple bring us close to Him. That's why I could never go back to my own people like Sayfah did. I want to worship the real God—your God, for the rest of my life."

"I have a hard time feeling forgiven sometimes," Reuben said, "even though I watch the sacrifices every day and pray with the other men."

"But it's true, Reuben. He forgives you. 'As high as the heavens are above the earth, so great is His love for those who fear Him.'"

He looked at her with a puzzled expression. "Then why don't you believe it?"

"What do you mean?"

"You believe the Holy One can forgive my past, yet you say I shouldn't have anything to do with someone like you, because you're an Edomite by birth. Isn't your past forgiven, too?"

Amina didn't know what to say. Why was it easier to have faith for someone else than for herself? Reuben reached out and gently stroked her hair, the way Hodaya used to do to comfort her. "And if God doesn't care about your past, Amina, then why should I?"

"But my leg—"

"What about it?" he said, frowning. "Why should something like that come between friends?" She couldn't reply. "But maybe you don't want to be friends with me now that I told you I'm a thief," he said, letting his hand drop.

"I would be honored to be your friend, Reuben."

"Then let's not talk about our past ever again. Promise?"

"I promise."

"Rebbe Ezra told me if the Holy One has forgiven me, then my past is forgotten, and I don't need to tell anyone about it. But I wanted to tell you, Amina. I wanted our friendship to start with the truth. But the same thing is true for you. If your past if forgiven and forgotten, you don't ever have to think of yourself as an Edomite again. It doesn't matter."

"We may have to remind each other to forget," she said, smiling.

"Yes. Let's promise to do that. . . . So where are you staying here in Jerusalem?"

"I live with two priests and their families, Joshua and Johanan. They're sons of the prophet Zechariah."

"Wow! Very important men!"

"I guess so. They're very nice. And very good to me. Where are you living?"

"For now, Rebbe Ezra has been kind enough to let me camp with his family down in the valley since I don't have a family of my own."

"Rebbe Ezra, the governor of Judah?" she asked in amazement. He nodded. "Now I'm impressed."

"Listen, if you would like . . . I'll ask Rebbe Ezra's family if you can join us for the Sabbath." Amina hesitated, feeling the old, familiar shame, the fear she would be rejected and humiliated. Would the governor want to eat with an Edomite? "They're very kind people," Reuben continued. "I know they would make you feel welcome. Please come."

At last she nodded, grateful for the chance to see Reuben again. "I would like that. Thank you."

Reuben smiled, and he was so handsome she couldn't seem to breathe. He had looked angry to her the first few times she'd seen him, but now that she knew his story, she realized the angry expression was probably a habit. He hadn't had a very happy life. "My family used to celebrate Shabbat in Casiphia when my father was alive," he said, "but I didn't want anything to do with God after he died. I'm trying to relearn all the laws and everything, and I'm still afraid I'll do something wrong. But the rebbe and his wife have been very understanding."

Amina told him how to find Johanan's house on the ridge in the City of David, and Reuben promised to come for her on the eve of Shabbat. "In the meantime, I'll look forward to seeing you again," he said.

"I will, too." She let him walk with her back to the courtyard, and she waved good-bye before sitting down in front of her loom. She picked up the shuttle but simply held it in her hands for several minutes, unable to concentrate on her work.

"Amina . . . ?" She looked up at the woman seated beside

her, fearing she was in trouble for not working. But the woman smiled. "He's very handsome."

"H-he wants to be my friend." For some reason, the other women burst into laughter.

"Her friend?" one of them asked. "Did you see the way he looked at her?"

"My husband used to look at me that way, too," another woman said with a sigh, "right before he asked my father if he could marry me."

Amina felt her cheeks burning. She returned to her work, picking up where she left off. All around her, the other women talked of falling in love and marrying their husbands, but Amina was afraid to dream of such a happy ending. In spite of Reuben's assurances that he didn't care if she was an Edomite or a cripple, Amina was afraid to hope. A man like him could never fall in love with someone like her.

JERUSALEM

Devorah knelt inside her tent in the dark to arrange their bedding for the night, unhappy with the news Ezra had just told her. "Do we really have to move into the governor's house?" she asked. "I won't be sorry to move out of this tent, of course, but I can't imagine living in a house that big. Who needs all that space? And servants to cook for us and wait on us? I'm happy with a simple life."

Ezra sat cross-legged near the door, writing in his journal, bending close to see it in the light of a single oil lamp. Ever since he'd traveled to Susa, he'd written in it each night, keeping a record of everything he did. Devorah could see the scroll was going to run out very soon. "I agree," he said without looking up, "but the elders insisted we live there."

Devorah shook the blanket as she spread it out, causing Ezra's lamp to flicker. "I'm very uncomfortable with such luxuries when Miriam and Asher and all the others are doing without. Why can't we build a house like the one we had in Babylon? That was big enough, wasn't it?"

"The elders believe it gives me stature and respect among the other provincial leaders if I live in the governor's residence."

"People should respect you for who you are and how well you lead us, not for where you live."

He made a helpless gesture, still not looking up from his work. "People have strange priorities sometimes."

"It can't be avoided, then?" she asked.

"I'm afraid not. I trust you'll soon get used to it."

Devorah poked the blankets, searching for lumps, smoothing the wrinkles, trying to imagine having servants hovering everywhere, intruding on their privacy. "When?" she asked. Ezra stopped writing and looked up at her, puzzled. "When do I have to move into this palace and be waited on by servants?" She didn't try to disguise her scorn.

"They said we could move in right away, but would you rather wait until I return from my travels next week?"

"Yes," she said, relieved. "I can't imagine living there with you, let alone without you." She dropped onto all fours to continue arranging their bedding, the goat hair tent hovering low above her head. Ezra had told her only a short time ago his work would require traveling, and she didn't like that idea any more than she liked the thought of moving into the palace. "After your trip to Susa, I hoped we'd never have to be apart again," she said.

"I know, Devorah. But I need to visit as many towns in Judah as I can. I need to assess where we stand and start teaching the people, putting judges in place, making sure the law is followed. The king's decree commands everyone who lives in the province of Judah to follow God's law. But how can they possibly follow it if no one explains it to them? And if they don't follow it, God's wrath may fall on us all over again."

"Is it safe to travel? What about the local people, the Samaritans and Edomites?"

"If they attack me, they're attacking the representative of the Persian Empire."

"Well, that's very comforting. I'm sure the highwaymen will quickly change their villainous ways when they hear that." Her sarcasm made him look up from his journal again. "Can't someone else go in your place?" she asked, sitting back.

He shook his head. "I'm the leader."

Devorah exhaled in frustration. "How long will you be gone? You'll be back in time for the Sabbath, I hope."

"Don't count on me getting back. The Sabbath isn't being honored here in Jerusalem, so I'm sure it's being desecrated in other towns, as well. I want to set an example in the places I visit by not traveling or working."

"Did you forget Reuben is bringing a friend this Shabbat for the evening meal?"

Ezra looked stricken. "I'm sorry—I did forget. But it's too late to change my plans."

"I really hoped you'd be here. Reuben says *she* is just a friend and she's an orphan, but he acted so nervous when he asked me if she could come, I think she might be much more than a friend."

"You don't need me. You're better at these things than I am, Devorah." He pulled the lamp closer to return to his journal.

"These *things*? Reuben and his new friend are real people, you know."

"I meant romantic things—courtships, engagements. Those things."

She sighed. "No one would ever accuse you of being a romantic, Ezra ben Seraiah—unless you count quoting Scripture to me as romantic. It's just that Reuben doesn't have parents here. He looks up to you for advice."

"I know, but he's a grown man. And when it comes to falling in love, very few men are willing to listen to advice, especially from a rebbe."

"Never mind, then. We'll miss you this Sabbath. . . . But, Ezra, what will I do all day in that great big house if I don't need to cook for our family?"

He looked up at her as if he was finally listening to what she was saying. "You have a greater purpose than cooking meals,

Devorah. It's no accident your father taught you the Torah so well. Now you'll have time to talk with the women God brings into your life and teach them what you know. Many don't know how important their role in the home is, how they're responsible for following the dietary laws, setting the religious tone in the home, and teaching their children from a very young age to fear God—as you've done with our children. Mothers are the ones who teach young people the stories of our ancestors before they attend the yeshiva. I know of no pagan religion that places such important tasks in the hands of their women."

If Devorah didn't know better, she would think Ezra was trying to flatter her to make up for going away and missing Shabbat. But her husband seemed immune to flattery himself and certainly lacked the ability to flatter someone else. "Which villages will you visit?" she asked, changing the subject.

"I'm off to Bethany first, just over the mountain, then on to Bethlehem. I'm still amazed to find myself in the land of the Torah, seeing places I've read about all my life. Sometimes I can't believe I'm really here and my feet are walking the same roads our ancestors walked. The hills and valleys and rivers and deserts—they're all unchanged from Abraham's time. It's remarkable!"

Devorah knew she always had Ezra's full attention whenever she asked about his work. Mundane things like hosting Reuben's new friend or moving to a huge house were never important to him. "What will you do? How will you begin your work?" she asked.

"Well, if the villagers have a house of assembly, I'll go there to teach the people, explaining what the Torah says in plain language so everyone can understand it. It's the same thing I tried to do back in Babylon, but I never dreamed I would be teaching Torah here in the Promised Land. I still wake up every morning amazed to find myself here, don't you?"

"Yes, Ezra." She rose and took the scroll from his hand, laying it aside, then blew out the lamp. She knelt in front of him, holding his face in her hands. "Your work can consume you all next week. But tonight I deserve to have you all to myself before you leave."

The next morning Devorah forced herself not to cry when Ezra left. Time always passed so slowly when she was alone, even with the needs of her children to fill her days. She was grateful for the distraction of meeting Reuben's friend when the week came to an end, but she decided to cook the Sabbath meal with Miriam, enlisting their daughters' help. "I think Reuben will be more comfortable with another man at the table besides my sons," Devorah told Miriam as she kneaded the bread. "Asher can preside over the meal and recite the prayers."

She and Miriam worked all day, preparing enough food for the evening meal and all the meals the next day. They lit the Sabbath lights just as the sun set, and a few minutes later Reuben arrived with his friend Amina. It was easy to see why he was attracted to her. She was small and slender and very pretty with the loveliest reddish-brown hair Devorah had ever seen. Her beautifully dyed robe in shades of rust and amber perfectly complemented her hair. She looked very young, but maybe it was just her tiny frame, especially when she stood beside Reuben, who was at least six feet tall.

"Welcome, Amina. *Shabbat shalom.* I'm so glad you could join us tonight," Devorah said.

"Thank you so much for inviting me." She seemed nervous— but then, who wouldn't be? To Devorah, Ezra was simply her husband; to everyone else he was a distinguished rebbe and the governor of Judah. She was glad for Reuben's and Amina's sakes that he wasn't here—and they hadn't moved into the governor's residence yet.

"I'm sorry my husband is out of town and won't be able to

join us tonight," Devorah told them. "But let me introduce you to everyone else. And don't worry if you can't tell our twin sons apart—few people can."

Later, as they sat down together to enjoy the meal, Devorah was surprised by how talkative Reuben was, for once. He described what a skilled weaver Amina was, and how she'd grown up in Bethlehem but lived with a priestly family while she wove linen for the temple garments. He didn't explain how she had become crippled or why she walked with a crutch, but it was clear to Devorah within a matter of minutes that Reuben was infatuated with her and wouldn't have cared if she was missing all of her limbs.

Everyone began to relax as they shared the familiar rituals, breaking bread and sipping the Sabbath wine. Devorah could see that Amina had been raised in a good Jewish home and was familiar with all the Sabbath traditions, more so than Reuben. Throughout the lengthy meal, Devorah caught Amina gazing up at Reuben as if he were the only person there. He looked at her the same way—making Devorah miss Ezra more than ever.

At the end of the evening, as soon as their guests were gone, Devorah couldn't wait to compare notes with Miriam. "Well? What did you think?"

"She's a beautiful girl. They make a handsome couple."

"Do you think they're falling in love, Miriam? Is there going to be a wedding?"

"No doubt at all about that!"

Devorah was so happy for Reuben she felt like dancing. Ezra was fond of Reuben, too, and would rejoice with him, in spite of his reluctance to get involved with romantic matters. She couldn't wait to have him home again and to tell him the good news.

JERUSALEM

Millions of stars shone in the heavens as Amina stood with Reuben in the courtyard of Johanan's home, gazing down at the Kidron Valley below. "My sister's village is just across the valley from here," she said, pointing beyond the dark void to the shadowy mountain in the distance. Reuben had eaten dinner with her and Johanan's family, and now they stood together, talking on this crisp, fall night.

"I wish you weren't going to a pagan village, Amina."

"It's only for one night. I'll be back the next day." Reuben's concern touched her. Over the past two months they had grown very close, their feelings for each other deepening. Amina couldn't believe a man as wonderful as Reuben cared for her.

"How far is it? Do you have to walk all the way there?" he asked.

"Johanan is letting me ride his donkey. One of his servants will walk there with me before sunset like he did the last time."

"But then he's going to leave you there all alone?"

"Don't worry. I'm visiting my sister, Sayfah."

"I know what pagan festivals were like in Casiphia and—"

"She's married and has a family." Amina longed to take

381

Reuben's strong hands in hers and soothe his concerns, but it wasn't proper. "Sayfah invited me to come to the festival months ago, before I met you, and I know it means a lot to have me visit. She doesn't know the Almighty One, and I want to help her understand Him."

"Are you sure it's safe to go?" he asked.

"Yes. They're Edomites, like me."

"I want to come with you."

"Reuben, they won't let you into their village. I'm allowed in because they know I'm one of them, but you're Jewish."

"At least let me walk as far as the village entrance with you. I won't worry as much if I know where you are and that you're safe."

"That would be very kind of you. Thank you."

But as they walked down the ramp from Jerusalem on the day of the festival and crossed the Kidron Valley to Sayfah's village, Amina could see Reuben's worry multiplying with each step they took. "What kind of festival is it?" he asked again, although Amina had already told him.

"Sayfah says they're celebrating the harvest." He exhaled heavily but didn't reply. "I'll be fine," she soothed.

The village elders at the entrance rose to their feet as if preparing for a confrontation as Amina approached with the two Jewish men. Reuben drew the donkey to a halt a dozen yards away and helped her down. "I wish you hadn't promised your sister you'd come. I'm worried about you, Amina. I don't want anything to happen to you."

"Sayfah will watch out for me. I promise I'll stay close to her." She left Reuben and the servant behind and walked forward alone to talk to the elders. They motioned for Amina to enter the village, but when she glanced over her shoulder at Reuben one last time, he still stood where she had left him, watching her. She gave a little wave, then didn't look back again as she hurried through the streets to Sayfah's house, afraid she would change her mind and run back to his strong, protective arms.

Sayfah seemed pleased to see her, hugging her tightly. "I didn't think you'd come," she said. "I was sure you'd change your mind."

"Of course I came. I've been looking forward to spending time with you, and I have so much to tell you." But they were quickly caught up in the preparations for the festival and didn't have a chance to talk quietly. Amina finally met Sayfah's husband, who seemed to be a pleasant man even if he didn't show his wife much affection. Amina had become accustomed to the loving ways of the Jewish couples she knew, and only now remembered that none of the men in her parents' village had treated their wives with such affection. Sayfah was a very good mother to her three boys and seemed to be content with her life, though Amina noticed she rarely smiled.

After sunset the entire community gathered in the village square, like people used to do in Amina's village. The harvest festival turned out to be a wild, raucous affair with lots of drinking and shouting and uninhibited dancing. It brought back memories from childhood, especially of the night her father and the other villagers planned to kill the Jews.

The women piled food on rugs and small tables in the middle of the square, and everyone jostled for position around the food as they filled their plates, the men pushing forward first. "You didn't take very much to eat," Sayfah said when they returned to their place with the other women on the side of the square.

"This is plenty for me," Amina replied. She didn't tell Sayfah that she couldn't eat the meat because it had been sacrificed to Edom's gods, nor did she know what animal it had come from. The Jews had special rules for how to kill and cook everything properly, so Amina ate only fruit and plain vegetables, knowing they would be safe, fearing she would break one of the dietary laws. The Edomites consumed gallons of wine, but Amina sipped from the same cup all evening, refusing the refills that Sayfah offered. The Jews never drank this much wine at their festivals, and Amina had never seen any of them get drunk and lose control. But even Sayfah seemed to feel the wine's euphoric effects as the evening continued.

When the food was gone, the men built a bonfire in the middle of the square, even though the fall evening was warm. The music grew louder and wilder, the thundering drums pounding so noisily she wondered if Reuben could hear them up on the ridge in Jerusalem. Close to midnight, Amina gradually became aware of something she hadn't noticed when she was a child—the young men and women were pairing off, moving away from the bonfire and into the shadows, their arms draped around each other. The Torah would call their behavior immoral and forbidden. She could see why. She was ready for the evening to end, ready to return to Sayfah's house. Amina's three nephews had fallen asleep on the rug beside her, but Sayfah showed no sign of leaving.

Late in the night, two young men walked over to where they sat and Sayfah introduced them as her husband's cousins. "Come dance with us," they told Amina.

"You should go," Sayfah said. "You don't need to stay here with the married women and children."

The thought of going off into the dark with these strangers terrified Amina. "I can't dance. I'm crippled." She lifted her hem to show them her shriveled leg. As she'd hoped, the men were repulsed and went away. Sayfah was furious with her.

"What did you do that for? They just wanted to have a little fun."

"I didn't want to go with them. . . . Sayfah, there's someone special in my life—"

"I'm done talking to you." Sayfah refused to listen, turning her back on Amina and ignoring her as she talked with the other married women seated around them. Amina wished she'd listened to Reuben and stayed home. If only this long, horrible night would end. When she was tired of having her sister ignore her, Amina tugged on her sleeve to get her attention. "I thought you wanted me to come to the festival so we could spend time with each other."

"I did. But I also wanted you to meet my husband's relatives. We're all one family now. Or isn't family important to you anymore?"

"Of course it's important, but . . ." She longed to tell Sayfah about Reuben, to talk about the feelings she had for him and how wonderful it felt to be falling in love. She wanted to laugh as she shared her hopes and dreams. But her sister would probably be angry to learn Amina was falling in love with a Jewish man.

Time passed, and Amina began to doze. Sayfah nudged her awake and pointed out a well-built young man weaving his way toward them with drunken, swaying steps. "That's my husband's brother walking toward us. If he stops and talks to us, be nice to him." Amina looked away, desperate for the man to ignore her and keep walking, hoping he wouldn't notice them in the dark. But Sayfah called to him as soon as he was near, and he stopped a few feet from where they sat, looking down at them.

"This is my sister, Amina," Sayfah said. "Remember I told you about her?"

"She's as pretty as you are. And not married? How did that happen? Come on, Amina, you don't want to sit here with the married women and little children. I'll introduce you to some of my friends." He extended his hand to pull her to her feet.

"But I really don't—"

"Go," Sayfah whispered, pushing her from behind. "Don't be difficult."

Amina ignored his outstretched hand and used her crutch to get up, hoping it would discourage him. Instead, her crutch slipped and fell to the ground as he grabbed her arm. She had to leave it behind as he pulled her toward the darkened lane where the other couples had disappeared. "I-I'd rather stay out here in the square by the bonfire," she said, dragging her feet.

"There are too many people out here. And you look like you could use a drink."

"I don't want any more wine. I've had enough already. . . ."

He stopped short and gave her a little shake. "What's wrong with you? Sayfah said you were looking for a good time."

"I-I'm not!"

"Well, I am!" He wouldn't let go as he pulled her toward the alley against her will. The more she resisted, the tighter he held on to her until she was sure he would leave bruises on her arm. She wanted to scream, to run, but he held her so tightly and the party had become so loud, no one would hear her above the noise and shrieks of laughter.

"No, stop! Let me go! Please!" she begged.

Her captor merely laughed at her futile struggles. "A cripple like you can't afford to be choosy, you know."

Was this her punishment for coming to a pagan feast? "Lord, help me, please!" she wept.

Out of nowhere, a shadow emerged from the darkness, racing toward them. It hurtled into the drunken Edomite, knocking Amina free. She knew it was Reuben, but it seemed impossible that he could be here, that he had come just in time to save her. Reuben punched the startled man in the stomach, then in the jaw, making him stumble backward and nearly fall. "Leave her alone, or I'll kill you!" he said. Then he lifted Amina in his arms and sprinted away with her before the man could protest.

"Oh, thank God, thank God." She wept against his chest.

"Are you okay, Amina?"

"Yes . . . yes . . . but I was so scared!" Her body trembled from head to toe, and she couldn't stop crying. Reuben stopped and set her down in a dark lane between two houses, holding her close and letting her cling to him and weep until her tears of fear and relief and shame were finally exhausted. Then he led her to Sayfah's house—she had no idea how he knew where it was. They sat side by side in Sayfah's courtyard until she finally stopped trembling, the music booming from the village square, the glow of the bonfire lighting up the night sky.

"I can't believe you're really here, Reuben. Why . . . ? How . . . ? How did you find me?"

"I followed you. I had Babylonian friends back in Casiphia, so I know what their festivals are like. As soon as I saw this village, I had a bad feeling about what would go on here tonight. I've been watching you from the shadows all night."

"No one saw you?"

He gave a short laugh. "I used to be a thief, Amina. I'm still pretty good at watching without being seen. Pretty good at sneaking into places, too. And waiting."

"I'm so glad you did!"

"Are you sure you're all right?"

"Yes. But I want to go home."

"What about your sister?"

"I don't care about her. She's the one who made me go with him, and she'll be furious with me when she finds out what happened. We don't have anything in common anymore."

"Are you sure you don't want to wait until she comes home? If you leave, she might worry about you. Besides, it's a long way back to Jerusalem in the dark."

"You're right. I guess I should wait here. It'll be dawn soon, won't it? How much longer will the festival last?"

"Probably until then. We can go home as soon as it's light."

Amina realized she was still clinging to him for protection like a drowning woman, unwilling to let go. He made her feel safe as he gently rubbed her back to soothe her. She wished she could stay in his embrace forever, but he released her after a while and held her at arms' length to look into her eyes.

"Amina, I feel like I've wasted so much of my life already. I don't want to waste another day or hour or minute of it. I've fallen in love with you, and I want to spend the rest of my life with you. Will you be my wife?"

She had finally stopped crying, but once again tears blurred her vision at his words. She couldn't believe it. A wonderful man like Reuben loved her? She couldn't speak. "Amina, say something, please."

"Yes, Reuben, yes! I haven't stopped thinking about you since the day you came to be measured for your robe, and I was so happy when I saw you again at the temple and you helped me. Whenever we're together, I feel like my heart is being woven into yours, like this"—she said, twining her fingers together—"but I was afraid to fall in love with you, afraid it couldn't possibly work out—a man like you with someone like me."

"I'm the lucky one, not you. So you'll really marry me?"

"Yes! Yes, I will!" He bent his head to kiss her, and the touch of his lips on hers—tender at first, then conveying all of his passion and love—was the most wonderful feeling she had ever known. "I'm sorry," he said when he finally pulled away. "That probably wasn't proper, but I couldn't resist a single moment longer."

"I'm not sorry," she said, letting him kiss her again.

"What do we do next?" he asked. "How long do we have to wait to get married?"

"I think our fathers are supposed to arrange our betrothal, but we don't have any parents. Jacob is the closest thing I have to a father or a guardian, but he isn't coming back to Jerusalem until the Feast of Passover, next spring."

"We'll go to Bethlehem and ask him, then."

"I don't have a dowry, Reuben."

"That doesn't matter—I don't have any money for a bride price. Let's just do it, Amina. I can't stand to say good-bye to you every day. I don't even know how I'll stand to go to work and be away from you once we're married."

"Where will we live?"

"I'll build a house for you in Jerusalem. I'll lay every stone myself, working day and night until it's finished. I'll even—" He paused, suddenly alert, listening. He rose to his feet. "Someone's coming. I have to go. Meet me at the village entrance at dawn. I'll be waiting for you." She saw him slink through the gate into the street, but then he seemed to vanish, disappearing as suddenly as he had appeared.

Amina hadn't heard a sound until then, but a few moments after Reuben left, Sayfah and her family stumbled home, looking bleary and tired, carrying the smaller children and Amina's crutch. "There you are," Sayfah said. "Why did you run off like that? My brother-in-law said you weren't very nice to him."

"I tried to tell you last night, but you wouldn't listen to me. I'm in love with a wonderful man named Reuben ben David and—"

"A Jew? Amina, how could you!"

"He loves me, too, and we hope to be married soon. I want you to come to our wedding and meet him."

"Never. Even if my husband allowed it, which he won't, I wouldn't come. The Jews are our enemies, Amina. Did you forget they killed Mama and Papa and our brothers? Did you forget what they did to our village?"

"That was a lifetime ago. And Reuben wasn't part of it. He just moved here from—"

"He's a Jew, isn't he?"

"Yes, but—"

"I guess we have nothing more to say to each other."

"Can't you be happy for me, Sayfah? I love Reuben. He doesn't care that I'm crippled or that I'm not Jewish."

"You shouldn't marry a Jew. It's wrong."

"I am going to marry him. But please don't be angry with me. We're sisters."

"You're marrying one of my people's enemies. That makes you my enemy."

"I don't feel that way about you and your family."

"My husband won't allow you to come back if you marry a

Jew. He hates the Jews. Don't come back to see me again unless you're coming back to live here for good." Sayfah turned away, and Amina knew she wouldn't change her mind.

The sky was quickly turning light. It was time to leave. The bonds of love joining her to Reuben were stronger than the bonds between her and Sayfah. She was about to break the final tie to her past. "I'm leaving now," she said. "Good-bye, Sayfah." She hugged her sister one last time, but Sayfah stood with her arms at her sides, not returning the embrace. Amina limped away, wiping her eyes, knowing she probably would never see her sister again.

Reuben stood just beyond the village entrance, waiting for her. Without a word, he took Amina's hand, and they started across the valley to Jerusalem and their new life together.

BETHLEHEM

One week later, Amina held tightly to the donkey she
rode as Reuben led it up the long climb to the top of
the Mount of Olives. Neither the bumpy, uncomfortable ride nor the dreary fall day and overcast skies could dampen
her happiness. Reuben loved her and wanted to marry her. She
decided to ask Hodaya's son Jacob and his wife, Rivkah, to
arrange their betrothal and wedding since they were Amina's
only family now. She and Reuben borrowed the donkey from
Joshua ben Zechariah for the trip to Bethlehem. Both Joshua
and his brother, Johanan, gave Amina and Reuben their blessing, as well as the donkey and a servant to accompany them on
the six-mile trip. Now each swaying step of the journey brought
Amina closer to her new life with Reuben.

At last they reached the top of the hill, and Amina longed to
spur the donkey into a gallop as the road descended, knowing
Reuben would gladly race all the way to Bethlehem with her.

"I hope Jacob is home," Amina said as they drew closer
to the village, "and not out in the desert somewhere with his
flocks." She worried that she hadn't seen any flocks in the fields
close to town.

"If he isn't home, I'll hike out to the desert to find him," Reuben said. He looked so serious and determined that Amina believed he would.

"Reuben, no!" she said in alarm. "You grew up in a city! You don't know how to find your way through those grazing lands."

"Then we'd better pray Jacob is home."

Thankfully, he was. Amina and Reuben arrived in Bethlehem before noon at the home where she'd lived for most of her life. Reuben wasted no time asking Jacob for her hand. "I'm Reuben ben David from the tribe of Levi," he said, introducing himself. "Amina and I want to get married. Will you help us do everything the proper way?"

"I would be honored," Jacob said with a broad grin. Rivkah hugged Amina tightly, tears of joy in her eyes.

"We don't need anything fancy," Amina said, "and I don't want you to fuss."

"And we don't want to wait any longer than we have to," Reuben added.

Amina looked up at him and smiled. "We just want to start our new life together as soon as possible."

"Well, then," Jacob said, clapping his hands together. "I believe I have just enough time to spread the word and gather our family and the village elders. We'll hold your betrothal right here after evening prayers. Is that soon enough?"

Amina threw her arms around him to hug him. "Yes! Thank you so much!"

They sat down to eat the noon meal Rivkah quickly laid out, then Jacob went off to spread the news through the village, inviting everyone to Amina's betrothal that evening. "Would you like me to show you around my village while we wait?" Amina asked. "It isn't raining at the moment."

"Yes, let's go."

She took Reuben to the market square first because of what it symbolized to her, even though today wasn't market day and the booths stood empty. "This is where my old life ended and my new one began," she told him as they slowly walked between the stalls. "Hodaya used to sell her cloth right here. I was running with my sister and our friends the first time I met her, and I fell right in front of her. Hodaya helped me up and cleaned my scraped knees. No one treated me so kindly before. She told me we had something in common because we were both crippled." Amina paused, overcome with sorrow as she remembered her precious friend. "Sayfah and I came here to hide in Hodaya's booth after our house was robbed and our village plundered by our own people, fleeing from the Jews. Hodaya found us and took us home with her."

"I wish I could have met her."

"Me too. . . . The village where I came from is just a short walk down that road," she said as they moved on. "We used to come to Bethlehem for market day every week."

"Is it still there?"

"No, the village is gone. Jacob took Sayfah and me back after the war, but everything had burned to the ground." Amina led him toward the narrow entrance where Mama and so many others had been trampled to death. She longed to hold Reuben's hand for comfort, but it wasn't proper. *Soon,* she told herself. Soon they'd never have to be apart.

She halted at the edge of the square, images of the massacre still as fresh as if it had happened yesterday. "I overheard my father and the others planning what they would do to Bethlehem's Jews on the Thirteenth of Adar," she said. "They had no compassion, only hatred and greed and a lust to kill. So I came to Hodaya's booth to warn her. I told her she and the other Jews needed to run away and hide." Amina closed her eyes for a moment, remembering Hodaya's beautiful smile, her deep faith. "She told me her God would save them. 'I don't know how He'll do it,' she said, 'and I know it looks hopeless right now, but they're telling us to trust God.' And she was right. I knew even then I wanted to be like her, not like my parents. My father's plans were evil, and he died because of them. Hodaya used to say whatever seed you plant in the ground, that's what crop you'll harvest. And he planted evil."

"Those were terrible days for all of us," Reuben said. "I couldn't get past the fact my father had been killed, and God had allowed it. But you lost everything. I can't imagine that."

"At the time, I saw my loss as a terrible thing," Amina said. "I didn't know how Sayfah and I would survive. But now I look back and see how the Almighty One brought something good out of something terrible. The changes in my life seemed unbearable, but they led to better things. . . . They led to you."

She saw Reuben check to see if anyone was watching, then he took her hand in his and squeezed it before letting go again. "I love you," he said. The knowledge still astounded her.

"I'm sorry you lost your father," Amina said. "He must have been a wonderful man. . . . I used to live in fear of my father." She shivered involuntarily, remembering how he beat her and Sayfah. "He was ashamed of me because I was crippled, and I lived with that shame every day. But being crippled probably saved my life. If I had gone with Mama and the other women that night, I might have been trampled to death, too. I've never felt shame or rejection with the Jewish people. They believe every life is precious, every person God created is valuable."

She turned her back on the road to her old village and began walking again. "But as wonderful as my life has been, all the images of that day are still burned into my heart and mind," she said. "I'm not sure I can ever erase them."

"I know what you mean," Reuben said. "So many people died. It was the first time I experienced death, and to see it come so violently . . ."

"Yes. But when we can look back on our past, no matter how painful it was, and see God at work, it gives us hope for the future. And right now, when I think of our future together, I can't imagine anything but joy—can you, Reuben? Think of it!"

"I wish we could get married today."

"Me too."

Amina thought only of their future that evening as her friends and adopted family members from Bethlehem gathered in the courtyard of Jacob's home to witness her betrothal. Reuben and Jacob signed the marriage contract the elders had drawn up for them, and she stood with Reuben beneath a canopy of branches hastily built by Jacob's sons. Reuben's hand was steady as he poured a cup of wine from the flask. "Amina . . . by offering you this cup, I vow I am willing to give my life for you," he said.

Amina gazed up at him and saw his eyes glisten as she accepted the cup from him. She drank from it, accepting his proposal and promising to give her life for him, too. A shout of joy erupted before a crowd of well-wishers enveloped Amina, women she'd known for most of her life and had grown to love. One by one, they congratulated her and promised to help her prepare for the wedding. God willing, she and Reuben would have only a short time to wait.

"I hate saying good-bye to you," she told Reuben the next morning as he prepared to leave for Jerusalem.

"I won't be long," he told her. "I'm going to prepare a new home for you, and when I come back, we'll never have to be apart again."

"I love you," she whispered.

He grasped her hand and squeezed it. "And I love you. Always and forever."

Reuben hefted a stone into place on the foundation of his new home, then paused to rest his aching muscles. The one-room house was tinier than the hideout where he and his friends used to meet in Babylon, the courtyard barren and rough and unpaved. If only he could build a palace for Amina, with servants to wait on her every need like the servants Rebbe Ezra had.

"A small house is much better," Amina had assured him before they'd said good-bye in Bethlehem. "I can't limp around a great big house with my bad leg." He smiled at her sweet nature, remembering how she'd added, "All we need is a hearth for cooking, a place for my loom, and a bedroom for you and me."

He lifted another stone into place, wishing he could build faster. The elders gave him this piece of property near the top of the sloping City of David, just below the temple mount, in a section of Jerusalem not rebuilt eighty years ago by the earlier settlers. Amina wouldn't have to walk too far to worship or visit the marketplace. And several other families from Rebbe Ezra's caravan were also building homes nearby, so they would have neighbors soon. The site already had a cistern, and once it was re-plastered, Amina would be spared the long trek to the spring for water. The home's foundation, leftover from when the Babylonians destroyed Jerusalem, needed only a few repairs before Reuben was able to build on it. But the winter rains would start before long, and if he didn't finish the house and set the roof in place by then, he'd be unable to finish until spring, unable to marry the woman he loved. The thought of waiting made him desperate. He bent to lift another stone.

"Need help, Reuben?" someone called. He looked up, surprised to see his friend Eli and five other Levites, including his Uncle Hashabiah, making their way toward him. Reuben still felt wary of his uncle, but Rebbe Ezra had explained that accepting the Holy One's forgiveness meant forgiving others, as well. Seeing help arrive now was like seeing the dawn after a long shift on night duty.

"I sure do!" He took a moment to stretch his aching back and shoulders.

"Well, we're here to help," Hashabiah said. "Tell us what to do."

Reuben assigned tasks, and they all worked steadily for the next few hours, accomplishing much more than he could have alone. Hashabiah proved adept at laying paving stones and created a smooth, level outdoor courtyard where Amina could work. The men came back for a second day and then a third, and when the cooking hearth was finished and the roof nearly complete, Reuben spread the word that his wedding was about to take place.

On their last day of work, Reuben was hanging the door on its hinges with Eli's help when he saw Rebbe Ezra's wife coming up the street followed by her daughters and two servants, all carrying bundles. "We thought you and your wife could use some household articles," she said, setting down her burden in his courtyard.

"Uncle Asher made these pots and bowls and jars for you," the rebbe's daughter said. She handed him the clay cooking pot she carried. Reuben was speechless.

"I'm so sorry we can't make it to your wedding in Bethlehem," Devorah said. "My husband is traveling and won't be home in time. So we decided to bring our presents here to your new home."

"Thank you, thank you so much! I'm . . . I'm overwhelmed!"

"Ezra and I are very fond of you, Reuben. And we wish you and your lovely wife many, many years of happiness."

Two days later after the evening sacrifice, Reuben put on his finest robe and set off with Eli and a group of friends and fellow Levites, including his uncle, to travel to Bethlehem and claim his bride. He wished he had wings and could fly all the way there. Joshua and Johanan and their families joined his procession, along with musicians playing drums and tambourines and flutes. They all carried torches to light their way after the sun set.

Amina had been right; the Almighty One was able to bring good things out of the terrible times in his life. Reuben remembered all the dark years he'd wasted with anger and bitterness after losing his father and the blacksmith shop, remembered breaking into homes and stealing with his friends, always searching for something and never finding it. But those wasted years seemed like nothing compared with the new beginning he'd been offered. He'd returned to the God of his ancestors and found forgiveness and a purpose. And now God gave him the wonderful gift of Amina for his wife. Could Adam have been any more overjoyed when he awoke in Eden to find Eve beside him? Reuben thought his heart would burst with happiness.

Everyone in his procession sang as they neared the outskirts of Bethlehem. Reuben heard shouts of "The bridegroom is coming! The bridegroom is coming!" Shofars trumpeted the news. Lamps and torches lit up the streets leading to Jacob's home and courtyard, and the villagers cheered and welcomed Reuben like a victorious king. And there was Amina, sitting beneath the canopy, as radiant as a queen on her throne. She would soon be his wife—his wife!

One of Amina's attendants hurried forward and presented Reuben with a gift as he entered the courtyard. "Amina made this new prayer shawl for you," she said. "She wove it herself." Hashabiah helped Reuben drape it around his shoulders. Amina's craftsmanship was exquisite, fit for royalty. She must have worked as hard on this as he had on their house to get it finished on time.

Reuben could scarcely breathe as he helped Amina to her feet and lifted her veil to gaze at her beautiful face. They stood beneath the canopy to speak their vows, then shared the cup of wine that would seal their marriage. He bent to kiss his new wife at last.

Shouts and cheers echoed around them as the music and feasting began. According to tradition, they were treated like a king and queen this night, and their guests' foremost task was to bring joy and laughter to the new bride and groom. The men formed a circle to whirl and dance in front of them, pulling

Reuben into the spinning circle with them. The women danced in a separate circle, lifting Amina high in the air on her chair. Reuben saw her beautiful smile, heard her joyous laughter, and silently thanked the Almighty One for blessing him. Food and wine flowed all evening, and their friends showered them with presents, everything they would need for their new life together.

At last it was time for Reuben to carry his wife into their bridal chamber. He was no longer aware of the music and festivities outside as he closed the door and held Amina in his arms. He could share all his love with her at last.

"You are a miracle," he whispered as he held her tightly. "A miracle!"

CHAPTER
51

JERUSALEM

Ezra said good-bye to his two sons after the morning sacrifice on the temple mount, then watched as they hurried off to their classes in the yeshiva. Four months after arriving in Jerusalem, they were maturing into fine young men, and he was proud of them. "Do you like your new life here in the Promised Land?" he had asked them just the other day.

"Yes, Abba!" they'd said in unison.

"I can't wait to learn how to be a priest," Shallum had said.

"Do you think one of us might become the high priest someday?" Judah had asked.

"It's possible. Some of your ancestors served as high priests."

"It's so beautiful here in Jerusalem," Shallum added. "I feel . . . free . . . without pagan Gentiles surrounding us all the time."

"You're glad we came, then? Even with all the rules and laws you're required to follow?"

The twins had looked at each other for a moment, then grinned. "You and Mama would have made us follow all the rules in Babylon anyway, right, Abba?" Judah asked.

Ezra had smiled in return. "That's true. We would have."

"I like living in our huge new house," Shallum said.

"It's like a king's palace!"

"Don't get used to it," Ezra had warned. "It is God who raises men up, and He can easily bring them down again."

Now as Ezra stood on the temple mount in the cold winter rain, inhaling the aroma of the sacrifice, he felt content. He had asked the people to join him in praying for the spiritual restoration his nation sorely needed, and he knew the abundant winter rain was a sign of God's favor.

Ezra thought his work was going well. He had traveled to nearly every town and village in the Province of Judah and spoken to the leaders about the need to teach the laws of the Torah. His reforms had met with very little resistance. He was satisfied that justice was being meted out according to the law by the tribunals of magistrates he'd set in place and by the judges he'd appointed. Now that the winter rains made travel difficult, he looked forward to uninterrupted time at home with his family and more time for his personal studies.

"Rebbe Ezra, if you can spare a moment . . ."

He turned to see three of Jerusalem's elders waiting to speak with him. He recognized them from the council meetings he held in the assembly hall. "Yes? How long have you been standing there?"

"We didn't want to interrupt your prayers . . . but there's something we need to bring to your attention. It's very important."

"I just met with all of you yesterday in my council chamber and was assured that any problems that arose during my absence have been taken care of."

"We weren't free to speak yesterday."

"What do you mean?"

"We need to talk with you alone, Rebbe. Please, if we could just have a moment . . . it's very important."

"Here? If it's important, why not discuss it when all of the elders and chief priests are together in my council chamber?"

"Because this matter concerns some of those leaders and elders. . . . Please, hear us out, Rebbe."

Ezra folded his arms across his chest. "I need to warn you that if this turns out to be malicious gossip, I will quickly cut you off. The Almighty One won't stand for gossip and neither will I."

"I wish it were only gossip instead of the truth."

Ezra studied the three men for a moment as he decided how to reply. They were among the youngest of Jerusalem's leaders, seldom speaking in the council meetings, sidelined by more dominant leaders like Eliezer. Today their spokesman was a man named Yonah, one of the chief Levites.

"Very well," Ezra said. "What is it, then?"

"Everyone knows how you feel about scrupulously keeping the law of God—"

"Our future as a people depends on it. Those laws are a matter of life and death."

"Yes, Rebbe. We agree. Which is why we thought you should know that many of the people of Israel, including some of the priests and Levites, have not kept themselves separate from the neighboring peoples with their detestable practices."

The chill Ezra felt had nothing to do with the rain. "What do you mean? Surely the people aren't worshiping idols?"

"Not openly . . . but they've taken some of the Gentiles' daughters as wives, and their sons have mingled the holy race with the peoples around them. And the leaders and officials have led the way in this unfaithfulness. Even if they haven't married Gentiles themselves, our leaders are aware this is happening and they've looked the other way, failing to speak up or to use their influence to stop these sinful marriages."

For a moment, Ezra couldn't speak, stunned by the devastating news. "But . . . this can't happen! Mixed marriages with Gentiles will destroy the Jewish nation just as surely as Haman's decree attempted to do—it just takes longer. A generation instead of a day."

"You're right, Rebbe," a second elder added. "Our people have fallen for the same temptation our ancestors did in the desert when they worshiped the Baal of Peor. God sent a plague to show His displeasure then, and we fear a similar disaster now. That's why we decided to speak up."

Ezra knew the plague in the desert was halted only after Phineas executed the wrongdoers. Ezra had the power to impose the death penalty, but he prayed it wouldn't come to that. Not since the news of Haman's decree had a report left Ezra this deeply shaken. Mixed marriages with pagan Gentiles? He wished he could sit down, but there was no place nearby in the temple's vast outer courtyard.

"The destructive power of intermarriage is the reason why God told our ancestors to destroy all the Gentiles when they entered the Promised Land," he said. "Anyone who marries a non-Jew has married their false gods. Such a marriage desecrates God's sanctity. Children of pagan mothers will never be considered Jewish. And a priest or Levite involved in such a marriage is unfit to serve in God's temple." The three men nodded their agreement. "How widespread is this?" he asked, fearing their answer.

"I'm sorry to say that along with the priests and Levites we're aware of, we estimate at least a hundred men in this province are married to foreign women. Maybe more."

Anger and disbelief made it hard for Ezra to breathe. "Who are the priests and Levites involved?"

The three men looked at each other as if reluctant to speak their names. "Eliezer the priest is married to a Gentile wife," Yonah finally replied.

Ezra closed his eyes. "That explains his opposition to some of my reforms. He has no business being a priest, let alone a chief priest. . . . Who else?"

"Three other priests, Maaseiah, Jarib, and Gedaliah. And at least five Levites, including Jozabad and Shimei. . . . And I regret to say the young Levite who traveled with you from Babylon has married an Edomite woman."

Ezra stared at the man. "Reuben has? Are you certain?" The man nodded before looking away, as if uncomfortable at having to relay such personal news. Devorah said Reuben had taken a wife, but she'd never told him the woman was an Edomite. He'd been traveling when Reuben's wedding took place. How long ago had that been? One month? Maybe two?

"I'm sorry, Rebbe. But as you can see, this isn't gossip. You can easily verify what we've just told you."

Ezra's anger and grief were more than he could bear. He grabbed the neck of his tunic with both hands and tore it in sorrow over this desecration of the Torah, this open rebellion against the Holy One who had forgiven them and returned them to their homeland. Overwhelmed, Ezra then tore his cloak, the ripping sound echoing the rending of his heart, which seemed to be tearing in two. He pulled his hair and his beard, but even the pain from those actions weren't enough to convey his despair at his people's unfaithfulness. He sank to his knees on the damp pavement, stunned and appalled, speechless with anguish.

The three men who had brought the news stood back, giving him time and space to confront his grief. But time only increased Ezra's sorrow instead of easing it. God's ban on intermarriage with Gentiles had been given to His people from their earliest days as a nation. Surely every Jew knew about the prohibition and the reason for it. They couldn't have forgotten—which meant they had willfully disobeyed. And Ezra was responsible for leading these people, responsible for enforcing the law with the strictest of punishments—because God would surely punish them all if he didn't.

But his grief was also for the men involved, young men like Reuben who must love his new bride, and like the elderly priest, Eliezer, who surely had been married to his pagan wife for many, many years. Could Ezra give up Devorah if he learned God forbade their marriage? Could he divorce her and send her and their children away? Because that's what his fellow Jews must do in order to avoid God's wrath.

The impossibility of their situation brought tears to his eyes. The consequences of their disobedience would be painful beyond words. The consequences if they didn't obey and divorce their wives and send their children away would be equally painful.

How long he remained that way, pouring out his distress in prayer, Ezra didn't know. But gradually, as the morning wore on, he became aware of talking and murmuring all around him. He looked up from his prayers and saw a large crowd gathering, but they didn't appear to be ordinary gawkers. Yonah and the other two elders explained the situation to them, and he saw genuine expressions of grief and sorrow as the men listened to the news. Yonah hurried over to Ezra when he saw he had looked up from his prayer.

"Rebbe, these men are all like us, men who tremble at the word of God. They've gathered here to grieve with you and to discuss what we should do."

Ezra silently thanked God for sending men who would support him and pray with him. "Have them sit down," he said.

"Here? Shouldn't we go someplace dry and get out of the rain?"

Ezra hadn't even been aware of the rain. Grief had rooted him to this spot, within sight of the temple and God's mercy seat. He couldn't move, wouldn't move. He shook his head. "Even the heavens are weeping with us."

The other men quickly found places to sit, forming a semi-circle around him like students seated before their teacher. Ezra knew he could easily issue a decree commanding the people to divorce their pagan spouses, and he knew he had the power to enforce it. But the Holy One saw the Jewish people as a single community—if one sinned, it was as if they'd all sinned because they'd failed to correct the transgressors. All His people went into exile, all had been punished. All faced punishment now. And as much as Ezra longed to dictate what needed to be done, he knew the decision had to come from the people themselves to show their willingness to live by God's laws. Otherwise, his leadership would be futile, and their conformity to the law would last no longer than his lifetime. But that didn't mean he couldn't guide them to the right decision.

"Our grief is only a fraction of the grief the Holy One feels when His law is disobeyed," he began. "In speaking of the Gentiles, God told us, 'Do not intermarry with them. Do not give your daughters to their sons or take their daughters for your sons. . . .' Do you remember His reasons why?"

"Yes," someone replied, "for they will turn our sons away from following the Holy One to serve other gods."

"And then what?"

"'And the Lord's anger will burn against you and quickly destroy you.'"

"The Almighty One has only recently turned His anger aside from us and given us a second chance. We have confessed and repented and promised to walk in a different direction. God separated us from the Babylonians and Persians and their abominable ways and gave us the Province of Judah where we can live under His law. Now He's watching to see how serious we are, waiting for proof we've learned our lesson. If not, He can revoke our pardon and destroy us in a single day, as Haman's decree had the power to do."

Ezra paused, gazing around at the other men, praying for the right words to say, words that would convict. "We've returned to the sins that brought the exile. Do you remember what the prophets said those reasons were?"

"Our worst offense was idolatry," Yonah said, "worshiping the gods of the pagan people around us."

"Yes. And as the Torah warns, pagan wives will entice our sons to worship idols. The gods of the Gentiles allow immorality and lust. It's part of their worship. When our people refuse to control their lust, they are drawn to idols that promise no moral restraints. Yet God exiled us to lands known for their sensuality and idolatry. He was testing us to see if we would learn our lesson there or become like them."

Ezra thought of the men who'd remained behind in Babylon, unwilling to give up its comforts and pleasures. How many generations would it take before their sons and grandsons adopted Gentile ways and forgot the God of Israel? And would the same thing happen here if His people continued to intermarry with Gentiles?

"What should we do about these mixed marriages, Rebbe Ezra?" someone asked. He recognized the man as one of the elders from his council, a man named Shecaniah ben Jehiel. But Ezra didn't reply, waiting for the community to reach their own conclusions rather than invoking his authority. "Six men from my clan have married Samaritan women," Shecaniah continued, "including my own father, who married a Samaritan after my mother died. None of the Gentile women who are now part of my clan have renounced their gods, although they say they also believe in the Holy One. But what should I do about it? What should all of us do?"

"What does the Torah teach?" Ezra asked.

"Abraham sent his pagan wife Hagar and their son Ishmael away," someone replied.

"Can you really expect a man to give up his wife of many years?" a Levite named Shabbathai asked. "And send his own children away? That's impossible. Doesn't God care about the bonds of love we have with our families?"

"Of course He does," Yonah replied. "Yet He told Abraham to send Hagar and Ishmael away. Then He commanded Abraham to sacrifice his son Isaac on Mount Moriah. Abraham needed to decide whom he loved more—the Almighty One or his own flesh and blood. He needed to decide if he would obey God no matter what."

"We recite God's greatest commandment every morning," someone else said. "'Love the Lord your God with *all* your heart and with all your soul and with all your strength.' Love for Him comes first."

"Yes," Ezra agreed. "And I have no doubt our brothers will suffer great pain at making such a sacrifice. But we can always expect pain as a consequence of disobedience. Did these pagan wives deceive their husbands into believing they were Jewish? Or did the men knowingly sin?"

"There was a shortage of women among the first group of exiles who returned from Babylon," a man named Meshullam said.

"That's no excuse," Yonah said. "Not when the Torah clearly warns us not to intermarry with Gentiles."

"Perhaps God caused the shortage of women to test our resolve," Ezra said. "One of the causes for our exile was idolatry, and so this challenge gave us an opportunity to triumph over the temptation to marry idolatrous wives and bring idols into our homes."

"And we clearly failed that challenge," Shecaniah said. "The six men from my clan are all guilty. My own father . . ." He shook his head, too overcome with emotion to speak.

"We all share the guilt of their sin," Ezra said. "All Jews are responsible for each other in the Holy One's sight."

"That's why we went into exile together," Yonah said. "And it's why we'll all suffer once again if this sin isn't dealt with."

The gathered men fell silent, the problem and its consequences clearly spelled out. There was nothing more to say. Ezra knew they were waiting for him to act, but he deliberately refrained from doing so, praying that the will to purge the province of mixed marriages would come from the people themselves. If it did, the guilty men would be opposing the entire community, not just him. Banishment was a severe punishment that could be fatal in such a small community surrounded by hostile neighbors. It should be clear by Ezra's anguish and torn garments just how severely he judged the matter. The silence lengthened, and the majority of men decided to sit in sorrow with him, some openly weeping as he was doing.

When it was time for the evening sacrifice, Ezra finally rose and went into the Court of Men to worship, shivering in his rain-soaked robes. The swelling crowds followed his every move. He watched as the priest sacrificed a lamb and laid it on the altar to be consumed, hoping the congregation saw a clear picture of sin's consequences in the animal's death. Disobedience led to death ever since Adam and Eve disobeyed God in Gan Eden. But the lamb's sacrificial death also pictured God's mercy and forgiveness in providing a way to atone for sin.

Afterward, the priest removed a coal from the altar of sacrifice and carried it into the sanctuary, where he would use it to light the incense on the golden altar before God's throne. The prayers of the people would ascend with the incense. Ezra fell to his knees with his hands spread out to the Lord, praying aloud on behalf of his people:

"O my God, I am too ashamed and disgraced to lift up my face to you. Our sins are higher than our heads and our guilt has reached to the heavens. Because of our sins, we have been subjected to the sword and captivity at the hand of foreign kings, as it is today. Yet the Lord our God has been gracious in leaving us a remnant and giving us relief from our bondage for a brief moment. He has shown us kindness in the sight of the kings of Persia."

Rain coursed down his face along with his tears as he continued. "But now, O our God, what can we say after this? For we have disregarded the commands you gave when you said do not give your daughters in marriage to their sons or take their daughters for your sons. Our evil deeds and our great guilt have led us to this result and yet, our God, you have punished us less than our sins deserve. Shall we again break your commands and intermarry with the peoples who commit such detestable practices? Would you not be angry enough to destroy us, leaving us no remnant or survivor? O Lord, God of Israel, you are righteous! We are left this day as a remnant. Here we are before you in our guilt, though because of it not one of us can stand in your presence."

When Ezra finished, he heard many in the crowd weeping along with him. As soon as the sacrifice ended and the last strains of music died away, Shecaniah stood before the men and said, "We have been unfaithful to our God by marrying foreign women, but in spite of this there is hope. Let's make a covenant with God to send away all these foreign women and their children. Let it be done according to the law and the will of all God-fearing people. Rebbe Ezra, we put this matter in your hands. We stand behind you, so take courage and do it."

Ezra rose to his feet, hearing in Shecaniah's words echoes of God's charge to Joshua and the Israelites: *"Be strong and very courageous. Be careful to obey all the law . . . that you may be successful wherever you go."* To see the people responding so quickly and decisively filled him with hope.

"Are we agreed?" he asked the crowd. "Are we ready to take an oath before the Almighty One, here in His temple, to send away all our foreign wives and their children?" A resounding *yes* filled the courtyard. When the voices died away again, he faced the sanctuary and lifted his right hand to make a covenant with God. "May God deal with us, be it ever so severely, if we don't rid our homes and our towns of all our Gentile wives and their children."

The men in the courtyard behind him, who had also raised their hands to swear the oath, confirmed Ezra's words with a loud, "Amen."

"Your oath now carries the same legal and moral force as the king's decree," he said, facing the crowd again. "Your willingness—" For a moment, Ezra's words all fled when he spotted Reuben in the crowd. The young Levite had a wild, frantic look on his face, and Ezra remembered he had married an Edomite woman. Ezra needed to talk with him privately and convince him of all the reasons why he must divorce her. Otherwise, not only would Reuben be stripped of his duties as a Levite, he would be excommunicated from his people.

"Your willingness to make this enormous sacrifice," Ezra continued after a moment, "is a testimony of your devotion to God and to His Torah. The proclamation I'll issue will be sent throughout the province of Judah, telling all men to assemble here in Jerusalem in three days' time to follow through on our oath. Anyone who fails to appear will forfeit all his property, in accordance with the decision of the officials and elders. He'll be expelled from the community of returned exiles. The survival of our people is at stake—just as it was after Haman's decree."

A man named Meshullam, who had argued with Ezra earlier that day, stepped forward to speak again. "Rebbe Ezra, it's winter. This proclamation presents a hardship for our people."

"I've traveled the length and breadth of our country," Ezra said. "No one is more than fifty miles from Jerusalem. Three days provides plenty of time."

"Why not assemble only the men who are involved?" Meshullam asked.

"Because we're accountable for one another and united in our collective guilt. Those who saw these mixed marriages and didn't protest are just as guilty as the men who married foreign wives. I don't think you realize how serious this is. Intermarriage will destroy us as a people."

"We are *one*!" someone shouted from the crowd.

"Draw up the proclamation," Ezra told Yonah and Shecaniah. "I'll sign it."

As the men dispersed, Ezra looked around for Reuben but didn't see him. The magnitude of this crisis and what it meant for his people's survival so overwhelmed Ezra that he sent word home to Devorah that he'd be spending the night here at the temple, fasting and praying. Ezra refused all offers of food and water as he continued to mourn, remembering how Moses had done the same thing after Israel sinned with the golden calf. Once again, the threat of divine judgment seemed to hover over his people because of their unfaithfulness. And although Ezra grieved, the community's quick and decisive action gave him hope. It remained to be seen how the entire province would respond.

He thought again of Reuben, how frightened and devastated he had looked, and Ezra dropped to his knees before God. Covering his face with his hands, Ezra prayed for Reuben to have the strength to do the right thing and divorce his Edomite wife.

CHAPTER
52

JERUSALEM

"I don't think you should wait up for your father any longer,"
Devorah told her sons. She had put their daughters to bed a
few hours ago and had nearly fallen asleep alongside them,
but the twins had asked to wait up for Ezra. He sent word
home last night not to expect him, but she hadn't heard from
him tonight.

"When do you think Abba will come home?" Judah asked.

"I don't know. This is a very difficult time for him, as you
can imagine. All Jerusalem is in an uproar."

"We saw the men taking the oath yesterday at the evening
sacrifice," Shallum said. "Not everyone seemed happy about
it."

"Even so, your father will do what the Torah says."

"But why is he staying at the temple? Why doesn't he come
home?"

Devorah thought she knew why. He needed to listen to God,
not to criticism and political maneuvering. He hadn't been to
his council chamber next door for two days, but the noise of
the disturbance among the elders had spilled over into her private living quarters. She was glad Ezra wasn't there to hear it.

She'd repeatedly told the elders he wasn't home and had finally instructed the servants to answer the door in her place and send everyone away.

"He needs time to pray, Shallum. I don't think he's coming home tonight, either, so you'd better go to bed now or you'll be too tired for school tomorrow."

Devorah was preparing for bed herself after they had fallen asleep when Ezra finally dragged home in the dark. She met him with an embrace, and he held her tightly in return. She felt his sigh as clearly as she heard it.

"You must be hungry. Can I get you something to eat?"

"I don't know. . . . Have you heard what's been going on, Devorah? Have you been up to the temple?"

"Yes. I was at the evening sacrifice yesterday. The entire city is talking about it. This must be quite an ordeal for you." She watched him remove his sandals and sink onto the cushions in their living area. He looked bone-weary, with dark circles beneath his eyes. His hair and beard seemed to have turned even whiter than before. Was it possible in only two days? She started toward the storeroom to get him something to eat and ran into one of their servants. Devorah was still unused to having them around. "Will you fetch the governor something to eat, please? Thank you." She knelt beside Ezra to rub his shoulders, feeling the tension in his muscles.

"Devorah . . . I need to ask you something," he said quietly.

"Yes?"

"Why didn't you tell me Reuben's new wife was an Edomite?"

She stopped massaging. "What are you talking about? Amina is Jewish!"

"If she told you that, then she lied to you."

"She did no such thing! We celebrated Shabbat together, and she knew the rituals and songs better than Reuben did. I just assumed . . ."

"Neither of them mentioned that she was a Gentile?"

414

"No. Are you certain it's true, Ezra? I think you must be mistaken."

"I'm not. The elders who brought the issue of mixed marriages to my attention told me Reuben had married an Edomite woman. So I asked Joshua ben Zechariah, one of the priests she used to live with here in Jerusalem, and he confirmed it was true. The woman is an Edomite from a village outside of Bethlehem."

"The *woman* has a name, Ezra—it's Amina."

The servant entered with a tray of food and set it on the low table in front of Ezra's cushion. "Thank you," he mumbled, though he appeared too weary to lean forward and eat it. When the servant was gone, he said, "They never should have allowed Reuben to marry her. Now he's embroiled in this whole mess, and his future is at risk."

"But they did marry. They love each other. We were invited to their wedding feast, but you were away. Look, I know Moses forbade mixed marriages when our ancestors conquered the Promised Land, but what about afterward? Ruth was a foreign woman, wasn't she? A Moabite? And what about all the prophecies saying the Gentiles will worship the Holy One with us one day?"

He leaned forward and picked up a piece of bread. "I can't find any place in the Torah reversing God's original ruling on mixed marriages."

Devorah's frustration grew as she remembered how happy Reuben and Amina had been. "So Ruth's marriage to Boaz should have been dissolved? Is that what you would have advised if you lived back then? Should the entire line of King David descended from Ruth be sent away as 'unclean' Gentiles, like the children of mixed marriages?"

"I can't answer that. It isn't the question that's before me. Foreign wives lead to idolatry. Even King Solomon, the wisest man who ever lived, ended up worshiping idols because of his foreign wives, remember?"

"What will happen to Reuben and Amina?"

"You were there at the temple. The people swore an oath before God saying anyone involved in a mixed marriage must put away his foreign wife and children. Reuben will have to comply. He will have to divorce her."

"Oh no . . ." Devorah felt sick at the thought. She watched Ezra swallow a few bites of food and wondered if his own hatred toward Gentiles influenced his decision. "And if these men don't divorce their wives?" she asked. "Will they be subject to 'banishment, imprisonment, death,' and all those other terrible things in the Persian king's decree?"

Ezra nodded. "Reuben won't be allowed to serve in the temple. His children won't be considered Jewish. The community will banish him."

"Where will he live? What will he do?" Ezra shrugged in reply, multiplying Devorah's frustration. "Listen, I care about Reuben. I can't imagine what he's going through. Nor can I imagine being asked to make a choice like this. You didn't see how much he and Amina love each other."

Ezra set down the bowl again. "The Torah forbids intermarriage. I can't change the law. And when we disobey God's law, it always causes pain in the long run. Reuben will suffer if he disobeys. I'll suffer if I disobey."

"Isn't there any room for God's grace? For His mercy? You showed Reuben grace once before, and it led him to God. Can't grace heal our community this time, too? Suppose the law made you divorce me and give up our children?"

"But you aren't a Gentile. You and I wouldn't have married a pagan spouse to begin with, any more than we would have married a dog. I've been appointed our nation's leader, and it's my job to enforce the law. That's my mandate, Devorah. I can't change what the law says, nor can I show favoritism to Reuben and look the other way, no matter how fond I am of him. He married a Gentile. Whether he knew that's what she was beforehand or not, I don't know. But now he must obey the law. Intermarriage is just as deadly to our people as Haman's decree."

"Every time you say the word *Gentile* I can hear the hatred in your voice. God doesn't hate them, you know. And neither do I."

"How can you say that? They tried to destroy our people. They would have killed every Jewish man, woman, and child. They killed Jude, remember?"

"Of course I remember. But I also remember that God promised Abraham all the nations on earth would be blessed through his offspring—through us! If you really want to understand God, then you need to understand that He loves the Gentiles, too."

"Devorah, I'm already facing opposition over this—men who don't want to live by the Torah's laws and who resent my leadership. Please don't fight with me at home, too."

For a moment, his words stunned her. Ezra promised before they married to share everything with her. She should be free to discuss this with him, giving her opinion on the matter. But maybe tonight wasn't the best time to remind him of his promise. He had come to her for solace and a respite from the heavy burden he carried.

"I'm sorry," she said. "I'll stop trying to convince you to show mercy—not because I agree with you, but because I can see you're not going to change your mind tonight." She rose to go to bed, but he stopped her.

"Please understand, there's so much more at stake here than Reuben's marriage. If our people fail to keep God's covenant, we'll face spiritual death, which is much worse than the physical death we faced when Haman ruled over us. And I'll be responsible for that death. I want our people to survive now just as badly as I did after Haman issued his decree. That's what I'm fighting for all over again—our survival."

"Then it looks like Reuben may be a casualty of this battle, just as Jude was the last time."

"I know, and I'm so sorry for him. But I can't sacrifice my integrity as a leader by showing favoritism. Nor will I compromise the integrity of God's law."

Devorah saw how trapped her husband was and knew there was nothing more she could say.

JERUSALEM

The past three days had been the longest ones in Reuben's life as he waited for all the men in the province to gather in response to Rebbe Ezra's proclamation. The chief Levite, Yonah, hadn't assigned Reuben to a guard post during that time, and he was afraid he knew why. Rebbe Ezra and the other leaders wouldn't make him give up Amina, would they? It was impossible to think of such a thing! They had been married for nearly two months now, the happiest months of Reuben's entire life.

Today was the twentieth day of the ninth month, and the waiting was over. People from all over the province had arrived in Jerusalem, streaming into the city in spite of the torrential rains. It was time for Reuben to join them on the temple mount to hear Rebbe Ezra's decision. Reuben had waited at home as long as he'd dared in order to avoid the rain and frigid cold, but now it was time to go.

"Please, stay home by the fire," he begged Amina. "You're going to make yourself sick going out in this weather."

"I need to hear what they say," she insisted. "This is our life they're deciding, Reuben. Our future." Amina had just learned she was expecting their first child. Their joy had been boundless. Now fear overshadowed their joy.

They left the house together and were drenched before they even reached the stairs to the top of the mount. The air felt nearly cold enough for Reuben to see his breath. The outer courtyard of the temple was packed already, the huddled men and women wearing their warmest wool robes. The huge crowd looked larger than for the fall feasts two months ago. He reached for Amina's hand so he wouldn't lose her in the throng.

"You're shivering!"

"I'm so scared, Reuben." Her teeth chattered when she spoke.

"I know. I'm scared, too. But no matter what, they can't make me leave you. They can't!" He squeezed her hand tightly to reassure her.

For the past two days, Reuben had tried to find Rebbe Ezra and ask for his help. Surely Amina wasn't a foreign wife, was she? Her Jewish family adopted her at a young age. She'd grown up in a Jewish home. She had certainly never worshiped idols. The sons of Zechariah the prophet knew her background, and they hadn't protested their wedding. In fact, Joshua and Johanan had celebrated with them in Bethlehem. And why had the priests given Amina the honor of weaving their robes if they believed she was a pagan Edomite? Reuben's efforts to find Ezra had been futile. The priests insisted he was in seclusion. And in spite of Reuben's attempts to reassure Amina and himself, nothing had diminished their terrible fear.

Reuben had been present in the temple courtyard to hear Rebbe Ezra's prayer at the evening sacrifice three days ago. He'd heard the men swearing an oath before God to send away their foreign wives and children. But Reuben hadn't raised his hand or sworn. How could he?

He searched for a place to sit as others were doing and managed to find a spot of pavement that didn't look too damp. He and Amina sat side-by-side in the crowded courtyard, the closeness of their neighbors offering a little warmth.

"Everything will be fine, Amina. Please don't worry. Rebbe Ezra will explain what he means by foreign wives, and I'm sure you and I will be safe. You can't possibly be considered a pagan." He took both of her hands in his. Her trembling fingers were icy cold.

At last Rebbe Ezra emerged from one of the priests' chambers. The crowd parted to make way for him as he walked to the platform set up in the outer courtyard. He looked weary and cold, his shoulders hunched against the rain. The murmuring died away, and as he began to speak, his voice sounded hoarse. "We've been unfaithful to our God and to His Torah. We've married foreign women, adding to Israel's guilt. Now repent and make confession to the Lord, the God of your fathers, and do His will."

Confess? Reuben wondered. *And then what?* The rebbe had taught him the proper steps: repent, confess, and then turn away from your sin. But how could Reuben confess and turn away from his sin when he hadn't done anything wrong? Amina wasn't an idolater. She worshiped the same God he did.

"For the sake of our people and our covenant with the Almighty One," Ezra continued, "you must now separate yourselves from the peoples of the land and from your foreign wives."

Reuben's heart raced faster as a murmur swept through the crowd. He slipped his arm around Amina's shoulder and drew her close, not caring who saw him.

"Our entire community decided on this action in conformity to the Torah," Ezra said. "I have a mandate from the king of Persia to enforce the Torah's laws. I prefer you divorce your pagan wives voluntarily so it won't be necessary to resort to stricter punishments. But our survival depends on our obedience to the Almighty One. Are we agreed?"

When the majority of people answered with a loud "Amen!"

Reuben was speechless. He heard shouts of "Yes, you're right!" and "We must do as you say." Then as the crowd quieted, he began hearing murmurs of protest. He felt the relief of a momentary reprieve as four men stood and made their way forward to the foot of Ezra's platform. Reuben recognized one of them as a fellow Levite, a man named Shabbethai.

"We stand opposed to this ruling," Shabbethai said, gesturing to the other men. "Jonathan ben Asahel, Jahzeiah ben Tikvah, Meshullam, and I oppose your decree."

"On what basis?" Ezra asked. "The Torah is very clear in this matter of mixed marriages."

"But exactly who gets to decide whether or not an individual is considered a Gentile? What if our wives have given up their gods to worship the God of Abraham? Doesn't a judgment need to be made on these matters?" Reuben held his breath, feeling a sliver of hope as Rebbe Ezra considered the question.

"History shows," he finally replied, "that while the ancestors of the Samaritans claimed to worship the Almighty One after they settled in our land, they continued to cling to their own gods, as well. The result is this unholy mixture of people and beliefs we see today among the Gentiles."

"But aren't we at least entitled to a fair, individual hearing before being forced to comply with your edict?" Shabbethai asked.

"I suppose each case could be decided separately," Ezra said, "after seeking the counsel of God." He lifted his hands as he appealed to the crowd. "Would convening a jury, here and now, as Shabbethai suggests, be acceptable to you?"

The crowd began to murmur, and Reuben couldn't tell what their answer would be. One of Judah's elders rose and stepped forward. "I believe we are agreed," he said, "but there are many people here and it's the rainy season. We can't remain outside while waiting for each case to be considered individually. Besides, we can't take care of this matter in a day or two because there are hundreds of marriages involved, scattered throughout the province."

Everyone in the audience began talking at once, and Ezra had to call for quiet. "Why not let our officials act for the whole assembly?" the elder continued. "Then let everyone in our towns who has married a foreign woman come at a set time, along with elders and judges of each town, so a decision can be made. It's important to do this quickly so the fierce anger of our God in this matter will be turned away from us."

Ezra turned to Shabbethai and Meshullam and the other men who'd protested. "If a jury listens to each case, will you agree to abide by their decision?" he asked them.

"We will. But we want our voices heard first."

"Then we will do as you have proposed," Ezra said. "I'll select a jury of men from among the family heads, one from each family division, to investigate individual cases. We'll draw lots to decide the order in which each town and village will stand before the jury, which will meet in my council chamber."

"May we bring witnesses to speak in our defense?" Shabbethai asked.

"Yes, of course. And I'll be present as a nonvoting member to make sure the jury's decisions adhere to the Torah. I'll need a few days to set everything up, so we'll begin on the first day of the tenth month. You are all dismissed."

"Let's go home and get warm," Reuben said. He helped his wife to her feet, and they shuffled from the crowded courtyard with all the others. Reuben's outer robe was so wet he could probably wring water from it. Amina's hair dripped beneath her soggy head covering. She looked pale with cold and fear.

"I'm scared, Reuben."

"It's going to be fine. Rebbe Ezra knows me. He'll listen to me and decide in our favor. You'll see." He helped Amina kindle a fire inside their tiny house and waited for her to dry off and change into warm clothes. But he didn't remove his outer robe.

"Aren't you going to put on dry clothes?" she asked.

"I need to go back up to the temple. I forgot to check when my next guard shift is scheduled."

"Can't you wait until the rain stops?"

"I'm already wet. . . . I won't be long." He kissed her and went back out into the cold.

Reuben wasn't surprised that his name still wasn't on the roster. He found one of the chief Levites who confirmed what he had already guessed. "We thought you should take some time off, Reuben, until this matter is cleared up."

"You mean the *matter* of my Gentile wife?" he asked angrily. "Amina is more devout than I am!"

"I'm sorry, Reuben."

He needed to find Rebbe Ezra. Now. He'd heard the rebbe spent his days praying in one of the temple's side rooms, so he made his way first to the Levites' changing room to put on his white robe, knowing it would give him access to all the sacred areas. When Reuben finally barged into the rebbe's room, he found him seated with his elbows on his knees, his hands covering his face. He looked up as Reuben entered.

"Reuben? What are you doing here?"

"I've come to beg for mercy, Rebbe," he said, closing the door behind him. "You're going to sit on the jury that decides Amina's and my case—"

"No, I'm not on the jury. I'm sorry. I'm simply serving as an advisor on matters of the law. The family heads will hear your case and—"

"And they'll tell me I have to divorce her? I won't do it! This is cruel!"

"Reuben, please listen—"

"Why? So you can tell me how terrible and sinful I am for marrying Amina? I've done everything you've said. I've cleaned up my life, repented of my sin, and worked hard to serve God and follow all His rules. And now God says my love for Amina is wrong? That falling in love with her was a sin? Then I'll live in that sin! Because our love and our marriage aren't wrong. Our child is a blessing, conceived within marriage vows—vows we spoke before God. You and your jury are wrong!"

"You have to understand, Reuben, that our wives set the tone of the home. They raise and influence our children until they're old enough to learn at the yeshiva. Women are responsible for keeping all the dietary laws in our homes, and for keeping the Sabbath and the feast days. They pass on our heritage as God's people. A Gentile wife can't do those things."

Reuben was ready to explode. "If you knew Amina, you'd know she's already doing all those things!"

"Listen, Reuben—"

"Are you saying God can forgive me for being a thief and for turning away from His laws for most of my life, but He can't forgive me for falling in love? That's crazy! What am I supposed to think of a God like that?"

"He's wiser than we are. We have to trust Him and—"

"I love her! Do you love your wife, Rebbe? Could you give her up?"

"I realize God is asking you to do a very difficult thing—"

"It's an impossible thing! I won't leave Amina. She's the best thing that's ever happened to me. I love her. If God says I can't serve in the temple because I'm married to her, then I'll turn in my robe and resign right now. If He says I have to divorce her and abandon our child, then He's unfair, and I don't want to serve Him."

"God is never unfair. He always has a good reason for His decrees."

"You said that about my father's death, too. How do you expect me to trust God when He does such incomprehensible things?"

"Reuben, if only you knew how much I long to help you—"

"Then do it! Help me! Figure something out! Come up with a different ruling!"

"I can't, don't you see? This is a moral dilemma for me, too. Either I disobey God and abandon the reforms I believe in and have worked for all my life, or I enforce God's law and hurt you and all the other people I love. I have to choose God. There's no other choice for me."

"What about mercy? You showed mercy to me once before and gave me another chance." Reuben dropped to his knees in front of Ezra. "Please! I'm begging you for mercy now, Rebbe Ezra. Please don't ask me to divorce Amina."

"Reuben, don't beg. Stand up," he said, pulling Reuben's arm.

"Amina is expecting our first child," he said, refusing to stand. "How can I abandon my wife and child? You're on the committee. You can decide in our favor."

Ezra dropped to his knees, as well, and gripped Reuben's shoulders. Tears filled his eyes as he said, "Reuben, I'm sorry. It's up to the jury. There's nothing I can do."

"You can! But you won't!" Reuben scrambled to his feet. "I'm finished with you. And with all of this!" He strode from the room, slamming the door behind him.

JERUSALEM

Amina performed her daily tasks of grinding flour and making bread in a daze of shock and grief. The leaders said her marriage to Reuben must be dissolved. She had tried not to weep in front of Reuben, believing his assurances that he'd never abandon her and their unborn child. But when she was alone, as she was now, her tears couldn't be stopped, anointing every task she performed.

She had believed God loved and accepted her, but it had been a lie. She was an Edomite, the enemy of His chosen people. Nothing could alter that fact. The rejection and shame that dogged her early years had caught up with her at last. She was worthless, a shameful disgrace. And the man she loved more than her own life would be rejected because of her. Reuben had told her the truth only this morning that he wasn't being assigned a shift at the temple because of her. He hadn't said *because of her*, but she knew that was the reason. He had kissed her before leaving home, saying he needed to talk with one of the local blacksmiths about a job.

She let the grinding stone slip from her hand as she covered her face and sobbed. Hodaya said the Almighty One was a God of mercy and grace. Why was He turning His back on Amina now? If He had always been against her, why not let her die when her family died years ago? Why give her hope and love . . . and then snatch it away again?

The heavens didn't reply. The flour remained unground, the bread unbaked. Amina knew she should finish preparing a meal for Reuben before he returned, but she lacked the strength. He was a Levite, not a blacksmith. How could she let him sacrifice his faith and his people and his calling as a Levite—for her? How could she let him face God's judgment for disobeying the Torah? Reuben was being asked to choose between her and God, and he had to choose God. For Reuben's sake, she needed to make certain he did.

Amina dried her eyes and rose to her feet. The only solution was for her to return to her own people where she belonged. Rebbe Ezra's jury was going to compel Reuben to divorce her, so she may as well leave now and spare him the pain of doing it or the penalty for refusing. She had been a fool to believe she would be accepted among the Jews—hadn't Sayfah been telling her that all along? Her sister said Amina would be welcome if she returned to their people for good. It was where she belonged. Her father had been right to treat a cripple like her with such contempt.

She tidied up the flour and put away the grinding stone. She raked the coals so the fire on the hearth would go out while she packed her meager belongings, tying them up in a small bundle. Then she gazed around one last time at the beautiful little home that Reuben had so lovingly built for her. The Almighty One had never intended for it to be hers.

The sky poured rain as if to punish Amina further as she limped through the city streets toward the ramp leading down to the valley. She slipped and fell twice on the slick cobblestones as she hurried to get away before Reuben returned. She fell three more times on the muddy road as she walked to Sayfah's village on the other side of the valley, skinning her knees, scraping the palms of her hands, dirtying her robe. She'd never walked this far on her own before, juggling her crutch and her unwieldy bundle of belongings, and the journey took Amina all day. She was soaked and shivering by the time she reached the seated elders at the entrance to Sayfah's village. "I'm here to visit my sister," she told them through chattering teeth. She saw their disdain as they waved her through.

Amina went around to the rear gate of her sister's house and knocked, aware of how filthy and bedraggled she must look. Sayfah answered with a toddler on her hip and seemed not to recognize her at first. "Amina? . . . What are you doing here?"

Amina dropped her bundle to hug her sister tightly, the child squirming and protesting between them. "May I stay with you, Sayfah? We're still sisters, aren't we? No matter what?"

Sayfah held her at arms' length beneath the overhanging roof to look her over. "What happened to you?"

"I had to walk all the way here . . . and I fell a few times."

"But . . . why did you come? What happened to the Jewish man you were going to marry?"

When Amina thought of Reuben and how she would miss his strong arms and the warmth of him by her side, the pain in her heart was nearly unbearable. But she knew she had been right to leave him. "Things didn't work out," she replied. "I've—I've left him. May I please stay with you until I figure out where else to go?"

Sayfah seemed to soften a little at the sight of her terrible grief. "I'll have to ask my husband when he comes home . . . but . . . but I think it will be all right."

Amina remembered how Hodaya had gladly taken the two of them into her home, not caring what her sons said or thought about her decision. Hodaya's kind heart had convinced Amina to believe that the Almighty One was a God of love and compassion. But He was compassionate only toward Jews, not toward

Gentiles like her. She wondered for the first time if the jury would have made Hodaya divorce her husband, too? Even now, would Jacob and Hodaya's other sons be rejected by the community because of their Gentile mother?

"Thank you," she told Sayfah. "I had no place else to go."

"What about all your Jewish friends?" Sayfah asked as she led her into the warmth of her house. Amina could only shake her head, forcing back the tears that threatened to give her away. "I tried to tell you that you belonged with our own people," Sayfah said.

"I know. You were right." And Sayfah had been right to treat Amina with such cold contempt, just as their parents had. Amina took a few minutes to clean up and change out of her wet clothes, then she went out to the courtyard to help Sayfah chop onions and garlic and soak the dried fish to prepare it for dinner. "Let me help you with the meal," she said and quickly went to work, freeing Sayfah to tend to her son. Amina decided not to mention that she was expecting Reuben's baby. Sayfah would eventually see the truth for herself. But in spite of the distractions, Amina couldn't take her mind off Reuben. How much time would have to pass until she could forget him? Months? Years?

Never. She would never stop thinking of him, loving him.

When Sayfah's husband returned home, Amina was careful to stay out of sight, just as she'd done in her home village. "I asked my husband if you may stay," Sayfah told her later, "and he says you may if you agree to work for us as a servant. I'm sorry, but we aren't wealthy people, and we can't afford to support you unless you earn your own way."

"Yes, that's as it should be. I don't mind being your servant." It would be better this way. If they considered her part of the family, they might force her to marry, and she could never be unfaithful to Reuben. She would never love anyone but him.

Sayfah served her husband and ate with him, but Amina ate alone, like a proper servant. She had returned to the place where she'd started, a rejected cripple, bringing shame on her family. "I'll fix a bed for you in the storeroom," Sayfah told her.

"That will be fine."

As Amina lay there later that night, shivering beneath the thin blanket, listening to the mice skittering among the storage jars, she knew this was her punishment for being born an Edomite. Her family had attacked God's people and had tried to destroy them. But as she tried to pray to the Almighty One, she still wondered why He had given her so much happiness, only to snatch it all away from her again.

CHAPTER
55

I'm sorry, Ezra," Devorah said, "but I can't hold my tongue any longer." She had listened all morning to the tumult in Ezra's nearby council chamber as the jury decided the fate of men who had married Gentile wives. Women wailed with grief in the courtyard outside Devorah's rooms. Grown men wept, and she wanted to weep along with them. Now the jury had finished their deliberations for the day, and Ezra had returned home, exhausted and haggard. But Devorah simply couldn't remain silent a moment longer. She met him at the door before he had a chance to take off his sandals and sit down.

"Has everyone in this province gone crazy?" she asked. "When is this heartache going to end?"

"Devorah, please . . ." he said wearily. "This doesn't concern you. . . ."

"Of course it does! It concerns everyone in this province! You promised before we were married that you would let me speak my mind, remember?"

"Yes, I remember." He sank down on a bench near the door and pulled off his sandals. "I'm listening."

"It seems as though you and the other men have become as

432

ruthless as hunters stalking their prey, chasing down Gentiles and punishing them. Why not go after all the Jews who've forsaken God? I'm sure there are plenty of those to hunt down, aren't there?"

"We're not stalking, we're conducting a rigorous inquiry. The jury is willing to accept testimonies and examine the beliefs of each of these Gentile women before deciding if the marriage must be dissolved."

"And have there been any marriages that you haven't dissolved?"

Ezra looked away. "No. Not yet."

"And you're a voting member of this jury?"

"No, I'm not voting. I'm consulted as an expert on the Torah. If a question of the law is involved, then it's up to me to give a legal ruling. We've never faced a situation like this in our history before. Each day I'm deciding precedents that will affect our people's future marriages."

"And what if there are children from these marriages? Does that matter at all to you?"

"According to the Torah, it can't matter. Having children is not an acceptable excuse for preventing the divorce."

"Oh, Ezra. That's so cruel!"

"It isn't up to me!" he said, spreading his hands.

"But it could be up to you. You're the leader. You have the final say."

He stood and walked past her, shaking his head. Devorah followed him into the room where they slept, wondering if she could still love a man who was so unbending. The law had brought about her marriage to Ezra and had given them children, but was it possible to have too much law? Why couldn't he see that if God had strictly imposed the law without showing compassion, they all would have died in Babylon?

"What about Reuben?" she asked. "Have he and Amina come before the jury yet?"

"No. The cases from Jerusalem won't be tried until next week." He stood looking around uselessly, as if he couldn't recall why he'd come into the room. "Reuben came to me and asked me to make an exception and help him," he said, "but I had to refuse. I told him I couldn't do that without breaking the law."

"But he's going to walk away from God if you don't help him. I know he won't divorce Amina." Ezra closed his eyes, and she feared he longed for her to go away and leave him alone. But she moved closer instead and took his hands in hers. "You're so faithful in following the law, but isn't God merciful to Gentiles who seek Him? Gentiles like Ruth?"

"You have no idea how I've struggled to walk the fine line between law and grace. But the difference between us and the Gentiles is that they are pagans who don't know God, and they make no attempt to follow His law. How can He show them mercy?"

She dropped his hands. "Ezra, I think you need to confront your hatred toward Gentiles."

"I don't hate them."

"I think you do. Be honest: Don't you believe this province would be a better place if every Gentile was banished outside its borders? In fact, what if we convinced the Persian king to issue a decree like Haman's, only this time all the Gentiles would be executed on the Thirteenth of Adar instead of us?"

It took a lot to make Ezra angry, but his eyes flashed as his temper flared. She heard the controlled rage in his tight voice as he replied. "The Gentiles will never stop hating us, Devorah. Never! Throughout the ages, time after time, they have tried to annihilate us just like Haman did. The Egyptians threw all our sons into the Nile to drown them. The Moabites hired Balaam to curse us. The Amalekites attacked us and our families when we were helpless in the wilderness. The Philistines hired a giant to lead their army and destroy us. The Assyrians killed millions of us when they conquered the northern tribes. The Babylonians slaughtered us mercilessly when they destroyed Jerusalem, and they did it gleefully! Our Edomite 'brethren' joined in pillaging us instead of helping us. In any given time or place, if given the chance to slaughter us, the Gentiles will gladly do it. They don't believe in the Almighty One. They blaspheme His name. They rebel against His authority and moral order. That's why they want to wipe out all traces of His people from the earth— because we represent Him and His Law."

"Not every Gentile hates us and our God. What about Rahab, who helped Joshua conquer Jericho? What about Ruth?"

"I'm sorry to say that they're the exceptions, not the rule."

"So, you hate Gentiles because you believe God hates them?" Ezra didn't reply. "I don't believe God hates them, Ezra. And if you do, I think you need to excuse yourself from these deliberations."

"I wish I could. But I'm under orders from the king of Persia to govern this province by the Torah. Believe me, I would gladly show mercy if I could. Do you think I enjoy what I'm doing? It's eating me up inside!"

She trailed her hand down his arm to comfort him. "Do you suppose this is how the Holy One feels? Loving us, wanting to show us mercy and grace, yet needing to balance it against His holiness and justice?"

"God is God. He has the wisdom to balance law and grace perfectly. I just wish He would show me how to do it under these circumstances."

"Ezra, why did God forgive us and bring us back here to start all over again?"

"Because He loves us and wants us to love Him and serve Him in return. He has a plan for us."

"Did our people receive the judgment we deserved, or did He show mercy?"

"He showed mercy, of course."

"Is it possible that He wants the Gentiles to love and serve

Him, too? Might some Jewish husbands lead their Gentile wives to God instead of the wives enticing their husbands to idols?"

"Of course . . . but the Torah forbids mixed marriages. I have to judge according to the revealed word of God."

"Then do what you do best, Ezra—study God's Word. Let Him show you His answer for this impossible situation. Ask Him to show you how He would balance law and grace in situations like Reuben's. Please, that's all I'm asking of you. Find the God of grace in the Torah—the God who forgave our people and gave us a second chance."

Ezra scrubbed his face with his hands, pressing his fingers against his closed eyes. Then he lowered his hands and looked at her again, nodding. "I can do that. I've been focusing on the law that forbids intermarriage. I can see what else God has said about marriage in His Word." He pulled her close for a long moment, holding her tightly, then released her and left the room, heading toward the front door.

"Where are you going?"

"I need to take a walk."

Devorah didn't know what to do with herself after Ezra left. Had he truly heard her? Would it change the way the jury made decisions? She thought about Reuben and Amina, wondering how their faith was holding up through this ordeal. Ezra said Reuben had spoken to him, but what if he and Amina gave up after Ezra refused to help them? What if they left Jerusalem instead of waiting for the jury to decide their future?

The more she thought about it, the more convinced Devorah was that she needed to talk with Reuben and Amina and encourage them to trust in God's mercy. She grabbed her shawl and left the house to hurry through the twisting streets to the young couple's home. Reuben answered the door when Devorah knocked. "Is Amina with you?" he asked before she had a chance to speak. He wore a frantic look on his face and sounded breathless, as if he'd been running.

"No. I haven't seen her. I came—"

"She's gone! Amina is gone, and I can't find her anywhere!" His panic became contagious, and Devorah's heart beat faster.

"Tell me what happened," she said.

"I went to see a blacksmith this morning, looking for work. I can't serve as a Levite in the temple anymore because of Amina. I just got home a few minutes ago, and she was gone! The house is empty! If something happened to her . . ."

Devorah bent to feel the hearth. It was cold. She saw no signs of food being prepared, as it should be this time of day. "Are any of her clothes or other things missing?"

She followed him as he ducked inside the house and looked around. "Yes! Her clothes are gone! So are all her things!"

"She must have given up hope," Devorah murmured. Why hadn't she come to see Amina sooner?

"I have to find her!" Reuben cried.

Devorah grabbed his arm as he started to rush from the room. "Wait. When you find her, tell her to trust God. That's what I came here to encourage you to do. I'm convinced Amina loves God, and I know He will judge fairly when you stand before the jury. God knows the truth about what she believes. He knows she doesn't worship idols. You just have to wait and have faith in His justice." Reuben nodded, but he was so distraught, Devorah wondered if he'd even heard her.

"I'll never stop searching for her! Never! . . . I'm sorry, but I have to go."

Devorah went back out into the drizzling rain to return home, wondering if it would change Ezra's mind and heart if he could see what his decisions were doing to the lives of real people. She was convinced the Holy One longed to have mercy on Reuben and Amina. Why couldn't her husband and the men on the jury show the same compassion?

JERUSALEM

Ezra was desperate for someone to talk to. Devorah's pleas for mercy broke his heart and eroded his resolve to continue as Judah's leader. Was she right about his hatred toward Gentiles? Was that what was motivating him? If so, he should resign.

Not knowing where else to go, he walked through the streets to his brother Asher's house. "He isn't here," Miriam told him. "He went down to the pottery yard on the south side of the city."

"The pottery yard? What's he doing down there?"

"Making pots," she said with a shrug. "He says it helps him relax."

Apprentices and workers bustled around the yard in spite of the misting rain when Ezra arrived. He could feel the heat of the kiln standing several feet away from it. The foreman saw Ezra and dropped what he was doing to hurry over to him. "Governor Ezra! May I help you?"

"I came to talk to my brother. I was told he was here."

"Yes, over there." He pointed to the clay pit.

Ezra saw him now, but Asher had blended in so thoroughly with the other workers in his leather apron and clay-smudged hands that he hadn't recognized him at first. Ezra walked closer, then stopped, remaining at a distance to watch unnoticed. Asher scooped a lump of clay from the treading pit and carried it to the worktable, wedging it to remove the air pockets. He finished the job with the speed and efficiency of an expert and carried it to one of the potters' wheels. As he sat down, he glanced up and noticed Ezra for the first time.

"What are you doing here?" he asked as Ezra walked closer.

"I could ask you the same question. Have you resigned from the priesthood already?"

"No. I'm not scheduled to serve this week." Asher dropped the clay in the center of the wheel with a firm thud, then kicked the lower wheel with his foot to start it spinning. He bent to dip his hands in the basin of water, shaking off the excess.

"Why come here, Asher? I'm sure you don't need to work as a potter anymore."

"Because," he replied with a vague lift of his shoulders. "There's so much in life that I don't understand, but this is one thing I do. It's comforting for me to see the finished product of all my hard work at the end of the day. How many other tasks in life give us the satisfaction of saying, 'There, it's finished, I accomplished something useful'?"

Ezra exhaled. "I doubt if I'll ever finish my reforms or turn all the people back to God." He watched as Asher spun the wheel faster with his foot, then pressed the sides of the clay with his hands until he formed a smooth, round mound. He dipped his hands in the water again, then pushed his thumbs into the center of the spinning lump and gently drew it upwards to form a cylinder.

"Does it do any good," Asher asked him without looking up, "to get people to follow all God's rules if they still don't know Him?"

"Maybe not—but that's what I'm supposed to do. The Persian emperor gave me the authority to enforce the Torah, even if it means breaking up marriages and sending children away from their fathers and their homes."

"Isn't this what you wanted? The authority to enforce the Torah?"

"I thought I did. . . . Devorah and Reuben both accused me of being cruel, and what I'm doing does seem cruel. These are real people, real families. Yet I know it has to be done. God's remnant people can't survive if we intermarry with idolaters. . . . But the process is just so painful."

"Remember when you were wounded during the battle? It was painful to have your wound cleaned and dressed, wasn't it?" Asher glanced up at him briefly before returning to his work. "But what would've happened to you if you'd let the contamination remain?"

"I would have died. You and I understand that, but men like Reuben, who love their Gentile wives, don't realize our future is at stake. All they know is they don't want to divorce their wives."

Ezra watched Asher's hands as he continued to shape the clay. It seemed almost fluid beneath his touch, obeying the pressure of his fingers. He wasn't simply creating a pot but something beautiful and graceful—and useful.

"I think I should resign, Asher. I can't lead anymore. I can't make these difficult decisions and try to enforce God's law among people who are determined to break it—people who think the law is wrong and should be changed to fit their particular circumstances. I can't keep apologizing for God's rules and trying to explain what He's doing. I can't carry the responsibility of them on my shoulders anymore."

"But we're priests, Ezra. We're responsible for these people. Even if you were no longer the governor, your job as a priest is to carry the people before God's throne, to offer sacrifices for their sins."

"It's one thing to have them sin in ignorance—that's what

the daily offerings are for. But these men who have married Gentiles knew what the law said and deliberately disobeyed it."

"It happens all the time," Asher said with a shrug. "A man came to me the other day to confess and bring his sin offering—and it was the same sin he had confessed to me a month ago! What was I supposed to tell him? Go away? I'm done with you and so is God?"

"That's what I mean. These men sinned when they married Gentiles, and now they want me to sin by looking the other way. I can't lead these people anymore. It's tearing me up inside. I'm not sleeping at night. Most days my stomach aches so badly I can barely eat. I'm not the Messiah, Asher."

"No one expects you to be." He halted the spinning wheel with his foot, then pinched the mouth of the clay jar to form a spout. He would add a handle to the finished flask so it could be used to dip olive oil or wine from a larger vessel.

"Anyway, I just came here to tell you that I'm planning to resign. I'll serve in the temple as a regular priest and—" Asher's loud laughter interrupted him. "What's so funny?"

"You can't resign! You didn't volunteer to lead these people in the first place, nor did they ask you to lead them. God gave you this task. Do you honestly think you can tell Him you're resigning and just walk away?"

"He's asking me to do the impossible."

"No, He's asking you to sound the warning like the prophet Ezekiel's watchman on the wall. If the people don't heed your warning, they'll die in their sins. But if you fail to warn them . . ."

"Their sins will be on my head."

"Yes." Asher took a thin cord and sliced the flask free from the wheel at its base. He rose from his stool and carried the finished pot to the drying shelf. "You're feeling the flames, Ezra, but that's part of the process. This pot I just made won't be useful for anything until it goes through that fire." He pointed to the kiln, where waves of heat shimmered above it. "The pots baking in there right now would be useless if they didn't endure the heat."

"I've also seen them crack inside the kiln," Ezra said. "And I feel near the breaking point myself. Even Devorah disagrees with me, and our marriage is suffering. She believes I should show mercy to men like Reuben and his Gentile wife. But how can I? How much more heat does the Almighty One think I can take before I break?"

"The pots that break under fire are the ones with flaws. Maybe the potter didn't shape the clay evenly because it wasn't centered on the wheel, or maybe the clay had impurities or air pockets. But you know the Torah better than any of us. You know God's Word is flawless. And I know you better than most other men do. I know you're a man of integrity and faith, whose life is truly centered on God. If you want to be useful to our people, then you need to stand firm through the fire until you come out on the other side."

"How?"

"Don't try to do this alone. Ask the Holy One to help you. Remember how we all pleaded with Him to help us before the Thirteenth of Adar? Do you think we would've been victorious that day without His help?"

That's what Devorah had advised him to do—to ask God to show him how to balance law and grace. "Thanks for listening, Asher. . . . And by the way," he gestured to the finished pot, "I'm glad to see you haven't lost your touch."

"You like it? I'll give it to you after it's been fired."

"Asher . . . you're still going to serve as a priest, aren't you?"

"Of course!" he said with a grin. "When I'm not making pots."

CHAPTER
57

THE EDOMITE VILLAGE OUTSIDE JERUSALEM

Amina went to bed early, exhausted from her slow, limping trek from Jerusalem to her sister's village. Despite the utter weariness of her body, she couldn't keep from weeping, however. The losses in her life seemed overwhelming, and she wondered how she had ever believed God would bring good from them. She touched her stomach, where Reuben's child grew inside her. At least she would have his baby to love—or would God punish her and take away this child, too?

She had trouble falling into a deep sleep, dozing fitfully until a chill from a sudden breeze awakened her. She heard a rustling sound near the door and rolled over to look, squinting in the darkness. The door slowly opened. Amina sat up, covering her mouth to keep from screaming—and recognized Reuben.

He came inside without a sound and knelt down on the mat to hold her tightly. "I was so afraid I wouldn't find you," he whispered. "So afraid I would never see you again. I would have searched for you as long as I lived."

"You shouldn't have come," she murmured as she hugged him tightly in return. Now she would have to endure the pain of losing him all over again.

"Why did you leave me, Amina?"

"They're going to make me leave you anyway."

"Never. They can't make me give you up."

"But you belong with your people—the law says so. And I belong with mine."

He didn't seem to be listening. He stood, pulling Amina to her feet, and helped her get dressed. He bent to pick up her crutch as she put on her sandals, then he glanced around the darkened storeroom as if searching for something. When he found her bundle of belongings, he scooped it up. "Is that everything?" he asked.

"Yes, but—" Reuben lifted her off her feet and into his arms. "What are you doing? Reuben, wait . . . we'll only have to go through this pain all over again."

"No, we won't. You belong with me."

Amina longed to return home to Jerusalem with him, and yet she was afraid. If he stayed married to her, he would have to give up everything else in his life. How could she explain to him that she wasn't worth such a sacrifice? She leaned her head against his chest as he carried her through the back lanes of Sayfah's village without making a sound. He knew exactly when to halt and when to move, peering around corners before proceeding with the skill of an expert.

When they were finally a short distance past the village, Reuben set her down so she could walk. It was nearly dawn. Behind them, the crimson sky above the mountain warned of more rain.

"Why did you leave me?" Reuben asked again.

"So you wouldn't be faced with this impossible choice. God called you to be a Levite. You can't walk away from the Holy One for my sake."

"I don't care about being a Levite. I found work as a blacksmith today. I talked to a shop owner, and he agreed to hire me. I'd rather work for him than serve a God who would take you away from me."

444

"They can enforce the death penalty in this province if you defy God."

"I've done plenty of things that deserved punishment, but loving you can't possibly be wrong."

"Reuben, please listen. I'd rather give you up than watch you sacrifice your faith and your heritage. There's no other God to worship, no other place to go. I'll still worship Him even if He makes me divorce you, and you have to do the same. Remember how Abraham offered up his son to God?"

They reached a fork in the road, where several large stones provided a place to rest. Amina sat gratefully, her legs trembling with weariness.

"I've been praying for an answer," Reuben said, "praying about what to do, and Rebbe Ezra's wife came to see me yesterday. She told us not to give up."

Amina felt a sliver of hope. "Can she convince Governor Ezra to show mercy? What else did she say?"

"She said God knew the truth about what you believe. He knows you don't worship idols. She said we could trust the Almighty One to do what was right."

"Then let's trust Him together, Reuben. Let's wait for the jury's judgment before we do anything else." She hoped it would give Reuben more time to think about what he would have to sacrifice for her. Because deep in her heart, Amina knew the jury would consider her an unclean Gentile. They would never make an exception for her.

"I feel so helpless," Reuben said, "and I hate feeling this way. I was helpless when my father died, helpless when my uncle sold the shop, helpless when I was boy and the gang of Babylonians jumped me and blindfolded me and tied me up. I swore I would never let other people decide my fate again, yet here I am in the same situation. People are forcing me to do things against my will."

"But you aren't fighting other people," Amina said, "you're

fighting God. His Torah clearly said not to marry a Gentile like me. So do we want our way, Reuben, or God's way?"

"I want my way. Our way."

"I do, too. But in the end we would have each other but not God. I know what my life was like before I found Him, and you told me what your life was like. Do you really want to go back to that emptiness? Do you want to live away from God and His people? To give up your work and the sacrifices at the temple? We would have no place to go, Reuben. Even the Gentiles wouldn't want us. Years from now, after being isolated and exiled, we would end up hating each other."

"I could never hate you."

"Let's ask God for mercy. Let's give Him our lives and then trust Him to do the best thing for us."

Reuben stood, facing her. "What are you saying?"

"Let's do what the rebbe's wife said and let the jury decide. Let's have faith in His justice. If they tell us to divorce—"

"Then we'll go away together and live someplace else. I won't stay here and serve an unfair God."

"I don't think faith works that way, Reuben. Before we can ask for mercy, we have to be prepared to obey the Almighty One no matter what happens. Abraham didn't know that God would provide a ram in the thicket in place of Isaac. He was willing to obey and sacrifice the son he loved no matter what."

"I don't want to live without you."

"Nor I without you. But maybe God is asking us to divorce for a reason—just as there must have been a reason why your father gave up his life. Was he willing to sacrifice his will for God's?"

Reuben closed his eyes and nodded. "Abba said we should trust in God's goodness even when all the evidence is to the contrary."

"Then let's submit to His will, Reuben. Let's promise God and each other that if He asks us to divorce, we'll obey Him.

It'll mean God has rejected me, and you should, too. I'll return to my people, and you'll stay here with yours. Agreed?"

She watched his face as he wrestled with the decision, knowing the pain in his heart was every bit as great as her own. He paced in the crossroad, his hands balled into fists, before finally turning back to her and falling to his knees in front of her. Reuben gripped her tightly in his arms, weeping. But at last she heard him whisper, "Agreed."

CHAPTER
58

JERUSALEM

One month into the hearings on mixed marriages, the cases involving men and women from Jerusalem were scheduled to appear before the court. Ezra had dreaded this day, and he guessed Reuben and his wife dreaded it, too. So far, in every case Ezra and the jury heard, the judgment had been for divorce. Evidence had always revealed the Gentile spouse still worshiped pagan gods. All the wives, as well as their children, had been forced to return to the Samaritan or Edomite villages where they'd come from. Ezra longed to show mercy as Devorah had pleaded with him to do, but he sat listening in the courtroom day after day, knowing what the law said, knowing there was nothing he could do but enforce it. God's people could not remain married to idolaters.

Day after day Ezra witnessed the anger and hatred among the rejected Gentile spouses. Why would God put them through this much pain? Was it because He hated the Gentiles? No, Ezra had searched the Scriptures and saw too much evidence to the contrary, too much proof that He didn't. Just this morning the Levite choir had sung, *"Declare His glory among the nations, His marvelous deeds among all peoples."* Why obey that command and declare His deeds if He didn't want the nations to know Him? No, the Almighty One didn't hate the Gentiles—He hated their pagan practices and idols. And if the Gentiles weren't willing to give up those practices, Ezra and the jury had no choice but to send them away.

The foreman called for the first case. The chamber door opened, and Ezra's gut twisted painfully as the former chief priest, Eliezer, shuffled into the room. Tears streamed down his wrinkled face as he stood before the jury and took an oath to tell the truth. Eliezer and his Gentile wife probably had been married for many years. They'd raised children and grandchildren. All of the men on the jury knew Eliezer, and Ezra could sense their discomfort at being forced to question him.

"Were you aware that your wife was a Gentile before you married her?" the foreman began by asking.

"Yes. I was aware. I met her at a festival in her Samaritan village."

"Did anyone try to warn you or prevent you from entering into this union?"

"My father, Jeshua, the high priest, did. But I wouldn't listen to him."

"As part of this hearing, the jury is willing to hear your wife's testimony and offer her a chance to tell us what she believes."

"My wife wouldn't come," Eliezer said, staring at his feet. "She's angry with what she calls Jewish racism. She says it's the same racism that led Joshua to destroy her Canaanite ancestors when he invaded this land."

"I'm sorry . . . but if she won't appear, then we'll have to ask you to testify on her behalf." The foreman paused to clear his throat. "Does she worship only the Almighty One? Does she follow the laws of the Torah? Is she careful to maintain a devout home and keep the dietary laws?" Eliezer shook his head in response to each question, wiping the tears that continued to flow.

"None of those things seemed important to me when I was

young and in love. Now my wife says she's too old to change her ways and start following all those rules. In fact, she already left me, knowing this jury would force me to divorce her. She returned to her home village yesterday and won't be back."

Ezra had to look away from Eliezer's obvious pain. And the questioning wasn't over yet. "Do you have children?" one of the jury members asked.

"Yes. And grandchildren. Our children are grown and married with children and homes of their own. My son married a Samaritan woman from his mother's village. He also left Jerusalem along with my wife, knowing that under the circumstances, he can never serve as a priest. My three daughters all married Jewish spouses, however, and they still live here in Jerusalem."

"Do your daughters understand that since their mother isn't Jewish, they and their husbands will have to come before this tribunal, as well?"

"Yes . . . they know. . . . They know that because of me, their husbands may have to divorce them, too. . . ." He covered his face and wept, unable to finish.

No matter how many times Ezra had been through this, it never got any easier. The room felt cold. He heard the wind blowing against the eaves, the rain slashing against the shutters. At last Eliezer looked up and nodded to indicate he was ready to continue.

"Did you swear an oath in the temple with the other men to divorce your Gentile wife?" the foreman asked.

"I was too cowardly."

"What about now? Are you willing to abide by our decision and put aside your wife if necessary?"

"Yes. As I said, she's already gone—and she made it clear that she won't be back. I was so blind when I was young! Now my disobedience has not only caused pain for the woman I love, my wife of all these years, but also for my children and grandchildren. I never would have believed years ago that my choice would have such terrible consequences."

"I'm so sorry, Rebbe Eliezer," Ezra said, unable to remain quiet. "I'm so sorry for your loss." And although he longed to show mercy, he saw no way to do it, even though it was very clear from Eliezer's life that his wife hadn't led him to worship idols.

"Would you please step outside for a moment?" the foreman asked Eliezer. "The jury needs time to confer."

"You don't need to confer in private. I already know what your verdict will be. There's no question my wife is a Gentile. Our marriage has already dissolved."

"You understand the divorce will have to be permanent?"

"Yes. I understand."

Eliezer would spend the rest of his years alone—an unbearable punishment. Still, by his own testimony, he had been warned years ago and had willfully chosen to disobey.

"Let's take a short break," Ezra said, rising to his feet. "We could all use some fresh air." This had been the first case involving someone Ezra knew, and the emotional ordeal caused more pain than the stab wound to his arm had. But as he made his way from the room, Eliezer pulled him aside.

"I've already passed the age of retirement and no longer serve as a priest," he said, "but I want you to know I'm resigning from your council as of today."

"That isn't necessary, Eliezer. You know as well as I do you'll receive forgiveness if you confess and offer a ram from the flock as a guilt offering. Your remorse is obvious, and your suffering is more than I can imagine—"

"I know, I know, but I still intend to resign. I have a request to make, Rebbe. Instead of serving on the council, I would like to spend my remaining years teaching the younger priests. My youthful sins have cost me everything, and I would like to stand before the next generation as an example, so they can see the painful results of disobeying the Torah."

"Of course. We'll make a place for you as a teacher right away. . . . Thank you." Ezra hurried outside to the courtyard for air and saw Reuben waiting in the corridor with his wife, a slender, pretty young woman. Reuben hovered over her protectively. *"She has a name,"* Devorah had chided him—*"Amina."* Ezra's stomach ached with grief at the thought of witnessing his young friend's suffering.

Knowing he couldn't be gone long, Ezra quickly climbed the stairs to the rooftop of his residence to gaze up toward the temple mount. Only the rooftop of the sanctuary housing God's mercy seat was visible. The column of smoke rising from the altar blended with the gray, scudding clouds. Ezra closed his eyes and prayed. *God, give me wisdom. . . . If there is a way to offer your grace—if that's what you want me to do—please show me.*

The jury was already seated when Ezra returned, and the foreman called for the next case. Reuben's wife entered first, limping with a crutch and accompanied by five men who all swore an oath to tell the truth. Ezra recognized two of the men as priests, sons of Zechariah the prophet. One of the other three men introduced himself first.

"My name is Jacob ben Aaron, and these are my two brothers. We're members of Amina's family—perhaps not by blood but by bonds of love. We traveled here from Bethlehem to stand with her and give testimony on her behalf, so she wouldn't have to face this jury alone." He paused to offer Amina a reassuring smile, but she stood with her head bowed, staring at the floor as if too ashamed to face the jury.

"Yes, Amina is a Gentile by birth," Jacob continued. "An Edomite who was orphaned at the age of eight after the battles on the Thirteenth of Adar. Our mother, Hodaya, adopted her. I'll admit my brothers and I weren't too happy about my mother's decision at first. Emotions were running very high after the events of that day, and the hatred we felt toward the enemies who had tried to annihilate us was still very strong. I was convinced

my mother was making a mistake by bringing Amina and her
sister into our home. But my mother's great faith in God soon
became Amina's faith. She loves the Holy One as much as any
Jewish woman I know. We've witnessed her devotion to Him
over the years. Amina has followed the Torah all of her life, and
we testify under oath that her conversion to our faith is genuine
and sincere." Again, he paused as if to reassure Amina, but she
still hadn't lifted her head.

"Amina had a chance to return to her people and live with
her Edomite uncle a number of years ago," Aaron continued.
"And although her sister decided to return, Amina chose to
stay with us. Because of her confession of faith in the God of
Abraham, we told her she was now considered one of us. She
bathed in the mikveh, put her trust in God, and renounced the
gods of her people long before she met her husband, Reuben."

"Thank you," the foreman said when he finished. The two
priests stepped forward to stand alongside Amina next. From
where he sat, Ezra could see Amina's hand trembling as she
wiped tears from her face.

"My name is Johanan ben Zechariah, and this is my brother
Joshua. We also are glad to testify on Amina's behalf. Our aunt
Hodaya adopted her after the Thirteenth of Adar, and she and
Amina loved each other very much. She was like a daughter to
our aunt, lovingly caring for her as our aunt's health deteriorated
in her final years. Besides the love bonding them like mother
and daughter, they also shared a bond of understanding because
our aunt was also lame." He paused to draw a breath, squar-
ing his shoulders. "We know Amina to be a godly woman who
worships God faithfully and joyfully. When Reuben asked to
marry her, we didn't hesitate to give them our blessing. We knew
Amina was a Gentile by birth, but our aunt Hodaya was also a
Gentile by birth, yet she had always been completely accepted
by our people as one of us. Our father, Zechariah, who was
both a priest and prophet, considered Hodaya Jewish and saw

her happily married to a Jewish man. Naturally, we considered Amina Jewish for all the same reasons."

"How old was Hodaya when she was adopted?" one of the men on the jury asked.

"She was a newborn baby. The Samaritans rejected her and left her to die right after her birth because she was crippled."

"So Hodaya never knew or lived with her people?"

"No."

"But Amina lived with her family until she was eight years old, correct?"

"Yes, that's true."

Ezra winced, seeing where this line of reasoning was going. Devorah's question still haunted him—*What about Ruth?* She was a Gentile, raised in the land of Moab. Why weren't Ruth's children—including King David's royal family—considered Gentiles?

Jacob held on to Amina's arm as she waited to be questioned next. "I have only a few questions for you," the jury foreman said. "Did your family take part in pagan rituals to false gods when you were growing up?"

"Yes, they did."

"And you participated with them?"

"As a child, yes."

"Have you ever returned to your people or to your village after you became an adult?"

Ezra saw fear in her eyes. A few seconds passed before she replied. "Y-yes, I returned to my sister Sayfah's village to visit her."

"And did you participate in any form of pagan worship as an adult?"

Amina took longer to reply this time. Her voice became softer. "I-I attended a harvest festival with Sayfah. But I was careful not to eat sacrificed meat or anything else unclean. I went to see my sister, not to worship. I didn't know what the festival would be like."

"And what was the festival like?"

She stared down at her feet, not at the men. "Embarrassing . . . unholy . . ."

"Did you leave when you saw it was a pagan festival?"

"No. I didn't leave, although I wanted to. I had no way to get home."

The foreman looked at the other men to see if they had any questions. When they shook their heads he said, "That's all. You may go."

Ezra stood. "Wait. I have a question, if I may. . . . What made you decide to leave your people and give up your family's gods to follow the Holy One?"

Amina raised her head to reply. "Because I saw that everything Hodaya taught me about Him was true. I learned how wonderful the Almighty One was, and that He was a God who loves His people and provides for them. I saw how He saved them on the Thirteenth of Adar. And He became my God when He saved me. My uncle tried to make me go back with him to live with my people, and Sayfah insisted I had to go. So I prayed and begged God to save me and allow me to stay with Hodaya so I could worship Him. The Holy One answered my prayer and made a way for me to stay. He has been my God ever since."

"Thank you. You may go," Ezra said, sitting down again. "Send Reuben in, please."

CHAPTER

59

JERUSALEM

Reuben paced the hallway while he waited for Amina to come out. He thought he might be sick. He hadn't known such fear since going into battle fifteen years ago. If only he could fight for Amina with arrows or a sword instead of waiting here helplessly. At least he might stand a chance of prevailing with a weapon. Would he have to live estranged from Amina at the end of the trial, or estranged from God? Amina said she wouldn't let him disobey God—and Reuben knew God well enough by now to fear turning his back on Him. He had turned away from God the first time because He had allowed Abba to die. Did he trust Him enough to believe it wouldn't happen again—that God wouldn't take Amina away from him, too?

Lord, help us. Please help us.

At last the door opened and Amina and the men came out. "How did it go?" Reuben asked.

"Hard to tell," Jacob said. "We did our best."

Amina pulled free from Jacob and ran into Reuben's arms. "I'm so sorry, Reuben . . . I should have listened to you . . . I never should have gone to the festival in Sayfah's village."

"It's going to be all right, Amina," he assured her, but his gut made a sickening turn at her words.

"They're waiting for you," Jacob told Reuben.

He squeezed her tightly, then released her again. "Don't let her out of your sight," he whispered to Jacob as he moved past him. "Please!"

Reuben stepped into the council chamber and faced the seated men, closing the door behind him. He saw Rebbe Ezra seated behind the others, and their gazes locked for a moment before the rebbe looked away. The jury foreman asked Reuben to take an oath before the Holy One to tell the truth, then Reuben remained standing before the men.

"We would like to ask you a few questions," one of the men on the jury began. "Were you aware your wife was a Gentile Edomite before you married her?"

"Yes. She told me so herself. But she was Jewish in every possible way and—"

The man lifted his hand to cut him off. "Were you warned by anyone that you would be disobeying the Torah if you married a Gentile?"

"No. In fact, the two priests who just testified gave us their blessing. I'm sure they must have told you—"

"Yes, they did." Again, the elder's raised hand stopped Reuben. "Have you ever known your wife to worship other gods?"

"Never! Amina is a devout woman who worships only the Almighty One."

"What about the pagan festival she attended with her sister?"

Reuben felt sick. So this is what Amina had meant. How had they found out about it? Reuben glanced at Ezra as anger and bitterness rose up inside him, and he thought he saw a warning look in the rebbe's eyes. "What about that festival?" Reuben asked.

"Your wife told us she attended a pagan festival before you were married. Did you know about it?"

"Yes. I took her there myself and—" The moment he spoke, Reuben knew he had said the wrong thing. It would sound as though Amina had led him astray, enticing him to her village to worship idols—the very reason mixed marriages were forbidden. "Please, let me explain," he begged. "The only reason Amina went there was because she loves her sister, and—" And her sister worshiped idols. Reuben was making a bad situation worse.

"Didn't her eagerness to go back to her people serve as a warning to you that she may not worship God wholeheartedly? That she might be drawn to pagan ways?"

"No, because it wasn't true. Amina wanted her sister to know about our God. That's why she went to visit her. I hid in the village and watched the festival from a distance the entire time so I could protect Amina. I swear under oath right now that she didn't participate in *any* way in that pagan festival."

"What about you? Have you ever participated in pagan rites?"

Reuben opened his mouth to deny it, then stopped.

"Remember, you've sworn to tell the truth, Reuben."

He swallowed a lump of bile. "When I lived in Casiphia, I attended some pagan festivals with my Babylonian friends. Not because I believed in their gods but for the pleasures they promised." If the jury asked what he had done there, Reuben couldn't have said. He used to drink until he passed out and often had no recollection of what he'd done the next day. "I committed those sins long before I met Amina. They have nothing to do with her. I've repented of my former life, and God has forgiven me. My wife and I worship Him alone."

"But you admit you were drawn to foreign gods?"

"No! I was never drawn to them. From the time I was very young, my father taught me the confession of our faith, 'Hear O Israel, the Lord our God, the Lord is One.' I attended the yeshiva and became a Son of the Commandments, and then my father was killed on the Thirteenth of Adar. I was attracted to the pagans' immoral celebrations, not to their gods. . . . Why are you even asking me about this? My past has nothing to do with Amina. That life left me feeling empty and alone. I would never go back to it. I've repented, and I've been assured that my past has been forgiven."

"One more question: Did you swear an oath in the temple with the other men that you would divorce your Gentile wife?"

He felt tears stinging his eyes. "No. I couldn't swear such a thing. I would rather lose my life than lose Amina."

"If the committee decides you need to divorce your Gentile wife, do you understand the consequences if you fail to abide by their decision?"

"Yes. I understand."

"Thank you. You may go."

JERUSALEM

Ezra's heart ached as he watched Reuben leave the room, his steps brisk with anger, his shoulders hunched with defeat. The jury had finished questioning him and would now discuss his case before reaching their decision. As much as Ezra longed to ask the jury to show mercy, he couldn't do it. But he could use the Torah to shed extra light on Reuben's case as Devorah had advised him to do. She had shown him the precedents in this situation weeks ago, but he hadn't listened. He rose from his seat as God began telling him what to say.

"Before you begin your deliberations, there is something I would like to add to this case," he said, walking around to face the men. "Ever since my brother Jude died on the Thirteenth of Adar, I've harbored a deep hatred for Gentiles. I've denied it all these years, but after consulting God's Word, I now understand that my hatred was greatly displeasing to God. I intend to repent and offer a sacrifice to ask for His forgiveness. Such hatred cannot remain in my heart, especially during these inquiries. It cannot remain because God doesn't hate the Gentiles. And what I'm about to explain from the Torah will show that." The men watched him eagerly as if surprised by his confession.

"This is our first case involving a Gentile who has completely abandoned her false gods to worship the Holy One. I've been searching the Torah for a precedent to see what God would say in this instance, but first I need to ask—is there anyone here who isn't convinced this woman's conversion is real?"

"It seemed genuine to me," one man said.

"We heard sworn testimony from two well-respected priests and from her adoptive family," another added.

"Does anyone believe Amina worships idols?" Ezra asked. "Even when she visited her sister's village?"

The men all shook their heads.

"Good. Then I think the precedent for this case is the story of Ruth, who was a Gentile and also a Moabite. The Torah not only forbids intermarriage with Gentiles, it also says, 'No Moabite or any of his descendants may enter the assembly of the Lord, even down to the tenth generation. For they did not come to meet you with bread and water when you came out of Egypt.' Yet Boaz was allowed to marry Ruth, who was clearly both a Gentile and a Moabite. And nowhere in the Torah or the writings do we see any hint that the Almighty One considered their marriage wrong or that their descendant, King David, was a Gentile because of his Gentile ancestress. Was God making an exception for David? Looking the other way? God said, 'No Moabite or any of his descendants may enter the assembly of the Lord,' yet David and his heir, Solomon, built the temple and worshiped in the assembly of God's people. God even made an everlasting covenant with David's family, promising that the Messiah would come through him."

Ezra paused to look around at his audience and saw the men following his line of reasoning with interest. "We know God is just and doesn't bend or change His laws. Therefore, the only way I can reconcile the Torah's two clear laws with David's history is by concluding that God did not consider Ruth a Gentile or a Moabite. We have the written record of her confession

of faith: 'Your people will be my people and your God my
God.' She faced a difficult decision—to stay with her people
and worship their gods, or turn her back on them and follow
her mother-in-law, Naomi. Ruth chose the Jewish people and
our God. She demonstrated her trust in Him by walking away
from a secure future with her own people to join a helpless,
impoverished widow with no hope or future, clearly trusting the
Almighty One's promises for provision. The important thing is
that God considered her conversion to the Jewish faith genuine.
From the moment she confessed her faith and then acted on it,
Ruth was no longer a Moabite. Therefore, her children weren't
considered Gentiles under the Moabite curse."

"That makes sense," the foreman said.

"God's Word confirms His acceptance of Gentile believers in
another case," Ezra continued. "In the scroll of Joshua we have
the story of another woman's conversion, a Canaanite woman
from Jericho named Rahab who lived before Ruth. She is also an
ancestress of King David. We see the same sequence of events
in Rahab's story. She confessed her faith to the Israelite spies
when she said, 'the Lord your God is God in heaven above and
on earth below.' She demonstrated that faith against tremendous
odds and at great risk to her own life by first hiding the spies,
and then by tying the scarlet cord in her window. Our ancestors
had demonstrated the same faith when they put the blood of
the lamb on their doorposts at Passover. Rahab chose to leave
her people and follow God, placing all her trust in Him. And
her faith led to her salvation. After her conversion, she married
an Israelite, who was Boaz's father, in fact. Again, there is no
indication at all in God's Word that this was a mixed marriage
or that their children weren't considered Jewish."

Ezra paused as he tried to read their faces. Was there agreement—or had hatred of the Gentiles infected some of them as
much as it had infected him? "We see the same pattern in both
cases," he continued after a moment. "These women forsook

their pagan gods and their own people. They confessed—then demonstrated—their faith in the Almighty One *before* they were married. Neither Rahab nor Ruth converted in order to marry a man they loved. From the moment they turned to God, they were no longer considered Gentiles in the Almighty One's eyes, but true Jews. The amazing truth is that someday the long-awaited Messiah will come through two Gentile women who put their trust in the God of Abraham." He paused to look at each of the men on the jury before saying, "It is my opinion that Amina's conversion to our faith clearly follows this pattern. She is not a Gentile but a Jew by faith."

Ezra felt as if he'd done a full day of hard labor as he returned to his seat. He listened as the other men deliberated, relieved when they decided that Reuben's marriage clearly followed the biblical precedent. "This woman is considered a Jew," the fore-man decided. "The marriage stands. Call them in, please."

Ezra stood. "May I tell them?" he asked. He could see how shaken Reuben and Amina were as they entered, their faces drawn and pale with worry. Ezra smiled as he tried to put them at ease. "Amina, the Almighty One rewards your faith and trust in Him. In God's eyes and in ours, you are a true daughter of Abraham by faith. Therefore, yours is not a mixed marriage between Jew and Gentile and does not need to be dissolved. May the Almighty One bless you both."

They fell into each other's arms, weeping.

CHAPTER

61

JERUSALEM

Amina leaned on Reuben's arm as she limped up the steps to the temple mount. People from Jerusalem and all the nearby villages were walking up to the temple's outer courtyard today to celebrate the Thirteenth of Adar. The joy Amina felt on this warm spring day matched the festive atmosphere all around her as men and women of all ages came to hear the story of Queen Esther. There would be parties and celebrations afterward, with feasting and gift exchanges and food for the poor.

"I didn't realize there would be so many people," she told Reuben.

"Me either. I know they used to celebrate this day in Casiphia, but I never went. Back then, I didn't want to remember the events of this day."

"I always stayed home while Hodaya and the others celebrated," Amina said. "I was so ashamed of what my father and the other people in my village plotted to do." But now the jury had declared her a daughter of Abraham, and Amina finally belonged. From now on, the Thirteenth of Adar would be the day her old life ended and her new life began.

They chose a place to sit in the sunny courtyard after stopping to greet dozens of people—Amina's friends from the House of the Weavers, Rebbe Ezra's wife and family, Reuben's Levite friends, and his uncle Hashabiah. When it was time to begin, the excited crowd hushed as Governor Ezra climbed onto a raised platform with a scroll in his hand. He was such a distinguished-looking man with his white beard and hair, yet he seemed so humble, an unlikely leader with none of the swagger or ego found in most men of power. Amina would never forget how happy he'd looked as he'd announced the jury's decision: "You are a true daughter of Abraham by faith. Therefore, yours is not a mixed marriage . . . and does not need to be dissolved."

Now he wore a faint smile on his face as he addressed the people. "This is the story of God's miracle of salvation," he said. "We will share it with our children and grandchildren each year for generations to come. We call today's holiday *Purim* because of the lots our enemy cast to decide which day to destroy us. But the Almighty One had a different plan. As the proverb says, 'The lot is cast into the lap, but its every decision is from the Lord.'"

Amina sat back to listen as he unrolled the scroll and began to read. The story described the grand banquet King Xerxes held for all of his royal officials, and told how he called for his queen to attend. Amina was shocked when the queen refused his request. How dare she refuse to come before the king? Xerxes was so enraged he took away her crown, and then held a beauty contest throughout the empire to find a beautiful, worthy wife to replace her.

"I've never heard this story before," Amina whispered to Reuben. "Have you?" He shook his head.

Governor Ezra unrolled more of the scroll as he continued to read. "'Now there was in the citadel of Susa a Jew of the tribe of Benjamin named Mordecai who had been carried into exile from Jerusalem. Mordecai had a cousin named Esther who was lovely in form and features, and he had taken her as his own daughter when her father and mother died.'"

Amina listened in amazement. This heroine who saved the lives of the Jewish people was an orphan, like her. The Holy One had been faithful to both of them, making sure a loving family adopted them. "If only we could see the end from the beginning," Amina whispered to Reuben. "If only we had eyes to see how God can weave all the broken strands of our life into something beautiful." On the tragic day when Amina lost both her parents, she never could have imagined that she would end up here, a daughter of the Holy One, with a wonderful husband by her side, and his child fluttering inside her as if it wore butterfly wings.

"'When the king's order and edict had been proclaimed,'" Ezra read in his calm, eloquent voice, "'many girls were brought to the citadel of Susa. And Esther was also taken to the king's palace.'"

"How terrible!" Amina whispered. "I can't imagine being taken from my home against my will to become part of the king's harem." She wondered what might have become of her if Uncle Abdel had forced her to go home with him. By God's grace, Amina had gone from an abusive home to a loving one, while poor Esther had been locked away from all the people she loved for the rest of her life. Esther surely must have thought God had abandoned her. She couldn't have known His plan and purpose for her life—a plan like the one taking shape so beautifully in Reuben and Amina's lives.

"'Esther was taken to King Xerxes in the royal residence in the tenth month in the seventh year of his reign. . . . Now the king was attracted to Esther more than to any of the other women, and she won his favor and approval. So he set a royal crown on her head and made her queen.'"

If this had been the end of the story, it would have been a wonderful one—an orphan who won the king's love and became queen of the entire empire. But there was more to Esther's story, and Amina leaned against her husband to hear the rest.

Reuben listened with interest as Rebbe Ezra read how their enemy Haman came to power in King Xerxes' court. Each time the rebbe said Haman's name, the children in the audience booed and hissed and made noise to try to drown it out. It was amusing—and yet it wasn't. Why had the Almighty One allowed evil to triumph, even for a short time? Reuben thought of his father, as he always did on this day. *"It's the highest form of praise,"* Abba had said, *"to keep believing that God is good even when it doesn't seem that way."*

"'When Haman saw that Mordecai the Jew would not kneel down or pay him honor, he was enraged,'" Rebbe Ezra read. "'Yet having learned who Mordecai's people were, he scorned the idea of killing only Mordecai. Instead, Haman looked for a way to destroy all Mordecai's people, the Jews, throughout the whole kingdom.'"

Rebbe Ezra read the king's edict next, and Reuben closed his eyes as he remembered the day he'd stood beside his father in the house of assembly in Casiphia and heard it read for the first time: *"Destroy, kill, and annihilate all the Jews—young and old, women and little children—on a single day, the thirteenth of Adar."* Everyone who'd heard the decree had been stunned. Reuben had been just a boy, twelve years old, yet he'd been sentenced to die in a less than one year's time. He remembered battling tears as he'd worked in the smithy with Abba, watching time trickle away. He hadn't wanted to die, but there seemed no way out. "Why don't we blend in with the Babylonians," he'd asked his father, "and go to their temples and festivals so they won't know we're Jews?"

"If we deny God, our lives aren't worth living," Abba had replied.

The truth of Abba's words was now very real to Reuben. When he'd turned his back on his Jewish community and had tried to blend in with his Babylonian friends in Casiphia, he had ended up feeling empty and alone. And his life would still be meaningless if the Holy One hadn't found him and drawn him back and given him direction and a purpose. God loved him even more than his own father had. What an astounding thought! For that reason alone, Reuben wanted to worship the Holy One for as long as he lived.

Amina was a gift from God, and so was the child she carried. Reuben vowed to be the kind of father Abba had been—fearless and brave, trusting in the Almighty One no matter how hopeless things appeared. Reuben knew the inheritance he had as a Jew and as a Levite was more valuable and enduring than Abba's blacksmith shop and all his tools—an inheritance no one could ever take away from him and his sons.

Devorah thought her heart would burst with love and pride as she listened to her husband read the scroll of Esther to the gathered crowd. Yet along with her happiness she remembered the devastating grief she'd felt as her beloved husband Jude had died in her arms. That grief had nearly consumed her. But God in His mercy had provided a way for Jude's memory and heritage to live on through her son Judah. He was seated beside her today, and she reached to ruffle his dark hair, grateful to God for him and for the marriage the Almighty One had arranged.

As she listened to Ezra read, it occurred to her that Queen Esther also faced a loveless, arranged marriage to King Xerxes, a marriage that had fulfilled God's purpose in the end. Devorah knew she never would have chosen to marry Ezra on her own. Nothing about the quiet, scholarly man had appealed to her at first, except that he could provide a son to carry on Jude's name. But God had clearly chosen them for each other, and His choice had proven to be a blessed one.

"'Mordecai sent Esther a copy of the edict,'" Ezra continued to read, "'that called for their annihilation. And he urged her to go into the king's presence to beg for mercy and plead with him for her people. Esther sent back this reply: "Any man or woman who approaches the king without being summoned will be put to death. The only exception is for the king to extend his gold scepter and spare his life. Besides, thirty days have passed since I was called to go to the king."'"

Devorah imagined how terrified Esther must have felt. How could Mordecai expect her to leave the safety and seclusion of the harem and enter the official throne room unbidden? It was as unthinkable for Esther to approach the king without being summoned as it was for his first queen to refuse his summons.

Ezra Read Mordecai's blunt reply: "'Do not think that because you are in the king's house you alone of all the Jews will escape. For if you remain silent at this time, relief and deliverance for the Jews will arise from another place, but you and your father's family will perish. And who knows but that you have come to royal position for such a time as this?'"

Devorah remembered her astonishment when she'd first learned a Jewish woman had saved her people. Their deliverance was even more amazing than the victory won by Devorah's namesake against the Canaanites. How amazing that God used women of faith, just as He used men of faith! She listened as Ezra read Queen Esther's courageous reply: "'I will go to the king, even though it is against the law. And if I perish, I perish.'" Devorah wondered if she would have had Esther's courage.

The story built in suspense as the queen prepared to beg King Xerxes to save her people. Devorah watched her children's faces as they listened to their father read the story. Her two daughters by Jude were both married and expecting children of their own. Her twins, Judah and Shallum, so alike in looks and temperament, were studying to become priests like their ancestors. And her three youngest daughters, born to her and Ezra after the twins, would grow up in Jerusalem and probably never remember their life in Babylon. Devorah's greatest wish for all her children was that they would become men and women of faith like Esther and Mordecai. Like their father.

"'Esther pleaded with the king,'" Ezra read, "'falling at his feet and weeping. She begged him to put an end to the evil plan of Haman, which he had devised against the Jews. "For how can I bear to see disaster fall on my people? How can I bear to see the destruction of my family?" King Xerxes replied to Queen Esther and to Mordecai the Jew, "Now write another decree in the king's name on behalf of the Jews and seal it with the king's signet ring—for no document written in the king's name and sealed with his ring can be revoked."'"

Devorah remembered the day her community received word her people could defend themselves against their enemies on the Thirteenth of Adar. Jude had been relieved and eager to fight. Devorah often described his bravery to her children, and also told them of Ezra's courage as he'd led their people in prayer and into battle. She was proud of both men.

The story came to a triumphant end: "'The Jews struck down all their enemies with the sword, killing and destroying them, and they did what they pleased to those who hated them. But they did not lay their hands on the plunder. Mordecai recorded these events, and he sent letters to all the Jews throughout the provinces of King Xerxes, near and far, to have them celebrate annually the fourteenth and fifteenth days of the month of Adar as the time when the Jews got relief from their enemies, and as the month when their sorrow was turned into joy and their mourning into a day of celebration.'"

Tonight Devorah and her family would celebrate the Almighty

One's faithfulness and His salvation with feasting and singing and joy.

Ezra sat with his family on the roof of the governor's residence that night, watching the festivities in the streets below. Songs and laughter filled the air as Jerusalem remembered God's miraculous deliverance. "Listen . . ." Ezra told his sons. "Hear how joyful our people are tonight? You can't imagine how different the atmosphere was when we first received news of Haman's decree. We were in shock, engulfed by hopelessness and despair. The only thing we could do in our helplessness was fast and pray and beg the Almighty One for mercy."

"And He answered, didn't He, Abba," Ezra's youngest daughter said.

"Yes, He surely did. If things ever look hopeless to you, remember how the Holy One answered our prayers. Don't ever forget to call on Him in your time of need."

"Mama says we should remember my father Jude, too," his son Judah said. "He died protecting her and Abigail and Michal."

"That's true. Your mother's right. Along with our happiness, we will always grieve for my brother Jude on this day." Ezra reached to encircle Devorah's shoulder and draw her close, marveling how joy and love had come from a time of great pain. "But tell me," Ezra continued, "did you listen closely as I read the story today?"

"Yes, Abba." Judah and Shallum answered simultaneously, the way they had since they'd first learned to talk. They made Ezra smile.

"Did you notice anything missing from the story?" he asked.

"What do you mean, Abba?" Shallum asked.

"I'll put the question another way—how many times was the Almighty One mentioned in Queen Esther's story? What part did He play?" The boys looked at each other as they tried to recall, both frowning the way Devorah did when she was deep in thought.

"How many times?" Shallum repeated. "I don't think . . ."

"Wait! You're right!" Judah interrupted. "I know what's missing! The story never mentioned the Almighty One at all."

"Are you sure?" one of Ezra's daughters asked him.

"I'm pretty sure . . ." Judah said. "Am I right, Abba?"

"Yes, you're right. God is never mentioned or even referred to in the scroll. His name is curiously missing, and He seems to play no part at all in the events. Now, we know Mordecai was a God-fearing man, so why do you suppose he had the story written and passed along to us this way? Why is the Almighty One never mentioned? Any thoughts?"

Ezra sat back to listen as his children discussed the mystery for several minutes, giving various reasons for His absence. Even Devorah joined in, offering a few guesses of her own. But as time passed, they all decided that none of their reasons was satisfactory.

"We give up, Abba," Judah finally said.

"Do you know the real reason, Abba?" Shallum asked.

Ezra shook his head. "No, Mordecai didn't provide an explanation. But I've given it a great deal of thought, and I think I know a possible reason why God is hidden behind the scenes in this story." His children sat forward, listening intently. "I believe Mordecai wrote it this way because this is how we most often experience the Holy One in our own lives. God's plan is often hidden from us in such a way that we can't see what He's doing. We may feel abandoned by Him and wonder what He is doing and why He has left us all alone. But of course He isn't 'missing' at all, just as He isn't really missing in Esther's story. He's always right beside us, only a prayer away, working out events for our salvation. He wants us to trust Him in faith, even when we can't see or understand what He is doing."

"I remember how abandoned we felt when we first heard Haman's decree," Devorah said. "No one could understand why He allowed evil to win."

"Yes. But now we know from Esther's story that God hadn't abandoned us after all. He was hard at work behind the scenes, arranging to save us through a Jewish queen."

"I think you're right, Abba," Shallum said. "I think that's why the Holy One is 'missing.'"

"Your father is the wisest man in Jerusalem," Devorah said, smiling up at him. She rose and passed around a tray of sweets to all their children.

Ezra leaned back and relaxed as he listened to his family laughing and talking among themselves. Never had he known such joy and contentment. He closed his eyes for a moment as he whispered a silent prayer of thanksgiving for the Almighty One's goodness and deliverance. God had used the events of Purim to not only give him this beautiful family, but to bring them here to Jerusalem.

Ezra had studied the Scriptures all his life, seeking to know and understand the God who loved him. But even after all these years, he knew he had barely begun to learn about Him—the God who balanced justice and mercy, law and grace. Tomorrow, when the celebration ended, he would return to his study and open the Torah scrolls to learn even more about his awesome God.

Glossary

Abba—Father, Daddy.

Apadna—A huge, open-air terrace used by Persian kings for formal ceremonies.

Aron Ha Kodesh—The sacred ark in the Jewish house of worship where the Torah and other sacred scrolls are kept.

Bar Mitzvah—Son of the commandments—The ceremony at age twelve or thirteen at which a Jewish boy is considered a man and can read Scripture in the synagogue.

Bimah—The raised platform in a Jewish house of worship where Scripture is read.

Gan Eden—The Garden of Eden.

Havdalah—Separation. Havdalah lights are lit as the Sabbath ends to mark the separation between that holy day and ordinary days.

Kidron Valley—The valley outside Jerusalem between the city and the Mount of Olives to the east.

Kippah—A small head covering worn by Jewish men.

Korban—To make a sacrifice. From the Hebrew root word meaning "to come near."

Levir—Brother-in-law.

Levite—A descendant of the tribe of Levi, one of Jacob's twelve sons, who later became temple assistants.

Mikveh / Mikvoth (pl)—A bath used for ritual cleansing and purity.

Phylacteries—Small boxes containing Scripture that Jewish men attach to their foreheads and arms while praying. (See Deuteronomy 6:8).

Purim—The plural of *Pur*, meaning to cast lots.

Rebbe—Rabbi, teacher.

Shabbat—The Sabbath, a Jewish day of rest. It begins at sundown on Friday and lasts until sundown on Saturday.

Shema—Hebrew for "hear." The *shema* is the Jewish confession of faith found in Deuteronomy 6:4. It begins, "Hear, O Israel . . ."

Torah—The first five books of the Bible, which contain God's Law.

Yeshiva—A Jewish school where Scripture is studied.

Ziggurat—A stepped pyramid used for worshipping pagan gods, like the Tower of Babel.

A Note to the Reader

Careful study of Scripture and commentaries support the fictionalization of this story. To create authentic speech, the author has paraphrased the words of biblical figures such as Ezra. However, the New International Version has been directly quoted when characters are reading, singing, or reciting Scripture passages.

Interested readers are encouraged to research the full accounts of these events in the Bible as they enjoy the RESTORATION CHRONICLES.

Scripture references for *Keepers of the Covenant:*

Ezra 7–10
Esther 1–10
Ruth 1–4
1 Samuel 15:1–35
Genesis 19:1–38; 36:1–12
Exodus 17:8–14; 28:1–42; 34:15–16
Numbers 1:47–53; 3:11–13; 8:5–26; 18:21; 25:1–15
Deuteronomy 25:5–10; 25:17–19
Joshua 2:1–22; 6:22–25
Judges 4–5
Matthew 1:5–6

More From Lynn Austin

To learn more about Lynn and her books, visit lynnaustin.org.

Don't Miss the First RESTORATION Novel!
Bringing to life the biblical books of Ezra and
Nehemiah, *Return to Me* is the compelling story of
Babylonian exiles Iddo and Zechariah, the women who
love them, and the faithful followers who struggle to
rebuild their lives in obedience to the God who
beckons them home.

Return to Me
THE RESTORATION CHRONICLES #1

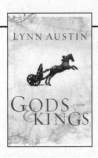

Experience the history and promises of the Old
Testament in these dramatic stories of struggle and
triumph. When invading armies, idol worship, and
infidelity plague the life and legacy of King Hezekiah,
can his faith survive the ultimate test?

CHRONICLES OF THE KINGS: *Gods and Kings, Song of Redemption,
Strength of His Hand, Faith of My Fathers, Among the Gods*

You May Also Enjoy

A powerful retelling of the story of Esther! In 1944, blond-haired and blue-eyed Jewess Hadassah Benjamin will do all she can to save her people—even if she cannot save herself.

For Such a Time by Kate Breslin
katebreslin.com

With the help of the lovely Miss Midwinter, can London dancing master Alec Valcourt unravel old mysteries and bring new life to the village of Beaworthy—and to one widow's hardened heart?

The Dancing Master by Julie Klassen
julieklassen.com

United in a quest to cure tuberculosis, physician Trevor McDonough and statistician Kate Livingston must overcome past secrets and current threats to find hope for their cause—and their hearts.

With Every Breath by Elizabeth Camden
elizabethcamden.com